THE MYSTERY
HALL OF FAME

THE MYSTERY HALL OF FAME

An Anthology of Classic Mystery and Suspense Stories Selected by the Mystery Writers of America

Edited by
BILL PRONZINI, MARTIN H. GREENBERG,
AND CHARLES G. WAUGH

William Morrow and Company, Inc.
New York   1984

Library of Congress Cataloging in Publication Data
Main entry under title:

The Mystery Hall of Fame.

  1. Detective and mystery stories, American.
2. Detective and mystery stories, English.
I. Pronzini, Bill. II. Greenberg, Martin Harry.
III. Waugh, Charles. IV. Mystery Writers of America.
PS648.D4M9 1984   813'.0872'08   83–13225
ISBN 0–688–02221–9

Printed in the United States of America

First Edition

1 2 3 4 5 6 7 8 9 10

CONTENTS

6 *Contents*

INTRODUCTION

The distinguished critic Howard Haycraft once said, "The short story has often been called the perfect and ideal form of expression for detective fiction. However that may be, it has surely been the most influential. Think of the authors and detective characters who have survived from an earlier day to the present: almost without exception they have flourished in the short medium!"

This was certainly the case up until the recent past, when changes in distribution patterns and rising costs wreaked havoc with the magazine business, killed off the pulps, and left only three digest-size periodicals specializing in mystery and suspense fiction—*Ellery Queen's Mystery Magazine, Alfred Hitchcock's Mystery Magazine,* and *Michael Shayne's Mystery Magazine* (the titles give further evidence of the importance of the series figure to crime fiction—can you imagine picking up Norman Mailer's *Mainstream Magazine?*). This is a far cry from the 1940s and 1950s, decades that saw newsstands overflowing with crime publications of every variety and quality.

This is not to say that the short crime story is dead—in addition to the three magazines mentioned above, numerous mystery and suspense tales appear in a wide variety of nonspecialist publications from *Cosmopolitan* to *Playboy,* as well as in anthologies and single-author collections. *The Mystery Hall of Fame* is not just another good anthology of

7

outstanding stories, but rather constitutes an ambitious attempt to immortalize those stories that represent the craft of mystery writing at its very best. And who better to choose stories for inclusion in the Hall of Fame than the men and women who write this brand of fiction—the members of the Mystery Writers of America, one of the most important and active writers' groups extant. These people are not only writers—they are heavy and constant readers and critics of the field and they know of what they speak, even if few of them have ever driven a knife between a pair of human ribs.

With this expertise in mind, we approached the leadership of the MWA with the concept of *The Mystery Hall of Fame* and received their enthusiastic permission to poll the membership. The most important part of our ballot reads as follows:

Dear MWA Member:

The purpose of this letter is to invite you to participate in an exciting anthology project co-sponsored by the Mystery Writers of America, to be called *The Mystery Hall of Fame.* The book, which will be published by William Morrow and Company in early 1984, will consist of the best mystery and suspense stories of all time as selected by a vote of those of you who write in the field.

Please list below your five favorite stories and their authors, in order of preference. They may be of any type, from any period, by writers living or deceased; the only restriction is that they should be under fifteen thousand words in length. You may also make additional selections on the back of this sheet, if you wish.

The response of the writers was heavy and uniformly positive, with the following stories receiving the largest numbers of votes (first-place votes, followed by total votes, in parentheses):

"The Specialty of the House," Stanley Ellin (13, 31)
"Lamb to the Slaughter," Roald Dahl (8, 25)
"The Purloined Letter," Edgar Allan Poe (8, 16)
"The Hands of Mr. Ottermole," Thomas Burke (4, 14)
"The Adventure of the Speckled Band," Sir Arthur
  Conan Doyle (3, 15)

It should be noted that two stories that received sufficient votes for inclusion do not appear in this collection: the
wonderful "Witness for the Prosecution" by Agatha Christie, because that author's stories that were made into movies
are not available for reprinting, and "The Lottery" by Shir-
ley Jackson, because of difficulties in securing permission to
reprint from the publisher.

The result of the voting lies before you—included are
such pioneering masterpieces as "The Problem of Cell 13"
by Jacques Futrelle, "The Monkey's Paw" by W. W. Jacobs,
and "The Two Bottles of Relish" by Lord Dunsany; great
hard-boiled fiction such as "The Gutting of Couffignal" by
Dashiell Hammett, "Rear Window" by Cornell Woolrich,
and "Red Wind" by Raymond Chandler; and wonderful
puzzles of detection like Harry Kemelman's "The Nine Mile
Walk," Agatha Christie's "Accident," and the late and lamented Ellery Queen's "No Parking." Certainly this is a rich
mix of categories and subgenres, a testimony to the vitality
of this field over so many decades.

We are particularly pleased with the selection of stories
by writers who are not as well known as they should be. For
example, Jacques Futrelle (1875–1912; he perished with the
Titanic) was a newspaper reporter whose stories about Professor Van Dusen, "The Thinking Machine," were outstanding early tales of classic detection. Another early pioneer,
Thomas Burke (1886–1945), wrote a wonderful series of
mystery and suspense stories set in London's Chinese district, and was one of the first authors to portray Orientals
with dignity in crime fiction.

Among more modern writers, the names of Fredric

Brown and Philip MacDonald are well known only to some
fans of the mystery/suspense genre but both were remarkable craftsmen whose best work was as good as any produced in the field. Brown (1906–1972) was a major science
fiction writer who also wrote numerous novels and short
stories in the mystery field, including such masterpieces as
The Fabulous Clipjoint (1947, a terrific first mystery novel),
The Screaming Mimi (1949), and *The Lenient Beast* (1956,
arguably his greatest work). Philip MacDonald was a noted
Hollywood screenwriter with many credits, including the
script for *Rebecca* (1940). His novels featuring his series detective Anthony Gethryn were popular in their time and
deserve to be more widely known. However, it was as a
short-story writer that MacDonald really excelled, and he
won an Edgar award from the Mystery Writers of America
for his collection *Something to Hide* (1952). It is a pleasure
to bring these lesser-known writers to the attention of a new
generation of readers.

These twenty stories—each and every one of them—
richly deserve the honor bestowed upon them by the Mystery Writers of America, and we are proud to have played
a small part in bringing them to your attention.*

BILL PRONZINI, MARTIN H. GREENBERG,
and CHARLES G. WAUGH
March 1983

---

*One final note: the voting produced a result that merits an additional
comment—"Sweet Fever" by Bill Pronzini received more than enough
votes to make the final table of contents, and his co-editors insisted that
it appear.

THE PURLOINED LETTER

Edgar Allan Poe

At Paris, just after dark one gusty evening in the autumn of 18—, I was enjoying the twofold luxury of meditation and a meerschaum, in company with my friend C. Auguste Dupin, in his little back library, or bookcloset, *au troisième,* No. 33 Rue Dunôt, Faubourg Saint-Germain. For one hour at least we had maintained a profound silence; while each, to any casual observer, might have seemed intently and exclusively occupied with the curling eddies of smoke that oppressed the atmosphere of the chamber. For myself, however, I was mentally discussing certain topics which had formed matter for conversation between us at an earlier period of the evening; I mean the affair of the Rue Morgue, and the mystery attending the murder of Marie Rogêt. I looked upon it, therefore, as something of a coincidence, when the door of our apartment was thrown open and admitted our old ac-

11

quaintance, Monsieur G——, the prefect of the Parisian police.

We gave him a hearty welcome; for there was nearly half as much of the entertaining as of the contemptible about the man, and we had not seen him for several years. We had been sitting in the dark, and Dupin now arose for the purpose of lighting a lamp, but sat down again, without doing so, upon G——'s saying that he had called to consult us, or rather to ask the opinion of my friend, about some official business which had occasioned a great deal of trouble.

"If it is any point requiring reflection," observed Dupin, as he forbore to enkindle the wick, "we shall examine it to better purpose in the dark."

"That is another of your odd notions," said the prefect, who had the fashion of calling everything "odd" that was beyond his comprehension, and thus lived amid an absolute legion of "oddities."

"Very true," said Dupin, as he supplied his visitor with a pipe, and rolled toward him a comfortable chair.

"And what is the difficulty now?" I asked. "Nothing more in the assassination way, I hope."

"Oh, no; nothing of that nature. The fact is, the business is *very* simple indeed, and I make no doubt that we can manage it sufficiently well ourselves; but then I thought Dupin would like to hear the details of it, because it is so excessively *odd*."

"Simple and odd," said Dupin.

"Why, yes; and not exactly that either. The fact is, we have all been a good deal puzzled because the affair *is* so simple, and yet baffles us altogether."

"Perhaps it is the very simplicity of the thing which puts you at fault," said my friend.

"What nonsense you *do* talk!" replied the prefect, laughing heartily.

"Perhaps the mystery is a little *too* plain," said Dupin.

"Oh, good heavens! who ever heard of such an idea?"

"A little *too* self-evident."

"Ha! ha! ha!—ha! ha! ha!—ho! ho! ho!" roared our visitor, profoundly amused, "oh, Dupin, you will be the death of me yet!"

"And what, after all, *is* the matter on hand?" I asked.

"Why, I will tell you," replied the prefect, as he gave a long, steady, and contemplative puff, and settled himself in his chair. "I will tell you in a few words; but, before I begin, let me caution you that this is an affair demanding the greatest secrecy, and that I should most probably lose the position I now hold, were it known that I confided it to anyone."

"Proceed," said I.

"Or not," said Dupin.

"Well, then; I have received personal information, from a very high quarter, that a certain document of the last importance has been purloined from the royal apartments. The individual who purloined it is known; this beyond a doubt; he was seen to take it. It is known, also, that it still remains in his possession."

"How is this known?" asked Dupin.

"It is clearly inferred," replied the prefect, "from the nature of the document, and from the nonappearance of certain results which would at once arise from its passing *out* of the robber's possession—that is to say, from his employing it as he must design in the end to employ it."

"Be a little more explicit," I said.

"Well, I may venture so far as to say that the paper gives its holder a certain power in a certain quarter where such power is immensely valuable." The prefect was fond of the cant of diplomacy.

"Still I do not quite understand," said Dupin.

"No? Well; the disclosure of the document to a third person, who shall be nameless, would bring in question the honor of a personage of most exalted station; and this fact gives the holder of the document an ascendancy over the illustrious personage whose honor and peace are so jeopardized."

"But this ascendancy," I interposed, "would depend upon the robber's knowledge of the loser's knowledge of the robber. Who would dare—"

"The thief," said G——, "is the minister D——, who dares all things, those unbecoming as well as those becoming a man. The method of the theft was not less ingenious than bold. The document in question—a letter, to be frank—had been received by the personage robbed while alone in the royal boudoir. During its perusal she was suddenly interrupted by the entrance of the other exalted personage from whom especially it was her wish to conceal it. After a hurried and vain endeavor to thrust it in a drawer, she was forced to place it, open as it was, upon a table. The address, however, was uppermost, and, the contents thus unexposed, the letter escaped notice. At this juncture enters the minister D——. His lynx eye immediately perceives the paper, recognizes the handwriting of the address, observes the confusion of the personage addressed, and fathoms her secret. After some business transactions, hurried through in his ordinary manner, he produces a letter somewhat similar to the one in question, opens it, pretends to read it, and then places it in close juxtaposition to the other. Again he converses, for some fifteen minutes, upon the public affairs. At length, in taking leave, he takes also from the table the letter to which he had no claim. Its rightful owner saw but, of course, dared not call attention to the act, in the presence of the third personage who stood at her elbow. The minister decamped, leaving his own letter—one of no importance—upon the table."

"Here, then," said Dupin to me, "you have precisely what you demand to make the ascendancy complete—the robber's knowledge of the loser's knowledge of the robber."

"Yes," replied the prefect; "and the power thus attained has, for some months past, been wielded, for political purposes, to a very dangerous extent. The personage robbed is more thoroughly convinced, every day, of the necessity of reclaiming her letter. But this, of course, cannot be done openly. In fine, driven to despair, she has committed the matter to me."

"Than whom," said Dupin, amid a perfect whirlwind of smoke, "no more sagacious agent could, I suppose, be desired, or even imagined."

"You flatter me," replied the prefect; "but it is possible that some such opinion may have been entertained."

"It is clear," said I, "as you observe, that the letter is still in the possession of the minister; since it is this possession, and not any employment of the letter, which bestows the power. With the employment the power departs."

"True," said G——; "and upon this conviction I proceeded. My first care was to make thorough search of the minister's hotel; and here my chief embarrassment lay in the necessity of searching without his knowledge. Beyond all things, I have been warned of the danger which would result from giving him reason to suspect our design."

"But," said I, "you are quite *au fait* in these investigations. The Parisian police have done this thing often before."

"Oh, yes; and for this reason I did not despair. The habits of the minister gave me, too, a great advantage. He is frequently absent from home all night. His servants are by no means numerous. They sleep at a distance from their master's apartment, and, being chiefly Neapolitans, are readily made drunk. I have keys, as you know, with which I can open any chamber or cabinet in Paris. For three months a night has not passed during the greater part of which I have not been engaged, personally, in ransacking the D—— Hotel. My honor is interested, and, to mention a great secret, the reward is enormous. So I did not abandon the search until I had become fully satisfied that the thief is a more astute man than myself. I fancy that I have investigated every nook and corner of the premises in which it is possible that the paper can be concealed."

"But is it not possible," I suggested, "that although the letter may be in possession of the minister, as it unquestionably is, he may have concealed it elsewhere than upon his own premises?"

"This is barely possible," said Dupin. "The present peculiar condition of affairs at court, and especially of those intrigues in which D—— is known to be involved, would render the instant availability of the document—its susceptibility of being produced at a moment's notice—a point of nearly equal importance with its possession."

"Its susceptibility of being produced?" said I.

"That is to say, of being *destroyed*," said Dupin.

"True," I observed; "the paper is clearly then upon the premises. As for its being upon the person of the minister, we may consider that as out of the question."

"Entirely," said the prefect. "He has been twice waylaid, as if by footpads, and his person rigidly searched under my own inspection."

"You might have spared yourself this trouble," said Dupin. "D——, I presume, is not altogether a fool, and, if not, must have anticipated these waylayings, as a matter of course."

"Not *altogether* a fool," said G——, "but then he is a poet, which I take to be only one remove from a fool."

"True," said Dupin, after a long and thoughtful whiff from his meerschaum, "although I have been guilty of certain doggerel myself."

"Suppose you detail," said I, "the particulars of your search."

"Why, the fact is, we took our time, and we searched *everywhere*. I have had long experience in these affairs. I took the entire building, room by room, devoting the nights of a whole week to each. We examined, first, the furniture of each apartment. We opened every possible drawer; and I presume you know that, to a properly trained police agent, such a thing as a 'secret' drawer is impossible. Any man is a dolt who permits a 'secret' drawer to escape him in a search of this kind. The thing is *so* plain. There is a certain amount of bulk—of space—to be accounted for in every cabinet.

Then we have accurate rules. The fiftieth part of a line could not escape us. After the cabinets we took the chairs. The cushions we probed with the fine long needles you have seen me employ. From the tables we removed the tops."

"Why so?"

"Sometimes the top of a table, or other similarly arranged piece of furniture, is removed by the person wishing to conceal an article; then the leg is excavated, the article deposited within the cavity, and the top replaced. The bottoms and tops of bedposts are employed in the same way."

"But could not the cavity be detected by sounding?" I asked.

"By no means, if, when the article is deposited, a sufficient wadding of cotton be placed around it. Besides, in our case, we were obliged to proceed without noise."

"But you could not have removed—you could not have taken to pieces *all* articles of furniture in which it would have been possible to make a deposit in the manner you mention. A letter may be compressed into a thin spiral roll, not differing much in shape or bulk from a large knitting needle, and in this form it might be inserted into the rung of a chair, for example. You did not take to pieces all the chairs?"

"Certainly not; but we did better—we examined the rungs of every chair in the hotel, and, indeed, the jointings of every description of furniture, by the aid of a most powerful microscope. Had there been any traces of recent disturbance we should not have failed to detect it instantly. A single grain of gimlet dust, for example, would have been as obvious as an apple. Any disorder in the gluing—any unusual gaping in the joints—would have sufficed to ensure detection."

"I presume you looked to the mirrors, between the boards and the plates, and you probed the beds and the bedclothes, as well as the curtains and carpets."

"That of course; and when we had absolutely completed every particle of the furniture in this way, then we examined the house itself. We divided its entire surface into compartments, which we numbered, so that none might be missed; then we scrutinized each individual square inch throughout the premises, including the two houses immediately adjoining, with the microscope, as before."

"The two houses adjoining!" I exclaimed; "you must have had a great deal of trouble."

"We had; but the reward offered is prodigious."

"You include the *grounds* about the houses?"

"All the grounds are paved with brick. They gave us comparatively little trouble. We examined the moss between the bricks, and found it undisturbed."

"You looked among D——'s papers, of course, and into the books of the library?"

"Certainly; we opened every package and parcel; we not only opened every book, but we turned over every leaf in each volume, not contenting ourselves with a mere shake, according to the fashion of some of our police officers. We also measured the thickness of every book *cover*, with the most accurate admeasurement, and applied to each the most jealous scrutiny of the microscope. Had any of the bindings been recently meddled with, it would have been utterly impossible that the fact should have escaped observation. Some five or six volumes, just from the hands of the binder, we carefully probed, longitudinally, with the needles."

"You explored the floors beneath the carpets?"

"Beyond doubt. We removed every carpet, and examined the boards with the microscope."

"And the paper on the walls?"

"Yes."

"You looked into the cellars?"

"We did."

"Then," I said, "you have been making a miscalculation, and the letter is *not* upon the premises as you suppose."

"I fear you are right there," said the prefect. "And now, Dupin, what would you advise me to do?"

"To make a thorough research of the premises."

"That is absolutely needless," replied G——. "I am not more sure that I breathe than I am that the letter is not at the hotel."

"I have no better advice to give you," said Dupin.

"You have, of course, an accurate description of the letter?"

"Oh, yes!"—and here the prefect, producing a memorandum book, proceeded to read aloud a minute account of the internal, and especially of the external, appearance of the missing document. Soon after finishing the perusal of this description, he took his departure, more entirely depressed in spirits than I had ever known the good gentleman before.

In about a month afterward he paid us another visit, and found us occupied very nearly as before. He took a pipe and a chair and entered into some ordinary conversation. At length I said:

"Well, but G——, what of the purloined letter? I presume you have at last made up your mind that there is no such thing as overreaching the minister?"

"Confound him, say I—yes; I made the reexamination, however, as Dupin suggested—but it was all labor lost, as I knew it would be."

"How much was the reward offered, did you say?" asked Dupin.

"Why, a very great deal—a *very* liberal reward—I don't like to say how much, precisely; but one thing I *will* say, that I wouldn't mind giving my individual check for fifty thousand francs to any one who could obtain me that letter. The fact is, it is becoming of more and more importance every day; and the reward has been lately doubled. If it were trebled, however, I could do no more than I have done."

"Why, yes," said Dupin, drawlingly, between the whiffs of his meerschaum, "I really—think, G——, you have not exerted yourself—to the utmost in this matter. You might—do a little more, I think, eh?"

"How?—in what way?"

"Why—*puff, puff*—you might—*puff, puff*—employ counsel in the matter, eh?—*puff, puff, puff*. Do you remember the story they tell of Abernethy?"

"No; hang Abernethy!"

"To be sure! hang him and welcome. But, once upon a time, a certain rich miser conceived the design of sponging upon this Abernethy for a medical opinion. Getting up, for this purpose, an ordinary conversation in a private company, he insinuated his case to the physician, as that of an imaginary individual.

" 'We will suppose,' said the miser, 'that his symptoms are such and such; now, doctor, what would *you* have directed him to take?'

" 'Take!' said the Abernethy, 'why, take *advice*, to be sure.' "

"But," said the prefect, a little discomposed, "*I* am *perfectly* willing to take advice, and to pay for it. I would *really* give fifty thousand francs to anyone who would aid me in the matter."

"In that case," replied Dupin, opening a drawer, and producing a checkbook, "you may as well fill me up a check for the amount mentioned. When you have signed it, I will hand you the letter."

I was astounded. The prefect appeared absolutely thunderstricken. For some minutes he remained speechless and motionless, looking incredulously at my friend with open mouth, and eyes that seemed starting from their sockets; then apparently recovering himself in some measure, he seized a pen, and after several pauses and vacant stares, finally filled up and signed a check for fifty thousand francs, and handed it across the table to Dupin. The latter examined it carefully and deposited it in his pocketbook; then, unlocking an escritoire, took thence a letter and gave it to the prefect. This functionary grasped it in a perfect agony of joy, opened it with a trembling hand, cast a rapid glance at its contents, and then, scrambling and struggling to the door rushed at length unceremoniously from the room and from the house, without having uttered a syllable since Dupin had requested him to fill up the check.

When he had gone, my friend entered into some explanations.

"The Parisian police," he said, "are exceedingly able in their way. They are persevering, ingenious, cunning, and thoroughly versed in the knowledge which their duties seem chiefly to demand. Thus, when G—— detailed to us his mode of searching the premises at the Hotel D——, I felt entire confidence in his having made a satisfactory investigation—so far as his labors extended."

"So far as his labors extended?" said I.

"Yes," said Dupin. "The measures adopted were not only the best of their kind, but carried out to absolute perfection. Had the letter been deposited within the range of their search, these fellows would, beyond a question, have found it."

I merely laughed—but he seemed quite serious in all that he said.

"The measures, then," he continued, "were good in their kind, and well executed; their defect lay in their being inapplicable to the case and to the man. A certain set of highly ingenious resources are, with the prefect, a sort of Procrustean bed, to which he forcibly adapts his designs. But he perpetually errs by being too deep or too shallow for the matter in hand; and many a schoolboy is a better reasoner than he. I knew one about eight years of age, whose success at guessing in the game of even and odd attracted universal admiration. This game is simple, and is played with marbles. One player holds in his hand a number of these toys, and demands of another whether that number is even or odd. If the guess is right, the guesser wins one; if wrong he loses one. The boy to whom I allude won all the marbles of the school. Of course he had some principle of guessing; and this lay in mere observation and admeasurement of the astuteness of his opponents. For example, an arrant simpleton is his opponent, and, holding up his closed hand, asks, 'Are they even or odd?' Our schoolboy replies, 'Odd,' and loses; but upon the second trial he wins, for he then says to himself: 'The simpleton had them even upon the first trial, and his amount of cunning is just sufficient to make him have them odd upon the second; I will therefore guess odd'; he guesses odd, and wins. Now, with a simpleton a degree above the first, he would have reasoned thus: 'This fellow finds that in the first instance I guessed odd, and, in the second, he will propose to himself, upon the first impulse, a simple variation from even to odd, as did the first simpleton; but then a second thought will suggest that this is too simple a variation and finally he will decide upon putting it even as before. I will therefore guess even'; he guesses even, and wins. Now this mode of reasoning in the schoolboy, whom his fellows termed 'lucky'—what, in its last analysis, is it?"

"It is merely," I said, "an identification of the reasoner's intellect with that of his opponent."

"It is," said Dupin; "and, upon inquiring of the boy by what means he effected the *thorough* identification in which his success consisted, I received answer as follows: 'When I wish to find out how wise, or how stupid, or how good, or how wicked is anyone, or what are his thoughts at the moment, I fashion the expression of my face, as accurately as possible, in accordance with the expression of his, and then wait to see what thoughts or sentiments arise in my mind or heart, as if to match or correspond with the expression.' This response of the schoolboy lies at the bottom of all the spurious profundity which has been attributed to Rochefoucauld, to La Bougive, to Machiavelli, and to Campanella."

"And the identification," I said, "of the reasoner's intellect with that of his opponent, depends, if I understand you aright, upon the accuracy with which the opponent's intellect is admeasured."

"For its practical value it depends upon this," replied Dupin; "and the prefect and his cohort fail so frequently, first, by default of this identification, and, secondly, by ill admeasurement, or rather through nonadmeasurement, of the intellect with which they are engaged. They consider only their *own* ideas of ingenuity; and, in searching for anything hidden, advert only to the modes in which *they* would have hidden it. They are right in this much—that their own ingenuity is a faithful representative of that of the *mass;* but when the cunning of the individual felon is diverse in character from their own, the felon foils them of course. This always happens when it is above their own, and very usually when it is below. They have no variation of principle in their investigations; at best, when urged by some unusual emergency—by some extraordinary reward—they extend or exaggerate their old modes of *practice,* without touching their principles. What, for example, in this case of D——, has been done to vary the principle of action? What is all this boring, and probing, and sounding, and scrutinizing with the microscope, and dividing the surface of the building into registered square inches—what is it all but an exaggeration of the *application* of the one principle or set of principles of search, which are based upon the one set of notions regarding human ingenuity, to which the prefect, in the long routine of his duty, has been accustomed? Do you not see he has taken it for granted that *all* men proceed to conceal a letter, not exactly in a gimlet hole bored in a chair leg, but, at least, in *some* out-of-the-way hole or corner suggested by the same tenor of thought which would urge a man to secrete a letter in a gimlet hole bored in a chair leg? And do you not see, also, that such *recherchés* nooks for concealment are adapted only for ordinary occasions, and would be adopted only by ordinary intellects; for, in all cases of concealment, a disposal of the article concealed—a disposal of it in this *recherché* manner—is, in the very first instance, presumable and presumed; and thus its discovery depends, not at all upon the acumen, but altogether upon the mere care, patience, and determination of the seekers; and where the case is of importance—or, what amounts to the same thing in the policial eyes, when the reward is of magnitude—the qualities in question have *never* been known to fail. You will now understand what I meant in suggesting that, had the purloined letter been hidden anywhere within the limits of the prefect's examination—in other words, had the principle of its concealment been comprehended within the principles of the prefect—its discovery would have been a matter altogether beyond question. This functionary, however, has been thoroughly mystified; and the remote source of his defeat lies in the supposition that the minister is a fool, because he has acquired renown as a poet. All fools are poets; this the prefect *feels;* and he is merely guilty of a *non distributio medii* in thence inferring that all poets are fools."

"But is this really the poet?" I asked. "There are two brothers, I know; and both have attained reputation in letters. The minister I believe has written learnedly on the differential calculus. He is a mathematician, and no poet."

"You are mistaken; I know him well; he is both. As poet *and* mathematician, he would reason well; as mere mathematician, he could not have reasoned at all, and thus would have been at the mercy of the prefect."

"You surprise me," I said, "by these opinions, which have been contradicted by the voice of the world. You do not mean to set at naught the well-digested idea of centuries? The mathematical reason has long been regarded as *the* reason *par excellence.*"

"'*Il y a à parier,*'" replied Dupin, quoting from Chamfort, "'*que toute idée publique, toute convention reçue, est une sottise, car elle a convenue au plus grand nombre.*' The mathematicians, I grant you, have done their best to promulgate the popular error to which you allude, and which is none the less an error for its promulgation as truth. With an art worthy a better cause, for example, they have insinuated the term 'analysis' into application to algebra. The French are the originators of this particular deception; but if a term is of any importance—if words derive any value from applicability—then 'analysis' conveys 'algebra' about as much as, in Latin, *ambitus* implies 'ambition,' *religio* 'religion,' or *homines honesti* a set of *honorable* men."

"You have a quarrel on hand, I see," said I, "with some of the algebraists of Paris; but proceed."

"I dispute the availability, and thus the value, of that reason which is cultivated in any especial form other than the abstractly logical. I dispute, in particular, the reason educed by mathematical study. The mathematics are the science of form and quantity; mathematical reasoning is merely logic applied to observation upon form and quantity. The great error lies in supposing that even the truths of what is called *pure* algebra are abstract or general truths. And this error is so egregious that I am confounded at the universality with which it has been received. Mathematical axioms are *not* axioms of general truth. What is true of *relation*— of form and quantity—is often grossly false in regard to morals, for example. In this latter science it is very usually *un*true that the aggregated parts are equal to the whole. In chemistry also the axiom fails. In the consideration of motive it fails; for two motives, each of a given value, have not, necessarily, a value when united equal to the sum of their values apart. There are numerous other mathematical truths which are only truths within the limits of *relation*. But the mathematician argues from his *finite truths,* through habit, as if they were of an absolutely general applicability —as the world indeed imagines them to be. Bryant, in his very learned *Mythology,* mentions an analogous source of error, when he says that 'although the pagan fables are not believed, yet we forget ourselves continually, and make inferences from them as existing realities.' With the algebraists, however, who are pagans themselves, the 'pagan fables' *are* believed, and the inferences are made, not so much through lapse of memory as through an unaccountable addling of the brains. In short, I never yet encountered the mere mathematician who could be trusted out of equal roots, or one who did not clandestinely hold it as a point of his faith that $x^2 + px$ was absolutely and unconditionally equal to q. Say to one of these gentlemen, by way of experiment, if you please, that you believe occasions may occur where $x^2 + px$ is *not* altogether equal to q, and, having made him understand what you mean, get out of his reach as speedily as convenient, for, beyond doubt, he will endeavor to knock you down.

"I mean to say," continued Dupin, while I merely laughed at his last observations, "that if the minister had been no more than a mathematician, the prefect would have been under no necessity of giving me this check. I knew him, however, as both mathematician and poet, and my measures were adapted to his capacity, with reference to the circumstances by which he was surrounded. I knew him as a courtier, too, and as a bold *intrigant*. Such a man, I considered, could not fail to be aware of the ordinary policial modes of action. He could not have failed to anticipate—and events have proved that he did not fail to anticipate—the waylayings to which he was subjected. He must have foreseen, I reflected, the secret investigations of his premises. His frequent absences from home at night, which were hailed by the prefect as certain aids to his success, I regarded only as *ruses,* to afford opportunity for thorough search to the police, and thus the sooner to impress them with the conviction to which G——, in fact, did finally arrive —the conviction that the letter was not upon the premises. I felt, also, that the whole train of thought, which I was at some pains in detailing to you just now, concerning the invariable principle of policial action in searches for articles concealed—I felt that this whole train of thought would necessarily pass through the mind of the minister. It would imperatively lead him to despise all the ordinary *nooks* of concealment. *He* could not, I reflected, be so weak as not to see that the most intricate and remote recess of his hotel would be as open as his commonest closets to the eyes, to the probes, to the gimlets, and to the microscopes of the prefect. I saw, in fine, that he would be driven, as a matter of course, to *simplicity,* if not deliberately induced to it as a matter of choice. You will remember, perhaps, how desperately the prefect laughed when I suggested, upon our first interview, that it was just possible this mystery troubled him so much on account of its being so *very* self-evident."

"Yes," said I, "I remember his merriment well. I really thought he would have fallen into convulsions."

"The material world," continued Dupin, "abounds with very strict analogies to the immaterial; and thus some color of truth has been given to the rhetorical dogma, that metaphor, or simile, may be made to strengthen an argument as well as to embellish a description. The principle of the *vis inertiae,* for example, seems to be identical in physics and metaphysics. It is not more true in the former, that a large body is with more difficulty set in motion than a smaller one, and that its subsequent *momentum* is commensurate with this difficulty, than it is, in the latter, that intellects of the vaster capacity, while more forcible, more constant, and more eventful in their movements than those of inferior grade, are yet the less readily moved, and more embarrassed, and full of hesitation in the first few steps of their progress. Again: have you ever noticed which of the street signs over the shop doors are the most attractive of attention?"

"I have never given the matter a thought," I said.

"There is a game of puzzles," he resumed, "which is played upon a map. One party playing requires another to find a given word—the name of town, river, state, or empire —any word, in short, upon the motley and perplexed surface of the chart. A novice in the game generally seeks to embarrass his opponents by giving them the most minutely lettered names; but the adept selects such words as stretch, in large characters, from one end of the chart to the other. These, like the overlargely lettered signs and placards of the street, escape observation by dint of being excessively obvious; and here the physical oversight is precisely analogous with the moral inapprehension by which the intellect suffers to pass unnoticed those considerations which are too obtrusively and too palpably self-evident. But this is a point, it appears, somewhat above or beneath the understanding of the prefect. He never once thought it probable, or possible, that the minister had deposited the letter immediately beneath the nose of the whole world, by way of best preventing any portion of that world from perceiving it.

"But the more I reflected upon the daring, dashing, and discriminating ingenuity of D——; upon the fact that the document must always have been *at hand,* if he intended to use it to good purpose; and upon the decisive evidence, obtained by the prefect, that it was not hidden within the limits of that dignitary's ordinary search—the more satisfied I became that, to conceal this letter, the minister had resorted to the comprehensive and sagacious expedient of not attempting to conceal it at all.

"Full of these ideas, I prepared myself with a pair of green spectacles, and called one fine morning, quite by accident, at the ministerial hotel. I found D—— at home, yawning, lounging, and dawdling, as usual, and pretending to be in the last extremity of ennui. He is, perhaps, the most really energetic human being now alive—but that is only when nobody sees him.

"To be even with him, I complained of my weak eyes, and lamented the necessity of the spectacles, under cover of which I cautiously and thoroughly surveyed the whole apartment, while seemingly intent only upon the conversation of my host.

"I paid especial attention to a large writing table near which he sat, and upon which lay confusedly some miscellaneous letters and other papers, with one or two musical instruments and a few books. Here, however, after a long and very deliberate scrutiny, I saw nothing to excite particular suspicion.

"At length my eyes, in going the circuit of the room, fell upon a trumpery filigree card rack of pasteboard that hung dangling by a dirty blue ribbon, from a little brass knob just beneath the middle of the mantelpiece. In this rack, which had three or four compartments, were five or six visiting cards and a solitary letter. This last was much soiled and crumpled. It was torn nearly in two, across the middle—as if a design, in the first instance, to tear it entirely up as worthless had been altered, or stayed, in the second. It had a large black seal, bearing the D—— cipher *very* conspicuously, and was addressed, in a diminutive female hand, to D —— the minister, himself. It was thrust carelessly, and even, as it seemed, contemptuously, into one of the uppermost divisions of the rack.

"No sooner had I glanced at this letter than I concluded it to be that of which I was in search. To be sure, it was, to all appearance, radically different from the one of which the prefect had read us so minute a description. Here the seal was large and black, with the D—— cipher; there it was small and red, with the ducal arms of the S—— family. Here, the address, to the minister, was diminutive and feminine; there, the superscription, to a certain royal personage, was markedly bold and decided; the size alone formed a point of correspondence. But, then, the *radicalness* of these differences, which was excessive; the dirt; the soiled and torn condition of the paper, so inconsistent with the *true* methodical habits of D——, and so suggestive of a design to delude the beholder into an idea of the worthlessness of the document—these things, together with the hyperobtrusive situation of this document, full in the view of every visitor, and thus exactly in accordance with the conclusions to which I had previously arrived; these things, I say, were strongly corroborative of suspicion, in one who came with the intention to suspect.

"I protracted my visit as long as possible, and, while I maintained a most animated discussion with the minister, upon a topic which I knew well had never failed to interest and excite him, I kept my attention really riveted upon the letter. In this examination, I committed to memory its external appearance and arrangement in the rack—and also fell, at length, upon a discovery which set at rest whatever trivial doubt I might have entertained. In scrutinizing the edges of the paper, I observed them to be more *chafed* than seemed necessary. They presented the *broken* appearance which is manifested when a stiff paper, having been once folded and pressed with a folder, is refolded in a reversed direction, in the same creases or edges which had formed the original fold. This discovery was sufficient. It was clear to me that the letter had been turned, as a glove, inside out, redirected, and resealed. I bade the minister good morning, and took my departure at once, leaving a gold snuffbox upon the table.

"The next morning I called for the snuffbox, when we resumed, quite eagerly, the conversation of the preceding day. While thus engaged, however, a loud report, as if of a pistol, was heard immediately beneath the windows of the hotel, and was succeeded by a series of fearful screams, and the shoutings of a terrified mob. D—— rushed to a casement, threw it open, and looked out. In the meantime I stepped to the card rack, took the letter, put it in my pocket, and replaced it by a facsimile (so far as regards externals) which I had carefully prepared at my lodgings—imitating the D—— cipher, very readily, by means of a seal formed of bread.

"The disturbance in the street had been occasioned by the frantic behavior of a man with a musket. He had fired it among a crowd of women and children. It proved, however, to have been without ball, and the fellow was suffered to go his way as a lunatic or a drunkard. When he had gone, D—— came from the window, whither I had followed him immediately upon securing the object in view. Soon afterward I bade him farewell. The pretended lunatic was a man in my own pay."

"But what purpose had you," I asked, "in replacing the letter by a facsimile? Would it not have been better, at the first visit, to have seized it openly, and departed?"

"D——," replied Dupin, "is a desperate man, and a man

of nerve. His hotel, too, is not without attendants devoted to his interests. Had I made the wild attempt you suggest, I might never have left the ministerial presence alive. The good people of Paris might have heard of me no more. But I had an object apart from these considerations. You know my political prepossessions. In this matter, I act as a partisan of the lady concerned. For eighteen months the minister has had her in his power. She has now him in hers—since, being unaware that the letter is not in his possession, he will proceed with his exactions as if it was. Thus will he inevitably commit himself, at once, to his political destruction. His downfall, too, will not be more precipitate than awkward. It is all very well to talk about the *facilis descensus Averni;* but in all kinds of climbing, as Catalani said of singing, it is far more easy to get up than to come down. In the present instance I have no sympathy—at least no pity—for him who descends. He is that *monstrum horrendum,* an unprincipled man of genius. I confess, however, that I should like very well to know the precise character of his thoughts when, being defied by her whom the prefect terms 'a certain personage,' he is reduced to opening the letter which I left for him in the card rack."

"How? Did you put anything particular in it?"

"Why, it did not seem altogether right to leave the interior blank—that would have been insulting. D——, at Vienna once, did me an evil turn, which I told him, quite good-humoredly, that I should remember. So, as I knew he would feel some curiosity in regard to the identity of the person who had outwitted him, I thought it a pity not to give him a clue. He is well acquainted with my MS., and I just copied into the middle of the blank sheet the words:

> *Un dessein si funeste,*
> *S'il n' est digne d' Atrée, est digne de Thyeste.*

They are to be found in Crébillon's *Atrée.*"

THE ADVENTURE OF THE SPECKLED BAND

Sir Arthur Conan Doyle

In glancing over my notes of the seventy-odd cases in which
I have during the last eight years studied the methods of my
friend Sherlock Holmes, I find many tragic, some comic, a
large number merely strange, but none commonplace; for
working as he did rather for the love of his art than for the
acquirement of wealth, he refused to associate himself with
any investigation which did not tend towards the unusual,
and even the fantastic. Of all these varied cases, however,
I cannot recall any which presented more singular features
than that which was associated with the well-known Surrey
family of the Roylotts of Stoke Moran. The events in question occurred in the early days of my association with
Holmes, when we were sharing rooms as bachelors, in Baker
Street. It is possible that I might have placed them upon
record before, but a promise of secrecy was made at the

time, from which I have only been freed during the last month by the untimely death of the lady to whom the pledge was given. It is perhaps as well that the facts should now come to light, for I have reasons to know there are widespread rumours as to the death of Dr. Grimesby Roylott which tend to make the matter even more terrible than the truth.

It was early in April, in the year '83, that I woke one morning to find Sherlock Holmes standing, fully dressed, by the side of my bed. He was a late riser as a rule, and, as the clock on the mantelpiece showed me that it was only a quarter past seven, I blinked up at him in some surprise, and perhaps just a little resentment, for I was myself regular in my habits.

"Very sorry to knock you up, Watson," said he, "but it's the common lot this morning. Mrs. Hudson has been knocked up, she retorted upon me, and I on you."

"What is it, then? A fire?"

"No, a client. It seems that a young lady has arrived in a considerable state of excitement, who insists upon seeing me. She is waiting now in the sitting room. Now, when young ladies wander about the metropolis at this hour of the morning, and knock sleepy people up out of their beds, I presume that it is something very pressing which they have to communicate. Should it prove to be an interesting case, you would, I am sure, wish to follow it from the outset. I thought at any rate that I should call you, and give you the chance."

"My dear fellow, I would not miss it for anything."

I had no keener pleasure than in following Holmes in his professional investigations, and in admiring the rapid deductions, as swift as intuitions, and yet always founded on a logical basis, with which he unravelled the problems which were submitted to him. I rapidly threw on my clothes, and was ready in a few minutes to accompany my friend down to the sitting room. A lady dressed in black and heavily veiled, who had been sitting in the window, rose as we entered.

"Good morning, madam," said Holmes cheerily. "My name is Sherlock Holmes. This is my intimate friend and associate, Dr. Watson, before whom you can speak as freely as before myself. Ha, I am glad to see that Mrs. Hudson has had the good sense to light the fire. Pray, draw up to it, and I shall order you a cup of hot coffee, for I observe that you are shivering."

"It is not cold which makes me shiver," said the woman in a low voice, changing her seat as requested.

"What then?"

"It is fear, Mr. Holmes. It is terror." She raised her veil as she spoke, and we could see that she was indeed in a pitiable state of agitation, her face all drawn and grey, with restless, frightened eyes, like those of some hunted animal. Her features and figure were those of a woman of thirty, but her hair was shot with premature grey, and her expression was weary and haggard. Sherlock Holmes ran her over with one of his quick, all-comprehensive glances.

"You must not fear," said he soothingly, bending forward and patting her forearm. "We shall soon set matters right, I have no doubt. You have come in by train this morning, I see."

"You know me, then?"

"No, but I observe the second half of a return ticket in the palm of your left glove. You must have started early, and yet you had a good drive in a dog cart, along heavy roads, before you reached the station."

The lady gave a violent start, and stared in bewilderment at my companion.

"There is no mystery, my dear madam," said he, smiling. "The left arm of your jacket is spattered with mud in no less than seven places. The marks are perfectly fresh. There is no vehicle save a dog cart which throws up mud in that way, and then only when you sit on the left-hand side of the driver."

"Whatever your reasons may be, you are perfectly correct," said she. "I started from home before six, reached

Leatherhead at twenty past, and came in by the first train to Waterloo. Sir, I can stand this strain no longer; I shall go mad if it continues. I have no one to turn to—none, save only one, who cares for me, and he, poor fellow, can be of little aid. I have heard of you, Mr. Holmes; I have heard of you from Mrs. Farintosh, whom you helped in the hour of her sore need. It was from her that I had your address. Oh, sir, do you not think you could help me too, and at least throw a little light through the dense darkness which surrounds me? At present it is out of my power to reward you for your services, but in a month or two, I shall be married, with the control of my own income, and then at least you shall not find me ungrateful."

Holmes turned to his desk, and unlocking it, drew out a small casebook which he consulted.

"Farintosh," said he. "Ah, yes, I recall the case; it was concerned with an opal tiara. I think it was before your time, Watson. I can only say, madam, that I shall be happy to devote the same care to your case as I did to that of your friend. As to reward, my profession is its reward; but you are at liberty to defray whatever expenses I may be put to, at the time which suits you best. And now I beg that you will lay before us everything that may help us in forming an opinion upon the matter."

"Alas!" replied our visitor. "The very horror of my situation lies in the fact that my fears are so vague, and my suspicions depend so entirely upon small points, which might seem trivial to another, that even he to whom of all others I have a right to look for help and advice looks upon all that I tell him about it as the fancies of a nervous woman. He does not say so, but I can read it from his soothing answers and averted eyes. But I have heard, Mr. Holmes, that you can see deeply into the manifold wickedness of the human heart. You may advise me how to walk amid the dangers which encompass me."

"I am all attention, madam."

"My name is Helen Stoner, and I am living with my

stepfather, who is the last survivor of one of the oldest Saxons families in England, the Roylotts of Stoke Moran, on the western border of Surrey."

Holmes nodded his head. "The name is familiar to me," said he.

"The family was at one time among the richest in England, and the estate extended over the borders into Berkshire in the north, and Hampshire in the west. In the last century, however, four successive heirs were of a dissolute and wasteful disposition, and the family ruin was eventually completed by a gambler, in the days of the Regency. Nothing was left save a few acres of ground and the two-hundred-year-old house, which is itself crushed under a heavy mortgage. The last squire dragged out his existence there, living the horrible life of an aristocratic pauper; but his only son, my stepfather, seeing that he must adapt himself to the new conditions, obtained an advance from a relative, which enabled him to take a medical degree, and went out to Calcutta, where, by his professional skill and his force of character, he established a large practice. In a fit of anger, however, caused by some robberies which had been perpetrated in the house, he beat his native butler to death, and narrowly escaped a capital sentence. As it was, he suffered a long term of imprisonment, and afterwards returned to England a morose and disappointed man.

"When Dr. Roylott was in India he married my mother, Mrs. Stoner, the young widow of Major General Stoner, of the Bengal Artillery. My sister Julia and I were twins, and we were only two years old at the time of my mother's remarriage. She had a considerable sum of money, not less than a thousand a year, and this she bequeathed to Dr. Roylott entirely whilst we resided with him, with a provision that a certain annual sum should be allowed to each of us in the event of our marriage. Shortly after our return to England my mother died—she was killed eight years ago in a railway accident near Crewe. Dr. Roylott then abandoned his attempts to establish himself in practice in London, and took us to live with him in the ancestral house at Stoke Moran. The money which my mother had left was enough for all our wants, and there seemed no obstacle to our happiness.

"But a terrible change came over our stepfather about this time. Instead of making friends and exchanging visits with our neighbours, who had at first been overjoyed to see a Roylott of Stoke Moran back in the old family seat, he shut himself up in his house, and seldom came out save to indulge in ferocious quarrels with whoever might cross his path. Violence of temper approaching to mania has been hereditary in the men of the family, and in my stepfather's case it had, I believe, been intensified by his long residence in the tropics. A series of disgraceful brawls took place, two of which ended in the police court, until at last he became the terror of the village, and the folks would fly at his approach, for he is a man of immense strength, and absolutely uncontrollable in his anger.

"Last week he hurled the local blacksmith over a parapet into a stream, and it was only by paying over all the money that I could gather together that I was able to avert another public exposure. He had no friends at all save the wandering gipsies, and he would give these vagabonds leave to encamp upon the few acres of bramble-covered land which represent the family estate, and would accept in return the hospitality of their tents, wandering away with them sometimes for weeks on end. He has a passion also for Indian animals, which are sent over to him by a correspondent, and he has at this moment a cheetah and a baboon, which wander freely over his grounds, and are feared by the villagers almost as much as their master.

"You can imagine from what I say that my poor sister Julia and I had no great pleasure in our lives. No servant would stay with us, and for a long time we did all the work of the house. She was but thirty at the time of her death, and yet her hair had already begun to whiten, even as mine has."

"Your sister is dead, then?"

"She died just two years ago, and it is of her death that

I wish to speak to you. You can understand that, living the life which I have described, we were little likely to see anyone of our own age and position. We had, however, an aunt, my mother's maiden sister, Miss Honoria Westphail, who lives near Harrow, and we were occasionally allowed to pay short visits at this lady's house. Julia went there at Christmas two years ago, and met there a half-pay major of marines, to whom she became engaged. My stepfather learned of the engagement when my sister returned, and offered no objection to the marriage; but within a fortnight of the day which had been fixed for the wedding, the terrible event occurred which has deprived me of my only companion."

Sherlock Holmes had been leaning back in his chair with his eyes closed, and his head sunk in a cushion, but he half opened his lids now, and glanced across at his visitor.

"Pray be precise as to details," said he.

"It is easy for me to be so, for every event of that dreadful time is seared into my memory. The manor house is, as I have already said, very old, and only one wing is now inhabited. The bedrooms in this wing are on the ground floor, the sitting rooms being in the central block of the buildings. Of these bedrooms, the first is Dr. Roylott's, the second my sister's, and the third my own. There is no communication between them, but they all open out into the same corridor. Do I make myself plain?"

"Perfectly so."

"The windows of the three rooms open out upon the lawn. The fatal night Dr. Roylott had gone to his room early, though we knew that he had not retired to rest, for my sister was troubled by the smell of the strong Indian cigars which it was his custom to smoke. She left her room, therefore, and came into mine, where she sat for some time, chatting about her approaching wedding. At eleven o'clock she rose to leave me, but she paused at the door and looked back.

" 'Tell me, Helen,' said she, 'have you ever heard anyone whistle in the dead of the night?'

" 'Never,' said I.

" 'I suppose that you could not possibly whistle yourself in your sleep?'

" 'Certainly not. But why?'

" 'Because during the last few nights I have always, about three in the morning, heard a low clear whistle. I am a light sleeper, and it has awakened me. I cannot tell where it came from—perhaps from the next room, perhaps from the lawn. I thought that I would just ask you whether you had heard it.'

" 'No, I have not. It must be those wretched gipsies in the plantation.'

" 'Very likely. And yet if it were on the lawn I wonder that you did not hear it also.'

" 'Ah, but I sleep more heavily than you.'

" 'Well, it is of no great consequence at any rate,' she smiled back at me, closed my door, and a few moments later I heard her key turn in the lock.'

"Indeed," said Holmes. "Was it your custom always to lock yourselves in at night?"

"Always."

"And why?"

"I think that I mentioned to you that the doctor kept a cheetah and a baboon. We had no feeling of security unless our doors were locked."

"Quite so. Pray proceed with your statement."

"I could not sleep that night. A vague feeling of impending misfortune impressed me. My sister and I, you will recollect, were twins, and you know how subtle are the links which bind two souls which are so closely allied. It was a wild night. The wind was howling outside, and the rain was beating and splashing against the windows. Suddenly, amidst all the hubbub of the gale, there burst forth the wild scream of a terrified woman. I knew that it was my sister's voice. I sprang from my bed, wrapped a shawl round me, and rushed into the corridor. As I opened my door I seemed to hear a low whistle, such as my sister described, and a few moments later a clanging sound, as if a mass of metal had fallen. As I ran down the passage my sister's door was un-locked, and revolved slowly upon its hinges. I stared at it horror stricken, not knowing what was about to issue from it. By the light of the corridor lamp I saw my sister appear in the opening, her face blanched with terror, her hands groping for help, her whole figure swaying to and fro like that of a drunkard. I ran to her and threw my arms round her, but at that moment her knees seemed to give way and she fell to the ground. She writhed as one who is in terrible pain, and her limbs were dreadfully convulsed. At first I thought that she had not recognized me, but as I bent over her she suddenly shrieked out in a voice which I shall never forget, 'Oh, my God! Helen! It was the band! The speckled band!' There was something else which she would have fain have said, and she stabbed with her finger into the air in the direction of the doctor's room, but a fresh convulsion seized her and choked her words. I rushed out, calling loudly for my stepfather, and I met him hastening from his room in his dressing gown. When he reached my sister's side she was unconscious, and though he poured brandy down her throat, and sent for medical aid from the village, all efforts were in vain, for she slowly sank and died without having recovered her consciousness. Such was the dreadful end of my sister."

"One moment," said Holmes; "are you sure about this whistle and metallic sound? Could you swear to it?"

"That was what the county coroner asked me at the inquiry. It is my strong impression that I heard it, and yet among the crash of the gale, and the creaking of an old house, I may possibly have been deceived."

"Was your sister dressed?"

"No, she was in her nightdress. In her right hand was found the charred stump of a match, and in her left a match-box."

"Showing that she had struck a light and looked about her when the alarm took place. That is important. And what conclusions did the coroner come to?"

"He investigated the case with great care, for Dr. Roylott's conduct had long been notorious in the county, but he was unable to find any satisfactory cause of death. My evidence showed that the door had been fastened upon the inner side, and the windows were blocked by old-fashioned shutters with broad iron bars, which were secured every night. The walls were carefully sounded, and were shown to be quite solid all round, and the flooring was also thoroughly examined, with the same result. The chimney is wide, but is barred up by four large staples. It is certain, therefore, that my sister was quite alone when she met her end. Besides, there were no marks of any violence upon her."

"How about poison?"

"The doctors examined her for it, but without success."

"What do you think that this unfortunate lady died of, then?"

"It is my belief that she died of pure fear and nervous shock, though what it was which frightened her I cannot imagine."

"Were there gipsies in the plantation at the time?"

"Yes, there are nearly always some there."

"Ah, and what did you gather from this allusion to a band—a speckled band?"

"Sometimes I have thought that it was merely the wild talk of delirium, sometimes that it may have referred to some band of people, perhaps to these very gipsies in the plantation. I do not know whether the spotted handkerchiefs which so many of them wear over their heads might have suggested the strange adjective which she used."

Holmes shook his head like a man who is far from being satisfied.

"These are very deep waters," said he; "pray go on with your narrative."

"Two years have passed since then, and my life has been until lately lonelier than ever. A month ago, however, a dear friend, whom I have known for many years, has done me the honour to ask my hand in marriage. His name is Armitage—Percy Armitage—the second son of Mr.

Armitage, of Crane Water, near Reading. My stepfather has offered no opposition to the match, and we are to be married in the course of the spring. Two days ago some repairs were started in the west wing of the building, and my bedroom wall has been pierced, so that I have had to move into the chamber in which my sister died, and to sleep in the very bed in which she slept. Imagine, then, my thrill of terror when last night, as I lay awake, thinking over her terrible fate, I suddenly heard in the silence of the night the low whistle which had been the herald of her own death. I sprang up and lit the lamp, but nothing was to be seen in the room. I was too shaken to go to bed again, however, so I dressed, and as soon as it was daylight I slipped down, got a dog cart at the Crown Inn, which is opposite, and drove to Leatherhead, from whence I have come on this morning, with the one object of seeing you and asking your advice."

"You have done wisely," said my friend. "But have you told me all?"

"Yes, all."

"Miss Roylott, you have not. You are screening your stepfather."

"Why, what do you mean?"

For answer Holmes pushed back the frill of black lace which fringed the hand that lay upon our visitor's knee. Five little livid spots, the marks of four fingers and a thumb, were printed upon the white wrist.

"You have been cruelly used," said Holmes.

The lady coloured deeply, and covered over her injured wrist. "He is a hard man," she said, "and perhaps he hardly knows his own strength."

There was a long silence, during which Holmes leaned his chin upon his hands and stared into the crackling fire.

"This is very deep business," he said at last. "There are a thousand details which I should desire to know before I decide upon our course of action. Yet we have not a moment to lose. If we were to come to Stoke Moran today, would it

be possible for us to see over these rooms without the knowledge of your stepfather?"

"As it happens, he spoke of coming into town today
upon some most important business. It is probable that he
will be away all day, and that there would be nothing to
disturb you. We have a housekeeper now, but she is old and
foolish, and I could easily get her out of the way."

"Excellent. You are not averse to this trip, Watson?"

"By no means."

"Then we shall both come. What are you going to do
yourself ?"

"I have one or two things which I would wish to do now
that I am in town. But I shall return by the twelve o'clock
train, so as to be there in time for your coming."

"And you may expect us early in the afternoon. I have
myself some small business matters to attend to. Will you not
wait and breakfast?"

"No, I must go. My heart is lightened already since I
have confided my trouble to you. I shall look forward to
seeing you again this afternoon." She dropped her thick
black veil over her face, and glided from the room.

"And what do you think of it all, Watson?" asked Sherlock Holmes, leaning back in his chair.

"It seems to me to be a most dark and sinister business."

"Dark enough and sinister enough."

"Yet if the lady is correct in saying that the flooring and
walls are sound, and that the door, window, and chimney are
impassable, then her sister must have been undoubtedly
alone when she met her mysterious end."

"What becomes, then, of these nocturnal whistles, and
what of the very peculiar words of the dying woman?"

"I cannot think."

"When you combine the ideas of whistles at night, the
presence of a band of gipsies who are on intimate terms with
this old doctor, the fact that we have every reason to believe
that the doctor has an interest in preventing his stepdaughter's marriage, the dying allusion to a band, and finally, the

fact that Miss Helen Stoner heard a metallic clang, which might have been caused by one of those metal bars which secured the shutters falling back into their place, I think there is good ground to think that the mystery may be cleared along those lines."

"But what, then, did the gipsies do?"

"I cannot imagine."

"I see many objections to any such a theory."

"And so do I. It is precisely for that reason that we are going to Stoke Moran this day. I want to see whether the objections are fatal, or if they may be explained away. But what, in the name of the devil!"

The ejaculation had been drawn from my companion by the fact that our door had been suddenly dashed open, and that a huge man framed himself in the aperture. His costume was a peculiar mixture of the professional and of the agricultural, having a black top hat, a long frock coat, and a pair of high gaiters, with a hunting crop swinging in his hand. So tall was he that his hat actually brushed the crossbar of the doorway, and his breadth seemed to span it across from side to side. A large face, seared with a thousand wrinkles, burned yellow with the sun, and marked with every evil passion, was turned from one to the other of us, while his deep-set, bile-shot eyes, and the high thin fleshless nose, gave him somewhat the resemblance to a fierce old bird of prey.

"Which of you is Holmes?" asked this apparition.

"My name, sir, but you have the advantage of me," said my companion quietly.

"I am Dr. Grimesby Roylott, of Stoke Moran."

"Indeed, doctor," said Holmes blandly. "Pray take a seat."

"I will do nothing of the kind. My stepdaughter has been here. I have traced her. What has she been saying to you?"

"It is a little cold for the time of the year," said Holmes.

"What has she been saying to you?" screamed the old man furiously.

"But I have heard that the crocuses promise well," continued my companion imperturbably.

"Ha! You put me off, do you?" said our new visitor, taking a step forward, and shaking his hunting crop. "I know you, you scoundrel! I have heard of you before. You are Holmes the meddler."

My friend smiled.

"Holmes the busybody!"

His smile broadened.

"Holmes the Scotland Yard jack-in-office."

Holmes chuckled heartily. "Your conversation is most entertaining," said he. "When you go out close the door, for there is a decided draught."

"I will go when I have had my say. Don't you dare to meddle with my affairs. I know that Miss Stoner has been here—I traced her! I am a dangerous man to fall foul of! See here." He stepped swiftly forward, seized the poker and bent it into a curve with his huge brown hands.

"See that you keep yourself out of my grip," he snarled, and hurling the twisted poker into the fireplace, he strode out of the room.

"He seems a very amiable person," said Holmes, laughing. "I am not quite so bulky, but if he had remained I might have shown him that my grip was not much more feeble than his own." As he spoke he picked up the steel poker, and with a sudden effort straightened it out again.

"Fancy his having the insolence to confound me with the official detective force! This incident gives zest to our investigation, however, and I only trust that our little friend will not suffer from her imprudence in allowing this brute to trace her. And now, Watson, we shall order breakfast, and afterwards I shall walk down to Doctors' Commons, where I hope to get some data which may help us in this matter."

It was nearly one o'clock when Sherlock Holmes returned from his excursion. He held in his hand a sheet of blue paper, scrawled over with notes and figures.

"I have seen the will of the deceased wife," said he. 'To

determine its exact meaning I have been obliged to work out the present prices of the investments with which it is concerned. The total income, which at the time of the wife's death was little short of eleven hundred pounds, is now through the fall in agricultural prices not more than seven hundred fifty. Each daughter can claim an income of two hundred fifty pounds, in case of marriage. It is evident, therefore, that if both girls had married this beauty would have had a mere pittance, while even one of them would cripple him to a serious extent. My morning's work has not been wasted, since it has proved that he has the very strongest motives for standing in the way of anything of the sort. And now, Watson, this is too serious for dawdling, especially as the old man is aware that we are interesting ourselves in his affairs, so if you are ready we shall call a cab and drive to Waterloo. I should be very much obliged if you would slip your revolver into your pocket. An Eley's number two is an excellent argument with gentlemen who can twist steel pokers into knots. That and a toothbrush are, I think, all that we need."

At Waterloo we were fortunate in catching a train for Leatherhead, where he hired a trap at the station inn, and drove for four or five miles through the lovely Surrey lanes. It was a perfect day, with a bright sun and a few fleecy clouds in the heavens. The trees and wayside hedges were just throwing out their first green shoots, and the air was full of the pleasant smell of the moist earth. To me at least there was a strange contrast between the sweet promise of the spring and this sinister quest upon which we were engaged. My companion sat in front of the trap, his arms folded, his hat pulled down over his eyes, and his chin sunk upon his breast, buried in the deepest thought. Suddenly, however, he started, tapped me on the shoulder, and pointed over the meadows.

"Look there!" said he.

A heavily timbered park stretched up in a gentle slope, thickening into a grove at the highest point. From amidst the branches there jutted out the grey gables and high roof-tree of a very old mansion.

"Stoke Moran?" said he.

"Yes, sir, that be the house of Dr. Grimesby Roylott," remarked the driver.

"There is some building going on there," said Holmes; "that is where we are going."

"There's the village," said the driver, pointing to a cluster of roofs some distance to the left; "but if you want to get to the house, you'll find it shorter to go over this stile, and so by the footpath over the fields. There it is, where the lady is walking."

"And the lady, I fancy, is Miss Stoner," observed Holmes, shading his eyes. "Yes, I think we had better do as you suggest."

We got off, paid our fare, and the trap rattled back on its way to Leatherhead.

"I thought it as well," said Holmes, as we climbed the stile, "that this fellow should think we had come here as architects, or on some definite business. It may stop his gossip. Good afternoon, Miss Stoner. You see that we have been as good as our word."

Our client of the morning had hurried forward to meet us with a face which spoke her joy. "I have been waiting so eagerly for you," she cried, shaking hands with us warmly. "All has turned out splendidly. Dr. Roylott has gone to town, and it is unlikely that he will be back before evening."

"We have had the pleasure of making the doctor's acquaintance," said Holmes, and in a few words he sketched out what had occurred. Miss Stoner turned white to the lips as she listened.

"Good heavens!" she cried, "he has followed me, then."

"So it appears."

"He is so cunning that I never know when I am safe from him. What will he say when he returns?"

"He must guard himself, for he may find that there is someone more cunning than himself upon his track. You must lock yourself from him tonight. If he is violent, we shall take you away to your aunt's at Harrow. Now, we must make the best use of our time, so kindly take us at once to the rooms which we are to examine."

The building was of grey, lichen-blotched stone, with a high central portion, and two curving wings, like the claws of a crab, thrown out on each side. In one of these wings the windows were broken, and blocked with wooden boards, while the roof was partly caved in, a picture of ruin. The central portion was in little better repair, but the right-hand block was comparatively modern, and the blinds in the windows, with the blue smoke curling up from the chimneys, showed that this was where the family resided. Some scaffolding had been erected against the end wall, and the stonework had been broken into, but there were no signs of any workmen at the moment of our visit. Holmes walked slowly up and down the ill-trimmed lawn, and examined with deep attention the outsides of the windows.

"This, I take it, belongs to the room in which you used to sleep, the centre one to your sister's, and the one next to the main building to Dr. Roylott's chamber?"

"Exactly so. But I am now sleeping in the middle one."

"Pending the alterations, as I understand. By the way, there does not seem to be any very pressing need for repairs at that end wall."

"There were none. I believe that it was an excuse to move me from my room."

"Ah! that is suggestive. Now, on the other side of this narrow wing runs the corridor from which these three rooms open. There are windows in it, of course?"

"Yes, but very small ones. Too narrow for anyone to pass through."

"As you both locked your doors at night your rooms were unapproachable from that side. Now, would you have the kindness to go into your room, and to bar your shutters."

Miss Stoner did so, and Holmes, after a careful examination through the open window, endeavoured in every way to force the shutter open, but without success. There was no slit through which a knife could be passed to raise the bar. Then with his lens he tested the hinges, but they were of solid iron, built firmly into the massive masonry. "Hum!" said he, scratching his chin in some perplexity, "my theory certainly presents some difficulty. No one could pass these shutters if they were bolted. Well, we shall see if the inside throws any light upon the matter."

A small side door led into the whitewashed corridor from which the three bedrooms opened. Holmes refused to examine the third chamber, so we passed at once to the second, that in which Miss Stoner was now sleeping, and in which her sister had met her fate. It was a homely little room, with a low ceiling and a gaping fireplace, after the fashion of old country houses. A brown chest of drawers stood in one corner, a narrow white-counterpaned bed in another, and a dressing table on the left-hand side of the window. These articles, with two small wickerwork chairs, made up all the furniture in the room, save for a square of Wilton carpet in the centre. The boards round and the panelling of the walls were brown, worm-eaten oak, so old and discoloured that it may have dated from the original building of the house. Holmes drew one of the chairs into a corner and sat silent, while his eyes travelled round and round and up and down, taking in every detail of the apartment.

'Where does that bell communicate with?' he asked at last, pointing to a thick bell rope which hung down beside the bed, the tassel actually lying upon the pillow.

"It goes to the housekeeper's room."

"It looks newer than the other things?"

"Yes, it was only put there a couple of years ago."

"Your sister asked for it, I suppose?"

"No, I never heard of her using it. We used always to get what we wanted for ourselves."

"Indeed, it seemed unnecessary to put so nice a bellpull there. You will excuse me for a few minutes while I satisfy myself as to this floor." He threw himself down upon his face with his lens in his hand, and crawled swiftly backwards and forwards, examining minutely the cracks between the boards. Then he did the same with the woodwork with which the chamber was panelled. Finally he walked over to the bed and spent some time in staring at it, and in running his eye up and down the wall. Finally he took the bell rope in his hand and gave it a brisk tug.

"Why, it's a dummy," said he.

"Won't it ring?"

"No, it is not even attached to a wire. This is very interesting. You can see now that it is fastened to a hook just above where the little opening of the ventilator is."

"How very absurd! I never noticed that before."

"Very strange!" muttered Holmes, pulling at the rope. "There are one or two very singular points about this room. For example, what a fool a builder must be to open a ventilator in another room, when, with the same trouble, he might have communicated with the outside air!"

"This is also quite modern," said the lady.

"Done about the same time as the bell rope," remarked Holmes.

"Yes, there were several little changes carried out about that time."

"They seem to have been of a most interesting character—dummy bell ropes, and ventilators which do not ventilate. With your permission, Miss Stoner, we shall now carry our researches into the inner apartment."

Dr. Grimesby Roylott's chamber was larger than that of his stepdaughter, but was as plainly furnished. A camp bed, a small wooden shelf full of books, mostly of a technical character, an armchair beside the bed, a plain wooden chair against the wall, a round table, and a large iron safe were the principal things which met the eye. Holmes walked slowly round and examined each and all of them with the keenest interest.

"What's in here?" he asked, tapping the safe.

"My stepfather's business papers."

"Oh! you have seen inside, then!"

"Only once, some years ago. I remember that it was full of papers."

"There isn't a cat in it, for example?"

"No. What a strange idea!"

"Well, look at this!" He took up a small saucer of milk which stood on the top of it.

"No; we don't keep a cat. But there is a cheetah and a baboon."

"Ah, yes, of course! Well, a cheetah is just a big cat, and yet a saucer of milk does not go very far in satisfying its wants, I dare say. There is one point which I should wish to determine." He squatted down in front of the wooden chair, and examined the seat of it with the greatest attention.

"Thank you. That is quite settled," said he, rising and putting his lens in his pocket. "Hullo! here is something interesting!"

The object which had caught his eye was a small dog lash hung on one corner of the bed. The lash, however, was curled upon itself, and tied so as to make a loop of whipcord.

"What do you make of that, Watson?"

"It's a common enough lash. But I don't know why it should be tied."

"That is not quite so common, is it? Ah, me! it's a wicked world, and when a clever man turns his brain to crime it is the worst of all. I think that I have seen enough now, Miss Stoner, and, with your permission, we shall walk out upon the lawn."

I had never seen my friend's face so grim, or his brow so dark, as it was when we turned from the scene of this investigation. We had walked several times up and down the lawn, neither Miss Stoner nor myself liking to break in upon his thoughts before he roused himself from his reverie.

"It is very essential, Miss Stoner," said he, "that you should absolutely follow my advice in every respect."

"I shall most certainly do so."

"The matter is too serious for any hesitation. Your life may depend upon your compliance."

"I assure you that I am in your hands."

"In the first place, both my friend and I must spend the night in your room."

Both Miss Stoner and I gazed at him in astonishment.

"Yes, it must be so. Let me explain. I believe that that is the village inn over there?"

"Yes, that is the Crown."

"Very good. Your windows would be visible from there?"

"Certainly."

"You must confine yourself to your room, on pretence of a headache, when your stepfather comes back. Then when you hear him retire for the night, you must open the shutters of your window, undo the hasp, put your lamp there as a signal to us, and then withdraw with everything which you are likely to want into the room which you used to occupy. I have no doubt that, in spite of the repairs, you could manage there for one night."

"Oh, yes, easily."

"The rest you will leave in our hands."

"But what will you do?"

"We shall spend the night in your room, and we shall investigate the cause of this noise which has disturbed you."

"I believe, Mr. Holmes, that you have already made up your mind," said Miss Stoner, laying her hand upon my companion's sleeve.

"Perhaps I have."

"Then for pity's sake tell me what was the cause of my sister's death."

"I should prefer to have clearer proofs before I speak."

"You can at least tell me whether my own thought is correct, and if she died from some sudden fright."

"No, I do not think so. I think that there was probably some more tangible cause. And now, Miss Stoner, we must leave you, for if Dr. Roylott returned and saw us, our journey would be in vain. Good-bye, and be brave, for if you will do what I have told you, you may rest assured that we shall soon drive away the dangers that threaten you."

Sherlock Holmes and I had no difficulty in engaging a bedroom and sitting room at the Crown Inn. They were on the upper floor, and from our window we could command a view of the avenue gate, and of the inhabited wing of Stoke Moran Manor House. At dusk we saw Dr. Grimesby Roylott drive past, his huge form looming up beside the little figure of the lad who drove him. The boy had some slight difficulty in undoing the heavy iron gates, and we heard the hoarse roar of the doctor's voice, and saw the fury with which he shook his clenched fists at him. The trap drove on, and a few minutes later we saw a sudden light spring up among the trees as the lamp was lit in one of the sitting rooms.

"Do you know, Watson," said Holmes, as we sat to-gether in the gathering darkness, "I have really some scru-ples as to taking you tonight. There is a distinct element of danger."

"Can I be of assistance?"

"Your presence might be invaluable."

"Then I shall certainly come."

"It is very kind of you."

"You speak of danger. You have evidently seen more in these rooms than was visible to me."

"No, but I fancy that I may have deduced a little more. I imagine that you saw all I did."

"I saw nothing remarkable save the bell rope, and what purpose that could answer I confess is more than I can imag-ine."

"You saw the ventilator, too?"

"Yes, but I do not think that it is such a very unusual thing to have a small opening between two rooms. It was so small that a rat could hardly pass through."

"I knew that we should find a ventilator before ever we came to Stoke Moran."

"My dear Holmes!"

"Oh, yes, I did. You remember in her statement she said that her sister could smell Dr. Roylott's cigar. Now, of course that suggests at once that there must be a communication between the two rooms. It could only be a small one, or it would have been remarked upon at the coroner's inquiry. I deduced a ventilator."

"But what harm can there be in that?"

"Well, there is at least a curious coincidence of dates. A ventilator is made, a cord is hung, and a lady who sleeps in the bed dies. Does not that strike you?"

"I cannot as yet see any connection."

"Did you observe anything very peculiar about that bed?"

"No."

"It was clamped to the floor. Did you ever see a bed fastened like that before?"

"I cannot say that I have."

"The lady could not move her bed. It must always be in the same relative position to the ventilator and to the rope —for so we may call it, since it was clearly never meant for a bellpull."

"Holmes," I cried, "I seem to see dimly what you are hitting at. We are only just in time to prevent some subtle and horrible crime."

"Subtle enough and horrible enough. When a doctor goes wrong he is the first of criminals. He has nerve and he has knowledge. Palmer and Pritchard were among the heads of their profession. This man strikes even deeper, but I think, Watson, that we shall be able to strike deeper still. But we shall have horrors enough before the night is over: for goodness' sake let us have a quiet pipe, and turn our minds for a few hours to something more cheerful."

About nine o'clock the light among the trees was extinguished, and all was dark in the direction of the manor house. Two hours passed slowly away, and then, suddenly, just at the stroke of eleven, a single bright light shone out right in front of us.

"That is our signal," said Holmes, springing to his feet; "it comes from the middle window." As we passed out he exchanged a few words with the landlord, explaining that we were going on a late visit to an acquaintance, and that it was possible that we might spend the night there. A moment later we were out on the dark road, a chill wind blowing in our faces, and one yellow light twinkling in front of us through the gloom to guide us on our sombre errand.

There was little difficulty in entering the grounds, for unrepaired breaches gaped in the old park wall. Making our way among the trees, we reached the lawn, crossed it, and were about to enter through the window when out from a clump of laurel bushes there darted what seemed to be a hideous and distorted child, who threw itself on the grass with writhing limbs, and then ran swiftly across the lawn into the darkness.

"My God!" I whispered, "did you see it?"

Holmes was for the moment as startled as I. His hand closed like a vice upon my wrist in agitation. Then he broke into a low laugh, and put his lips to my ear.

"It is a nice household," he murmured; "that is the baboon."

I had forgotten the strange pets which the doctor affected. There was a cheetah, too; perhaps we might find it upon our shoulders at any moment. I confess that I felt easier in my mind when, after following Holmes's example and slipping off my shoes, I found myself inside the bedroom. My companion noiselessly closed the shutters, moved the lamp onto the table, and cast his eyes round the room. All was as we had seen it in the daytime. Then creeping up to me and making a trumpet of his hand, he whispered into my ear again so gently that it was all that I could do to distinguish the words:

"The least sound would be fatal to our plans."

I nodded to show that I had heard.

"We must sit without a light. He would see it through the ventilator."

I nodded again.

"Do not go to sleep; your very life may depend upon it. Have your pistol ready in case we should need it. I will sit on the side of the bed, and you in that chair."

I took out my revolver and laid it on the corner of the table.

Holmes had brought up a long thin cane, and this he placed upon the bed beside him. By it he laid the box of matches and the stump of a candle. Then he turned down the lamp and we were left in darkness.

How shall I ever forget that dreadful vigil? I could not hear a sound, not even the drawing of a breath, and yet I knew that my companion sat open-eyed, within a few feet of me, in the same state of nervous tension in which I was myself. The shutters cut off the least ray of light, and we waited in absolute darkness. From outside came the occasional cry of a night bird, and once at our very window a long-drawn, catlike whine, which told us that the cheetah was indeed at liberty. Far away we could hear the deep tones of the parish clock, which boomed out every quarter of an hour. How long they seemed, those quarters! Twelve o'clock, and one, and two, and three, and still we sat waiting silently for whatever might befall.

Suddenly there was the momentary gleam of a light up in the direction of the ventilator, which vanished immediately, but was succeeded by a strong smell of burning oil and heated metal. Someone in the next room had lit a dark lantern. I heard a gentle sound of movement, and then all was silent once more, though the smell grew stronger. For half an hour I sat with straining ears. Then suddenly another sound became audible—a very gentle, soothing sound, like that of a small jet of steam escaping continually from a kettle. The instant that we heard it, Holmes sprang from the bed, struck a match, and lashed furiously with his cane at the bell-pull.

"You see it, Watson?" he yelled. "You see it?"

But I saw nothing. At the moment when Holmes struck the light I heard a low, clear whistle, but the sudden glare flashing into my weary eyes made it impossible for me to tell what it was at which my friend lashed so savagely. I could, however, see that his face was deadly pale, and filled with horror and loathing.

He had ceased to strike, and was gazing up at the ventilator, when suddenly there broke from the silence of the night the most horrible cry to which I have ever listened. It swelled up louder and louder, a hoarse yell of pain and fear and anger all mingled in the one dreadful shriek. They say that away down in the village, and even in the distant parsonage, that cry raised the sleepers from their beds. It struck cold to our hearts, and I stood gazing at Holmes, and he at me, until the last echoes of it had died away into the silence from which it rose.

"What can it mean?" I gasped.

"It means that it is all over," Holmes answered. "And perhaps, after all, it is for the best. Take your pistol, and we shall enter Dr. Roylott's room."

With a grave face he lit the lamp, and led the way down the corridor. Twice he struck at the chamber door without any reply from within. Then he turned the handle and entered, I at his heels, with the cocked pistol in my hand.

It was a singular sight which met our eyes. On the table stood a dark lantern with the shutter half-open, throwing a brilliant beam of light upon the iron safe, the door of which was ajar. Beside this table, on the wooden chair, sat Dr. Grimesby Roylott, clad in a long grey dressing gown, his bare ankles protruding beneath, and his feet thrust into red heelless Turkish slippers. Across his lap lay the short stock with the long lash which we had noticed during the day. His chin was cocked upwards, and his eyes were fixed in a dreadful rigid stare at the corner of the ceiling. Round his brow he had a peculiar yellow band, with brownish speckles, which seemed to be bound tightly round his head. As we entered he made neither sound nor motion.

"The band! the speckled band!" whispered Holmes.

I took a step forward. In an instant his strange headgear began to move, and there reared itself from among his hair the squat diamond-shaped head and puffed neck of a loathsome serpent.

"It was a swamp adder!" cried Holmes, "—the deadliest snake in India. He had died within ten seconds of being bitten. Violence does, in truth, recoil upon the violent, and the schemer falls into the pit which he digs for another. Let us thrust this creature back into its den, and we can then remove Miss Stoner to some place of shelter, and let the county police know what has happened."

As he spoke he drew the dog whip swiftly from the dead man's lap, and throwing the noose round the reptile's neck, he drew it from its horrid perch, and carrying it at arm's length, threw it into the iron safe, which he closed upon it.

Such are the true facts of the death of Dr. Grimesby Roylott, of Stoke Moran. It is not necessary that I should prolong a narrative which has already run to too great a length by telling how we broke the sad news to the terrified girl, how we conveyed her by the morning train to the care of her good aunt at Harrow, of how the slow process of official inquiry came to the conclusion that the doctor met his fate while indiscreetly playing with a dangerous pet. The little which I had yet to learn of the case was told me by Sherlock Holmes as we travelled back next day.

"I had," said he, "come to an entirely erroneous conclusion, which shows, my dear Watson, how dangerous it always is to reason from insufficient data. The presence of the gipsies, and the use of the word 'band,' which was used by the poor girl, no doubt, to explain the appearance which she had caught a horrid glimpse of by the light of her match, were sufficient to put me upon an entirely wrong scent. I can only claim the merit that I instantly reconsidered my position when, however, it became clear to me that whatever danger threatened an occupant of the room could not come either from the window or the door. My attention was speedily drawn, as I have already remarked to you, to this ventilator, and to the bell rope which hung down to the bed. The discovery that this was a dummy, and that the bed was clamped to the floor, instantly gave rise to a suspicion that the rope was there as a bridge for something passing through the hole, and coming to the bed. The idea of a snake instantly occurred to me, and when I coupled it with my knowledge that the doctor was furnished with a supply of creatures from India, I felt that I was probably on the right track. The idea of using a form of poison which could not possibly be discovered by any chemical test was just such a one as would occur to a clever and ruthless man who had had an Eastern training. The rapidity with which such a poison would take effect would also, from his point of view, be an advantage. It would be a sharp-eyed coroner indeed who could distinguish the two little dark punctures which would show where the poison fangs had done their work. Then I thought of the whistle. Of course, he must recall the snake before the morning light revealed it to the victim. He had trained it, probably by the use of the milk which we saw, to return to him when summoned. He would put it through the ventilator at the hour that he thought best, with the certainty that it would crawl down the rope, and land on the bed. It might or might not bite the occupant, perhaps she might escape every night for a week, but sooner or later she must fall a victim.

"I had come to these conclusions before ever I had entered his room. An inspection of his chair showed me that he had been in the habit of standing on it, which, of course, would be necessary in order that he should reach the ventilator. The sight of the safe, the saucer of milk, and the loop of whipcord were enough to finally dispel any doubts which may have remained. The metallic clang heard by Miss Stoner was obviously caused by her father hastily closing the door of his safe upon its terrible occupant. Having once made up my mind, you know the steps which I took in order to put the matter to the proof. I heard the creature hiss, as I have no doubt that you did also, and I instantly lit the light and attacked it."

"With the result of driving it through the ventilator."

"And also with the result of causing it to turn upon its master at the other side. Some of the blows of my cane came home, and roused its snakish temper, so that it flew upon the first person it saw. In this way I am no doubt indirectly responsible for Dr. Grimesby Roylott's death, and I cannot say that it is likely to weigh very heavily upon my conscience."

THE ORACLE OF THE DOG

G. K. Chesterton

"Yes," said Father Brown, "I always like a dog so long as he isn't spelt backwards."

Those who are quick in talking are not always quick in listening. Sometimes even their brilliancy produces a sort of stupidity. Father Brown's friend and companion was a young man with a stream of ideas and stories, an enthusiastic young man named Fiennes, with eager blue eyes and blond hair that seemed to be brushed back, not merely with a hairbrush, but with the wind of the world as he rushed through it. But he stopped in the torrent of his talk in a momentary bewilderment before he saw the priest's very simple meaning.

"You mean that people make too much of them?" he said. "Well, I don't know. They're marvellous creatures. Sometimes I think they know a lot more than we do."

Father Brown said nothing, but continued to stroke the head of the big retriever in a half-abstracted but apparently soothing fashion.

"Why," said Fiennes, warming again to his monologue, "there was a dog in the case I've come to see you about; what they call the 'Invisible Murder Case,' you know. It's a strange story, but from my point of view the dog is about the strangest thing in it. Of course, there's the mystery of the crime itself, and how old Druce can have been killed by somebody else when he was all alone in the summer house—"

The hand stroking the dog stopped for a moment in its rhythmic movement; and Father Brown said calmly, "Oh, it was a summer house, was it?"

"I thought you'd read all about it in the papers," answered Fiennes. "Stop a minute; I believe I've got a cutting that will give you all the particulars." He produced a strip of newspaper from his pocket and handed it to the priest, who began to read it, holding it close to his blinking eyes with one hand while the other continued its half-conscious caress of the dog. It looked like the parable of a man not letting his right hand know what his left hand did.

Many mystery stories, about men murdered behind locked doors and windows, and murderers escaping without means of entrance and exit, have come true in the course of the extraordinary events at Cranston on the coast of Yorkshire, where Colonel Druce was found stabbed from behind by a dagger that has entirely disappeared from the scene, and apparently even from the neighbourhood.

The summer house in which he died was indeed accessible at one entrance, the ordinary doorway which looked down the central walk of the garden towards the house. But by a combination of events almost to be called a coincidence, it appears that both the path and the entrance were watched during the crucial time, and there is a chain of witnesses who confirm each other. The summer house stands at the extreme end of the garden, where there is no exit or entrance of any kind. The central garden path is a lane between two ranks of tall delphiniums, planted so close that any stray step off the path would leave its traces; and both path and plants run right up to the very mouth of the summer house, so that no straying from the straight path could fail to be observed, and no other mode of entrance can be imagined.

Patrick Floyd, secretary of the murdered man, testified that he had been in a position to overlook the whole garden from the time when Colonel Druce last appeared alive in the doorway to the time when he was found dead; as he, Floyd, had been on the top of a stepladder clipping the garden hedge. Janet Druce, the dead man's daughter, confirmed this, saying that she had sat on the terrace of the house throughout that time and had seen Floyd at his work. Touching some part of the time, this is again supported by Donald Druce, her brother, who overlooked the garden standing at his bedroom window in his dressing gown, for he had risen late. Lastly the account is consistent with that given by Dr. Valentine, a neighbour, who called for a time to talk with Miss Druce on the terrace, and by the colonel's solicitor, Mr. Aubrey Traill, who was apparently the last to see the murdered man alive—presumably with the exception of the murderer.

All are agreed that the course of events was as follows: about half past three in the afternoon, Miss Druce went down the path to ask her father when he would like tea; but he said he did not want any and was waiting to see Traill, his lawyer, who was to be sent to him in the summer house. The girl then came away and met Traill coming down the path; she directed him to her father and he went in as directed. About half an hour afterwards he came out again, the colonel coming with him to the door and showing himself to all appearance in health and even high spirits. He had been somewhat annoyed earlier in the day by his son's irregular hours, but seemed to recover his temper in a perfectly normal fashion, and had been rather markedly genial in receiving other visitors, including two of his nephews who came over for the day. But as these were out walking during the whole period of the tragedy, they had no evidence to give. It is said, indeed, that the colonel was not on very good terms with Dr. Valentine, but that gentleman only had a brief interview with the daughter of the house, to whom he is supposed to be paying serious attentions.

Traill, the solicitor, says he left the colonel entirely alone in the summer house, and this is confirmed by Floyd's bird's-eye view of the garden, which showed nobody else passing the only entrance. Ten minutes later Miss Druce again went down the garden and had not reached the end of the path when she saw her father, who was conspicuous by his white linen coat, lying in a heap on the floor. She uttered a scream which brought others to the spot, and on entering the place they found the colonel lying dead beside his basket-chair, which was also upset. Dr. Valentine, who was still in the immediate neighbourhood, testified that the wound was made by some sort of stiletto, entering under the shoulder blade and piercing the heart. The police have searched the neighbourhood for such a weapon, but no trace of it can be found.

"So Colonel Druce wore a white coat, did he?" said Father Brown as he put down the paper.

"Trick he learnt in the tropics," replied Fiennes with some wonder. "He'd had some queer adventures there, by his own account; and I fancy his dislike of Valentine was connected with the doctor coming from the tropics too. But it's all an infernal puzzle. The account there is pretty accurate; I didn't see the tragedy, in the sense of the discovery; I was out walking with the young nephews and the dog—the dog I wanted to tell you about. But I saw the stage set for it as described: the straight lane between the blue flowers right up to the dark entrance, and the lawyer going down it in his blacks and his silk hat, and the red head of the secretary showing high above the green hedge as he worked on it with his shears. Nobody could have mistaken that red head at any distance; and if people say they saw it there all the time, you may be sure they did. This red-haired secretary Floyd is quite a character: breathless, bounding sort of fellow, always doing everybody's work as he was doing the gardener's. I think he is an American; he's certainly got the American way of life; what they call the viewpoint, bless 'em."

"What about the lawyer?" asked Father Brown.

There was a silence and then Fiennes spoke quite slowly for him. "Traill struck me as a singular man. In his fine black clothes he was almost foppish, yet you can hardly call him fashionable. For he wore a pair of long, luxuriant black whiskers such as haven't been seen since Victorian times. He had rather a fine grave face and a fine grave manner, but every now and then he seemed to remember to smile. And when he showed his white teeth he seemed to lose a little of his dignity and there was something faintly fawning about him. It may have been only embarrassment, for he would also fidget with his cravat and his tiepin, which were at once handsome and unusual, like himself. If I could think of anybody—but what's the good, when the whole thing's impossible? Nobody knows who did it. Nobody knows how it could be done. At least there's only one exception I'd make, and that's why I really mentioned the whole thing. The dog knows."

Father Brown sighed and then said absently, "You were there as a friend of young Donald, weren't you? He didn't go on your walk with you?"

"No," replied Fiennes, smiling. "The young scoundrel

had gone to bed that morning and got up that afternoon. I went with his cousins, two young officers from India, and our conversation was trivial enough. I remember the elder, whose name I think is Herbert Druce and who is an authority on horse breeding, talked about nothing but a mare he had bought and the moral character of the man who sold her; while his brother Harry seemed to be brooding on his bad luck at Monte Carlo. I only mention it to show you, in the light of what happened on our walk, that there was nothing psychic about us. The dog was the only mystic in our company."

"What sort of a dog was he?" asked the priest.

"Same breed as that one," answered Fiennes. "That's what started me off on the story, your saying you didn't believe in believing in a dog. He's a big black retriever named Nox, and a suggestive name too; for I think what he did a darker mystery than the murder. You know Druce's house and garden are by the sea; we walked about a mile from it along the sands and then turned back, going the other way. We passed a rather curious rock called the Rock of Fortune, famous in the neighbourhood because it's one of those examples of one stone barely balanced on another, so that a touch would knock it over. It is not really very high, but the hanging outline of it makes it look a little wild and sinister; at least it made it look so to me, for I don't imagine my jolly young companions were afflicted with the picturesque. But it may be that I was beginning to feel an atmosphere; for just then the question arose of whether it was time to go back to tea, and even then I think I had a premonition that time counted for a good deal in the business. Neither Herbert Druce nor I had a watch, so we called out to his brother, who was some paces behind, having stopped to light his pipe under the hedge. Hence it happened that he shouted out the hour, which was twenty past four, in his big voice through the growing twilight; and somehow the loudness of it made it sound like the proclamation of something tremendous. His unconsciousness seemed to make it all the more so; but that was always the way with omens; and particular ticks of the clock were really very ominous things that afternoon. According to Dr. Valentine's testimony, poor Druce had actually died just about half past four.

"Well, they said we needn't go home for ten minutes and we walked a little farther along the sands, doing nothing in particular—throwing stones for the dog and throwing sticks into the sea for him to swim after. But to me the twilight seemed to grow oddly oppressive and the very shadow of the top-heavy Rock of Fortune lay on me like a load. And then the curious thing happened. Nox had just brought back Herbert's walking stick out of the sea and his brother had thrown his in also. The dog swam out again, but just about what must have been the stroke of the half hour, he stopped swimming. He came back again on to the shore and stood in front of us. Then he suddenly threw up his head and sent up a howl or wail of woe, if ever I heard one in the world.

" 'What the devil's the matter with the dog?' asked Herbert; but none of us could answer. There was a long silence after the brute's wailing and whining died away on the desolate shore; and then the silence was broken. As I live, it was broken by a faint and far-off shriek, like the shriek of a woman from beyond the hedges inland. We didn't know what it was then; but we knew afterwards. It was the cry the girl gave when she first saw the body of her father."

"You went back, I suppose," said Father Brown patiently. "What happened then?"

"I'll tell you what happened then," said Fiennes with a grim emphasis. "When we got back into that garden the first thing we saw was Traill the lawyer; I can see him now with his black hat and black whiskers relieved against the perspective of the blue flowers stretching down to the summer house, with the sunset and the strange outline of the Rock of Fortune in the distance. His face and figure were in shadow against the sunset; but I swear the white teeth were showing in his head and he was smiling.

"The moment Nox saw that man, the dog dashed forward and stood in the middle of the path barking at him madly, murderously, volleying out curses that were almost verbal in their dreadful distinctness of hatred. And the man doubled up and fled along the path between the flowers."

Father Brown sprang to his feet with a startling impatience.

"So the dog denounced him, did he?" he cried. "The oracle of the dog condemned him. Did you see what birds were flying, and are you sure whether they were on the right hand or the left? Did you consult the augers about the sacrifices? Surely you didn't omit to cut open the dog and examine his entrails. That is the sort of scientific test you heathen humanitarians seem to trust, when you are thinking of taking away the life and honour of a man."

Fiennes sat gaping for an instant before he found breath to say, "Why, what's the matter with you? What have I done now?"

A sort of anxiety came back into the priest's eyes—the anxiety of a man who has run against a post in the dark and wonders for a moment whether he has hurt it.

"I'm most awfully sorry," he said with sincere distress. "I beg your pardon for being so rude; pray forgive me."

Fiennes looked at him curiously. "I sometimes think you are more of a mystery than any of the mysteries," he said. "But anyhow, if you don't believe in the mystery of the dog, at least you can't get over the mystery of the man. You can't deny that at the very moment when the beast came back from the sea and bellowed, his master's soul was driven out of his body by the blow of some unseen power that no mortal man can trace or even imagine. And as for the lawyer, I don't go only by the dog; there are other curious details too. He struck me as a smooth, smiling, equivocal sort of person; and one of his tricks seemed like a sort of hint. You know the doctor and the police were on the spot very quickly; Valentine was brought back when walking away from the house, and he telephoned instantly. That, with the secluded house, small numbers, and enclosed space, made it pretty possible to search everybody who could have been near; and everybody was thoroughly searched—for a weapon. The whole house, garden, and shore were combed for a weapon. The disappearance of the dagger is almost as crazy as the disappearance of the man."

"The disappearance of the dagger," said Father Brown, nodding. He seemed to have become suddenly attentive.

"Well," continued Fiennes, "I told you that man Traill had a trick of fidgeting with his tie and tiepin—especially his tiepin. His pin, like himself, was at once showy and old-fashioned. It had one of those stones with concentric col-oured rings that look like an eye; and his own concentration on it got on my nerves, as if he had been a Cyclops with one eye in the middle of his body. But the pin was not only large but long; and it occurred to me that his anxiety about its adjustment was because it was even longer than it looked; as long as a stiletto in fact."

Father Brown nodded thoughtfully. "Was any other in-strument ever suggested?" he asked.

"There was another suggestion," answered Fiennes, "from one of the young Druces—the cousins, I mean. Nei-ther Herbert nor Harry Druce would have struck one at first as likely to be of assistance in scientific detection; but while Herbert was really the traditional type of heavy dragoon, caring for nothing but horses and being an ornament to the Horse Guards, his younger brother Harry had been in the Indian Police and knew something about such things. In-deed in his own way he was quite clever; and I rather fancy he had been too clever; I mean he had left the police through breaking some red-tape regulations and taking some sort of risk and responsibility of his own. Anyhow, he was in some sense a detective out of work, and threw himself in this business with more than the ardour of an amateur. And it was with him that I had an argument about the weapon—an argument that led to something new. It began by his countering my description of the dog barking at

Traill; and he said that a dog at his worst didn't bark, but growled."

"He was quite right there," observed the priest.

"This young fellow went on to say that, if it came to that, he'd heard Nox growling at other people before then; and among others at Floyd the secretary. I retorted that his own argument answered itself; for the crime couldn't be brought home to two or three people, and least of all to Floyd, who was as innocent as a harum-scarum schoolboy, and had been seen by everybody all the time perched above the garden hedge with his fan of red hair as conspicuous as a scarlet cockatoo. 'I know there's difficulties anyhow,' said my colleague, 'but I wish you'd come with me down the garden a minute. I want to show you something I don't think anyone else has seen.' This was on the very day of the discovery, and the garden was just as it had been: the stepladder was still standing by the hedge, and just under the hedge my guide stooped and disentangled something from the deep grass. It was the shears used for clipping the hedge, and on the point of one of them was a smear of blood."

There was a short silence, and then Father Brown said suddenly, "What was the lawyer there for?"

"He told us the colonel sent for him to alter his will," answered Fiennes. "And, by the way, there was another thing about the business of the will that I ought to mention. You see, the will wasn't actually signed in the summer house that afternoon."

"I suppose not," said Father Brown; "there would have to be two witnesses."

"The lawyer actually came down the day before and it was signed then; but he was sent for again next day because the old man had a doubt about one of the witnesses and had to be reassured."

"Who were the witnesses?" asked Father Brown.

"That's just the point," replied his informant eagerly, "the witnesses were Floyd the secretary and this Dr. Valentine, the foreign sort of surgeon or whatever he is; and the two have a quarrel. Now I'm bound to say that the secretary is something of a busybody. He's one of those hot and headlong people whose warmth of temperament has unfortunately turned mostly to pugnacity and bristling suspicion; to distrusting people instead of to trusting them. That sort of red-haired red-hot fellow is always either universally credulous or universally incredulous; and sometimes both. He was not only a jack-of-all-trades, but he knew better than all tradesmen. He not only knew everything, but he warned everybody against everybody. All that must be taken into account in his suspicions about Valentine; but in that particular case there seems to have been something behind it. He said the name of Valentine was not really Valentine. He said he had seen him elsewhere known by the name of De Villon. He said it would invalidate the will; of course he was kind enough to explain to the lawyer what the law was on that point. They were both in a frightful wax."

Father Brown laughed. "People often are when they are to witness a will," he said. "For one thing it means that they can't have any legacy under it. But what did Dr. Valentine say? No doubt the universal secretary knew more about the doctor's name than the doctor did. But even the doctor might have some information about his own name."

Fiennes paused a moment before he replied.

"Dr. Valentine took it in a curious way. Dr. Valentine is a curious man. His appearance is rather striking but very foreign. He is young but wears a beard cut square; and his face is very pale, dreadfully pale and dreadfully serious. His eyes have a sort of ache in them, as if he ought to wear glasses or had given himself a headache thinking; but he is quite handsome and always very formally dressed, with a top hat and a dark coat and a little red rosette. His manner is rather cold and haughty, and he has a way of staring at you which is very disconcerting. When thus charged with having changed his name, he merely stared like a sphinx and then said with a little laugh that he supposed Americans had no names to change. At that I think the colonel also got into a fuss and said all sorts of angry things to the doctor; all the more angry because of the doctor's pretensions to a future place in his family. But I shouldn't have thought much of that but for a few words that I happened to hear later, early in the afternoon of the tragedy. I don't want to make a lot of them, for they weren't the sort of words on which one would like, in the ordinary way, to play the eavesdropper. As I was passing out towards the front gate with my two companions and the dog, I heard voices which told me that Dr. Valentine and Miss Druce had withdrawn for a moment into the shadow of the house, in an angle behind a row of flowering plants, and were talking to each other in passionate whisperings—sometimes almost like hissings; for it was something of a lovers' quarrel as well as a lovers' tryst. Nobody repeats the sorts of things they said for the most part; but in an unfortunate business like this I'm bound to say that there was repeated more than once a phrase about killing somebody. In fact, the girl seemed to be begging him not to kill somebody, or saying that no provocation could justify killing anybody; which seems an unusual sort of talk to address to a gentleman who has dropped in to tea."

"Do you know," asked the priest, "whether Dr. Valentine seemed to be very angry after the scene with the secretary and the colonel—I mean about witnessing the will?"

"By all accounts," replied the other, "he wasn't half so angry as the secretary was. It was the secretary who went away raging after witnessing the will."

"And now," said Father Brown, "what about the will itself?"

"The colonel was a very wealthy man, and his will was important. Traill wouldn't tell us the alternation at that stage, but I have since heard, only this morning in fact, that most of the money was transferred from the son to the daughter. I told you that Druce was wild with my friend Donald over his dissipated hours."

"The question of motive has been rather overshadowed by the question of method," observed Father Brown thoughtfully. "At that moment, apparently, Miss Druce was the immediate gainer by the death."

"Good God! What a cold-blooded way of talking," cried Fiennes, staring at him. "You don't really mean to hint that she—"

"Is she going to marry that Dr. Valentine?" asked the other.

"Some people are against it," answered his friend. "But he is liked and respected in the place and is a skilled and devoted surgeon."

"So devoted a surgeon," said Father Brown, "that he had surgical instruments with him when he went to call on the young lady at teatime. For he must have used a lancet or something, and he never seems to have gone home."

Fiennes sprang to his feet and looked at him in a heat of inquiry. "You suggest he might have used the very same lancet—"

Father Brown shook his head. "All these suggestions are fancies just now," he said. "The problem is not who did it or what did it, but how it was done. We might find many men and even many tools—pins and shears and lancets. But how did a man get into the room? How did even a pin get into it?"

He was staring reflectively at the ceiling as he spoke, but as he said the last words his eye cocked in an alert fashion as if he had suddenly seen a curious fly on the ceiling.

"Well, what would you do about it?" asked the young man. "You have a lot of experience; what would you advise now?"

"I'm afraid I'm not much use," said Father Brown with a sigh. "I can't suggest very much without having ever been near the place or the people. For the moment you can only go on with local inquiries. I gather that your friend from the Indian Police is more or less in charge of your inquiry down there. I should run down and see how he is getting on. See what he's been doing in the way of amateur detection. There may be news already."

As his guests, the biped and the quadruped, disappeared, Father Brown took up his pen and went back to his
interrupted occupation of planning a course of lectures on
the encyclical *Rerum Novarum*. The subject was a large one
and he had to recast it more than once, so that he was
somewhat similarly employed some two days later when the
big black dog again came bounding into the room and
sprawled all over him with enthusiasm and excitement. The
master who followed the dog shared the excitement if not
the enthusiasm. He had been excited in a less pleasant fashion, for his blue eyes seemed to start from his head and his
eager face was even a little pale.

"You told me," he said abruptly and without preface,
"to find out what Harry Druce was doing. Do you know
what he's done?"

The priest did not reply, and the young man went on
in jerky tones: "I'll tell you what's he's done. He's killed
himself."

Father Brown's lips moved only faintly, and there was
nothing practical about what he was saying—nothing that
has anything to do with this story or this world.

"You give me the creeps sometimes," said Fiennes.
"Did you—expect this?"

"I thought it possible," said Father Brown; "that was
why I asked you to go and see what he was doing. I hoped
you might not be too late."

"It was I who found him," said Fiennes rather huskily.
"It was the ugliest and most uncanny thing I ever knew. I
went down that old garden again and I knew there was
something new and unnatural about it besides the murder.
The flowers still tossed about in blue masses on each side of
the black entrance into the old grey summer house; but to me
the blue flowers looked like devils dancing before some dark
cavern of the underworld. I looked all round; everything
seemed to be in its ordinary place. But the queer notion grew
on me that there was something wrong with the very shape
of the sky. And then I saw what it was. The Rock of Fortune

always rose in the background beyond the garden hedge and against the sea. And the Rock of Fortune was gone."

Father Brown had lifted his head and was listening intently.

"It was as if a mountain had walked away out of a landscape or a moon fallen from the sky; though I knew, of course, that a touch at any time would have tipped the thing over. Something possessed me and I rushed down that garden path like the wind and went crashing through that hedge as if it were a spider's web. It was a thin hedge really, though its undisturbed trimness had made it serve all the purposes of a wall. On the shore I found the loose rock fallen from its pedestal; and poor Harry Druce lay like a wreck underneath it. One arm was thrown round it in a sort of embrace as if he had pulled it down on himself; and on the broad brown sands beside it, in large crazy lettering, he had sprawled the words 'The Rock of Fortune falls on the Fool.' "

"It was the Colonel's will that did that," observed Father Brown. "The young man had staked everything on profiting himself by Donald's disgrace, especially when his uncle sent for him on the same day as the lawyer, and welcomed him with so much warmth. Otherwise he was done; he'd lost his police job; he was beggared at Monte Carlo. And he killed himself when he found he'd killed his kinsman for nothing."

"Here, stop a minute!" cried the staring Fiennes. "You're going too fast for me."

"Talking about the will, by the way," continued Father Brown calmly, "before I forget it, or we go on to bigger things, there was a simple explanation, I think, of all that business about the doctor's name. I rather fancy I have heard both names before somewhere. The doctor is really a French nobleman with the title of the Marquis de Villon. But he is also an ardent Republican and has abandoned his title and and fallen back on the forgotten family surname. 'With your Citizen Requetti you have puzzled Europe for ten days.' "

"What is that?" asked the young man blankly.

"Never mind," said the priest. "Nine times out of ten it is a rascally thing to change one's name; but this was a piece of fine fanaticism. That's the point of his sarcasm about Americans having no names—that is, no titles. Now in England the Marquis of Hartington is never called Mr. Hartington; but in France the Marquis de Villon is called Monsieur de Villon. So it might well look like a change of names. As for the talk about killing, I fancy that also was a point of French etiquette. The doctor was talking about challenging Floyd to a duel, and the girl was trying to dissuade him."

"Oh, I *see*," cried Fiennes slowly. "Now I understand what she meant."

"And what is that about?" asked his companion, smiling.

"Well," said the young man, "it was something that happened to me just before I found that poor fellow's body; only the catastrophe drove it out of my head. I suppose it's hard to remember a little romantic idyll when you've just come on top of a tragedy. But as I went down the lanes leading to the colonel's old place, I met his daughter walking with Dr. Valentine. She was in mourning of course, and he always wore black as if he were going to a funeral; but I can't say that their faces were very funereal. Never have I seen two people looking in their way more respectably radiant and cheerful. They stopped and saluted me and then she told me they were married and living in a little house on the outskirts of the town, where the doctor was continuing his practice. This rather surprised me, because I knew that her old father's will had left her his property; and I hinted at it delicately by saying I was going along to her father's old place and had half expected to meet her there. But she only laughed and said, 'Oh, we've given up all that. My husband doesn't like heiresses.' And I discovered with some astonishment that they really had insisted on restoring the property to poor Donald; so I hope he's had a healthy shock and will treat it sensibly. There was never much really the matter with him; he was very young and his father was not very wise. But it was in connection with that that she said something I didn't understand at the time; but now I'm sure it must be as you say. She said with a sort of sudden and splendid arrogance that was entirely altruistic, "I hope it'll stop that red-haired fool from fussing any more about the will. Does he think my husband, who has given up a crest and a coronet as old as the Crusades for his principles, would kill an old man in a summer house for a legacy like that?' Then she laughed again and said, 'My husband isn't killing anybody except in the way of business. Why, he didn't even ask his friends to call on the secretary.' Now, of course, I see what she meant."

"I see part of what she meant, of course," said Father Brown. "What did she mean exactly by the secretary fussing about the will?"

Fiennes smiled as he answered, "I wish you knew the secretary, Father Brown. It would be a joy to you to watch him make things hum, as he calls it. He made the house of mourning hum. He filled the funeral with all the snap and zip of the brightest sporting event. There was no holding him, after something had really happened. I've told you how he used to oversee the gardener as he did the garden, and how he instructed the lawyer in the law. Needless to say, he also instructed the surgeon in the practice of surgery; and as the surgeon was Dr. Valentine, you may be sure it ended in accusing him of something worse than bad surgery. The secretary got it fixed in his red head that the doctor had committed the crime; and when the police arrived he was perfectly sublime. Need I say that he became on the spot the greatest of all amateur detectives? Sherlock Holmes never towered over Scotland Yard with more titanic intellectual pride and scorn than Colonel Druce's private secretary over the police investigating Colonel Druce's death. I tell you it was a joy to see him. He strode about with an abstracted air, tossing his scarlet crest of hair and giving curt impatient replies. Of course it was his demeanour during these days that made Druce's daughter so wild with him. Of course he had a theory. It's just the sort of theory a man would have in a book; and Floyd is the sort of man who ought to be in a book. He'd be better fun and less bother in a book."

"What was his theory?" asked the other.

"Oh, it was full of pep," replied Fiennes gloomily. "It would have been glorious copy if it could have held together for ten minutes longer. He said the colonel was still alive when they found him in the summer house and the doctor killed him with the surgical instrument on pretence of cutting the clothes."

"I see," said the priest. "I suppose he was lying flat on his face on the mud floor as a form of siesta."

"It's wonderful what hustle will do," continued his informant. "I believe Floyd would have got his great theory into the papers at any rate, and perhaps had the doctor arrested, when all these things were blown sky high as if by dynamite by the discovery of that dead body lying under the Rock of Fortune. And that's what we come back to after all. I suppose the suicide is almost a confession. But nobody will ever know the whole story."

There was a silence, and then the priest said modestly, "I rather think I know the whole story."

Fiennes stared. "But look here," he cried, "How do you come to know the whole story, or to be sure it's the true story? You've been sitting here a hundred miles away writing a sermon; do you mean to tell me you really know what happened already? If you've really come to the end, where in the world do you begin? What started you off with your own story?"

Father Brown jumped up with a very unusual excitement and his first exclamation was like an explosion.

"The dog!" he cried. "The dog, of course! You had the whole story in your hands in the business of the dog on the beach, if you'd only noticed the dog properly."

Fiennes stared still more. "But you told me just now that my feelings about the dog were all nonsense, and the dog had nothing to do with it."

"The dog had everything to do with it," said Father Brown, "as you'd have found out, if you'd only treated the dog as a dog and not as God Almighty, judging the souls of men."

He paused in an embarrassed way for a moment, and then said, with a rather pathetic air of apology:

"The truth is, I happen to be awfully fond of dogs. And it seemed to me that in all this lurid halo of dog superstitions nobody was really thinking about the poor dog at all. To begin with a small point, about his barking at the lawyer or growling at the secretary. You asked how I guess things a hundred miles away; but honestly it's mostly to your credit, for you described people so well that I know the types. A man like Traill who frowns usually and smiles suddenly, a man who fiddles with things, especially at his throat, is a nervous, easily embarrassed man. I shouldn't wonder if Floyd, the efficient secretary, is nervy and jumpy too; those Yankee hustlers often are. Otherwise he wouldn't have cut his fingers on the shears and dropped them when he heard Janet Druce scream.

"Now dogs hate nervous people. I don't know whether they make the dog nervous too; or whether, being after all a brute, he is a bit of a bully; or whether his canine vanity (which is colossal) is simply offended at not being liked. But anyhow there was nothing in poor Nox protesting against those people, except that he disliked them for being afraid of him. Now I know you're awfully clever, and nobody of sense sneers at cleverness. But I sometimes fancy, for instance, that you are too clever to understand animals. Sometimes you are too clever to understand men, especially when they act almost as simply as animals. Animals are very literal; they live in a world of truisms. Take this case; a dog barks at a man and a man runs away from a dog. Now you do not seem to be quite simple enough to see the fact; that the dog barked because he disliked the man and the man fled because he was frightened of the dog. They had no other motives and they needed none. But you must read psychological mysteries into it and suppose the dog had supernormal vision, and was a mysterious mouthpiece of doom. You must suppose the man was running away, not from the dog, but from the hangman. And yet, if you come to think of it, all this deeper psychology is exceedingly improbable. If the dog really could completely and consciously realize the murderer of his master, he wouldn't stand yapping as he might at a curate at a tea party; he's much more likely to fly at his throat. And on the other hand, do you really think a man who had hardened his heart to murder an old friend and then walk about smiling at the old friend's family, under the eyes of his old friend's daughter and post mortem doctor—do you think a man like that could be doubled up by mere remorse because a dog barked? He might feel the tragic irony of it; it might shake his soul, like any other tragic trifle. But he wouldn't rush madly the length of a garden to escape from the only witness whom he knew to be unable to talk. People have a panic like that when they are frightened, not of tragic ironies, but of teeth. The whole thing is simpler than you can understand. But when we come to that business by the seashore, things are much more interesting. As you stated them, they were much more puzzling. I didn't understand that tale of the dog going in and out of the water; it didn't seem to me a doggy thing to do. If Nox had been very much upset about something else, he might possibly have refused to go after the stick at all. He'd probably go off nosing in whatever direction he suspected the mischief. But when once a dog is actually chasing a thing, a stone or a stick or a rabbit, my experience is that he won't stop for anything but the most peremptory command, and not always for that. That he should turn round because his mood changed seems to me unthinkable."

"But he did turn round," insisted Fiennes, "and came back without the stick."

"He came back without the stick for the best reason in the world," replied the priest. "He came back because he couldn't find it. He whined because he couldn't find it.

That's the sort of thing a dog really does whine about. A dog is a devil of a ritualist. He is as particular about the precise routine of a game as a child about the precise repetition of a fairy tale. In this case something had gone wrong with the game. He came back to complain seriously of the conduct of the stick. Never had such a thing happened before. Never had an eminent and distinguished dog been so treated by a rotten old walking stick."

"Why, what had the walking stick done?" inquired the young man.

"It had sunk," said Father Brown.

Fiennes said nothing, but continued to stare, and it was the priest who continued:

"It had sunk because it was not really a stick, but a rod of steel with a very thin shell of cane and a sharp point. In other words, it was a sword stick. I suppose a murderer never got rid of a bloody weapon so oddly and yet so naturally as by throwing it into the sea for a retriever."

"I begin to see what you mean," admitted Fiennes; "but even if a sword stick was used, I have no guess of how it was used."

"I had a sort of guess," said Father Brown, "right at the beginning when you said the words 'summer house.' And another when you said that Druce wore a white coat. As long as everybody was looking for a short dagger, nobody thought of it; but if we admit a rather long blade like a rapier, it's not so impossible."

He was leaning back, looking at the ceiling, and began like one going back to his own first thoughts and fundamentals.

"All that discussion about detective stories like the Yellow Room, about a man found dead in sealed chambers which no one could enter, does not apply to the present case, because it is a summer house. When we talk of a Yellow Room, or any room, we imply walls that are really homogeneous and impenetrable. But a summer house is not made like that; it is often made, as it was in this case, of closely interlaced but still separate boughs and strips of wood, in which there are chinks here and there. There was one of them just behind Druce's back as he sat in his chair up against the wall. But just as the room was a summer house, so the chair was a basketchair. That also was a lattice of loopholes. Lastly, the summer house was close up under the hedge; and you have just told me that it was really a thin hedge. A man standing outside it could easily see, amid a network of twigs and branches and canes, one white spot of the colonel's coat as plain as the white of a target.

"Now, you left the geography a little vague; but it was possible to put two and two together. You said the Rock of Fortune was not really high; but you said it could be seen dominating the garden like a mountain peak. In other words, it was very near the end of the garden, though your walk had taken you a long way round to it. Also, it isn't likely the young lady really howled so as to be heard half a mile. She gave an ordinary involuntary cry, and yet you heard it on the shore. And among other interesting things that you told me, may I remind you that you said Harry Druce had fallen behind to light his pipe under a hedge."

Fiennes shuddered slightly. "You mean he drew his blade there and sent it through the hedge at the white spot. But surely it was a very odd chance and a very sudden choice. Besides, he couldn't be certain the old man's money had passed to him, and as a fact it hadn't."

Father Brown's face became animated.

"You misunderstand the man's character," he said, as if he himself had known the man all his life. "A curious but not unknown type of character. If he had really *known* the money would come to him, I seriously believe he wouldn't have done it. He would have seen it as the dirty thing it was."

"Isn't that rather paradoxical?" asked the other.

"This man was a gambler," said the priest, "and a man in disgrace for having taken risks and anticipated orders. It was probably for something pretty unscrupulous, for every imperial police is more like a Russian secret police than we like to think. But he had gone beyond the line and failed. Now, the temptation of that type of man is to do a mad thing precisely because the risk will be wonderful in retrospect. He wants to say, 'Nobody but I could have seized that chance or seen that it was then or never. What a wild and wonderful guess it was, when I put all those things together: Donald in disgrace; and the lawyer being sent for; and Herbert and I sent for at the same time—and then nothing more but the way the old man grinned at me and shook hands. Anybody would say I was mad to risk it; but that is how fortunes are made, by the man mad enough to have a little foresight.' In short, it is the vanity of guessing. It is the megalomania of the gambler. The more incongruous the coincidence, the more instantaneous the decision, the more likely he is to snatch the chance. The accident, the very triviality, of the white speck and the hole in the hedge intoxicated him like a vision of the world's desire. Nobody clever enough to see such a combination of accidents could be cowardly enough not to use them! That is how the devil talks to the gambler. But the devil himself would hardly have induced that unhappy man to go down in a dull, deliberate way and kill an old uncle from whom he'd always had expectations. It would be too respectable."

He paused a moment; and then went on with a certain quiet emphasis.

"And now try to call up the scene, even as you saw it yourself. As he stood there, dizzy with his diabolical opportunity, he looked up and saw that strange outline that might have been the image of his own tottering soul—the one great crag poised perilously on the other like a pyramid on its point—and remembered that it was called the Rock of Fortune. Can you guess how such a man at such a moment would read such a signal? I think it strung him up to action and even to vigilance. He who would be a tower must not fear to be a toppling tower. Anyhow he acted; his next difficulty was to cover his tracks. To be found with a sword stick, let alone a blood-stained sword stick, would be fatal in the search that was certain to follow. If he left it anywhere, it would be found and probably traced. Even if he threw it into the sea the action might be noticed, and thought noticeable —unless indeed he could think of some more natural way of covering the action. As you know, he did think of one, and a very good one. Being the only one of you with a watch, he told you it was not yet time to return, strolled a little farther, and started the game of throwing in sticks for the retriever. But how his eyes must have rolled darkly over all that desolate seashore before they alighted on the dog!"

Fiennes nodded, gazing thoughtfully into space. His mind seemed to have drifted back to a less practical part of the narrative.

"It's queer," he said, "that the dog really was in the story after all."

"The dog could almost have told you the story, if he could talk," said the priest. "All I complain of is that because he couldn't talk, you made up his story for him, and made him talk with the tongues of men and angels. It's part of something I've noticed more and more in the modern world, appearing in all sorts of newspaper rumours and conversational catchwords; something that's arbitrary without being authoritative. People readily swallow the untested claims of this, that, or the other. It's drowning all your old rationalism and scepticism, it's coming in like a sea; and the name of it is superstition." He stood up abruptly, his face heavy with a sort of frown, and went on talking almost as if he were alone. "It's the first effect of not believing in God that you lose your common sense, and can't see things as they are. Anything that anybody talks about, and says there's a good deal in it, extends itself indefinitely like a vista in a nightmare. And a dog is an omen and a cat is a mystery and a pig is a mascot and a beetle is a scarab, calling up all the menagerie of polytheism from Egypt and old India; Dog Anubis and great green-eyed Pasht and all the holy howling Bulls of Bashan; reeling back to the bestial gods of the beginning, escaping into elephants and snakes and crocodiles; and all because you are frightened of four words: 'He was made Man.' "

The young man got up with a little embarrassment, almost as if he had overheard a soliloquy. He called to the dog and left the room with vague but breezy farewells. But he had to call the dog twice, for the dog had remained behind quite motionless for a moment, looking up steadily at Father Brown as the wolf looked at Saint Francis.

THE MONKEY'S PAW

W. W. Jacobs

I

Without, the night was cold and wet, but in the small parlour of Laburnum Villa the blinds were drawn and the fire burned brightly. Father and son were at chess; the former, who possessed ideas about the game involving radical changes, putting his king into such sharp and unnecessary perils that it even provoked comment from the white-haired old lady knitting placidly by the fire.

"Hark at the wind," said Mr. White, who, having seen a fatal mistake after it was too late, was amiably desirous of preventing his son from seeing it.

"I'm listening," said the latter, grimly surveying the board as he stretched out his hand. "Check."

"I should hardly think that he'd come tonight," said his father, with his hand poised over the board.

"Mate," replied the son.

"That's the worst of living so far out," bawled Mr. White, with sudden and unlooked-for violence; "of all the beastly, slushy, out-of-the-way places to live in, this is the worst. Path's a bog, and the road's a torrent. I don't know what people are thinking about. I suppose because only two houses in the road are let, they think it doesn't matter."

"Never mind, dear," said his wife soothingly; "perhaps you'll win the next one."

Mr. White looked up sharply, just in time to intercept a knowing glance between mother and son. The words died away on his lips, and he hid a guilty grin in his thin grey beard.

"There he is," said Herbert White, as the gate banged to loudly and heavy footsteps came towards the door.

The old man rose with hospitable haste, and opening the door, was heard condoling with the new arrival. The new arrival also condoled with himself, so that Mrs. White said, "Tut, tut!" and coughed gently as her husband entered the room, followed by a tall, burly man, beady of eye and rubicund of visage.

"Sergeant Major Morris," he said, introducing him.

The sergeant major shook hands, and taking the proffered seat by the fire, watched contentedly while his host got out whisky and tumblers and stood a small copper kettle on the fire.

At the third glass his eyes got brighter, and he began to talk, the little family circle regarding with eager interest this visitor from distant parts, as he squared his broad shoulders in the chair, and spoke of wild scenes and doughty deeds; of wars and plagues, and strange peoples.

"Twenty-one years of it," said Mr. White, nodding at his wife and son. "When he went away he was a slip of a youth in the warehouse. Now look at him."

"He don't look to have taken much harm," said Mrs. White politely.

"I'd like to go to India myself," said the old man, "just to look round a bit, you know."

"Better where you are," said the sergeant major, shaking his head. He put down the empty glass, and sighing softly, shook it again.

"I should like to see those old temples and fakirs and jugglers," said the old man. "What was that you started telling me the other day about a monkey's paw or something, Morris?"

"Nothing," said the soldier hastily. "Leastways nothing worth hearing."

"Monkey's paw?" said Mrs. White curiously.

"Well, it's just a bit of what you might call magic, perhaps," said the sergeant major offhandedly.

His three listeners leaned forward eagerly. The visitor absentmindedly put his empty glass to his lips and then set it down again. His host filled it for him.

"To look at," said the sergeant major, fumbling in his pocket, "it's just an ordinary little paw, dried to a mummy."

He took something out of his pocket and proffered it. Mrs. White drew back with a grimace, but her son, taking it, examined it curiously.

"And what is there special about it?" inquired Mr. White as he took it from his son, and having examined it, placed it upon the table.

"It had a spell put on it by an old fakir," said the sergeant major, "a very holy man. He wanted to show that fate ruled people's lives, and that those who interfered with it did so to their sorrow. He put a spell on it so that three separate men could each have three wishes from it."

His manner was so impressive that his hearers were conscious that their light laughter jarred somewhat.

"Well, why don't you have three, sir?" said Herbert White cleverly.

The soldier regarded him in the way that middle age is wont to regard presumptuous youth. "I have," he said quietly, and his blotchy face whitened.

"And did you really have the three wishes granted?" asked Mrs. White.

"I did," said the sergeant major, and his glass tapped against his strong teeth.

"And has anybody else wished?" persisted the old lady.

"The first man had his three wishes. Yes," was the reply; "I don't know what the first two were, but the third was for death. That's how I got the paw."

His tones were so grave that a hush fell upon the group.

"If you've had your three wishes, it's no good to you now, then, Morris," said the old man at last. "What do you keep it for?"

The soldier shook his head. "Fancy, I suppose," he said slowly. "I did have some idea of selling it, but I don't think I will. It has caused enough mischief already. Besides, people won't buy. They think it's a fairy tale, some of them; and those who do think anything of it want to try it first and pay me afterwards."

"If you could have another three wishes," said the old man, eyeing him keenly, "would you have them?"

"I don't know," said the other. "I don't know."

He took the paw, and dangling it between his forefinger and thumb, suddenly threw it upon the fire. White, with a slight cry, stooped down and snatched it off.

"Better let it burn," said the soldier solemnly.

"If you don't want it, Morris," said the other, "give it to me."

"I won't," said his friend doggedly. "I threw it on the fire. If you keep it, don't blame me for what happens. Pitch it on the fire again like a sensible man."

The other shook his head and examined his new possession closely. "How do you do it?" he inquired.

"Hold it up in your right hand and wish aloud," said the sergeant major, "but I warn you of the consequences."

"Sounds like the *Arabian Nights*," said Mrs. White, as she rose and began to set the supper. "Don't you think you might wish for four pairs of hands for me?"

Her husband drew the talisman from his pocket, and then all three burst into laughter as the sergeant major, with a look of alarm on his face, caught him by the arm.

"If you must wish," he said gruffly, "wish for something sensible."

Mr. White dropped it back in his pocket, and placing chairs, motioned his friend to the table. In the business of supper the talisman was partly forgotten, and afterwards the three sat listening in an enthralled fashion to a second instalment of the soldier's adventures in India.

"If the tale about the monkey's paw is not more truthful than those he has been telling us," said Herbert, as the door closed behind their guest, just in time to catch the last train, "we shan't make much out of it."

"Did you give him anything for it, Father?" inquired Mrs. White, regarding her husband closely.

"A trifle," said he, colouring slightly. "He didn't want it, but I made him take it. And he pressed me again to throw it away."

"Likely," said Herbert, with pretended horror. "Why, we're going to be rich, and famous, and happy. Wish to be an emperor, Father, to begin with; then you can't be henpecked."

He darted round the table, pursued by the maligned Mrs. White armed with an antimacassar.

Mr. White took the paw from his pocket and eyed it dubiously. "I don't know what to wish for, and that's a fact," he said slowly. "It seems to me I've got all I want."

"If you only cleared the house, you'd be quite happy, wouldn't you!" said Herbert, with his hand on his shoulder. "Well, wish for two hundred pounds, then; that'll just do it."

His father, smiling shamefacedly at his own credulity, held up the talisman, as his son, with a solemn face, somewhat marred by a wink at his mother, sat down at the piano and struck a few impressive chords.

"I wish for two hundred pounds," said the old man distinctly.

A fine crash from the piano greeted the words, interrupted by a shuddering cry from the old man. His wife and son ran towards him.

"It moved," he cried, with a glance of disgust at the

object as it lay on the floor. "As I wished, it twisted in my hand like a snake."

"Well, I don't see the money," said his son, as he picked it up and placed it on the table, "and I bet I never shall."

"It must have been your fancy, Father," said his wife, regarding him anxiously.

He shook his head. "Never mind, though; there's no harm done, but it gave me a shock all the same."

They sat down by the fire again while the two men finished their pipes. Outside, the wind was higher than ever, and the old man started nervously at the sound of a door banging upstairs. A silence unusual and depressing settled upon all three, which lasted until the old couple arose to retire for the night.

"I expect you'll find the cash tied up in a big bag in the middle of your bed," said Herbert, as he bade them good night, "and something horrible squatting up on top of the wardrobe watching you as you pocket your ill-gotten gains."

He sat alone in the darkness, gazing at the dying fire, and seeing faces in it. The last face was so horrible and so simian that he gazed at it in amazement. It got so vivid that, with a little uneasy laugh, he felt on the table for a glass containing a little water to throw over it. His hand grasped the monkey's paw, and with a little shiver he wiped his hand on his coat and went up to bed.

II

In the brightness of the wintry sun next morning as it streamed over the breakfast table he laughed at his fears. There was an air of prosaic wholesomeness about the room which it had lacked on the previous night, and the dirty, shrivelled little paw was pitched on the sideboard with a carelessness which betokened no great belief in its virtues.

"I suppose all old soldiers are the same," said Mrs. White. "The idea of our listening to such nonsense! How could wishes be granted in these days? And if they could, how could two hundred pounds hurt you, father?"

"Might drop on his head from the sky," said the frivolous Herbert.

"Morris said the things happened so naturally," said his father, "that you might if you so wished attribute it to coincidence."

"Well, don't break into the money before I come back," said Herbert as he rose from the table. "I'm afraid it'll turn you into a mean, avaricious man, and we shall have to disown you."

His mother laughed, and following him to the door, watched him down the road; and returning to the breakfast table, was very happy at the expense of her husband's credulity. All of which did not prevent her from scurrying to the door at the postman's knock, nor prevent her from referring somewhat shortly to retired sergeant majors of bibulous habits when she found that the post brought a tailor's bill.

"Herbert will have some more of his funny remarks, I expect, when he comes home," she said, as they sat at dinner.

"I daresay," said Mr. White, pouring himself out some beer; "but for all that, the thing moved in my hand; that I'll swear to."

"You thought it did," said the old lady soothingly.

"I say it did," replied the other. "There was no thought about it; I had just—what's the matter?"

His wife made no reply. She was watching the mysterious movements of a man outside, who, peering in an undecided fashion at the house, appeared to be trying to make up his mind to enter. In mental connection with the two hundred pounds, she noticed that the stranger was well dressed, and wore a silk hat of glossy newness. Three times he paused at the gate, and then walked on again. The fourth time he stood with his hand upon it, and then with sudden resolution flung it open and walked up the path. Mrs. White at the same moment placed her hands behind her, and hurriedly unfastening the strings of her apron, put that useful article of apparel beneath the cushion of her chair.

She brought the stranger, who seemed ill at ease, into the room. He gazed at her furtively, and listened in a preoccupied fashion as the old lady apologized for the appearance of the room, and her husband's coat, a garment which he usually reserved for the garden. She then waited as patiently as her sex would permit, for him to broach his business, but he was at first strangely silent.

"I—was asked to call," he said at last, and stooped and picked a piece of cotton from his trousers. "I come from Maw and Meggins."

The old lady started. "Is anything the matter?" she asked breathlessly. "Has anything happened to Herbert? What is it? What is it?"

Her husband interposed. "There, there, mother," he said hastily. "Sit down, and don't jump to conclusions. You've not brought bad news, I'm sure, sir"; and he eyed the other wistfully.

"I'm sorry—" began the visitor.

"Is he hurt?" demanded the mother wildly.

The visitor bowed in assent. "Badly hurt," he said quietly, "but he is not in any pain."

"Oh, thank God!" said the old woman, clasping her hands. "Thank God for that! Thank—"

She broke off suddenly as the sinister meaning of the assurance dawned upon her, and she saw the awful confirmation of her fears in the other's averted face. She caught her breath, and turning to her slower-witted husband, laid a trembling old hand upon his. There was a long silence.

"He was caught in the machinery," said the visitor at length in a low voice.

"Caught in the machinery," repeated Mr. White, in a dazed fashion, "yes."

He sat staring blankly out at the window, and taking his wife's hand between his own, pressed it as he had been wont to do in their old courting days nearly forty years before.

"He was the only one left to us," he said, turning gently to the visitor. "It is hard."

The other coughed, and rising, walked slowly to the window. "The firm wished me to convey their sincere sympathy with you in your great loss," he said, without looking round. "I beg that you will understand I am only their servant and merely obeying orders."

There was no reply; the old woman's face was white, her eyes staring, and her breath inaudible; on the husband's face was a look such as his friend the sergeant might have carried into his first action.

"I was to say that Maw and Meggins disclaim all responsibility," continued the other. "They admit no liability at all, but in consideration of your son's services, they wish to present you with a certain sum as compensation."

Mr. White dropped his wife's hand, and rising to his feet, gazed with a look of horror at his visitor. His dry lips shaped the words, "How much?"

"Two hundred pounds," was the answer.

Unconscious of his wife's shriek, the old man smiled faintly, put out his hands like a sightless man, and dropped, a senseless heap, to the floor.

III

In the huge new cemetery, some two miles distant, the old people buried their dead, and came back to the house steeped in shadow and silence. It was all over so quickly that at first they could hardly realise it, and remained in a state of expectation as though of something else to happen— something else which was to lighten this load, too heavy for old hearts to bear.

But the days passed, and expectation gave place to resignation—the hopeless resignation of the old, sometimes miscalled apathy. Sometimes they hardly exchanged a word, for now they had nothing to talk about, and their days were long to weariness.

It was about a week after, that the old man, waking suddenly in the night, stretched out his hand and found himself alone. The room was in darkness, and the sound of subdued weeping came from the window. He raised himself in bed and listened.

"Come back," he said tenderly. "You will be cold."

"It is colder for my son," said the old woman, and wept afresh.

The sound of her sobs died away on his ears. The bed was warm, and his eyes heavy with sleep. He dozed fitfully, and then slept until a sudden wild cry from his wife awoke him with a start.

"The paw!" she cried wildly. "The monkey's paw!"

He started up in alarm. "Where? Where is it? What's the matter?"

She came stumbling across the room toward him. "I want it," she said quietly. "You've not destroyed it?"

"It's in the parlour, on the bracket," he replied, marvelling. "Why?"

She cried and laughed together, and bending over, kissed his cheek.

"I only just thought of it," she said hysterically. "Why didn't I think of it before? Why didn't *you* think of it?"

"Think of what?" he questioned.

"The other two wishes," she replied rapidly. "We've only had one."

"Was not that enough?" he demanded fiercely.

"No," she cried triumphantly; "we'll have one more. Go down and get it quickly, and wish our boy alive again."

The man sat up in bed and flung the bedclothes from his quaking limbs. "Good God, you are mad!" he cried, aghast.

"Get it," she panted; "get it quickly, and wish—oh, my boy, my boy!"

Her husband struck a match and lit the candle. "Get

back to bed," he said unsteadily. "You don't know what you are saying."

"We had the first wish granted," said the old woman feverishly; "why not the second?"

"A coincidence," stammered the old man.

"Go and get it and wish," cried his wife, quivering with excitement.

The old man turned and regarded her, and his voice shook. "He has been dead ten days, and besides he—I would not tell you else, but—I could only recognize him by his clothing. If he was too terrible for you to see then, how now?"

"Bring him back," cried the old woman, and dragged him towards the door. "Do you think I fear the child I have nursed?"

He went down in the darkness, and felt his way to the parlour, and then to the mantelpiece. The talisman was in its place, and a horrible fear that the unspoken wish might bring his mutilated son before him ere he could escape from the room seized upon him, and he caught his breath as he found that he had lost the direction of the door. His brow cold with sweat, he felt his way round the table, and groped along the wall until he found himself in the small passage with the unwholesome thing in his hand.

Even his wife's face seemed changed as he entered the room. It was white and expectant, and to his fears seemed to have an unnatural look upon it. He was afraid of her.

"*Wish!*" she cried, in a strong voice.

"It is foolish and wicked," he faltered.

"*Wish!*" repeated his wife.

He raised his hand. "I wish my son alive again."

The talisman fell to the floor, and he regarded it fearfully. Then he sank trembling into a chair as the old woman, with burning eyes, walked to the window and raised the blind.

He sat until he was chilled with the cold, glancing occasionally at the figure of the old woman peering through the window. The candle end, which had burned below the rim of the china candlestick, was throwing pulsating shadows on the ceiling and walls, until, with a flicker larger than the rest it expired. The old man, with an unspeakable sense of relief at the failure of the talisman, crept back to his bed, and a minute or two afterwards the old woman came silently and apathetically beside him.

Neither spoke, but lay silently listening to the ticking of the clock. A stair creaked, and a squeaky mouse scurried noisily through the wall. The darkness was oppressive, and after lying for some time screwing up his courage, he took the box of matches, and striking one, went downstairs for a candle.

At the foot of the stairs the match went out, and he paused to strike another; and at the same moment a knock, so quiet and stealthy as to be scarcely audible, sounded on the front door.

The matches fell from his hand and spilled in the passage. He stood motionless, his breath suspended until the knock was repeated. Then he turned and fled swiftly back to his room, and closed the door behind him. A third knock sounded through the house.

"*What's that?*" cried the old woman, starting up.

"A rat," said the old man in shaking tones, "—a rat. It passed me on the stairs."

His wife sat up in bed listening. A loud knock resounded through the house.

"It's Herbert!" she screamed. "It's Herbert!"

She ran to the door, but her husband was before her, and catching her by the arm, held her tightly.

"What are you going to do?" he whispered hoarsely.

"It's my boy; it's Herbert!" she cried, struggling mechanically. "I forgot it was two miles away. What are you holding me for? Let go. I must open the door."

"For God's sake don't let it in," cried the old man, trembling.

"You're afraid of your own son," she cried, struggling. "Let me go. I'm coming, Herbert; I'm coming."

There was another knock, and another. The old woman with a sudden wrench broke free and ran from the room. Her husband followed to the landing, and called after her appealingly as she hurried downstairs. He heard the chain rattle back and the bottom bolt drawn slowly and stiffly from the socket. Then the old woman's voice, strained and panting.

"The bolt," she cried loudly. "Come down. I can't reach it."

But her husband was on his hands and knees groping wildly on the floor in search of the paw. If he could only find it before the thing outside got in. A perfect fusillade of knocks reverberated through the house, and he heard the scraping of a chair as his wife put it down in the passage against the door. He heard the creaking of the bolt as it came slowly back, and at the same moment he found the monkey's paw, and frantically breathed his third and last wish.

The knocking ceased suddenly, although the echoes of it were still in the house. He heard the chair drawn back, and the door opened. A cold wind rushed up the staircase, and a long loud wail of disappointment and misery from his wife gave him courage to run down to her side, and then to the gate beyond. The street lamp flickering opposite shone on a quiet and deserted road.

THE PROBLEM OF CELL 13

Jacques Futrelle

Practically all those letters remaining in the alphabet after Augustus S.F.X. Van Dusen was named were afterward acquired by that gentleman in the course of a brilliant scientific career, and, being honorably acquired, were tacked on to the other end. His name, therefore, taken with all that belonged to it, was a wonderfully imposing structure. He was a Ph.D., an LL.D., an F.R.S., an M.D., and an M.D.S. He was also some other things—just what he himself couldn't say—through recognition of his ability by various foreign educational and scientific institutions.

In appearance he was no less striking than in nomenclature. He was slender with the droop of the student in his thin shoulders and the pallor of a close, sedentary life on his clean-shaven face. His eyes wore a perpetual, forbidding squint—the squint of a man who studies little things—and when they could be seen at all through his thick spectacles, were mere slits of watery blue. But above his eyes was his most striking feature. This was a tall, broad brow, almost abnormal in height and width, crowned by a heavy shock of bushy, yellow hair. All these things conspired to give him a peculiar, almost grotesque, personality.

Professor Van Dusen was remotely German. For generations his ancestors had been noted in the sciences; he was the logical result, the mastermind. First and above all he was a logician. At least thirty-five years of the half century or so of his existence had been devoted exclusively to proving that two and two always equal four, except in unusual cases, where they equal three or five, as the case may be. He stood broadly on the general proposition that all things that start must go somewhere, and was able to bring the concentrated mental force of his forefathers to bear on a given problem. Incidentally it may be remarked that Professor Van Dusen wore a No. 8 hat.

The world at large had heard vaguely of Professor Van Dusen as The Thinking Machine. It was a newspaper catchphrase applied to him at the time of a remarkable exhibition at chess; he had demonstrated then that a stranger to the game might, be the force of inevitable logic, defeat a champion who had devoted a lifetime to its study. The Thinking Machine! Perhaps that more nearly described him than all his honorary initials, for he spent week after week, month after month, in the seclusion of his small laboratory from which had gone forth thoughts that staggered scientific associates and deeply stirred the world at large.

It was only occasionally that The Thinking Machine had visitors, and these were usually men who, themselves high in the sciences, dropped in to argue a point and perhaps convince themselves. Two of these men, Dr. Charles Ransome and Alfred Fielding, called one evening to discuss some theory which is not of consequence here.

"Such a thing is impossible," declared Dr. Ransome emphatically, in the course of the conversation.

"Nothing is impossible," declared The Thinking Machine with equal emphasis. He always spoke petulantly. "The mind is master of all things. When science fully recognizes that fact a great advance will have been made."

"How about the airship?" asked Dr. Ransome.

"That's not impossible at all," asserted The Thinking Machine. "It will be invented sometime. I'd do it myself, but I'm busy."

Dr. Ransome laughed tolerantly.

"I've heard you say such things before," he said. "But they mean nothing. Mind may be master of matter, but it hasn't yet found a way to apply itself. There are some things that can't be *thought* out of existence, or rather which would not yield to any amount of thinking."

"What, for instance?" demanded The Thinking Machine.

Dr. Ransome was thoughtful for a moment as he smoked.

"Well, say prison walls," he replied. "No man can *think* himself out of a cell. If he could, there would be no prisoners."

"A man can so apply his brain and ingenuity that he can leave a cell, which is the same thing," snapped The Thinking Machine.

Dr. Ransome was slightly amused.

"Let's suppose a case," he said, after a moment. "Take a cell where prisoners under sentence of death are confined —men who are desperate and, maddened by fear, would take any chance to escape—suppose you were locked in such a cell. Could you escape?"

"Certainly," declared The Thinking Machine.

"Of course," said Mr. Fielding, who entered the conversation for the first time, "you might wreck the cell with an explosive—but inside, a prisoner, you couldn't have that."

"There would be nothing of that kind," said The Thinking Machine. "You might treat me precisely as you treated prisoners under sentence of death, and I would leave the cell."

"Not unless you entered it with tools prepared to get out," said Dr. Ransome.

The Thinking Machine was visibly annoyed and his blue eyes snapped.

"Lock me in any cell in any prison anywhere at any time, wearing only what is necessary, and I'll escape in a week," he declared, sharply.

Dr. Ransome sat up straight in the chair, interested. Mr. Fielding lighted a new cigar.

"You mean you could actually *think* yourself out?" asked Dr. Ransome.

"I would get out," was the response.

"Are you serious?"

"Certainly I am serious."

Dr. Ransome and Mr. Fielding were silent for a long time.

"Would you be willing to try it?" asked Mr. Fielding, finally.

"Certainly," said Professor Van Dusen, and there was a trace of irony in his voice. "I have done more asinine things than that to convince other men of less important truths."

The tone was offensive and there was an undercurrent strongly resembling anger on both sides. Of course it was an absurd thing, but Professor Van Dusen reiterated his willingness to undertake the escape and it was decided upon.

"To begin now," added Dr. Ransome.

"I'd prefer that it begin tomorrow," said The Thinking Machine, "because—"

"No, now," said Mr. Fielding, flatly. "You are arrested, figuratively, of course, without any warning locked in a cell with no chance to communicate with friends, and left there with identically the same care and attention that would be given to a man under sentence of death. Are you willing?"

"All right, now, then," said The Thinking Machine, and he arose.

"Say, the death cell in Chisholm Prison."

"The death cell in Chisholm Prison."

"And what will you wear?"

"As little as possible," said The Thinking Machine. "Shoes, stockings, trousers, and a shirt."

"You will permit yourself to be searched, of course?"

"I am to be treated precisely as all prisoners are treated," said The Thinking Machine. "No more attention and no less."

There were some preliminaries to be arranged in the matter of obtaining permission for the test, but all three were influential men and everything was done satisfactorily by telephone, albeit the prison commissioners, to whom the experiment was explained on purely scientific grounds, were sadly bewildered. Professor Van Dusen would be the most distinguished prisoner they had ever entertained.

When The Thinking Machine had donned those things which he was to wear during his incarceration he called the little old woman who was his housekeeper, cook, and maid-servant all in one.

"Martha," he said, "it is now twenty-seven minutes past nine o'clock. I am going away. One week from tonight, at half past nine, these gentlemen and one, possibly two, others will take supper with me here. Remember Dr. Ransome is very fond of artichokes."

The three men were driven to Chisholm Prison, where the warden was awaiting them, having been informed of the matter by telephone. He understood merely that the eminent Professor Van Dusen was to be his prisoner, if he could keep him, for one week; that he had committed no crime, but that he was to be treated as all other prisoners were treated.

"Search him," instructed Dr. Ransome.

The Thinking Machine was searched. Nothing was found on him; the pockets of the trousers were empty; the white, stiff-bosomed shirt had no pocket. The shoes and stockings were removed, examined, then replaced. As he watched all these preliminaries, and noted the pitiful, child-like physical weakness of the man—the colorless face, and the thin, white hands—Dr. Ransome almost regretted his part in the affair.

"Are you sure you want to do this?" he asked.

"Would you be convinced if I did not?" inquired The Thinking Machine in turn.

"No."

"All right. I'll do it."

What sympathy Dr. Ransome had was dissipated by the tone. It nettled him, and he resolved to see the experiment to the end; it would be a stinging reproof to egotism.

"It will be impossible for him to communicate with anyone outside?" he asked.

"Absolutely impossible," replied the warden. "He will not be permitted writing materials of any sort."

"And your jailers, would they deliver a message from him?"

"Not one word, directly or indirectly," said the warden. "You may rest assured of that. They will report anything he might say or turn over to me, anything he might give them."

"That seems entirely satisfactory," said Mr. Fielding, who was frankly interested in the problem.

"Of course, in the event he fails," said Dr. Ransome, "and asks for his liberty, you understand you are to set him free?"

"I understand," replied the warden.

The Thinking Machine stood listening, but had nothing to say until this was all ended, then:

"I should like to make three small requests. You may grant them or not, as you wish."

"No special favors, now," warned Mr. Fielding.

"I am asking none," was the stiff response. "I should like to have some tooth powder—buy it yourself to see that it is tooth powder—and I should like to have one five-dollar and two ten-dollar bills."

Dr. Ransome, Mr. Fielding and the warden exchanged

astonished glances. They were not surprised at the request for tooth powder, but were at the request for money.

"Is there any man with whom our friend would come in contact that he could bribe with twenty-five dollars?"

"Not for twenty-five hundred dollars" was the positive reply.

"Well, let him have them," said Mr. Fielding. "I think they are harmless enough."

"And what is the third request?" asked Dr. Ransome.

"I should like to have my shoes polished."

Again the astonished glances were exchanged. This last request was the height of absurdity, so they agreed to it. These things all being attended to, The Thinking Machine was led back into the prison from which he had undertaken to escape.

"Here is Cell Thirteen," said the warden, stopping three doors down the steel corridor. "This is where we keep condemned murderers. No one can leave it without my permission; and no one in it can communicate with the outside. I'll stake my reputation on that. It's only three doors back of my office and I can readily hear any unusual noise."

"Will this cell do, gentlemen?" asked The Thinking Machine. There was a touch of irony in his voice.

"Admirably," was the reply.

The heavy steel door was thrown open, there was a great scurrying and scampering of tiny feet, and The Thinking Machine passed into the gloom of the cell. Then the door was closed and double-locked by the warden.

"What is that noise in there?" asked Dr. Ransome, through the bars.

"Rats—dozens of them," replied The Thinking Machine, tersely.

The three men, with final good nights, were turning away when The Thinking Machine called:

"What time is it exactly, Warden?"

"Eleven-seventeen," replied the warden.

"Thanks. I will join you gentlemen in your office at half

past eight o'clock one week from tonight," said The Thinking Machine.

"And if you do not?"

"There is no 'if' about it."

Chisholm Prison was a great, spreading structure of granite, four stories in all, which stood in the center of acres of open space. It was surrounded by a wall of solid masonry eighteen feet high, and so smoothly finished inside and out as to offer no foothold to a climber, no matter how expert. Atop of this fence, as a further precaution, was a five-foot fence of steel rods, each terminating in a keen point. This fence in itself marked an absolute deadline between freedom and imprisonment, for, even if a man escaped from his cell, it would seem impossible for him to pass the wall.

The yard, which on all sides of the prison building was twenty-five feet wide, that being the distance from the building to the wall, was by day an exercise ground for those prisoners to whom was granted the boon of occasional semi-liberty. But that was not for those in Cell 13. At all times of the day there were armed guards in the yard, four of them, one patrolling each side of the prison building.

By night the yard was almost as brilliantly lighted as by day. On each of the four sides was a great arc light which rose above the prison wall and gave to the guards a clear sight. The lights, too, brightly illuminated the spiked top of the wall. The wires which fed the arc lights ran up the side of the prison building on insulators and from the top story led out to the poles supporting the arc lights.

All these things were seen and comprehended by The Thinking Machine, who was only enabled to see out his closely barred cell window by standing on his bed. This was on the morning following his incarceration. He gathered, too, that the river lay over there beyond the wall somewhere, because he heard faintly the pulsation of a motor boat and high up in the air saw a river bird. From that same direction came the shouts of boys at play and the occasional crack of a batted ball. He knew then that between the prison wall and the river was an open space, a playground.

Chisholm Prison was regarded as absolutely safe. No man had ever escaped from it. The Thinking Machine, from his perch on the bed, seeing what he saw, could readily understand why. The walls of the cell, though built he judged twenty years before, were perfectly solid, and the window bars of new iron had not a shadow of rust on them. The window itself, even with the bars out, would be a difficult mode of egress because it was small.

Yet, seeing these things, The Thinking Machine was not discouraged. Instead, he thoughtfully squinted at the great arc light—there was bright sunlight now—and traced with his eyes the wire which led from it to the building. That electric wire, he reasoned, must come down the side of the building not a great distance from his cell. That might be worth knowing.

Cell 13 was on the same floor with the offices of the prison—that is, not in the basement, nor yet upstairs. There were only four steps up to the office floor, therefore the level of the floor must be only three or four feet above the ground. He couldn't see the ground directly beneath his window, but he could see it further out toward the wall. It would be an easy drop from the window. Well and good.

Then The Thinking Machine fell to remembering how he had come to the cell. First, there was the outside guard's booth, a part of the wall. There were two heavily barred gates there, both of steel. At this gate was one man always on guard. He admitted persons to the prison after much clanking of keys and locks, and let them out when ordered to do so. The warden's office was in the prison building, and in order to reach that official from the prison yard one had to pass a gate of solid steel with only a peephole in it. Then coming from that inner office to Cell 13, where he was now, one must pass a heavy wooden door and two steel doors into the corridors of the prison; and always there was the double-locked door of Cell 13 to reckon with.

There were then, The Thinking Machine recalled, seven doors to be overcome before one could pass from Cell 13 into the outer world, a free man. But against this was the fact that he was rarely interrupted. A jailer appeared at his cell door at six in the morning with a breakfast of prison fare; he would come again at noon, and again at six in the afternoon. At nine o'clock at night would come the inspection tour. That would be all.

"It's admirably arranged, this prison system," was the mental tribute paid by The Thinking Machine. "I'll have to study it a little when I get out. I had no idea there was such great care exercised in the prisons."

There was nothing, positively nothing, in his cell, except his iron bed, so firmly put together that no man could tear it to pieces save with sledges or a file. He had neither of these. There was not even a chair, or a small table, or a bit of tin or crockery. Nothing! The jailer stood by when he ate, then took away the wooden spoon and bowl which he had used.

One by one these things sank into the brain of The Thinking Machine. When the last possibility had been considered he began an examination of his cell. From the roof, down the walls on all sides, he examined the stones and the cement between them. He stamped over the floor carefully time after time, but it was cement, perfectly solid. After the examination he sat on the edge of the iron bed and was lost in thought for a long time. For Professor Augustus S.F.X. Van Dusen, The Thinking Machine, had something to think about.

He was disturbed by a rat, which ran across his foot, then scampered away into a dark corner of the cell, frightened at its own daring. After a while The Thinking Machine, squinting steadily into the darkness of the corner where the rat had gone, was able to make out in the gloom many little beady eyes staring at him. He counted six pair, and there were perhaps others; he didn't see very well.

Then The Thinking Machine, from his seat on the bed,

noticed for the first time the bottom of his cell door. There was an opening there of two inches between the steel bar and the floor. Still looking steadily at this opening, The Thinking Machine backed suddenly into the corner where he had seen the beady eyes. There was a great scampering of tiny feet, several squeaks of frightened rodents, and then silence.

None of the rats had gone out the door, yet there were none in the cell. Therefore there must be another way out of the cell, however small. The Thinking Machine, on hands and knees, started a search for this spot, feeling in the darkness with his long, slender fingers.

At last his search was rewarded. He came upon a small opening in the floor, level with the cement. It was perfectly round and somewhat larger than a silver dollar. This was the way the rats had gone. He put his fingers deep into the opening; it seemed to be a disused drainage pipe and was dry and dusty.

Having satisfied himself on this point, he sat on the bed again for an hour, then made another inspection of his surroundings through the small cell window. One of the outside guards stood directly opposite, beside the wall, and happened to be looking at the window of Cell 13 when the head of The Thinking Machine appeared. But the scientist didn't notice the guard.

Noon came and the jailer appeared with the prison dinner of repulsively plain food. At home The Thinking Machine merely ate to live; here he took what was offered without comment. Occasionally he spoke to the jailer who stood outside the door watching him.

"Any improvements made here in the last few years?" he asked.

"Nothing particularly," replied the jailer. "New wall was built four years ago."

"Anything done to the prison proper?"

"Painted the woodwork outside, and I believe about seven years ago a new system of plumbing was put in."

"Ah!" said the prisoner. "How far is the river over there?"

"About three hundred feet. The boys have a baseball ground between the wall and the river."

The Thinking Machine had nothing further to say just then, but when the jailer was ready to go he asked for some water.

"I get very thirsty here," he explained. "Would it be possible for you to leave a little water in a bowl for me?"

"I'll ask the warden," replied the jailer, and he went away.

Half an hour later he returned with water in a small earthen bowl.

"The warden says you may keep this bowl," he informed the prisoner. "But you must show it to me when I ask for it. If it is broken, it will be the last."

"Thank you," said The Thinking Machine. "I shan't break it."

The jailer went on about his duties. For just the fraction of a second it seemed that The Thinking Machine wanted to ask a question, but he didn't.

Two hours later this same jailer, in passing the door of Cell No. 13, heard a noise inside and stopped. The Thinking Machine was down on his hands and knees in a corner of the cell, and from that same corner came several frightened squeaks. The jailer looked on interestedly.

"Ah, I've got you," he heard the prisoner say.

"Got what?" he asked, sharply.

"One of these rats," was the reply. "See?" And between the scientist's long fingers the jailer saw a small gray rat struggling. The prisoner brought it over to the light and looked at it closely.

"It's a water rat," he said.

"Ain't you got anything better to do than to catch rats?" asked the jailer.

"It's disgraceful that they should be here at all," was the irritated reply. "Take this one away and kill it. There are dozens more where it came from."

The jailer took the wriggling, squirmy rodent and flung it down on the floor violently. It gave one squeak and lay still. Later he reported the incident to the warden, who only smiled.

Still later that afternoon the outside armed guard on the Cell 13 side of the prison looked up again at the window and saw the prisoner looking out. He saw a hand raised to the barred window and then something white fluttered to the ground, directly under the window of Cell 13. It was a little roll of linen, evidently of white shirting material, and tied around it was a five-dollar bill. The guard looked up at the window again, but the face had disappeared.

With a grim smile he took the little linen roll and the five-dollar bill to the warden's office. There together they deciphered something which was written on it with a queer sort of ink, frequently blurred. On the outside was this:

"Finder of this please deliver to Dr. Charles Ransome."

"Ah," said the warden, with a chuckle. "Plan of escape number one has gone wrong." Then, as an afterthought: "But why did he address it to Dr. Ransome?"

"And where did he get the pen and ink to write with?" asked the guard.

The warden looked at the guard and the guard looked at the warden. There was no apparent solution of that mystery. The warden studied the writing carefully, then shook his head.

"Well, let's see what he was going to say to Dr. Ransome," he said at length, still puzzled, and he unrolled the inner piece of linen.

"Well, if that—what—what do you think of that?" he asked, dazed.

The guard took the bit of linen and read this:

"Epa cseot d'net niiy awe htto n'si sih. T."

The warden spent an hour wondering what sort of a cipher it was, and half an hour wondering why his prisoner should attempt to communicate with Dr. Ransome, who was the cause of his being there. After this the warden devoted some thought to the question of where the prisoner got writing materials, and what sort of writing materials he had. With the idea of illuminating this point, he examined the linen again. It was a torn part of a white shirt and had ragged edges.

Now it was possible to account for the linen, but what the prisoner had used to write with was another matter. The warden knew it would have been impossible for him to have either pen or pencil, and, besides, neither pen nor pencil had been used in this writing. What, then? The warden decided to investigate personally. The Thinking Machine was his prisoner; he had orders to hold his prisoners; if this one sought to escape by sending cipher messages to persons outside, he would stop it, as he would have stopped it in the case of any other prisoner.

The warden went back to Cell 13 and found The Thinking Machine on his hands and knees on the floor, engaged in nothing more alarming than catching rats. The prisoner heard the warden's step and turned to him quickly.

"It's disgraceful," he snapped, "these rats. There are scores of them."

"Other men have been able to stand them," said the warden. "Here is another shirt for you—let me have the one you have on."

"Why?" demanded The Thinking Machine, quickly. His tone was hardly natural, his manner suggested actual perturbation.

"You have attempted to communicate with Dr. Ransome," said the warden severely. "As my prisoner, it is my duty to put a stop to it."

The Thinking Machine was silent for a moment.

"All right," he said, finally. "Do your duty."

The warden smiled grimly. The prisoner arose from the floor and removed the white shirt, putting on instead a striped convict shirt the warden had brought. The warden took the white shirt eagerly, and then and there compared the pieces of linen on which was written the cipher with certain torn places in the shirt. The Thinking Machine looked on curiously.

"The guard brought *you* those, then?" he asked.

"He certainly did," replied the warden triumphantly. "And that ends your first attempt to escape."

The Thinking Machine watched the warden as he, by comparison, established to his own satisfaction that only two pieces of linen had been torn from the white shirt.

"What did you write this with?" demanded the warden.

"I should think it a part of your duty to find out," said The Thinking Machine, irritably.

The warden started to say some harsh things, then restrained himself and made a minute search of the cell and of the prisoner instead. He found absolutely nothing; not even a match or toothpick which might have been used for a pen. The same mystery surrounded the fluid with which the cipher had been written. Although the warden left Cell 13 visibly annoyed, he took the torn shirt in triumph.

"Well, writing notes on a shirt won't get him out, that's certain," he told himself with some complacency. He put the linen scraps into his desk to await developments. "If that man escapes from that cell I'll—hang it—I'll resign."

On the third day of his incarceration The Thinking Machine openly attempted to bribe his way out. The jailer had brought his dinner and was leaning against the barred door, waiting, when The Thinking Machine began the conversation.

"The drainage pipes of the prison lead to the river, don't they?" he asked.

"Yes," said the jailer.

"I suppose they are very small."

"Too small to crawl through, if that's what you're thinking about," was the grinning response.

There was silence until The Thinking Machine finished his meal. Then:

"You know I'm not a criminal, don't you?"

"Yes."

"And that I've a perfect right to be freed if I demand it?"

"Yes."

"Well, I came here believing that I could make my escape," said the prisoner, and his squint eyes studied the face of the jailer. "Would you consider a financial reward for aiding me to escape?"

The jailer, who happened to be an honest man, looked at the slender, weak figure of the prisoner, at the large head with its mass of yellow hair, and was almost sorry.

"I guess prisons like these were not built for the likes of you to get out of," he said, at last.

"But would you consider a proposition to help me get out?" the prisoner insisted, almost beseechingly.

"No," said the jailer, shortly.

"Five hundred dollars," urged The Thinking Machine. "I am not a criminal."

"No," said the jailer.

"A thousand?"

"No," again said the jailer, and he started away hurriedly to escape further temptation. Then he turned back. "If you should give me ten thousand dollars I couldn't get you out. You'd have to pass through seven doors, and I only have the keys to two."

Then he told the warden all about it.

"Plan number two fails," said the warden, smiling grimly. "First a cipher, then bribery."

When the jailer was on his way to Cell 13 at six o'clock, again bearing food to The Thinking Machine, he paused, startled by the unmistakable scrape, scrape of steel against steel. It stopped at the sound of his steps, then craftily the jailer, who was beyond the prisoner's range of vision, resumed his tramping, the sound being apparently that of a man going away from Cell 13. As a matter of fact he was in the same spot.

After a moment there came again the steady scrape, scrape, and the jailer crept cautiously on tiptoes to the door and peered between the bars. The Thinking Machine was standing on the iron bed working at the bars of the little window. He was using a file, judging from the backward and forward swing of his arms.

Cautiously the jailer crept back to the office, summoned the warden in person, and they returned to Cell 13 on tiptoes. The steady scrape was still audible. The warden listened to satisfy himself and then suddenly appeared at the door.

"Well?" he demanded, and there was a smile on his face.

The Thinking Machine glanced back from his perch on the bed and leaped suddenly to the floor, making frantic efforts to hide something. The warden went in, with hand extended.

"Give it up," he said.

"No," said the prisoner, sharply.

"Come, give it up," urged the warden. "I don't want to have to search you again."

"No," repeated the prisoner.

"What was it—a file?" asked the warden.

The Thinking Machine was silent and stood squinting at the warden with something very nearly approaching disappointment on his face—nearly, but not quite. The warden was almost sympathetic.

"Plan number three fails, eh?" he asked, good-naturedly. "Too bad, isn't it?"

The prisoner didn't say.

"Search him," instructed the warden.

The jailer searched the prisoner carefully. At last, artfully concealed in the waistband of the trousers, he found a piece of steel about two inches long, with one side curved like a half moon.

"Ah," said the warden, as he received it from the jailer. "From your shoe heel," and he smiled pleasantly.

The jailer continued his search and on the other side of the trousers waistband found another piece of steel identical with the first. The edge showed where they had been worn against the bars of the window.

"You couldn't saw a way through those bars with these," said the warden.

"I could have," said The Thinking Machine firmly.

"In six months, perhaps," said the warden, good-naturedly.

The warden shook his head slowly as he gazed into the slightly flushed face of his prisoner.

"Ready to give it up?" he asked.

"I haven't started yet," was the prompt reply.

Then came another exhaustive search of the cell. Carefully the two men went over it, finally turning out the bed and searching that. Nothing. The warden in person climbed upon the bed and examined the bars of the window where the prisoner had been sawing. When he looked he was amused.

"Just made it a little bright by hard rubbing," he said to the prisoner, who stood looking on with a somewhat crestfallen air. The warden grasped the iron bars in his strong hands and tried to shake them. They were immovable, set firmly in the solid granite. He examined each in turn and found them all satisfactory. Finally he climbed down from the bed.

"Give it up, Professor," he advised.

The Thinking Machine shook his head and the warden and jailer passed on again. As they disappeared down the corridor The Thinking Machine sat on the edge of the bed with his head in his hands.

"He's crazy to try to get out of that cell," commented the jailer.

"Of course he can't get out," said the warden. "But he's clever. I would like to know what he wrote that cipher with."

It was four o'clock next morning when an awful, heart-racking shriek of terror resounded through the great prison.

It came from a cell, somewhere about the center, and its tone told a tale of horror, agony, terrible fear. The warden heard and with three of his men rushed into the long corridor leading to Cell 13.

As they ran there came again that awful cry. It died away in a sort of wail. The white faces of prisoners appeared at cell doors upstairs and down, staring out wonderingly, frightened.

"It's that fool in Cell Thirteen," grumbled the warden.

He stopped and stared in as one of the jailers flashed a lantern. "That fool in Cell Thirteen" lay comfortably on his cot, flat on his back with his mouth open, snoring. Even as they looked there came again the piercing cry, from somewhere above. The warden's face blanched a little as he started up the stairs. There on the top floor he found a man in Cell 43, directly above Cell 13, but two floors higher, cowering in a corner of his cell.

"What's the matter?" demanded the warden.

"Thank God you've come," exclaimed the prisoner, and he cast himself against the bars of his cell.

"What is it?" demanded the warden again.

He threw open the door and went in. The prisoner dropped on his knees and clasped the warden about the body. His face was white with terror, his eyes were widely distended, and he was shuddering. His hands, icy cold, clutched at the warden's.

"Take me out of this cell, please take me out," he pleaded.

"What's the matter with you, anyhow?" insisted the warden, impatiently.

"I heard something—something," said the prisoner, and his eyes roved nervously around the cell.

"What did you hear?"

"I—I can't tell you," stammered the prisoner. Then, in a sudden burst of terror: "Take me out of this cell—put me anywhere—but take me out of here."

The warden and the three jailers exchanged glances.

"Who is this fellow? What's he accused of?" asked the warden.

"Joseph Ballard," said one of the jailers. "He's accused of throwing acid in a woman's face. She died from it."

"But they can't prove it," gasped the prisoner. "They can't prove it. Please put me in some other cell."

He was still clinging to the warden, and that official threw his arms off roughly. Then for a time he stood looking at the cowering wretch, who seemed possessed of all the wild, unreasoning terror of a child.

"Look here, Ballard," said the warden, finally, "if you heard anything, I want to know what it was. Now tell me."

"I can't, I can't," was the reply. He was sobbing.

"Where did it come from?"

"I don't know. Everywhere—nowhere. I just heard it."

"What was it—a voice?"

"Please don't make me answer," pleaded the prisoner.

"You must answer," said the warden, sharply.

"It was a voice—but—but it wasn't human," was the sobbing reply.

"Voice, but not human?" repeated the warden, puzzled.

"It sounded muffled and—and far away—and ghostly," explained the man.

"Did it come from inside or outside the prison?"

"It didn't seem to come from anywhere—it was just here, here, everywhere. I heard it. I heard it."

For an hour the warden tried to get the story, but Ballard had become suddenly obstinate and would say nothing —only pleaded to be placed in another cell, or to have one of the jailers remain near him until daylight. These requests were gruffly refused.

"And see here," said the warden, in conclusion, "if there's any more of this screaming I'll put you in the padded cell."

Then the warden went his way, a sadly puzzled man. Ballard sat at his cell door until daylight, his face, drawn and white with terror, pressed against the bars, and looked out into the prison with wide, staring eyes.

That day, the fourth since the incarceration of The Thinking Machine, was enlivened considerably by the volunteer prisoner, who spent most of his time at the little window of his cell. He began proceedings by throwing another piece of linen down to the guard, who picked it up dutifully and took it to the warden. On it was written:

"Only three days more."

The warden was in no way surprised at what he read; he understood that The Thinking Machine meant only three days more of his imprisonment, and he regarded the note as a boast. But how was the thing written? Where had The Thinking Machine found this new piece of linen? Where? How? He carefully examined the linen. It was white, of fine texture, shirting material. He took the shirt which he had taken and carefully fitted the two original pieces of the linen to the torn places. This third piece was entirely superfluous; it didn't fit anywhere, and yet it was unmistakably the same goods.

"And where—where does he get anything to write with?" demanded the warden of the world at large.

Still later on the fourth day The Thinking Machine, through the window of his cell, spoke to the armed guard outside.

"What day of the month is it?" he asked.

"The fifteenth," was the answer.

The Thinking Machine made a mental astronomical calculation and satisfied himself that the moon would not rise until after nine o'clock that night. Then he asked another question:

"Who attends to those arc lights?"

"Man from the company."

"You have no electricians in the building?"

"No."

"I should think you could save money if you had your own man."

"None of my business," replied the guard.

The guard noticed The Thinking Machine at the cell window frequently during that day, but always the face seemed listless and there was a certain wistfulness in the squint eyes behind the glasses. After a while he accepted the presence of the leonine head as a matter of course. He had seen other prisoners do the same thing; it was the longing for the outside world.

That afternoon, just before the day guard was relieved, the head appeared at the window again, and The Thinking Machine's hand held something out between the bars. It fluttered to the ground and the guard picked it up. It was a five-dollar bill.

"That's for you," called the prisoner.

As usual, the guard took it to the warden. That gentleman looked at it suspiciously; he looked at everything that came from Cell 13 with suspicion.

"He said it was for me," explained the guard.

"It's a sort of a tip, I suppose," said the warden. "I see no particular reason why you shouldn't accept—"

Suddenly he stopped. He had remembered that The Thinking Machine had gone into Cell 13 with one five-dollar bill and two ten-dollar bills; twenty-five dollars in all. Now a five-dollar bill had been tied around the first pieces of linen that came from the cell. The warden still had it, and to convince himself he took it out and looked at it. It was five dollars; yet here was another five dollars, and The Thinking Machine had only had ten-dollar bills.

"Perhaps somebody changed one of the bills for him," he thought at last, with a sigh of relief.

But then and there he made up his mind. He would search Cell 13 as a cell was never before searched in this world. When a man could write at will, and change money, and do other wholly inexplicable things, there was something radically wrong with his prison. He planned to enter the cell at night—three o'clock would be an excellent time. The Thinking Machine must do all the weird things he did sometime. Night seemed the most reasonable. Thus it happened that the warden stealthily descended upon Cell 13 that night at three o'clock. He paused at the door and listened. There was no sound save the steady, regular breathing of the prisoner. The keys unfastened the double locks with scarcely a clank, and the warden entered, locking the door behind him. Suddenly he flashed his dark lantern in the face of the recumbent figure.

If the warden had planned to startle The Thinking Machine he was mistaken, for that individual merely opened his eyes quietly, reached for his glasses, and inquired, in a most matter-of-fact tone:

"Who is it?"

It would be useless to describe the search that the warden made. It was minute. Not one inch of the cell or the bed was overlooked. He found the round hole in the floor, and with a flash of inspiration thrust his thick fingers into it. After a moment of fumbling there he drew up something and looked at it in the light of his lantern.

"Ugh!" he exclaimed.

The thing he had taken out was a rat—a dead rat. His inspiration fled as a mist before the sun. But he continued the search. The Thinking Machine, without a word, arose and kicked the rat out of the cell into the corridor.

The warden climbed on the bed and tried the steel bars in the tiny window. They were perfectly rigid; every bar of the door was the same.

Then the warden searched the prisoner's clothing, beginning at the shoes. Nothing hidden in them! Then the trousers waistband. Still nothing! Then the pockets of the trousers. From one side he drew out some paper money and examined it.

"Five one-dollar bills," he gasped.

"That's right," said the prisoner.

"But the—you had two tens and a five—what the—how do you do it?"

"That's my business," said The Thinking Machine.

"Did any of my men change this money for you—on your word of honor?"

The Thinking Machine paused just a fraction of a second.

"No," he said.

"Well, do you make it?" asked the warden. He was prepared to believe anything.

"That's my business," again said the prisoner.

The warden glared at the eminent scientist fiercely. He felt—he knew—that this man was making a fool of him, yet he didn't know how. If he were a real prisoner he would get the truth—but, then, perhaps, those inexplicable things which had happened would not have been brought before him so sharply. Neither of the men spoke for a long time, then suddenly the warden turned fiercely and left the cell, slamming the door behind him. He didn't dare to speak, then.

He glanced at the clock. It was ten minutes to four. He had hardly settled himself in bed when again came that heart-breaking shriek through the prison. With a few muttered words, which, while not elegant, were highly expressive, he relighted his lantern and rushed through the prison again to the cell on the upper floor.

Again Ballard was crushing himself against the steel door, shrieking, shrieking at the top of his voice. He stopped only when the warden flashed his lamp in the cell.

"Take me out, take me out," he screamed. "I did it, I did it, I killed her. Take it away."

"Take what away?" asked the warden.

"I threw the acid in her face—I did it—I confess. Take me out of here."

Ballard's condition was pitiable; it was only an act of mercy to let him out into the corridor. There he crouched in a corner, like an animal at bay, and clasped his hands to his ears. It took half an hour to calm him sufficiently for him to speak. Then he told incoherently what had happened. On the night before at four o'clock he had heard a voice—a sepulchral voice, muffled and wailing in tone. "What did it say?" asked the warden, curiously.

"Acid—acid—acid!" gasped the prisoner. "It accused me. Acid! I threw the acid, and the woman died. Oh!" It was a long, shuddering wail of terror.

"Acid?" echoed the warden, puzzled. The case was beyond him.

"Acid. That's all I heard—that one word, repeated several times. There were other things, too, but I didn't hear them."

"That was last night, eh?" asked the warden. "What happened tonight—what frightened you just now?"

"It was the same thing," gasped the prisoner. "Acid—acid—acid!" He covered his face with his hands and sat shivering. "It was acid I used on her, but I didn't mean to kill her. I just heard the words. It was something accusing me—accusing me." He mumbled, and was silent.

"Did you hear anything else?"

"Yes—but I couldn't understand—only a little bit—just a word or two."

"Well, what was it?"

"I heard 'acid' three times, then I heard a long, moaning sound, then—then—I heard 'number eight hat.' I heard that twice."

"Number eight hat," repeated the warden. "What the devil—number eight hat? Accusing voices of conscience have never talked about number eight hats, so far as I ever heard."

"He's insane," said one of the jailers, with an air of finality.

"I believe you," said the warden. "He must be. He probably heard something and got frightened. He's trembling now. Number eight hat! What the—"

When the fifth day of The Thinking Machine's imprisonment rolled around the warden was wearing a hunted look. He was anxious for the end of the thing. He could not help but feel that his distinguished prisoner had been amusing himself. And if this were so, The Thinking Machine had lost none of his sense of humor. For on this fifth day he flung down another linen note to the outside guard, bearing the words "Only two days more." Also he flung down half a dollar.

Now the warden knew—he *knew*—that the man in Cell 13 didn't have any half dollars—he *couldn't* have any half dollars, no more than he could have pen and ink and linen, and yet he did have them. It was a condition, not a theory; that is one reason why the warden was wearing a hunted look.

That ghastly, uncanny thing, too, about "acid" and "number eight hat" clung to him tenaciously. They didn't mean anything, of course, merely the ravings of an insane murderer who had been driven by fear to confess his crime, still there were so many things that "didn't mean anything" happening in the prison now since The Thinking Machine was there.

On the sixth day the warden received a postal stating that Dr. Ransome and Mr. Fielding would be at Chisholm Prison on the following evening, Thursday, and in the event Professor Van Dusen had not yet escaped—and they presumed he had not because they had not heard from him—they would meet him there.

"In the event he had not yet escaped!" The warden smiled grimly. Escaped!

The Thinking Machine enlivened this day for the warden with three notes. They were on the usual linen and bore generally on the appointment at half past eight o'clock Thursday night, which appointment the scientist had made at the time of his imprisonment.

On the afternoon of the seventh day the warden passed Cell 13 and glanced in. The Thinking Machine was lying on the iron bed, apparently sleeping lightly. The cell appeared precisely as it always did from a casual glance. The warden would swear that no man was going to leave it between that hour—it was then four o'clock—and half past eight o'clock that evening.

On his way back past the cell the warden heard the steady breathing again, and coming closer to the door looked in. He wouldn't have done so if The Thinking Machine had been looking, but now—well, it was different.

A ray of light came through the high window and fell on the face of the sleeping man. It occurred to the warden for the first time that his prisoner appeared haggard and weary. Just then The Thinking Machine stirred slightly and the warden hurried on up the corridor guiltily. That evening after six o'clock he saw the jailer.

"Everything all right in Cell Thirteen?" he asked.

"Yes, sir," replied the jailer. "He didn't eat much, though."

It was with a feeling of having done his duty that the warden received Dr. Ransome and Mr. Fielding shortly after seven o'clock. He intended to show them the linen notes and lay before them the full story of his woes, which was a long one. But before this came to pass the guard from the river side of the prison yard entered the office.

"The arc light in my side of the yard won't light," he informed the warden.

"Confound it, that man's a hoodoo," thundered the official. "Everything has happened since he's been here."

The guard went back to his post in the darkness, and the warden phoned to the electric light company.

"This is Chisholm Prison," he said through the phone. "Send three or four men down here quick, to fix an arc light."

The reply was evidently satisfactory, for the warden hung up the receiver and passed out into the yard. While Dr. Ransome and Mr. Fielding sat waiting the guard at the outer gate came in with a special-delivery letter. Dr. Ransome happened to notice the address, and, when the guard went out, looked at the letter more closely.

"By George!" he exclaimed.

"What is it?" asked Mr. Fielding.

Silently the doctor offered the letter. Mr. Fielding examined it closely.

"Coincidence," he said. "It must be."

It was nearly eight o'clock when the warden returned to his office. The electricians had arrived in a wagon, and were now at work. The warden pressed the buzz-button communicating with the man at the outer gate in the wall.

"How many electricians came in?" he asked, over the short phone. "Four? Three workmen in jumpers and overalls and the manager? Frock coat and silk hat? All right. Be certain that only four go out. That's all."

He turned to Dr. Ransome and Mr. Fielding.

"We have to be careful here—particularly," and there was broad sarcasm in his tone, "since we have scientists locked up."

The warden picked up the special-delivery letter carelessly, and then began to open it.

"When I read this I want to tell you gentlemen something about how—Great Caesar!" he ended, suddenly, as he glanced at the letter. He sat with mouth open, motionless, from astonishment.

"What is it?" asked Mr. Fielding.

"A special-delivery letter from Cell Thirteen," gasped the warden. "An invitation to supper."

"What?" and the two others arose, unanimously.

The warden sat dazed, staring at the letter for a moment, then called sharply to a guard outside in the corridor.

"Run down to Cell Thirteen and see if that man's in there."

The guard went as directed, while Dr. Ransome and Mr. Fielding examined the letter.

"It's Van Dusen's handwriting; there's no question of that," said Dr. Ransome. "I've seen too much of it."

Just then the buzz on the telephone from the outer gate sounded, and the warden, in a semitrance, picked up the receiver.

"Hello! Two reporters, eh? Let 'em come in." He turned suddenly to the doctor and Mr. Fielding. "Why, the man *can't* be out. He must be in his cell."

Just at that moment the guard returned.

"He's still in his cell, sir," he reported. "I saw him. He's lying down."

"There, I told you so," said the warden, and he breathed freely again. "But how did he mail that letter?"

There was a rap on the steel door which led from the jail yard into the warden's office.

"It's the reporters," said the warden. "Let them in," he instructed the guard; then to the two other gentlemen: "Don't say anything about this before them, because I'd never hear the last of it."

The door opened, and the two men from the front gate entered.

"Good evening, gentlemen," said one. That was Hutchinson Hatch; the warden knew him well.

"Well?" demanded the other, irritably. "I'm here."

That was The Thinking Machine.

He squinted belligerently at the warden, who sat with mouth agape. For the moment that official had nothing to say. Dr. Ransome and Mr. Fielding were amazed, but they didn't know what the warden knew. They were only amazed; he was paralyzed. Hutchinson Hatch, the reporter, took in the scene with greedy eyes.

"How—how—how did you do it?" gasped the warden, finally.

"Come back to the cell," said The Thinking Machine, in the irritated voice which his scientific associates knew so well.

The warden, still in a condition bordering on trance, led the way.

"Flash your light in there," directed The Thinking Machine.

The warden did so. There was nothing unusual in the appearance of the cell, and there—there on the bed lay the figure of The Thinking Machine. Certainly! There was the yellow hair! Again the warden looked at the man beside him and wondered at the strangeness of his own dreams.

With trembling hands he unlocked the cell door and The Thinking Machine passed inside.

"See here," he said.

He kicked at the steel bars in the bottom of the cell door and three of them were pushed out of place. A fourth broke off and rolled away in the corridor.

"And here, too," directed the erstwhile prisoner as he stood on the bed to reach the small window. He swept his hand across the opening and every bar came out.

"What's this in bed?" demanded the warden, who was slowly recovering.

"A wig," was the reply. "Turn down the cover."

The warden did so. Beneath it lay a large coil of strong rope, thirty feet or more, a dagger, three files, ten feet of electric wire, a thin, powerful pair of steel pliers, a small tack hammer with its handle, and—and a derringer pistol.

"How did you do it?" demanded the warden.

"You gentlemen have an engagement to supper with me at half past nine o'clock," said The Thinking Machine. "Come on, or we shall be late."

"But how did you do it?" insisted the warden.

"Don't ever think you can hold any man who can use his brain," said The Thinking Machine. "Come on; we shall be late."

It was an impatient supper party in the rooms of Professor Van Dusen and a somewhat silent one. The guests were Dr. Ransome, Alfred Fielding, the warden, and Hutchinson Hatch, reporter. The meal was served to the minute, in accordance with Professor Van Dusen's instructions of one week before; Dr. Ransome found the artichokes delicious. At last the supper was finished and The Thinking Machine turned full on Dr. Ransome and squinted at him fiercely.

"Do you believe it now?" he demanded.

"I do," replied Dr. Ransome.

"Do you admit that it was a fair test?"

"I do."

With the others, particularly the warden, he was waiting anxiously for the explanation.

"Suppose you tell us how—" began Mr. Fielding.

"Yes, tell us how," said the warden.

The Thinking Machine readjusted his glasses, took a couple of preparatory squints at his audience, and began the story. He told it from the beginning logically; and no man ever talked to more interested listeners.

"My agreement was," he began, "to go into a cell, carrying nothing except what was necessary to wear, and to leave that cell within a week. I had never seen Chisholm Prison. When I went into the cell I asked for tooth powder, two ten- and one five-dollar bills, and also to have my shoes blacked. Even if these requests had been refused it would not have mattered seriously. But you agreed to them.

"I knew there would be nothing in the cell which you thought I might use to advantage. So when the warden locked the door on me I was apparently helpless, unless I could turn three seemingly innocent things to use. They were things which would have been permitted any prisoner under sentence of death, were they not, warden?"

"Tooth powder and polished shoes, yes, but not money," replied the warden.

"Anything is dangerous in the hands of a man who knows how to use it," went on The Thinking Machine. "I did nothing that first night but sleep and chase rats." He glared at the warden. "When the matter was broached I knew I could do nothing that night, so suggested next day. You gentlemen thought I wanted time to arrange an escape with outside assistance, but this was not true. I knew I could communicate with whom I pleased, when I pleased."

The warden stared at him a moment, then went on smoking solemnly.

"I was aroused next morning at six o'clock by the jailer

with my breakfast," continued the scientist. "He told me dinner was at twelve and supper at six. Between these times, I gathered, I would be pretty much to myself. So immediately after breakfast I examined my outside surroundings from my cell window. One look told me it would be useless to try to scale the wall, even should I decide to leave my cell by the window, for my purpose was to leave not only the cell, but the prison. Of course, I could have gone over the wall, but it would have taken me longer to lay my plans that way. Therefore, for the moment, I dismissed all idea of that.

"From this first observation I knew the river was on that side of the prison, and that there was also a playground there. Subsequently these surmises were verified by a keeper. I knew then one important thing—that anyone might approach the prison wall from that side if necessary without attracting any particular attention. That was well to remember. I remembered it.

"But the outside thing which most attracted my attention was the feed wire to the arc light which ran within a few feet— probably three or four—of my cell window. I knew that would be valuable in the event I found it necessary to cut off that arc light."

"Oh, you shut it off tonight, then?" asked the warden.

"Having learned all I could from that window," resumed The Thinking Machine, without heeding the interruption, "I considered the idea of escaping through the prison proper. I recalled just how I had come into the cell, which I knew would be the only way. Seven doors lay between me and the outside. So, also for the time being, I gave up the idea of escaping that way. And I couldn't go through the solid granite walls of the cell."

The Thinking Machine paused for a moment and Dr. Ransome lighted a new cigar. For several minutes there was silence, then the scientific jailbreaker went on:

"While I was thinking about these things a rat ran across my foot. It suggested a new line of thought. There were at least half a dozen rats in the cell—I could see their beady eyes. Yet I had noticed none come under the cell door. I frightened them purposely and watched the cell door to see if they went out that way. They did not, but they were gone. Obviously they went another way. Another way meant another opening.

"I searched for this opening and found it. It was an old drain pipe, long unused and partly choked with dirt and dust. But this was the way the rats had come. They came from somewhere. Where? Drain pipes usually lead outside prison grounds. This one probably led to the river, or near it. The rats must therefore come from that direction. If they came a part of the way, I reasoned that they came all the way, because it was extremely unlikely that a solid iron or lead pipe would have any hole in it except at the exit.

"When the jailer came with my luncheon he told me two important things, although he didn't know it. One was that a new system of plumbing had been put in the prison seven years before; another that the river was only three hundred feet away. Then I knew positively that the pipe was a part of an old system; I knew, too, that it slanted generally toward the river. But did the pipe end in the water or on land?

"This was the next question to be decided. I decided it by catching several of the rats in the cell. My jailer was surprised to see me engaged in this work. I examined at least a dozen of them. They were perfectly dry; they had come through the pipe, and, most important of all, they were *not house rats, but field rats.* The other end of the pipe was on land, then, outside the prison walls. So far, so good.

"Then, I knew that if I worked freely from this point I must attract the warden's attention in another direction. You see, by telling the warden that I had come there to escape you made the test more severe, because I had to trick him by false scents."

The warden looked up with a sad expression in his eyes.

"The first thing was to make him think I was trying to communicate with you, Dr. Ransome. So I wrote a note on a piece of linen I tore from my shirt, addressed it to Dr. Ransome, tied a five-dollar bill around it, and threw it out the window. I knew the guard would take it to the warden, but I rather hoped the warden would send it as addressed. Have you that first linen note, Warden?"

The warden produced the cipher.

"What the deuce does it mean, anyhow?" he asked.

"Read it backward, beginning with the *T* signature and disregard the division into words," instructed The Thinking Machine.

The warden did so.

"*T-h-i-s*, this," he spelled, studied it a moment, then read it off, grinning:

"This is not the way I intend to escape."

"Well, now what do you think o' that?" he demanded, still grinning.

"I knew that would attract your attention, just as it did," said The Thinking Machine, "and if you really found out what it was it would be a sort of gentle rebuke."

"What did you write it with?" asked Dr. Ransome, after he had examined the linen and passed it to Mr. Fielding.

"This," said the erstwhile prisoner, and he extended his foot. On it was the shoe he had worn in prison, though the polish was gone—scraped off clean. "The shoe blacking, moistened with water, was my ink; the metal tip of the shoelace made a fairly good pen."

The warden looked up and suddenly burst into a laugh, half of relief, half of amusement.

"You're a wonder," he said, admiringly. "Go on."

"That precipitated a search of my cell by the warden, as I had intended," continued The Thinking Machine. "I was anxious to get the warden into the habit of searching my cell, so that finally, constantly finding nothing, he would get disgusted and quit. This at last happened, practically."

The warden blushed.

"He then took my white shirt away and gave me a prison shirt. He was satisfied that those two pieces of the shirt were all that was missing. But while he was searching my cell I had another piece of that same shirt, about nine inches square, rolled into a small ball in my mouth."

"Nine inches of that shirt?" demanded the warden. "Where did it come from?"

"The bosoms of all stiff white shirts are of triple thickness," was the explanation. "I tore out the inside thickness, leaving the bosom only two thicknesses. I knew you wouldn't see it. So much for that."

There was a little pause, and the warden looked from one to another of the men with a sheepish grin.

"Having disposed of the warden for the time being by giving him something else to think about, I took my first serious step toward freedom," said Professor Van Dusen. "I knew, within reason, that the pipe led somewhere to the playground outside; I knew a great many boys played there; I knew that rats came into my cell from out there. Could I communicate with some one outside with these things at hand?

"First was necessary, I saw, a long and fairly reliable thread, so—but here," he pulled up his trousers legs and showed that the tops of both stockings, of fine, strong lisle, were gone. "I unraveled those—after I got them started it wasn't difficult—and I had easily a quarter of a mile of thread that I could depend on.

"Then on half of my remaining linen I wrote, laboriously enough I assure you, a letter explaining my situation to this gentleman here," and he indicated Hutchinson Hatch. "I knew he would assist me—for the value of the newspaper story. I tied firmly to this linen letter a ten-dollar bill—there is no surer way of attracting the eye of anyone —and wrote on the linen: 'Finder of this deliver to Hutchinson Hatch, *Daily American,* who will give another ten dollars for the information.

"The next thing was to get this note outside on that playground where a boy might find it. There were two ways, but I chose the best. I took one of the rats—I became adept in catching them—tied the linen and money firmly to one leg, fastened my lisle thread to another, and turned him loose in the drain pipe. I reasoned that the natural fright of the rodent would make him run until he was outside the pipe and then out on earth he would probably stop to gnaw off the linen and money.

"From the moment the rat disappeared into that dusty pipe I became anxious. I was taking so many chances. The rat might gnaw the string, of which I held one end; other rats might gnaw it; the rat might run out of the pipe and leave the linen and money where they would never be found; a thousand other things might have happened. So began some nervous hours, but the fact that the rat ran on until only a few feet of the string remained in my cell made me think he was outside the pipe. I had carefully instructed Mr. Hatch what to do in case the note reached him. The question was: would it reach him?

"This done, I could only wait and make other plans in case this one failed. I openly attempted to bribe my jailer, and learned from him that he held the keys to only two of seven doors between me and freedom. Then I did something else to make the warden nervous. I took the steel supports out of the heels of my shoes and made a pretense of sawing the bars of my cell window. The warden raised a pretty row about that. He developed, too, the habit of shaking the bars of my cell window to see if they were solid. They were—then."

Again the warden grinned. He had ceased being astonished.

"With this one plan I had done all I could and could only wait to see what happened," the scientist went on. "I couldn't know whether my note had been delivered or even found, or whether the mouse had gnawed it up. And I didn't dare to draw back through the pipe that one slender thread which connected me with the outside.

"When I went to bed that night I didn't sleep, for fear there would come the slight signal twitch at the thread which was to tell me that Mr. Hatch had received the note. At half past three o'clock, I judge, I felt this twitch, and no prisoner actually under sentence of death ever welcomed a thing more heartily."

The Thinking Machine stopped and turned to the reporter.

"You'd better explain just what you did," he said.

"The linen note was brought to me by a small boy who had been playing baseball," said Mr. Hatch. "I immediately saw a big story in it, so I gave the boy another ten dollars, and got several spools of silk, some twine, and a roll of light, pliable wire. The professor's note suggested that I have the finder of the note show me just where it was picked up, and told me to make my search from there, beginning at two o'clock in the morning. If I found the other end of the thread I was to twitch it gently three times, then a fourth.

"I began the search with a small-bulb electric light. It was an hour and twenty minutes before I found the end of the drain pipe, half-hidden in weeds. The pipe was very large there, say twelve inches across. Then I found the end of the lisle thread, twitched it as directed and immediately I got an answering twitch.

"Then I fastened the silk to this and Professor Van Dusen began to pull it into his cell. I nearly had heart disease for fear the string would break. To the end of the silk I fastened the twine, and when that had been pulled in I tied on the wire. Then that was drawn into the pipe and we had a substantial line, which rats couldn't gnaw, from the mouth of the drain into the cell."

The Thinking Machine raised his hand and Hatch stopped.

"All this was done in absolute silence," said the scientist. "But when the wire reached my hand I could have shouted. Then we tried another experiment, which Mr. Hatch was prepared for. I tested the pipe as a speaking tube. Neither of us could hear very clearly, but I dared not speak loud for fear of attracting attention in the prison. At last I made him understand what I wanted immediately. He seemed to have great difficulty in understanding when I asked for nitric acid, and I repeated the word 'acid' several times.

"Then I heard a shriek from a cell above me. I knew instantly that someone had overheard, and when I heard you coming, Mr. Warden, I feigned sleep. If you had entered my cell at that moment that whole plan of escape would have ended there. But you passed on. That was the nearest I ever came to being caught.

"Having established this improvised trolley it is easy to see how I got things in the cell and made them disappear at will. I merely dropped them back into the pipe. You, Mr. Warden, could not have reached the connecting wire with your fingers; they are too large. My fingers, you see, are longer and more slender. In addition I guarded the top of that pipe with a rat—you remember how."

"I remember," said the warden, with a grimace.

"I thought that if anyone were tempted to investigate that hole the rat would dampen his ardor. Mr. Hatch could not send me anything useful through the pipe until next night, although he did send me change for ten dollars as a test, so I proceeded with other parts of my plan. Then I evolved the method of escape which I finally employed.

"In order to carry this out successfully it was necessary for the guard in the yard to get accustomed to seeing me at the cell window. I arranged this by dropping linen notes to him, boastful in tone, to make the warden believe, if possible, one of his assistants was communicating with the outside for me. I would stand at my window for hours gazing out, so the guard could see, and occasionally I spoke to him. In that way I learned that the prison had no electricians of its own, but was dependent upon the lighting company if anything should go wrong.

"That cleared the way to freedom perfectly. Early in the evening of the last day of my imprisonment, when it was dark, I planned to cut the feed wire which was only a few feet from my window, reaching it with an acid-tipped wire

I had. That would make that side of the prison perfectly dark while the electricians were searching for the break. That would also bring Mr. Hatch into the prison yard.

"There was only one more thing to do before I actually began the work of setting myself free. This was to arrange final details with Mr. Hatch through our speaking tube. I did this within half an hour after the warden left my cell on the fourth night of my imprisonment. Mr. Hatch again had serious difficulty in understanding me, and I repeated the word 'acid' to him several times, and later on the words 'number eight hat'—that's my size—and these were the things which made a prisoner upstairs confess to murder, so one of the jailers told me next day. This prisoner heard our voices, confused of course, through the pipe, which also went to his cell. The cell directly over me was not occupied, hence no one else heard.

"Of course the actual work of cutting the steel bars out of the window and door was comparatively easy with nitric acid, which I got through the pipe in tin bottles, but it took time. Hour after hour on the fifth and sixth and seventh days the guard below was looking at me as I worked on the bars of the window with the acid on a piece of wire. I used the tooth powder to prevent the acid spreading. I looked away abstractedly as I worked and each minute the acid cut deeper into the metal. I noticed that the jailers always tried the door by shaking the upper part, never the lower bars; therefore I cut the lower bars, leaving them hanging in place by thin strips of metal. But that was a bit of daredeviltry. I could not have gone that way so easily."

The Thinking Machine sat silent for several minutes.

"I think that makes everything clear," he went on. "Whatever points I have not explained were merely to confuse the warden and jailers. These things in my bed I brought in to please Mr. Hatch, who wanted to improve the story. Of course, the wig was necessary in my plan. The special-delivery letter I wrote and directed in my cell with

Mr. Hatch's fountain pen, then sent it out to him and he mailed it. That's all, I think."

"But your actually leaving the prison grounds and then coming in through the outer gate to my office?" asked the warden.

"Perfectly simple," said the scientist. "I cut the electric light wire with acid, as I said, when the current was off. Therefore when the current was turned on the arc didn't light. I knew it would take some time to find out what was the matter and make repairs. When the guard went to report to you the yard was dark. I crept out the window—it was a tight fit, too—replaced the bars by standing on a narrow ledge, and remained in a shadow until the force of electricians arrived. Mr. Hatch was one of them.

"When I saw him I spoke and he handed me a cap, a jumper, and overalls, which I put on within ten feet of you, Mr. Warden, while you were in the yard. Later Mr. Hatch called me, presumably as a workman, and together we went out the gate to get something out of the wagon. The gate guard let us pass out readily as two workmen who had just passed in. We changed our clothing and reappeared, asking to see you. We saw you. That's all."

There was silence for several minutes. Dr. Ransome was first to speak.

"Wonderful!" he exclaimed. "Perfectly amazing."

"How did Mr. Hatch happen to come with the electricians?" asked Mr. Fielding.

"His father is manager of the company," replied The Thinking Machine.

"But what if there had been no Mr. Hatch outside to help?"

"Every prisoner has one friend outside who would help him escape if he could."

"Suppose—just suppose—there had been no old plumbing system there?" asked the warden, curiously.

"There were two other ways out," said The Thinking Machine, enigmatically.

Ten minutes later the telephone bell rang. It was a request for the warden.

"Light all right, eh?" the warden asked, through the phone. "Good. Wire cut beside Cell Thirteen? Yes, I know. One electrician too many? What's that? Two came out?"

The warden turned to the others with a puzzled expression.

"He only let in four electricians; he has let out two and says there are three left."

"I was the odd one," said The Thinking Machine.

"Oh," said the warden. "I see." Then through the phone: "Let the fifth man go. He's all right."

THE HANDS
OF MR. OTTERMOLE

Thomas Burke

At six o'clock of a January evening Mr. Whybrow was walking home through the cobweb alleys of London's East End. He had left the golden clamour of the great High Street to which the tram had brought him from the river and his daily work, and was now in the chessboard of byways that is called Mallon End. None of the rush and gleam of the High Street trickled into these byways. A few paces south—a flood tide of life, foaming and beating. Here—only slow-shuffling figures and muffled pulses. He was in the sink of London, the last refuge of European vagrants.

As though in tune with the street's spirit, he too walked slowly, with head down. It seemed that he was pondering some pressing trouble, but he was not. He had no trouble. He was walking slowly because he had been on his feet all day, and he was bent in abstraction because he was wonder-

ing whether the Missis would have herrings for his tea, or
haddock; and he was trying to decide which would be the
more tasty on a night like this. A wretched night it was, of
damp and mist, and the mist wandered into his throat and
his eyes, and the damp had settled on pavement and road-
way, and where the sparse lamplight fell it sent up a greasy
sparkle that chilled one to look at. By contrast it made his
speculations more agreeable, and made him ready for that
tea—whether herring or haddock. His eye turned from the
glum bricks that made his horizon, and went forward half a
mile. He saw a gas-lit kitchen, a flamy fire, and a spread tea
table. There was toast in the hearth and a singing kettle on
the side and a piquant effusion of herrings, or maybe of
haddock, or perhaps sausages. The vision gave his aching
feet a throb of energy. He shook imperceptible damp from
his shoulders, and hastened towards its reality.

But Mr. Whybrow wasn't going to get any tea that evening—or any other evening. Mr. Whybrow was going to die.
Somewhere within a hundred yards of him another man was
walking: a man much like Mr. Whybrow and much like any
other man, but without the only quality that enables man-
kind to live peaceably together and not as madmen in a
jungle. A man with a dead heart eating into itself and bringing forth the foul organisms that arise from death and cor-
ruption. And that thing in man's shape, on a whim or a
settled idea—one cannot know—had said within himself
that Mr. Whybrow should never taste another herring. Not
that Mr. Whybrow had injured him. Not that he had any
dislike of Mr. Whybrow. Indeed, he knew nothing of him
save as a familiar figure about the streets. But, moved by a
force that had taken possession of his empty cells, he had
picked on Mr. Whybrow with that blind choice that makes
us pick one restaurant table that has nothing to mark it from
four or five other tables, or one apple from a dish of half a
dozen equal apples; or that drives nature to send a cyclone
upon one corner of this planet, and destroy five hundred
lives in that corner, and leave another five hundred in the

same corner unharmed. So this man had picked on Mr. Whybrow, as he might have picked on you or me, had we been
within his daily observation; and even now he was creeping
through the blue-toned streets, nursing his large white
hands, moving ever closer to Mr. Whybrow's tea table, and
so closer to Mr. Whybrow himself.

He wasn't, this man, a bad man. Indeed, he had many
of the social and amiable qualities, and passed as a respectable man, as most successful criminals do. But the thought
had come into his mouldering mind that he would like to
murder somebody, and, as he held no fear of God or man,
he was going to do it, and would then go home to *his* tea.
I don't say that flippantly, but as a statement of fact. Strange
as it may seem to the humane, murderers must and do sit
down to meals after a murder. There is no reason why they
shouldn't, and many reasons why they should. For one thing,
they need to keep their physical and mental vitality at full
beat for the business of covering their crime. For another,
the strain of their effort makes them hungry, and satisfaction
at the accomplishment of a desired thing brings a feeling of
relaxation towards human pleasures. It is accepted among
nonmurderers that the murderer is always overcome by fear
for his safety and horror at his act; but this type is rare. His
own safety is, of course, his immediate concern, but vanity
is a marked quality of most murderers, and that, together
with the thrill of conquest, makes him confident that he can
secure it, and when he has restored his strength with food
he goes about securing it as a young hostess goes about the
arranging of her first big dinner—a little anxious, but no
more. Criminologists and detectives tell us that *every* murderer, however intelligent or cunning, always makes one
slip in his tactics—one little slip that brings the affair home
to him. But that is only half-true. It is true only of the murderers who are caught. Scores of murderers are not caught:
therefore scores of murderers do not make any mistake at
all. This man didn't.

As for horror or remorse, prison chaplains, doctors, and

lawyers have told us that of murderers they have inter-
viewed under condemnation and the shadow of death, only
one here and there has expressed any contrition for his act,
or shown any sign of mental misery. Most of them display
only exasperation at having been caught when so many have
gone undiscovered, or indignation at being condemned for
a perfectly reasonable act. However normal and humane
they may have been before the murder, they are utterly
without conscience after it. For what is conscience? Simply
a polite nickname for superstition, which is a polite nickname for fear. Those who associate remorse with murder
are, no doubt, basing their ideas on the world legend of the
remorse of Cain, or are projecting their own frail minds into
the mind of the murderer, and getting false reactions.
Peaceable folk cannot hope to make contact with this mind,
for they are not merely different in mental type from the
murderer: they are different in their personal chemistry and
construction. Some men can and do kill, not one man, but
two or three, and go calmly about their daily affairs. Other
men could not, under the most agonising provocation, bring
themselves even to wound. It is men of this sort who imagine the murderer in torments of remorse and fear of the law,
whereas he is actually sitting down to his tea.

The man with the large white hands was as ready for his
tea as Mr. Whybrow was, but he had something to do before
he went to it. When he had done that something, and made
no mistake about it, he would be even more ready for it, and
would go to it as comfortably as he went to it the day before,
when his hands were stainless.

Walk on, then, Mr. Whybrow, walk on; and as you walk,
look your last upon the familiar features of your nightly
journey. Follow your jack-o'-lantern tea table. Look well
upon its warmth and colour and kindness; feed your eyes
with it, and tease your nose with its gentle domestic odours;
for you will never sit down to it. Within ten minutes' pacing
of you a pursuing phantom has spoken in his heart, and you
are doomed. There you go—you and phantom—two nebu-

lous dabs of mortality, moving through green air along pavements of powder-blue, the one to kill, the other to be killed. Walk on. Don't annoy your burning feet by hurrying, for the more slowly you walk, the longer you will breathe the green air of this January dusk, and see the dreamy lamplight and the little shops, and hear the agreeable commerce of the London crowd and the haunting pathos of the street organ. These things are dear to you, Mr. Whybrow. You don't know it now, but in fifteen minutes you will have two seconds in which to realise how inexpressibly dear they are.

Walk on, then, across this crazy chessboard. You are in Lagos Street now, among the tents of the wanderers of Eastern Europe. A minute or so, and you are in Loyal Lane, among the lodging houses that shelter the useless and the beaten of London's camp followers. The lane holds the smell of them, and its soft darkness seems heavy with the wail of the futile. But you are not sensitive to impalpable things, and you plod through it, unseeing, as you do every evening, and come to Blean Street, and plod through that. From basement to sky rise the tenements of an alien colony. Their windows slot the ebony of their walls with lemon. Behind those windows strange life is moving, dressed with forms that are not of London or of England, yet, in essence, the same agreeable life that you have been living, and tonight will live no more. From high above you comes a voice crooning *The Song of Katta.* Through a window you see a family keeping a religious rite. Through another you see a woman pouring out tea for her husband. You see a man mending a pair of boots; a mother bathing her baby. You have seen all these things before, and never noticed them. You do not notice them now, but if you knew that you were never going to see them again, you would notice them. You never *will* see them again, not because your life has run its natural course, but because a man whom you have often passed in the street has at his own solitary pleasure decided to usurp the awful authority of nature, and destroy you. So perhaps it's as well that you don't notice them, for your part in them is ended. No more for you these pretty moments of our earthly travail: only one moment of terror, and then a plunging darkness.

Closer to you this shadow of massacre moves, and now he is twenty yards behind you. You can hear his footfall, but you do not turn your head. You are familiar with footfalls. You are in London, in the easy security of your daily territory, and footfalls behind you, your instinct tells you, are no more than a message of human company.

But can't you hear something in those footfalls—something that goes with a widdershins beat? Something that says: *Look out, look out. Beware, beware.* Can't you hear the very syllables of *mur-der-er, mur-der-er?* No; there is nothing in footfalls. They are neutral. The foot of villainy falls with the same quiet note as the foot of honesty. But those footfalls, Mr. Whybrow, are bearing on to you a pair of hands, and there *is* something in hands. Behind you that pair of hands is even now stretching its muscles in preparation for your end. Every minute of your days you have been seeing human hands. Have you ever realised the sheer horror of hands—those appendages that are a symbol for our moments of trust and affection and salutation? Have you thought of the sickening potentialities that lie within the scope of that five-tentacled member? No, you never have; for all the human hands that you have seen have been stretched to you in kindness or fellowship. Yet, though the eyes can hate, and the lips can sting, it is only that dangling member that can gather the accumulated essence of evil, and electrify it into currents of destruction. Satan may enter into man by many doors, but in the hands alone can he find the servants of his will.

Another minute, Mr. Whybrow, and you will know all about the horror of human hands.

You are nearly home now. You have turned into your street—Caspar Street—and you are in the centre of the chessboard. You can see the front window of your little four-roomed house. The street is dark, and its three lamps give only a smut of light that is more confusing than darkness. It is dark—empty, too. Nobody about; no lights in the front parlours of the houses, for the families are at tea in their kitchens; and only a random glow in a few upper rooms occupied by lodgers. Nobody about but you and your following companion, and you don't notice him. You see him so often that he is never seen. Even if you turned your head and saw him, you would only say good evening to him, and walk on. A suggestion that he was a possible murderer would not even make you laugh. It would be too silly.

And now you are at your gate. And now you have found your door key. And now you are in, and hanging up your hat and coat. The Missis has just called a greeting from the kitchen, whose smell is an echo of that greeting (herrings!) and you have answered it, when the door shakes under a sharp knock.

Go away, Mr. Whybrow. Go away from that door. Don't touch it. Get right away from it. Get out of the house. Run with the Missis to the back garden, and over the fence. Or call the neighbours. But don't touch that door. Don't, Mr. Whybrow, don't open . . .

Mr. Whybrow opened the door.

That was the beginning of what became known as London's Strangling Horrors. Horrors they were called because they were something more than murders: they were motiveless, and there was an air of black magic about them. Each murder was committed at a time when the street where the bodies were found was empty of any perceptible or possible murderer. There would be an empty alley. There would be a policeman at its end. He would turn his back on the empty alley for less than a minute. Then he would look round and run into the night with news of another strangling. And in any direction he looked nobody to be seen and no report to be had of anybody being seen. Or he would be on duty in a long-quiet street, and suddenly be called to a house of dead people whom a few seconds earlier he had seen alive. And, again, whichever way he looked nobody to be seen; and although police whistles put an immediate cordon around the area, and searched all houses, no possible murderer to be found.

The first news of the murder of Mr. and Mrs. Whybrow was brought by the station sergeant. He had been walking through Caspar Street on his way to the station for duty, when he noticed the open door of No. 98. Glancing in, he saw by the gaslight of the passage a motionless body on the floor. After a second look he blew his whistle, and when the constables answered him he took one to join him in a search of the house, and sent others to watch all neighbouring streets, and make inquiries at adjoining houses. But neither in the house nor in the streets was anything found to indicate the murderer. Neighbours on either side, and opposite, were questioned, but they had seen nobody about, and had heard nothing. One had heard Mr. Whybrow come home— the scrape of his latchkey in the door was so regular an evening sound, he said, that you could set your watch by it for half past six—but he had heard nothing more than the sound of the opening door until the sergeant's whistle. Nobody had been seen to enter the house or leave it, by front or back, and the necks of the dead people carried no fingerprints or other traces. A nephew was called in to go over the house, but he could find nothing missing; and anyway his uncle possessed nothing worth stealing. The little money in the house was untouched, and there were no signs of any disturbance of the property, or even of struggle. No signs of anything but brutal and wanton murder.

Mr. Whybrow was known to neighbours and workmates as a quiet, likeable, home-loving man; such a man as could not have any enemies. But, then, murdered men seldom have. A relentless enemy who hates a man to the point of wanting to hurt him seldom wants to murder him, since to do that puts him beyond suffering. So the police were left with an impossible situation: no clue to the murderer and no motive for the murders; only the fact that they had been done.

The first news of the affair sent a tremor through London generally, and an electric thrill through all Mallon End. Here was a murder of two inoffensive people, not for gain and not for revenge; and the murderer, to whom, apparently, killing was a casual impulse, was at large. He had left no traces, and, provided he had no companions, there seemed no reason why he should not remain at large. Any clear-headed man who stands alone, and has no fear of God or man, can, if he chooses, hold a city, even a nation, in subjection; but your everyday criminal is seldom clear-headed, and dislikes being lonely. He needs, if not the support of confederates, at least somebody to talk to; his vanity needs the satisfaction of perceiving at first hand the effect of his work. For this he will frequent bars and coffee shops and other public places. Then, sooner or later, in a glow of comradeship, he will utter the one word too much; and the nark, who is everywhere, has an easy job.

But though the doss houses and saloons and other places were combed and set with watches, and it was made known by whispers that good money and protection were assured to those with information, nothing attaching to the Whybrow case could be found. The murderer clearly had no friends and kept no company. Known men of this type were called up and questioned, but each was able to give a good account of himself; and in a few days the police were at a dead end. Against the constant public gibe that the thing had been done almost under their noses, they became restive, and for four days each man of the force was working his daily beat under a strain. On the fifth day they became still more restive.

It was the season of annual teas and entertainments for the children of the Sunday schools, and on an evening of fog, when London was a world of groping phantoms, a small girl, in the bravery of best Sunday frock and shoes, shining face and new-washed hair, set out from Logan Passage for St. Michael's Parish Hall. She never got there. She was not actually dead until half past six, but she was as good as dead from the moment she left her mother's door. Somebody like a man, pacing the street from which the passage led, saw her come out; and from that moment she was dead. Through the fog somebody's large white hands reached after her, and in fifteen minutes they were about her.

At half past six a whistle screamed trouble, and those answering it found the body of little Nellie Vrinoff in a warehouse entry in Minnow Street. The sergeant was first among them, and he posted his men to useful points, ordering them here and there in the tart tones of repressed rage, and berating the officer whose beat the street was. "I saw you, Magson, at the end of the lane. What were you up to there? You were there ten minutes before you turned." Magson began an explanation about keeping an eye on a suspicious-looking character at that end, but the sergeant cut him short: "Suspicious characters be damned. You don't want to look for suspicious characters. You want to look for *murderers.* Messing about . . . and then this happens right where you ought to be. Now think what they'll say."

With the speed of ill news came the crowd, pale and perturbed; and on the story that the unknown monster had appeared again, and this time to a child, their faces streaked the fog with spots of hate and horror. But then came the ambulance and more police, and swiftly they broke up the crowd; and as it broke the sergeant's thought was thickened into words, and from all sides came low murmurs of "Right under their noses." Later inquiries showed that four people of the district, above suspicion, had passed that entry at intervals of seconds before the murder, and seen nothing and heard nothing. None of them had passed the child alive or seen her dead. None of them had seen anybody in the street except themselves. Again the police were left with no motive and with no clue.

And now the district, as you will remember, was given over, not to panic, for the London public never yields to that, but to apprehension and dismay. If these things were happening in their familiar streets, then anything might happen. Wherever people met—in the streets, the markets and the shops—they debated the one topic. Women took to bolting their windows and doors at the first fall of dusk. They kept their children closely under their eye. They did their shopping before dark, and watched anxiously, while pretending they weren't watching, for the return of their husbands from work. Under the Cockney's semihumorous resignation to disaster, they hid an hourly foreboding. By the whim of one man with a pair of hands the structure and tenor of their daily life were shaken, as they always can be shaken by any man contemptuous of humanity and fearless of its laws. They began to realise that the pillars that supported the peaceable society in which they lived were mere straws that anybody could snap; that laws were powerful only so long as they were obeyed; that the police were potent only so long as they were feared. By the power of his hands this one man had made a whole community do something new: he had made it think, and left it gasping at the obvious.

And then, while it was yet gasping under his first two strokes, he made his third. Conscious of the horror that his hands had created, and hungry as an actor who has once tasted the thrill of the multitude, he made fresh advertisement of his presence; and on Wednesday morning, three days after the murder of the child, the papers carried to the breakfast tables of England the story of a still more shocking outrage.

At 9:32 on Tuesday night a constable was on duty in Jarnigan Road, and at that time spoke to a fellow officer named Petersen at the top of Clemming Street. He had seen this officer walk down that street. He could swear that the street was empty at that time, except for a lame bootblack whom he knew by sight, and who passed him and entered a tenement on the side opposite that on which his fellow officer was walking. He had the habit, as all constables had just then, of looking constantly behind him and around him, whichever way he was walking, and he was certain that the street was empty. He passed his sergeant at 9:33, saluted him, and answered his inquiry for anything seen. He reported that he had seen nothing, and passed on. His beat ended at a short distance from Clemming Street, and, having paced it, he turned and came again at 9:34 to the top of the street. He had scarcely reached it before he heard the hoarse voice of the sergeant: "Gregory! You there? Quick. Here's another. My God, it's Petersen! Garrotted. Quick, call 'em up!"

That was the third of the Strangling Horrors, of which there were to be a fourth and a fifth; and the five horrors were to pass into the unknown and unknowable. That is, unknown as far as authority and the public were concerned. The identity of the murderer *was* known, but to two men only. One was the murderer himself; the other was a young journalist.

This young man, who was covering the affairs for his paper, the *Daily Torch,* was no smarter than the other zealous newspapermen who were hanging about these byways in the hope of a sudden story. But he was patient, and he hung a little closer to the case than the other fellows, and by continually staring at it he at last raised the figure of the murderer like a genie from the stones on which he had stood to do his murders.

After the first few days the men had given up any attempt at exclusive stories, for there was none to be had. They met regularly at the police station, and what little information there was they shared. The officials were agreeable to them, but no more. The sergeant discussed with them the details of each murder; suggested possible explanations of the man's methods; recalled from the past those cases that had some similarity; and on the matter of motive reminded them of the motiveless Neil Cream and the wanton John Williams, and hinted that work was being done which would soon bring the business to an end; but about that work he would not say a word. The inspector, too, was gracefully garrulous on the thesis of Murder, but whenever one of the party edged the talk towards what was being done in this immediate matter, he glided past it. Whatever the officials knew, they were not giving it to newspapermen. The business had fallen heavily upon them, and only by a capture made by their own efforts could they rehabilitate themselves in official and public esteem. Scotland Yard, of course, was at work, and had all the station's material; but the station's hope was that they themselves would have the honour of settling the affair; and however useful the cooperation of the press might be in other cases, they did not want to risk a defeat by a premature disclosure of their theories and plans.

So the sergeant talked at large, and propounded one interesting theory after another, all of which the newspaper men had thought of themselves.

The young man soon gave up these morning lectures on the Philosophy of Crime, and took to wandering about the streets and making bright stories out of the effect of the murders on the normal life of the people. A melancholy job made more melancholy by the district. The littered roadways, the crestfallen houses, the bleared windows—all held the acid misery that evokes no sympathy: the misery of the frustrated poet. The misery was the creation of the aliens, who were living in this makeshift fashion because they had no settled homes, and would neither take the trouble to make a home where they *could* settle nor get on with their wandering.

There was little to be picked up. All he saw and heard were indignant faces, and wild conjectures of the murderer's identity and of the secret of his trick of appearing and disappearing unseen. Since a policeman himself had fallen a victim, denunciations of the force had ceased, and the unknown was now invested with a cloak of legend. Men eyed other men, as though thinking: "It might be *him*. It might be *him*." They were no longer looking for a man who had the air of a Madame Tussaud murderer; they were looking for a man, or perhaps some harridan woman, who had done these particular murders. Their thoughts ran mainly on the foreign set. Such ruffianism could scarcely belong to England, nor could the bewildering cleverness of the thing. So they turned to Romanian gipsies and Turkish carpet sellers. There, clearly, would be found the warm spot. These Eastern fellows—they knew all sorts of tricks, and they had no real religion—nothing to hold them within bounds. Sailors returning from those parts had told tales of conjurors who made themselves invisible; and there were tales of Egyptian and Arab potions that were used for abysmally queer purposes. Perhaps it *was* possible to them; you never knew. They were so slick and cunning, and they had such gliding movements; no Englishman could melt away as they could. Almost certainly the murderer would be found to be one of that sort—with some dark trick of his own—and just because they were sure that he *was* a magician, they felt that it was useless to look for him. He was a power, able to hold them in subjection and to hold himself untouchable. Superstition, which so easily cracks the frail shell of reason, had got into them. He could do anything he chose: he would never be discovered. These two points they settled, and they went about the streets in a mood of resentful fatalism.

They talked of their ideas to the journalist in half tones, looking right and left, as though *he* might overhear them and visit them. And though all the district was thinking of him and ready to pounce upon him, yet so strongly had he worked upon them that if any man in the street—say, a small man of commonplace features and form—had cried, "*I* am the monster!" would their stifled fury have broken into flood and have borne him down and engulfed him? Or would they not suddenly have seen something unearthly in that everyday face and figure, something unearthly in his everyday boots, something unearthly about his hat, something that marked him as one whom none of their weapons could alarm or pierce? And would they not momentarily have fallen back from this devil, as the devil fell back from the Cross made by the sword of Faust, and so have given him

time to escape? I do not know; but so fixed was their belief
in his invincibility that it is at least likely that they would
have made this hesitation, had such an occasion arisen. But
it never did. Today this commonplace fellow, his murder
lust glutted, is still seen and observed among them as he was
seen and observed all the time; but because nobody then
dreamt, or now dreams, that he was what he was, they observed him then, and observe him now, as people observe
a lamppost.

Almost was their belief in his invincibility justified; for,
five days after the murder of the policeman Petersen, when
the experience and inspiration of the whole detective force
of London were turned towards his identification and capture, he made his fourth and fifth strokes.

At nine o'clock that evening, the young newspaperman,
who hung about every night until his paper was away, was
strolling along Richards Lane. Richards Lane is a narrow
street, partly a stall market, and partly residential. The
young man was in the residential section, which carries on
one side small working-class cottages, and on the other the
wall of a railway goods yard. The great wall hung a blanket
of shadow over the lane, and the shadow and the cadaverous
outline of the now deserted market stalls gave it the appearance of a living lane that had been turned to frost in the
moment between breath and death. The very lamps, that
elsewhere were nimbuses of gold, had here the rigidity of
gems. The journalist, feeling this message of frozen eternity,
was telling himself that he was tired of the whole thing,
when in one stroke the frost was broken. In the moment
between one pace and another silence and darkness were
racked by a high scream and through the scream a voice:
"Help! help! *He's here!*"

Before he could think what movement to make, the
lane came to life. As though its invisible populace had been
waiting on that cry, the door of every cottage was flung
open, and from them and from the alleys poured shadowy
figures bent in question mark form. For a second or so they

stood as rigid as the lamps; then a police whistle gave them direction, and the flock of shadows sloped up the street. The journalist followed them, and others followed him. From the main street and from surrounding streets they came, some risen from unfinished suppers, some disturbed in their ease of slippers and shirt sleeves, some stumbling on infirm limbs, and some upright, and armed with pokers or the tools of their trade. Here and there above the wavering cloud of heads moved the bold helmets of policemen. In one dim mass they surged upon a cottage whose doorway was marked by the sergeant and two constables; and voices of those behind urged them on with "Get in! Find him! Run round the back! Over the wall!" and those in front cried: "Keep back! Keep back!"

And now the fury of a mob held in thrall by unknown peril broke loose. He was here—on the spot. Surely this time he *could not* escape. All minds were bent upon the cottage; all energies thrust towards its doors and windows and roof; all thought was turned upon one unknown man and his extermination. So that no one man saw any other man. No man saw the narrow, packed lane and the mass of struggling shadows, and all forgot to look among themselves for the monster who never lingered upon his victims. All forgot, indeed, that they, by their mass crusade of vengeance, were affording him the perfect hiding place. They saw only the house, and they heard only the rending of woodwork and the smash of glass at back and front, and the police giving orders or crying with the chase; and they pressed on.

But they found no murderer. All they found was news of murder and a glimpse of the ambulance, and for their fury there was no other object than the police themselves, who fought against this hampering of their work.

The journalist managed to struggle through to the cottage door, and to get the story from the constable stationed there. The cottage was the home of a pensioned sailor and his wife and daughter. They had been at supper, and at first it appeared that some noxious gas had smitten all three in midaction. The daughter lay dead on the hearthrug, with a piece of bread and butter in her hand. The father had fallen sideways from his chair, leaving on his plate a filled spoon of rice pudding. The mother lay half under the table, her lap filled with the pieces of a broken cup and splashes of cocoa. But in three seconds the idea of gas was dismissed. One glance at their necks showed that this was the Strangler again; and the police stood and looked at the room and momentarily shared the fatalism of the public. They were helpless.

This was his fourth visit, making seven murders in all. He was to do, as you know, one more—and to do it that night; and then he was to pass into history as the unknown London horror, and return to the decent life that he had always led, remembering little of what he had done, and worried not at all by the memory. Why did he stop? Impossible to say. Why did he begin? Impossible again. It just happened like that; and if he thinks at all of those days and nights, I surmise that he thinks of them as we think of foolish or dirty little sins that we committed in childhood. We say that they were not really sins, because we were not then consciously ourselves: we had not come to realisation; and we look back at that foolish little creature that we once were, and forgive him because he didn't know. So, I think, with this man.

There are plenty like him. Eugene Aram, after the murder of Daniel Clarke, lived a quiet, contented life for fourteen years, unhaunted by his crime and unshaken in his self-esteem. Dr. Crippen murdered his wife, and then lived pleasantly with his mistress in the house under whose floor he had buried the wife. Constance Kent, found not guilty of the murder of her young brother, led a peaceful life for five years before she confessed. George Joseph Smith and William Palmer lived amiably among their fellows untroubled by fear or by remorse for their poisonings and drownings. Charles Peace, at the time he made his one unfortunate essay, had settled down into a respectable citizen with an interest in antiques. It happened that, after a lapse of time, these men were discovered, but more murderers than we guess are living decent lives today, and will die in decency, undiscovered and unsuspected. As this man will.

But he had a narrow escape, and it was perhaps this narrow escape that brought him to a stop. The escape was due to an error of judgement on the part of the journalist.

As soon as he had the full story of the affair, which took some time, he spent fifteen minutes on the telephone, sending the story through, and at the end of the fifteen minutes, when the stimulus of the business had left him, he felt physically tired and mentally dishevelled. He was not yet free to go home; the paper would not go away for another hour; so he turned into a bar for a drink and some sandwiches.

It was then, when he had dismissed the whole business from his mind, and was looking about the bar and admiring the landlord's taste in watch chains and his air of domination, and was thinking that the landlord of a well-conducted tavern had a more comfortable life than a newspaperman, that his mind received from nowhere a spark of light. He was not thinking about the Strangling Horrors; his mind was on his sandwich. As a public-house sandwich, it was a curiosity. The bread had been thinly cut, it was buttered, and the ham was not two months stale; it was ham as it should be. His mind turned to the inventor of this refreshment, the earl of Sandwich, and then to George IV, and then to the Georges, and to the legend of that George who was worried to know how the apple got into the apple dumpling. He wondered whether George would have been equally puzzled to know how the ham got into the ham sandwich, and how long it would have been before it occurred to him that the ham could not have got there unless somebody had put it there. He got up to order another sandwich, and in that moment a little active corner of his mind settled the affair. If there was ham in his sandwich, somebody must have put it there. If seven people had been murdered, somebody must have been there to murder them. There was no aeroplane or automobile that would go into a man's pocket; therefore that somebody must have escaped either by running away or standing still; and again therefore—

He was visualising the front-page story that his paper would carry if his theory were correct, and if—a matter of conjecture—his editor had the necessary nerve to make a bold stroke, when a cry of "Time, gentlemen, please! All out!" reminded him of the hour. He got up and went out into a world of mist, broken by the ragged discs of roadside puddles and the streaming lightning of motor buses. He was certain that he had *the* story, but, even if it were proved, he was doubtful whether the policy of his paper would permit him to print it. It had one great fault. It was truth, but it was impossible truth. It rocked the foundations of everything that newspaper readers believed and that newspaper editors helped them to believe. They might believe that Turkish carpet sellers had the gift of making themselves invisible. They would not believe this.

As it happened, they were not asked to, for the story was never written. As his paper had by now gone away, and as he was nourished by his refreshment and stimulated by his theory, he thought he might put in an extra half hour by testing that theory. So he began to look about for the man he had in mind—a man with white hair, and large white hands; otherwise an everyday figure whom nobody would look twice at. He wanted to spring his idea on this man without warning, and he was going to place himself within reach of a man armoured in legends of dreadfulness and grue. This might appear to be an act of supreme courage— that one man, with no hope of immediate outside support, should place himself at the mercy of one who was holding a whole parish in terror. But it wasn't. He didn't think about the risk. He didn't think about his duty to his employers or loyalty to his paper. He was moved simply by an instinct to follow a story to its end.

He walked slowly from the tavern and crossed into Fingal Street, making for Deever Market, where he had hope of finding his man. But his journey was shortened. At the corner of Lotus Street he saw him—or a man who looked like him. This street was poorly lit, and he could see little of the man: but he *could* see white hands. For some twenty paces he stalked him; then drew level with him; and at a point where the arch of a railway crossed the street, he saw that this was his man. He approached him with the current conversational phrase of the district: "Well, seen anything of the murderer?" The man stopped to look sharply at him; then, satisfied that the journalist was not the murderer, said:

"Eh? No, nor's anybody else, curse it. Doubt if they ever will."

"I don't know. I've been thinking about them, and I've got an idea."

"So?"

"Yes. Came to me all of a sudden. Quarter of an hour ago. And I'd felt that we'd all been blind. It's been staring us in the face."

The man turned again to look at him, and the look and the movement held suspicion of this man who seemed to know so much. "Oh? Has it? Well, if you're so sure, why not give us the benefit of it?"

"I'm going to." They walked level, and were nearly at the end of the little street where it meets Deever Market, when the journalist turned casually to the man. He put a finger on his arm. "Yes, it seems to me quite simple now. But there's still one point I don't understand. One little thing I'd like to clear up. I mean the motive. Now, as man to man, tell me, Sergeant Ottermole, just *why* did you kill all those inoffensive people?"

The sergeant stopped, and the journalist stopped. There was just enough light from the sky, which held the reflected light of the continent of London, to give him a sight of the sergeant's face, and the sergeant's face was turned to him with a wide smile of such urbanity and charm that the journalist's eyes were frozen as they met it. The smile stayed for some seconds. Then said the sergeant: "Well, to tell you the truth, Mr. Newspaperman, I don't know. I really don't know. In fact, I've been worried about it myself. But I've got an idea—just like you. Everybody knows that we can't control the workings of our minds. Don't they? Ideas come into our minds without asking. But everybody's supposed to be able to control his body. Why? Eh? We get our minds from Lord-knows-where—from people who were dead hundreds of years before we were born. Mayn't we get our bodies in the same way? Our faces—our legs—our heads—they aren't completely ours. We don't make 'em. They come to us. And couldn't ideas come into our bodies like ideas come into our minds? Eh? Can't ideas live in nerve and muscle as well as in brain? Couldn't it be that parts of our bodies aren't really us, and couldn't ideas come into those parts all of a sudden, like ideas come into —into"—he shot his arms out, showing the great white-gloved hands and hairy wrists; shot them out so swiftly to the journalist's throat that his eyes never saw them—"into *my hands!*"

THE TWO BOTTLES OF RELISH

Lord Dunsany

Smithers is my name. I'm what you might call a small man and in a small way of business. I travel for Num-numo, a relish for meats and savouries—the world-famous relish, I ought to say. It's really quite good, no deleterious acids in it, and does not affect the heart; so it is quite easy to push. I wouldn't have got the job if it weren't. But I hope some day to get something that's harder to push, as of course the harder they are to push, the better the pay. At present I can just make my way, with nothing at all over; but then I live in a very expensive flat. It happened like this, and that brings me to my story. And it isn't the story you'd expect from a small man like me, yet there's nobody else to tell it. Those that know anything of it besides me are all for hushing it up. Well, I was looking for a room to live in in London when first I got my job. It had to be in London, to be central;

and I went to a block of buildings, very gloomy they looked, and saw the man that ran them and asked him for what I wanted. Flats they called them; just a bedroom and a sort of a cupboard. Well, he was showing a man round at the time who was a gent, in fact more than that, so he didn't take much notice of me—the man that ran all those flats didn't, I mean. So I just ran behind for a bit, seeing all sorts of rooms and waiting till I could be shown my class of thing. We came to a very nice flat, a sitting room, bedroom and bathroom, and a sort of little place that they called a hall. And that's how I came to know Linley. He was the bloke that was being shown round.

"Bit expensive," he said.

And the man that ran the flats turned away to the window and picked his teeth. It's funny how much you can show by a simple thing like. What he meant to say was that he'd hundreds of flats like that, and thousands of people looking for them, and he didn't care who had them or whether they all went on looking. There was no mistaking him, somehow. And yet he never said a word, only looked away out of the window and picked his teeth. And I ventured to speak to Mr. Linley then; and I said, "How about it, sir, if I paid half, and shared it? I wouldn't be in the way, and I'm out all day, and whatever you said would go, and really I wouldn't be no more in your way than a cat."

You may be surprised at my doing it; and you'll be much more surprised at him accepting it—at least, you would if you knew me, just a small man in a small way of business. And yet I could see at once that he was taking to me more than he was taking to the man at the window.

"But there's only one bedroom," he said.

"I could make up my bed easy in that little room there," I said.

"The hall," said the man, looking round from the window, without taking his toothpick out.

"And I'd have the bed out of the way and hid in the cupboard by any hour you like," I said.

He looked thoughtful, and the other man looked out over London; and in the end, do you know, he accepted.

"Friend of yours?" said the flat man.

"Yes," answered Mr. Linley.

It was really very nice of him.

I'll tell you why I did it. Able to afford it? Of course not. But I heard him tell the flat man that he had just come down from Oxford and wanted to live for a few months in London. It turned out he wanted just to be comfortable and do nothing for a bit while he looked things over and chose a job, or probably just as long as he could afford it. Well, I said to myself, what's the Oxford manner worth in business, especially a business like mine? Why, simply everything you've got. If I picked up only a quarter of it from this Mr. Linley I'd be able to double my sales, and that would soon mean I'd be given something a lot harder to push, with perhaps treble the pay. Worth it every time. And you can make a quarter of an education go twice as far again, if you're careful with it. I mean you don't have to quote the whole of the *Inferno* to show that you've read Milton; half a line may do it.

Well, about that story I have to tell. And you mightn't think that a little man like me could make you shudder. Well, I soon forgot about the Oxford manner when we settled down in our flat. I forgot it in the sheer wonder of the man himself. He had a mind like an acrobat's body, like a bird's body. It didn't want education. You didn't notice whether he was educated or not. Ideas were always leaping up in him, things you'd never have thought of. And not only that, but if any ideas were about, he'd sort of catch them. Time and again I've found him knowing just what I was going to say. Not thought reading, but what they call intuition. I used to try to learn a bit about chess, just to take my thoughts off Num-numo in the evening, when I'd done with it. But problems I never could do. Yet he'd come along and glance at my problem and say, "You probably move that piece first," and I'd say, "But where?" and he'd say, "Oh, one of those three squares." And I'd say, "But it will be taken on all of them." And the piece a queen all the time, mind you. And he'd say, "Yes, it's doing no good there: you're probably meant to lose it."

And, do you know, he'd be right.

You see, he'd been following out what the other man had been thinking. That's what he'd been doing.

Well, one day there was that ghastly murder at Unge. I don't know if you remember it. But Steeger had gone down to live with a girl in a bungalow on the North Downs, and that was the first we had heard of him.

The girl had two hundred pounds, and he got every penny of it, and she utterly disappeared. And Scotland Yard couldn't find her.

Well, I'd happened to read that Steeger had bought two bottles of Num-numo; for the Otherthorpe police had found out everything about him, except what he did with the girl; and that of course attracted my attention, or I should have never thought again about the case or said a word of it to Linley. Num-numo was always on my mind, as I always spent every day pushing it, and that kept me from forgetting the other thing. And so one day I said to Linley, "I wonder with all that knack you have for seeing through a chess problem, and thinking of one thing and another, that you don't have a go at that Otherthorpe mystery. It's a problem as much as chess," I said.

"There's not the mystery in ten murders that there is in one game of chess," he answered.

"It's beaten Scotland Yard," I said.

"Has it?" he asked.

"Knocked them endwise," I said.

"It shouldn't have done that," he said. And almost immediately after he said, "What are the facts?"

We were both sitting at supper, and I told him the facts, as I had them straight from the papers. She was a pretty blonde, she was small, she was called Nancy Elth, she had two hundred pounds, they lived at the bungalow for five days. After that he stayed there for another fortnight, but nobody ever saw her alive again. Steeger said she had gone to South America, but later said he had never said South America, but South Africa. None of her money remained in the bank where she had kept it, and Steeger was shown to have come by at least a hundred fifty pounds just at that time. Then Steeger turned out to be a vegetarian, getting all his food from the greengrocer, and that made the constable in the village of Unge suspicious of him, for a vegetarian was something new to the constable. He watched Steeger after that, and it's well he did, for there was nothing that Scotland Yard asked him that he couldn't tell them about him, except of course the one thing. And he told the police at Other-thorpe five or six miles away, and they came and took a hand at it too. They were able to say for one thing that he never went outside the bungalow and its tidy garden ever since she disappeared. You see, the more they watched him the more suspicious they got, as you naturally do if you're watching a man; so that very soon they were watching every move he made, but if it hadn't been for his being a vegetarian they'd never have started to suspect him, and there wouldn't have been enough evidence even for Linley. Not that they found out anything much against him, except that hundred fifty pounds dropping in from nowhere, and it was Scotland Yard that found that, not the police of Other-thorpe. No, what the constable of Unge found out was about the larch trees, and that beat Scotland Yard utterly, and beat Linley up to the very last, and of course it beat me. There were ten larch trees in the bit of a garden, and he'd made some sort of an arrangement with the landlord, Steeger had, before he took the bungalow, by which he could do what he liked with the larch trees. And then from about the time that little Nancy Elth must have died he cut every one of them down. Three times a day he went at it for nearly a week, and when they were all down he cut them all up into logs no more than two foot long and laid them all in neat heaps. You never saw such work. And what for? To give an excuse for the axe was one theory. But the excuse was bigger than the axe; it took him a fortnight, hard work every day. And he could have killed a little thing like Nancy Elth without an axe, and cut her up too. Another theory was that he wanted firewood, to make away with the body. But he never used it. He left it all standing there in those neat stacks. It fairly beat everybody.

Well, those are the facts I told Linley. Oh yes, and he bought a big butcher's knife. Funny thing, they all do. And yet it isn't so funny after all; if you've got to cut a woman up, you've got to cut her up; and you can't do that without a knife. Then, there were some negative facts. He hadn't burned her. Only had a fire in the small stove now and then, and only used it for cooking. They got on to that pretty smartly, the Unge constable did, and the men that were lending him a hand from Otherthorpe. There were some little woody places lying round, shaws they call them in that part of the country, the country people do, and they could climb a tree handy and unobserved and get a sniff at the smoke in almost any direction it might be blowing. They did that now and then, and there was no smell of flesh burning, just ordinary cooking. Pretty smart of the Otherthorpe police that was, though of course it didn't help to hang Steeger. Then later on the Scotland Yard men went down and got another fact—negative, but narrowing things down all the while. And that was that the chalk under the bungalow and under the little garden had none of it been disturbed. And he'd never been outside it since Nancy disappeared. Oh yes, and he had a big file besides the knife. But there was no sign of any ground bones found on the file, or any blood on the knife. He'd washed them of course. I told all that to Linley.

Now I ought to warn you before I go any further. I am a small man myself and you probably don't expect anything horrible from me. But I ought to warn you this man was a murderer, or at any rate somebody was; the woman had been made away with, a nice pretty little girl too, and the man that had done that wasn't necessarily going to stop at things you might think he'd stop at. With the mind to do a thing like that, and with the long thin shadow of the rope to drive him further, you can't say what he'll stop at. Murder tales seem nice things sometimes for a lady to sit and read all by herself by the fire. But murder isn't a nice thing, and when a murderer's desperate and trying to hide his tracks he isn't even as nice as he was before. I'll ask you to bear that in mind. Well, I've warned you.

So I says to Linley, "And what do you make of it?"

"Drains?" said Linley.

"No," I says, "you're wrong there. Scotland Yard has been into that. And the Otherthorpe people before them. They've had a look in the drains, such as they are, a little thing running into a cesspool beyond the garden; and nothing has gone down it—nothing that oughtn't to have, I mean."

He made one or two other suggestions, but Scotland Yard had been before him in every case. That's really the crab of my story, if you'll excuse the expression. You want a man who sets out to be a detective to take his magnifying glass and go down to the spot; to go to the spot before everything; and then to measure the footmarks and pick up the clues and find the knife that the police have overlooked. But Linley never even went near the place, and he hadn't got a magnifying glass, not as I ever saw, and Scotland Yard were before him every time.

In fact they had more clues than anybody could make head or tail of. Every kind of clue to show that he'd murdered the poor little girl; every kind of clue to show that he hadn't disposed of the body; and yet the body wasn't there. It wasn't in South America either, and not much more likely in South Africa. And all the time, mind you, that enormous bunch of chopped larchwood, a clue that was staring everyone in the face and leading nowhere. No, we didn't seem to want any more clues, and Linley never went near the place. The trouble was to deal with the clues we'd got. I was completely mystified; so was Scotland Yard; and Linley seemed to be getting no forwarder; and all the while the mystery was hanging on me. I mean if it were not for the trifle I'd chanced to remember, and if it were not for one chance word I said to Linley, that mystery would have gone the way of all the other mysteries that men have made nothing of, a darkness, a little patch of night in history.

Well, the fact was Linley didn't take much interest in it at first, but I was so absolutely sure that he could do it that I kept him to the idea. "You can do chess problems," I said.

"That's ten times harder," he said, sticking to his point.

"Then why don't you do this?" I said.

"Then go and take a look at the board for me," said Linley.

That was his way of talking. We'd been a fortnight together, and I knew it by now. He meant to go down to the bungalow at Unge. I know you'll say why didn't he go himself; but the plain truth of it is that if he'd been tearing about the countryside he'd never have been thinking, whereas sitting there in his chair by the fire in our flat there was no limit to the ground he could cover, if you follow my meaning. So down I went by train next day, and got out at Unge station. And there were the North Downs rising up before me, somehow like music.

"It's up there, isn't it?" I said to the porter.

"That's right," he said. "Up there by the lane; and mind to turn to your right when you get to the old yew tree, a very big tree, you can't mistake it, and then . . ." and he told me the way so that I couldn't go wrong. I found them all like that, very nice and helpful. You see, it was Unge's day at last. Everyone had heard of Unge now; you could have got a letter there any time just then without putting the county or post town; and this was what Unge had to show. I dare say if you tried to find Unge now . . . well, anyway, they were making hay while the sun shone.

Well, there the hill was, going up into sunlight, going up like a song. You don't want to hear about the spring, and all the May rioting, and the colour that came down over everything later on in the day, and all those birds; but I thought,

"What a nice place to bring a girl to." And then when I
thought that he'd killed her there, well, I'm only a small
man, as I said, but when I thought of her on that hill with
all the birds singing, I said to myself, "Wouldn't it be odd if
it turned out to be me after all that got that man killed, if
he did murder her." So I soon found my way up to the
bungalow and began prying about, looking over the hedge
into the garden. And I didn't find much, and I found nothing
at all that the police hadn't found already, but there were
those heaps of larch logs staring me in the face and looking
very queer.

I did a lot of thinking, leaning against the hedge, breathing the smell of the may, and looking over the top of it at
the larch logs, and the neat little bungalow the other side of
the garden. Lots of theories I thought of, till I came to the
best thought of all; and that was that if I left the thinking to
Linley, with his Oxford and Cambridge education, and only
brought him the facts, as he had told me, I should be doing
more good in my way than if I tried to do any big thinking.
I forgot to tell you that I had gone to Scotland Yard in the
morning. Well, there wasn't really much to tell. What they
asked me was what I wanted. And, not having an answer
exactly ready, I didn't find out very much from them. But
it was quite different at Unge; everyone was most obliging;
it was their day there, as I said. The constable let me go
indoors, so long as I didn't touch anything, and he gave me
a look at the garden from the inside. And I saw the stumps
of the ten larch trees, and I noticed one thing that Linley
said was very observant of me, not that it turned out to be
any use, but anyway I was doing my best: I noticed that the
stumps had been all chopped anyhow. And from that I
thought that the man that did it didn't know much about
chopping. The constable said that was a deduction. So then
I said that the axe was blunt when he used it; and that
certainly made the constable think, though he didn't actually say I was right this time. Did I tell you that Steeger
never went outdoors, except to the little garden to chop

wood, ever since Nancy disappeared? I think I did. Well, it was perfectly true. They'd watched him night and day, one or another of them, and the Unge constable told me that himself. That limited things a good deal. The only thing I didn't like about it was that I felt Linley ought to have found all that out instead of ordinary policemen, and I felt that he could have too. There'd have been romance in a story like that. And they'd never have done it if the news hadn't gone round that the man was a vegetarian and only dealt at the greengrocer's. Likely as not even that was only started out of pique by the butcher. It's queer what little things may trip a man up. Best to keep straight is my motto. But perhaps I'm straying a bit away from my story. I should like to do that forever—forget that it ever was; but I can't.

Well, I picked up all sorts of information; clues I suppose I should call it in a story like this, though they none of them seemed to lead anywhere. For instance, I found out everything he ever bought at the village, I could even tell you the kind of salt he bought, quite plain with no phosphates in it, that they sometimes put in to make it tidy. And then he got ice from the fishmonger's, and plenty of vegetables, as I said, from the greengrocer, Mergin & Sons. And I had a bit of a talk over it all with the constable. Slugger he said his name was. I wondered why he hadn't come in and searched the place as soon as the girl was missing. "Well, you can't do that," he said. "And besides, we didn't suspect at once, not about the girl, that is. We only suspected there was something wrong about him on account of him being a vegetarian. He stayed a good fortnight after the last that was seen of her. And then we slipped in like a knife. But, you see, no one had been inquiring about her; there was no warrant out."

"And what did you find," I asked Slugger, "when you went in?"

"Just a big file," he said, "and the knife and the axe that he must have got to chop her up with."

"But he got the axe to chop trees with," I said.

"Well, yes," he said, but rather grudgingly.

"And what did he chop them for?" I asked.

"Well, of course, my superiors has theories about that," he said, "that they mightn't tell to everybody."

You see, it was those logs that were beating them.

"But did he cut her up at all?" I asked.

"Well, he said that she was going to South America," he answered. Which was really very fair-minded of him.

I don't remember now much else that he told me. Steeger left the plates and dishes all washed up and very neat, he said.

Well, I brought all this back to Linley, going up by the train that started just about sunset. I'd like to tell you about the late spring evening, so calm over that grim bungalow, closing in with a glory all round it as though it were blessing it; but you'll want to hear of the murder. Well, I told Linley everything, though much of it didn't seem to me to be worth the telling. The trouble was that the moment I began to leave anything out, he'd know it, and make me drag it in. "You can't tell what may be vital," he'd say. "A tin tack swept away by a housemaid might hang a man."

All very well, but be consistent, even if you are educated at Eton and Harrow, and whenever I mentioned Num-numo, which after all was the beginning of the whole story, because he wouldn't have heard of it if it hadn't been for me, and my noticing that Steeger had bought two bottles of it, why then he said that things like that were trivial and we should keep to the main issues. I naturally talked a bit about Num-numo, because only that day I had pushed close on fifty bottles of it in Unge. A murder certainly stimulates people's minds, and Steeger's two bottles gave me an opportunity that only a fool could have failed to make something of. But of course all that was nothing at all to Linley.

You can't see a man's thoughts, and you can't look into his mind, so that all the most exciting things in the world can never be told of. But what I think happened all that evening with Linley, while I talked to him before supper, and all through supper, and sitting smoking afterwards in front of our fire, was that his thoughts were stuck at a barrier there was no getting over. And the barrier wasn't the difficulty of finding ways and means by which Steeger might have made away with the body, but the impossibility of finding why he chopped those masses of wood every day for a fortnight, and paid, as I'd just found out, twenty-five pounds to his landlord to be allowed to do it. That's what was beating Linley. As for the ways by which Steeger might have hidden the body, it seemed to me that every way was blocked by the police. If you said he buried it, they said the chalk was undisturbed; if you said he carried it away, they said he never left the place; if you said he burned it, they said no smell of burning was ever noticed when the smoke blew low, and when it didn't they climbed trees after it. I'd taken to Linley wonderfully, and I didn't have to be educated to see there was something big in a mind like his, and I thought that he could have done it. When I saw the police getting in before him like that, and no way that I could see of getting past them, I felt real sorry.

Did anyone come to the house, he asked me once or twice. Did anyone take anything away from it? But we couldn't account for it that way. Then perhaps I made some suggestion that was no good, or perhaps I started talking of Num-numo again, and he interrupted me rather sharply.

"But what would you do, Smithers?" he said. "What would you do yourself?"

"If I'd murdered poor Nancy Elth?" I asked.

"Yes," he said.

"I can't ever imagine doing such a thing," I told him.

He sighed at that, as though it were something against me.

"I suppose I should never be a detective," I said. And he just shook his head.

Then he looked broodingly into the fire for what seemed an hour. And then he shook his head again. We both went to bed after that.

I shall remember the next day all my life. I was till evening, as usual, pushing Num-numo. And we sat down to supper about nine. You couldn't get things cooked at those flats, so of course we had it cold. And Linley began with a salad. I can see it now, every bit of it. Well, I was still a bit full of what I'd done in Unge, pushing Num-numo. Only a fool, I know, would have been unable to push it there; but still, I *had* pushed it; and about fifty bottles, forty-eight to be exact, are something in a small village, whatever the circumstances. So I was talking about it a bit; and then all of a sudden I realized that Num-numo was nothing to Linley, and I pulled myself up with a jerk. It was really very kind of him; do you know what he did? He must have known at once why I stopped talking, and he just stretched out a hand and said, "Would you give me a little of your Num-numo for my salad?"

I was so touched I nearly gave it him. But of course you don't take Num-numo with salad. Only for meats and savouries. That's on the bottle.

So I just said to him, "Only for meats and savouries." Though I don't know what savouries are. Never had any.

I never saw a man's face go like that before.

He seemed still for a whole minute. And nothing speaking about him but that expression. Like a man that's seen a ghost, one is tempted to write. But it wasn't really at all. I'll tell you what he looked like. Like a man that's seen something that no one has ever looked at before, something he thought couldn't be.

And then he said in a voice that was all quite changed, more low and gentle and quiet it seemed, "No good for vegetables, eh?"

"Not a bit," I said.

And at that he gave a kind of sob in his throat. I hadn't thought he could feel things like that. Of course I didn't know what it was all about; but, whatever it was, I thought all that sort of thing would have been knocked out of him at Eton and Harrow, an educated man like that. There were no tears in his eyes, but he was feeling something horribly.

And then he began to speak with big spaces between his words, saying, "A man might make a mistake perhaps, and use Num-numo with vegetables."

"Not twice," I said. What else could I say?

And he repeated that after me as though I had told of the end of the world, and adding an awful emphasis to my words, till they seemed all clammy with some frightful significance, and shaking his head as he said it.

Then he was quite silent.

"What is it?" I asked.

"Smithers," he said.

"Yes," I said.

"Smithers," said he.

And I said, "Well?"

"Look here, Smithers," he said, "you must phone down to the grocer at Unge and find out from him this."

"Yes?" I said.

"Whether Steeger bought those two bottles, as I expect he did, on the same day, and not a few days apart. He couldn't have done that."

I waited to see if any more was coming, and then I ran out and did what I was told. It took me some time, being after nine o'clock, and only then with the help of the police. About six days apart they said; and so I came back and told Linley. He looked up at me so hopefully when I came in, but I saw that it was the wrong answer by his eyes.

You can't take things to heart like that without being ill, and when he didn't speak I said, "What you want is a good brandy, and go to bed early."

And he said, "No. I must see someone from Scotland Yard. Phone round to them. Say here at once."

But I said, "I can't get an inspector from Scotland Yard to call on us at this hour."

His eyes were all lit up. He was all there all right.

"Then tell them," he said, "they'll never find Nancy Elth. Tell one of them to come here, and I'll tell him why."

And he added, I think only for me, "They must watch Steeger, till one day they get him over something else."

And, do you know, he came. Inspector Ulton; he came himself.

While we were waiting I tried to talk to Linley. Partly curiosity, I admit. But I didn't want to leave him to those thoughts of his, brooding away by the fire. I tried to ask him what it was all about. But he wouldn't tell me. "Murder is horrible," is all he would say. "And as a man covers his tracks up it only gets worse."

He wouldn't tell me. "There are tales," he said, "that one never wants to hear."

That's true enough. I wish I'd never heard this one. I never did actually. But I guessed it from Linley's last words to Inspector Ulton, the only ones that I overheard. And perhaps this is the point at which to stop reading my story, so that you don't guess it too; even if you think you want murder stories. For don't you rather want a murder story with a bit of a romantic twist, and not a story about real foul murder? Well, just as you like.

In came Inspector Ulton, and Linley shook hands in silence, and pointed the way to his bedroom; and they went in there and talked in low voices, and I never heard a word.

A fairly hearty-looking man was the inspector when they went into that room.

They walked through our sitting room in silence when they came out, and together they went into the hall, and there I heard the only words they said to each other. It was the inspector that first broke that silence.

"But why," he said, "did he cut down the trees?"

"Solely," said Linley, "in order to get an appetite."

THE GUTTING OF COUFFIGNAL

Dashiell Hammett

Wedge-shaped Couffignal is not a large island, and not far from the mainland, to which it is linked by a wooden bridge. Its western shore is a high, straight cliff that jumps abruptly up out of San Pablo Bay. From the top of this cliff the island slopes eastward, down to a smooth pebble beach that runs into the water again, where there are piers and a clubhouse and moored pleasure boats.

Couffignal's main street, paralleling the beach, has the usual bank, hotel, moving-picture theater, and stores. But it differs from most main streets of its size in that it is more carefully arranged and preserved. There are trees and hedges and strips of lawn on it, and no glaring signs. The buildings seem to belong beside one another, as if they had been designed by the same architect, and in the stores you will find goods of a quality to match the best city stores.

The intersecting streets—running between rows of neat cottages near the foot of the slope—become winding hedged roads as they climb toward the cliff. The higher these roads get, the farther apart and larger are the houses they lead to. The occupants of these higher houses are the owners and rulers of the island. Most of them are well-fed old gentlemen who, the profits they took from the world with both hands in their younger days now stowed away at safe percentages, have bought into the island colony so they may spend what is left of their lives nursing their livers and improving their golf among their kind. They admit to the island only as many storekeepers, working people, and similar riffraff as are needed to keep them comfortably served.

That is Couffignal.

It was some time after midnight. I was sitting in a second-story room in Couffignal's largest house, surrounded by wedding presents whose value would add up to something between fifty and a hundred thousand dollars.

Of all the work that comes to a private detective (except divorce work, which the Continental Detective Agency doesn't handle) I like weddings as little as any. Usually I manage to avoid them, but this time I hadn't been able to. Dick Foley, who had been slated for the job, had been handed a black eye by an unfriendly pickpocket the day before. That let Dick out and me in. I had come up to Couffignal—a two-hour ride from San Francisco by ferry and auto-stage—that morning, and would return the next.

This had been neither better nor worse than the usual wedding detail. The ceremony had been performed in a little stone church down the hill. Then the house had begun to fill with reception guests. They had kept it filled to overflowing until some time after the bride and groom had sneaked off to their eastern train.

The world had been well represented. There had been an admiral and an earl or two from England; an ex-president of a South American country; a Danish baron; a tall young Russian princess surrounded by lesser titles, including a fat, bald, jovial, and black-bearded Russian general, who had talked to me for a solid hour about prize fights, in which he had a lot of interest, but not so much knowledge as was possible; an ambassador from one of the Central European countries; a justice of the Supreme Court; and a mob of people whose prominence and near prominence didn't carry labels.

In theory, a detective guarding wedding presents is supposed to make himself indistinguishable from the other guests. In practice, it never works out that way. He has to spend most of his time within sight of the booty, so he's easily spotted. Besides that, eight or ten people I recognized among the guests were clients or former clients of the agency, and so knew me. However, being known doesn't make so much difference as you might think, and everything had gone off smoothly.

A couple of the groom's friends, warmed by wine and the necessity of maintaining their reputations as cutups, had tried to smuggle some of the gifts out of the room where they were displayed and hide them in the piano. But I had been expecting that familiar trick, and blocked it before it had gone far enough to embarrass anybody.

Shortly after dark a wind smelling of rain began to pile storm clouds up over the bay. Those guests who lived at a distance, especially those who had water to cross, hurried off for their homes. Those who lived on the island stayed until the first raindrops began to patter down. Then they left.

The Hendrixson house quieted down. Musicians and extra servants left. The weary house servants began to disappear in the direction of their bedrooms. I found some sandwiches, a couple of books and a comfortable armchair, and took them up to the room where the presents were now hidden under gray-white sheeting.

Keith Hendrixson, the bride's grandfather—she was an orphan—put his head in at the door. "Have you everything you need for your comfort?" he asked.

"Yes, thanks."

He said good night and went off to bed—a tall old man, slim as a boy.

The wind and the rain were hard at it when I went downstairs to give the lower windows and doors the up-and-down. Everything on the first floor was tight and secure, everything in the cellar. I went upstairs again.

Pulling my chair over by a floor lamp, I put sandwiches, books, ashtray, gun, and flashlight on a small table beside it. Then I switched off the other lights, set fire to a Fatima, sat down, wriggled my spine comfortably into the chair's padding, picked up one of the books, and prepared to make a night of it.

The book was called *The Lord of the Sea,* and had to do with a strong, tough, and violent fellow named Hogarth, whose modest plan was to hold the world in one hand. There were plots and counterplots, kidnappings, murders, prison breakings, forgeries and burglaries, diamonds large as hats, and floating forts larger than Couffignal. It sounds dizzy here, but in the book it was as real as a dime.

Hogarth was still going strong when the lights went out.

In the dark, I got rid of the glowing end of my cigarette by grinding it in one of the sandwiches. Putting the book down, I picked up gun and flashlight, and moved away from the chair.

Listening for noises was no good. The storm was making hundreds of them. What I needed to know was why the lights had gone off. All the other lights in the house had been turned off some time ago. So the darkness of the hall told me nothing.

I waited. My job was to watch the presents. Nobody had touched them yet. There was nothing to get excited about.

Minutes went by, perhaps ten of them.

The floor swayed under my feet. The windows rattled with a violence beyond the strength of the storm. The dull boom of a heavy explosion blotted out the sounds of wind and falling water. The blast was not close at hand, but not far enough away to be off the island.

Crossing to the window, peering through the wet glass, I could see nothing. I should have seen a few misty lights far down the hill. Not being able to see them settled one point. The lights had gone out all over Couffignal, not only in the Hendrixson house.

That was better. The storm could have put the lighting system out of whack, could have been responsible for the explosion—maybe.

Staring through the black window, I had an impression of great excitement down the hill, of movement in the night. But all was too far away for me to have seen or heard even had there been lights, and all too vague to say what was moving. The impression was strong but worthless. It didn't lead anywhere. I told myself I was getting feebleminded, and turned away from the window.

Another blast spun me back to it. This explosion sounded nearer than the first, maybe because it was stronger. Peering through the glass again, I still saw nothing. And still had the impression of things that were big moving down there.

Bare feet pattered in the hall. A voice was anxiously calling my name. Turning from the window again, I pocketed my gun and snapped on the flashlight. Keith Hendrixson, in pajamas and bathrobe, looking thinner and older than anybody could be, came into the room.

"Is it—"

"I don't think it's an earthquake," I said, since that is the first calamity your Californian thinks of. "The lights went off a little while ago. There have been a couple of explosions down the hill since the—"

I stopped. Three shots, close together, had sounded. Rifle shots, but of the sort that only the heaviest of rifles could make. Then, sharp and small in the storm, came the report of a faraway pistol.

"What is it?" Hendrixson demanded.

"Shooting."

More feet were pattering in the halls, some bare, some shod. Excited voices whispered questions and exclamations.

The butler, a solemn, solid block of a man, partly dressed and carrying a lighted five-pronged candlestick, came in.

"Very good, Brophy," Hendrixson said as the butler put the candlestick on the table beside my sandwiches. "Will you try to learn what is the matter?"

"I have tried, sir. The telephone seems to be out of order, sir. Shall I send Oliver down to the village?"

"No-o. I don't suppose it's that serious. Do you think it is anything serious?" he asked me.

I said I didn't think so, but I was paying more attention to the outside than to him. I had heard a thin screaming that could have come from a distant woman, and a volley of small-arms shots. The racket of the storm muffled these shots, but when the heavier firing we had heard before broke out again, it was clear enough.

To have opened the window would have been to let in gallons of water without helping us to hear much clearer. I stood with an ear tilted to the pane, trying to arrive at some idea of what was happening outside.

Another sound took my attention from the window— the ringing of the bellpull at the front door. It rang loudly and persistently.

Hendrixson looked at me. I nodded. "See who it is, Brophy," he said.

The butler went solemnly away, and came back even more solemnly. "Princess Zhukovski," he announced.

She came running into the room—the tall Russian girl I had seen at the reception. Her eyes were wide and dark with excitement. Her face was very white and wet. Water ran in streams down her blue waterproof cape, the hood of which covered her dark hair.

"Oh, Mr. Hendrixson!" She had caught one of his hands in both of hers. Her voice, with nothing foreign in its accents, was the voice of one who is excited over a delightful surprise. "The bank is being robbed, and the—what do you call him?—marshal of police has been killed!"

"What's that?" the old man exclaimed, jumping awkwardly because water from her cape had dripped down on one of his bare feet. "Weegan killed? And the bank robbed?"

"Yes! Isn't it terrible?" She said it as if she were saying wonderful. "When the first explosion woke us, the general sent Ignati down to find out what was the matter, and he got down there just in time to see the bank blown up. Listen!"

We listened, and heard a wild outbreak of mixed gunfire.

"That will be the general arriving!" she said. "He'll enjoy himself most wonderfully. As soon as Ignati returned with the news, the general armed every male in the household from Aleksandr Sergeyevich to Ivan the cook, and led them out happier than he's been since he took his division to East Prussia in 1914."

"And the duchess?" Hendrixson asked.

"He left her at home with me, of course, and I furtively crept out and away from her while she was trying for the first time in her life to put water in a samovar. This is not the night for one to stay at home!"

"Hm-m," Hendrixson said, his mind obviously not on her words. "And the bank!"

He looked at me. I said nothing. The racket of another volley came to us.

"Could you do anything down there?" he asked.

"Maybe, but—" I nodded at the presents under their covers.

"Oh, those!" the old man said. "I'm as much interested in the bank as in them; and besides, we will be here."

"All right!" I was willing enough to carry my curiosity down the hill. 'I'll go down. You'd better have the butler stay in here, and plant the chauffeur inside the front door. Better give them guns if you have any. Is there a raincoat I can borrow? I brought only a light overcoat with me."

Brophy found a yellow slicker that fit me. I put it on, stowed gun and flashlight conveniently under it, and found my hat while Brophy was getting and loading an automatic pistol for himself and a rifle for Oliver, the mulatto chauffeur.

Hendrixson and the princess followed me downstairs. At the door I found she wasn't exactly following me—she was going with me.

"But, Sonya!" the old man protested.

"I'm not going to be foolish, though I'd like to," she promised him. "But I'm going back to my Irina Androvna, who will perhaps have the samovar watered by now."

"That's a sensible girl!" Hendrixson said, and let us out into the rain and the wind.

It wasn't weather to talk in. In silence we turned downhill between two rows of hedging, with the storm driving at our backs. At the first break in the hedge I stopped, nodding toward the black blot a house made. "That is your—"

Her laugh cut me short. She caught my arm and began to urge me down the road again. "I only told Mr. Hendrixson that so he would not worry," she explained. "You do not think I am not going down to see the sights."

She was tall. I am short and thick. I had to look up to see her face—to see as much of it as the rainy-gray night would let me see. "You'll be soaked to the hide, running around in this rain," I objected.

"What of that? I am dressed for it." She raised a foot to show me a heavy waterproof boot and a woolen-stockinged leg.

"There's no telling what we'll run into down there, and I've got work to do," I insisted. "I can't be looking out for you."

"I can look out for myself." She pushed her cape aside to show me a square automatic pistol in one hand.

"You'll be in my way."

"I will not," she retorted. "You'll probably find I can help you. I'm as strong as you, and quicker, and I can shoot."

The reports of scattered shooting had punctuated our argument, but now the sound of heavier firing silenced the dozen objections to her company that I could still think of. After all, I could slip away from her in the dark if she became too much of a nuisance.

"Have it your own way," I growled, "but don't expect anything from me."

"You're so kind," she murmured as we got under way again, hurrying now, with the wind at our backs speeding us along.

Occasionally dark figures moved on the road ahead of us, but too far away to be recognizable. Presently a man passed us, running uphill—a tall man whose nightshirt hung out of his trousers, down below his coat, identifying him as a resident.

"They've finished the bank and are at Medcraft's!" he yelled as he went by.

"Medcraft is the jeweler," the girl informed me.

The sloping under our feet grew less sharp. The houses—dark but with faces vaguely visible here and there at windows—came closer together. Below, the flash of a gun could be seen now and then—orange streaks in the rain.

Our road put us into the lower end of the main street just as a staccato rat-tat-tat broke out.

I pushed the girl into the nearest doorway, and jumped in after her.

Bullets ripped through walls with the sound of hail tapping on leaves.

That was the thing I had taken for an exceptionally heavy rifle—a machine gun.

The girl had fallen back in a corner, all tangled up with something. I helped her up. That something was a boy of seventeen or so, with one leg and a crutch.

"It's the boy who delivers papers," Princess Zhukovski said, "and you've hurt him with your clumsiness."

The boy shook his head, grinning as he got up. "No'm, I ain't hurt none, but you kind of scared me, jumping on me like that."

She had to stop and explain that she hadn't jumped on him, that she had been pushed into him by me, and that she was sorry and so was I.

"What's happening?" I asked the newsboy when I could get a word in.

"Everything," he boasted, as if some of the credit were his. "There must be a hundred of them, and they've blowed the bank wide open, and now some of 'em is in Medcraft's, and I guess they'll blow that up, too. And they killed Tom Weegan. They got a machine gun on a car in the middle of the street. That's it shooting now."

"Where's everybody—all the merry villagers?"

"Most of 'em are up behind the Hall. They can't do nothing, though, because the machine gun won't let 'em get near enough to see what they're shooting at, and that smart Bill Vincent told me to clear out, 'cause I've only got one leg, as if I couldn't shoot as good as the next one, if I only had something to shoot with!"

"That wasn't right of them," I sympathized. "But you can do something for me. You can stick here and keep your eye on this end of the street, so I'll know if they leave in this direction."

"You're not just saying that so I'll stay here out of the way, are you?"

"No," I lied. "I need somebody to watch. I was going to leave the princess here, but you'll do better."

"Yes," she backed me up, catching the idea. "This gentleman is a detective, and if you do what he asks you'll be helping more than if you were up with the others."

The machine gun was still firing, but not in our direction now.

"I'm going across the street," I told the girl. "If you—"

"Aren't you going to join the others?"

"No. If I can get around behind the bandits while they're busy with the others, maybe I can turn a trick.

"Watch sharp now?" I ordered the boy, and the princess and I made a dash for the opposite sidewalk.

We reached it without drawing lead, sidled along a building for a few yards, and turned into an alley. From the alley's other end came the smell and wash and the dull blackness of the bay.

While we moved down this alley I composed a scheme by which I hoped to get rid of my companion, sending her off on a safe wild-goose chase. But I didn't get a chance to try it out.

The big figure of a man loomed ahead of us.

Stepping in front of the girl, I went on toward him. Under my slicker I held my gun on the middle of him. He stood still. He was larger than he had looked at first. A big, slope-shouldered, barrel-bodied husky. His hands were empty. I spotted the flashlight on his face for a split second. A flat-cheeked, thick-featured face, with high cheekbones and a lot of ruggedness in it.

"Ignati!" the girl exclaimed over my shoulder.

He began to talk what I suppose was Russian to the girl. She laughed and replied. He shook his big head stubbornly, insisting on something. She stamped her foot and spoke sharply. He shook his head again and addressed me. "General Pleshskev, he tell me bring Princess Sonya to home."

His English was almost as hard to understand as his Russian. His tone puzzled me. It was as if he was explaining some absolutely necessary thing that he didn't want to be blamed for, but that nevertheless he was going to do.

While the girl was speaking to him again, I guessed the answer. This big Ignati had been sent out by the general to bring the girl home, and he was going to obey his orders if he had to carry her. He was trying to avoid trouble with me by explaining the situation.

"Take her," I said, stepping aside.

The girl scowled at me, laughed. "Very well, Ignati," she said in English, "I shall go home," and she turned on her heel and went back up the alley, the big man close behind her.

Glad to be alone, I wasted no time in moving in the opposite direction until the pebbles of the beach were under my feet. The pebbles ground harshly under my heels. I moved back to more silent ground and began to work my way as swiftly as I could up the shore toward the center of action. The machine gun barked on. Smaller guns snapped.

Three concussions, close together—bombs, hand grenades, my ears and my memory told me.

The stormy sky glared pink over a roof ahead of me and to the left. The boom of the blast beat my eardrums. Fragments I couldn't see fell around me. That, I thought, would be the jeweler's safe blowing apart.

I crept on up the shore line. The machine gun went silent. Lighter guns snapped, snapped. Another grenade went off. A man's voice shrieked pure terror.

Risking the crunch of pebbles, I turned down to the water's edge again. I had seen no dark shape on the water that could have been a boat. There had been boats moored along this beach in the afternoon. With my feet in the water of the bay I still saw no boat. The storm could have scattered them, but I didn't think it had. The island's western height shielded this shore. The wind was strong here, but not violent.

My feet sometimes on the edge of the pebbles, sometimes in the water, I went on up the shoreline. Now I saw a boat. A gently bobbing black shape ahead. No light was on it. Nothing I could see moved on it. It was the only boat on that shore. That made it important.

Foot by foot, I approached.

A shadow moved between me and the dark rear of a building. I froze. The shadow, man size, moved again, in the direction from which I was coming.

Waiting, I didn't know how nearly invisible, or how plain, I might be against my background. I couldn't risk giving myself away by trying to improve my position.

Twenty feet from me the shadow suddenly stopped.

I was seen. My gun was on the shadow.

"Come on," I called softly. "Keep coming. Let's see who you are."

The shadow hesitated, left the shelter of the building, drew nearer. I couldn't risk the flashlight. I made out dimly a handsome face, boyishly reckless, one cheek dark-stained.

"Oh, how d'you do?" the face's owner said in a musical

baritone voice. "You were at the reception this afternoon."

"Yes."

"Have you seen Princess Zhukovski? You know her?"

"She went home with Ignati ten minutes or so ago."

"Excellent!" He wiped his stained cheek with a stained handkerchief, and turned to look at the boat. "That's Hendrixson's boat," he whispered. "They've got it and they've cast the others off."

"That would mean they are going to leave by water."

"Yes" he agreed, "unless—shall we have a try at it?"

"You mean jump it?"

"Why not?" he asked. "There can't be very many aboard. God knows there are enough of them ashore. You're armed. I've a pistol."

"We'll size it up first," I decided, "so we'll know what we're jumping."

"That is wisdom," he said, and led the way back to the shelter of the buildings.

Hugging the rear walls of the buildings, we stole toward the boat.

The boat grew clearer in the night. A craft perhaps forty-five feet long, its stern to the shore, rising and falling beside a small pier. Across the stern something protruded. Something I couldn't quite make out. Leather soles scuffled now and then on the wooden deck. Presently a dark head and shoulders showed over the puzzling thing in the stern.

The Russian lad's eyes were better than mine.

"Masked," he breathed in my ear. "Something like a stocking over his head and face."

The masked man was motionless where he stood. We were motionless where we stood.

"Could you hit him from here?" the lad asked.

"Maybe, but night and rain aren't a good combination for sharpshooting. Our best bet is to sneak as close as we can, and start shooting when he spots us."

"That is wisdom," he agreed.

Discovery came with our first step forward. The man in the boat grunted. The lad at my side jumped forward. I recognized the thing in the boat's stern just in time to throw out a leg and trip the young Russian. He tumbled down, all sprawled out on the pebbles. I dropped behind him.

The machine gun in the boat's stern poured metal over our heads.

"No good rushing that!" I said. "Roll out of it!"

I set the example by revolving toward the back of the building we had just left.

The man at the gun sprinkled the beach, but sprinkled it at random, his eyes no doubt spoiled for night seeing by the flash of his gun.

Around the corner of the building, we sat up.

"You saved my life by tripping me," the lad said coolly.

"Yes. I wonder if they've moved the machine gun from the street, or if—"

The answer to that came immediately. The machine gun in the street mingled its vicious voice with the drumming of the one in the boat.

"A pair of them!" I complained. "Know anything about the layout?"

"I don't think there are more than ten or twelve of them," he said, "although it is not easy to count in the dark. The few I have seen are completely masked—like the man in the boat. They seem to have disconnected the telephone and light lines first and then to have destroyed the bridge. We attacked them while they were looting the bank, but in front they had a machine gun mounted in an automobile, and we were not equipped to combat on equal terms."

"Where are the islanders now?"

"Scattered, and most of them in hiding, I fancy, unless General Pleshskev has succeeded in rallying them again."

I frowned and beat my brains together. You can't fight machine guns and hand grenades with peaceful villagers and retired capitalists. No matter how well led and armed they are, you can't do anything with them. For that matter, how could anybody do much against a game of that toughness?

"Suppose you stick here and keep your eye on the boat," I suggested. "I'll scout around and see what's doing farther up, and if I can get a few good men together, I'll try to jump the boat again, probably from the other side. But we can't count on that. The getaway will be by boat. We can count on that, and try to block it. If you lie down you can watch the boat around the corner of the building without making much of a target of yourself. I wouldn't do anything to attract attention until the break for the boat comes. Then you can do all the shooting you want."

"Excellent!" he said. "You'll probably find most of the islanders up behind the church. You can get to it by going straight up the hill until you come to an iron fence, and then follow that to the right."

"Right."

I moved off in the direction he had indicated.

At the main street I stopped to look around before venturing across. Everything was quiet there. The only man I could see was spread out face down on the sidewalk near me.

On hands and knees I crawled to his side. He was dead. I didn't stop to examine him further, but sprang up and streaked for the other side of the street.

Nothing tried to stop me. In a doorway, flat against a wall, I peeped out. The wind had stopped. The rain was no longer a driving deluge, but a steady downpouring of small drops. Couffignal's main street, to my senses, was a deserted street.

I wondered if the retreat to the boat had already started. On the sidewalk, walking swiftly toward the bank, I heard the answer to that guess.

High up on the slope, almost up to the edge of the cliff by the sound, a machine gun began to hurl out its stream of bullets.

Mixed with the racket of the machine gun were the sounds of smaller arms, and a grenade or two.

At the first crossing, I left the main street and began to run up the hill. Men were running toward me. Two of them passed, paying no attention to my shouted "What's up now?"

The third man stopped because I grabbed him—a fat man whose breath bubbled, and whose face was fishbelly-white.

"They've moved the car with the machine gun on it up behind us," he gasped when I had shouted my question into his ear again.

"What are you doing without a gun?" I asked.

"I—I dropped it."

"Where's General Pleshskev?"

"Back there somewhere. He's trying to capture the car, but he'll never do it. It's suicide! Why don't help come?"

Other men had passed us, running downhill, as we talked. I let the white-faced man go, and stopped four men who weren't running so fast as the others.

"What's happening now?" I questioned them.

"They's going through the houses up the hill," a sharp-featured man with a small moustache and a rifle said.

"Has anybody got word off the island yet?" I asked.

"Can't," another informed me. "They blew up the bridge first thing."

"Can't anybody swim?"

"Not in that wind. Young Catlan tried it and was lucky to get out again with a couple of broken ribs."

"The wind's gone down," I pointed out.

The sharp-featured man gave his rifle to one of the others and took off his coat. "I'll try it," he promised.

"Good! Wake up the whole country, and get word through to the San Francisco police boat and to the Mare Island Navy Yard. They'll lend a hand if you tell 'em the bandits have machine guns. Tell 'em the bandits have an armed boat waiting to leave in. It's Hendrixson's."

The volunteer swimmer left.

"A boat?" two of the men asked together.

"Yes. With a machine gun on it. If we're going to do anything, it'll have to be now, while we're between them and their getaway. Get every man and every gun you can find down there. Tackle the boat from the roofs if you can. When the bandits' car comes down there, pour it into it. You'll do better from the buildings than from the street."

The three men went on downhill. I went uphill, toward the crackling of firearms ahead. The machine gun was working irregularly. It would pour out its rat-tat-tat for a second or so, and then stop for a couple of seconds. The answering fire was thin, ragged.

I met more men, learned from them the general, with less than a dozen men, was still fighting the car. I repeated the advice I had given the other men. My informants went down to join them. I went on up.

A hundred yards farther along, what was left of the general's dozen broke out of the night, around and past me, flying downhill, with bullets hailing after them.

The road was no place for mortal man. I stumbled over two bodies, scratched myself in a dozen places getting over a hedge. On soft, wet sod I continued my uphill journey.

The machine gun on the hill stopped its clattering. The one in the boat was still at work.

The one ahead opened again, firing too high for anything near at hand to be its target. It was helping its fellow below, spraying the main street.

Before I could get closer it had stopped. I heard the car's motor racing. The car moved toward me.

Rolling into the hedge, I lay there, straining my eyes through the spaces between the stems. I had six bullets in a gun that hadn't yet been fired on this night that had seen tons of powder burned.

When I saw wheels on the lighter face of the road, I emptied my gun, holding it low.

I sprang out of my hiding-place.

The car was suddenly gone from the empty road.

There was a grinding sound. A crash. The noise of metal folding on itself. The tinkle of glass.

I raced toward those sounds.

Out of a black pile where an engine sputtered, a black figure leaped—to dash off across the soggy lawn. I cut after it, hoping that the others in the wreck were down for keeps.

I was less than fifteen feet behind the fleeing man when he cleared a hedge. I'm no sprinter, but neither was he. The wet grass made slippery going.

He stumbled while I was vaulting the hedge. When we straightened out again I was not more than ten feet behind him.

Once I clicked my gun at him, forgetting I had emptied it. Six cartridges were wrapped in a piece of paper in my vest pocket, but this was no time for loading.

I was tempted to chuck the empty gun at his head. But that was too chancy.

A building loomed ahead. My fugitive bore off to the right, to clear the corner.

To the left a heavy shotgun went off.

The running man disappeared around the house corner.

"Sweet God!" General Pleshskev's mellow voice complained. "That with a shotgun I should miss all of a man at the distance!"

"Go round the other way!" I yelled, plunging around the corner after my quarry.

His feet thudded ahead. I could not see him. The general puffed around from the other side of the house.

"You have him?"

"No."

In front of us was a stone-faced bank, on top of which ran a path. On either side of us was a high and solid hedge.

"But, my friend," the general protested. "How could he have—?"

A pale triangle showed on the path above—a triangle

that could have been a bit of shirt showing above the opening of a vest.

"Stay here and talk!" I whispered to the general, and crept forward.

"It must be that he has gone the other way," the general carried out my instructions, rambling on as if I were standing beside him, "because if he had come my way I should have seen him, and if he had raised himself over either of the hedges or the embankment, one of us would surely have seen him against . . ."

He talked on and on while I gained the shelter of the bank on which the path sat, while I found places for my toes in the rough stone facing.

The man on the road, trying to make himself small with his back in a bush, was looking at the talking general. He saw me when I had my feet on the path.

He jumped, and one hand went up.

I jumped, with both hands out.

A stone, turning under my foot, threw me sidewise, twisting my ankle, but saving my head from the bullet he sent at it.

My outflung left arm caught his legs as I spilled down. He came over on top of me. I kicked him once, caught his gun arm, and had just decided to bite it when the general puffed up over the edge of the path and prodded the man off me with the muzzle of the shotgun.

When it came my turn to stand up, I found it not so good. My twisted ankle didn't like to support its share of my hundred and eighty-some pounds. Putting most of my weight on the other leg, I turned my flashlight on the prisoner.

"Hello, Flippo!" I exclaimed.

"Hello!" he said without joy in the recognition.

He was a roly-poly Italian youth of twenty-three or -four. I had helped send him to San Quentin four years ago for his part in a payroll stick-up. He had been out on parole for several months now.

"The prison board isn't going to like this," I told him.

"You got me wrong," he pleaded. "I ain't been doing a thing. I was up here to see some friends. And when this thing busted loose I had to hide, because I got a record, and if I'm picked up I'll be railroaded for it. And now you got me, and you think I'm in on it!"

"You're a mind reader," I assured him, and asked the general, "Where can we pack this bird away for a while, under lock and key?"

"In my house there is a lumber room with a strong door and not a window."

"That'll do it. March, Flippo!"

General Pleshskev collared the youth, while I limped along behind them, examining Flippo's gun, which was loaded except for the one shot he had fired at me, and reloading my own.

We had caught our prisoner on the Russian's grounds, so we didn't have far to go.

The general knocked on the door and called out something in his language. Bolts clicked and grated, and the door was swung open by a heavily moustached Russian servant. Behind him the princess and a stalwart older woman stood.

We went in while the general was telling his household about the capture, and took the captive up to the lumber room. I frisked him for his pocketknife and matches—he had nothing else that could help him get out—locked him in and braced the door solidly with a length of board. Then we went downstairs again.

"You are injured!" the princess cried, seeing me limp across the floor.

"Only a twisted ankle," I said. "But it does bother me some. Is there any adhesive tape around?"

"Yes," and she spoke to the moustached servant, who went out of the room and presently returned, carrying rolls of gauze and tape and a basin of steaming water.

"If you'll sit down," the princess said, taking these things from the servant.

But I shook my head and reached for the adhesive tape. "I want cold water, because I've got to go out in the wet again. If you'll show me the bathroom, I can fix myself up in no time."

We had to argue about that, but I finally got to the bathroom, where I ran cold water on my foot and ankle, and strapped it with adhesive tape, as tight as I could without stopping the circulation altogether. Getting my wet shoe on again was a job, but when I was through I had two firm legs under me, even if one of them did hurt some.

When I rejoined the others I noticed that sounds of firing no longer came up the hill, and that the patter of rain was lighter, and a gray streak of coming daylight showed under a drawn blind.

I was buttoning my slicker when the knocker rang on the front door. Russian words came through, and the young Russian I had met on the beach came in.

"Aleksandr, you're—" The stalwart older woman screamed, when she saw the blood on his cheek, and fainted.

He paid no attention to her at all, as if he was used to having her faint.

"They've gone in the boat," he told me while the girl and two men servants gathered up the woman and laid her on an ottoman.

"How many?" I asked.

"I counted ten, and I don't think I missed more than one or two, if any."

"The men I sent down there couldn't stop them?"

He shrugged. "What would you do? It takes a strong stomach to face a machine gun. Your men had been cleared out of the buildings almost before they arrived."

The woman who had fainted had revived by now and was pouring anxious questions in Russian at the lad. The princess was getting into her blue cape. The woman stopped questioning the lad and asked her something.

"It's all over," the princess said. "I am going to view the ruins."

That suggestion appealed to everybody. Five minutes later all of us, including the servants, were on our way downhill, hurrying along in the drizzle that was very gentle now, their faces tired and excited in the bleak morning light.

Halfway down, a woman ran out of a cross-path and began to tell me something. I recognized her as one of Hendrixson's maids.

I caught some of her words.

"Presents gone ... Mr. Brophy murdered ... Oliver ..."

"I'll be down later," I told the others, and set out after the maid.

She was running back to the Hendrixson house. I couldn't run, couldn't even walk fast. She and Hendrixson and more of his servants were standing on the front porch when I arrived.

"They killed Oliver and Brophy," the old man said.

"How?"

"We were in the back of the house, the rear second story, watching the flashes of the shooting down in the village. Oliver was down here, just inside the front door, and Brophy in the room with the presents. We heard a shot in there, and immediately a man appeared in the doorway of our room, threatening us with two pistols, making us stay there for perhaps ten minutes. Then he shut and locked the door and went away. We broke the door down—and found Brophy and Oliver dead."

"Let's look at them."

The chauffeur was just inside the front door. He lay on his back, with his brown throat cut straight across the front, almost back to the vertebrae. His rifle was under him. I pulled it out and examined it. It had not been fired.

Upstairs, the butler Brophy was huddled against a leg of one of the tables on which the presents had been spread. His gun was gone. I turned him over, straightened him out, and found a bullet hole in his chest. Around the hole his coat was charred in a large area.

Most of the presents were still there. But the valuable

pieces were gone. The others were in disorder, lying around any which way, their covers pulled off.

"What did the one you saw look like?" I asked.

"I didn't see him very well," Hendrixson said. "There was no light in our room. He was simply a dark figure against the candle burning in the hall. A large man in a black rubber raincoat, with some sort of black mask that covered his whole head and face, with small eyeholes."

"No hat?"

"No, just the mask over his entire face and head."

As we went downstairs again I gave Hendrixson a brief account of what I had seen and heard and done since I had left them. There wasn't enough of it to make a long tale.

"Do you think you can get information about the others from the one you caught?" he asked, as I prepared to go out.

"No. But I expect to bag them just the same."

Couffignal's main street was jammed with people when I limped into it again. A detachment of marines from Mare Island was there, and men from a San Francisco police boat. Excited citizens in all degrees of partial nakedness boiled around them. A hundred voices were talking at once, re-counting their personal adventures and braveries and losses and what they had seen. Such words as "machine gun," "bomb," "bandit," "car," "shot," "dynamite," and "killed" sounded again and again, in every variety of voice and tone.

The bank had been completely wrecked by the charge that had blown the vault. The jewelry store was another ruin. A grocer's across the street was serving as a field hospital. Two doctors were there, patching up damaged villagers.

I recognized a familiar face under a uniform cap—Sergeant Roche of the harbor police—and pushed through the crowd to him.

"Just get here?" he asked as we shook hands. "Or were you in on it?"

"In on it."

"What do you know?"

"Everything."

"Who ever heard of a private detective that didn't," he joshed as I led him out of the mob.

"Did you people run into an empty boat out in the bay?" I asked when we were away from audiences.

"Empty boats have been floating around the bay all night," he said.

I hadn't thought of that.

"Where's your boat now?" I asked him.

"Out trying to pick up the bandits. I stayed with a couple of men to lend a hand here."

"You're in luck," I told him. "Now sneak a look across the street. See the stout old boy with the black whiskers, standing in front of the druggist's?"

General Pleshskev stood there, with the woman who had fainted, the young Russian whose bloody cheek had made her faint, and a pale, plump man of forty-something who had been with them at the reception. A little to one side stood big Ignati, the two menservants I had seen at the house, and another who was obviously one of them. They were chatting together and watching the excited antics of a red-faced property owner who was telling a curt lieutenant of marines that it was his own personal private automobile that the bandits had stolen to mount their machine gun on, and what he thought should be done about it.

"Yes," said Roche, "I see your fellow with the whiskers."

"Well, he's your meat. The woman and two men with him are also your meat. And those four Russians standing to the left are some more of it. There's another missing, but I'll take care of that one. Pass the word to the lieutenant, and you can round up those babies without giving them a chance to fight back. They think they're safe as angels."

"Sure, are you?" the sergeant asked.

"Don't be silly!" I growled, as if I had never made a mistake in my life.

I had been standing on my one good prop. When I put my weight on the other to turn away from the sergeant, it stung me all the way to the hip. I pushed my back teeth together and began to work painfully through the crowd to the other side of the street.

The princess didn't seem to be among those present. My idea was that, next to the general, she was the most important member of the push. If she was at their house, and not yet suspicious, I figured I could get close enough to yank her in without a riot.

Walking was hell. My temperature rose. Sweat rolled out on me.

"Mister, they didn't none of 'em come down that way."

The one-legged newsboy was standing at my elbow. I greeted him as if he were my paycheck.

"Come on with me," I said, taking his arm. "You did fine down there, and now I want you to do something else for me."

Half a block from the main street I led him up on the porch of a small yellow cottage. The front door stood open, left that way when the occupants ran down to welcome police and marines, no doubt. Just inside the door, beside a hall rack, was a wicker porch chair. I committed unlawful entry to the extent of dragging that chair out on the porch.

"Sit down, son," I urged the boy.

He sat, looking up at me with puzzled freckled face. I took a firm grip on his crutch and pulled it out of his hand.

"Here's five bucks for rental," I said, "and if I lose it I'll buy you one of ivory and gold."

And I put the crutch under my arm and began to propel myself up the hill.

It was my first experience with a crutch. I didn't break any records. But it was a lot better than tottering along on an unassisted bum ankle.

The hill was longer and steeper than some mountains I've seen, but the gravel walk to the Russians' house was finally under my feet.

I was still some dozen feet from the porch when Princess Zhukovski opened the door.

"Oh!" she exclaimed, and then, recovering from her

surprise, "your ankle is worse!" She ran down the steps to help me climb them. As she came I noticed that something heavy was sagging and swinging in the right-hand pocket of her gray flannel jacket.

With one hand under my elbow, the other arm across my back, she helped me up the steps and across the porch. That assured me she didn't think I had tumbled to the game. If she had, she wouldn't have trusted herself within reach of my hands. Why, I wondered, had she come back to the house after starting downhill with the others?

While I was wondering we went into the house, where she planted me in a large and soft leather chair.

"You must certainly be starving after your strenuous night," she said. "I will see if—"

"No, sit down." I nodded at a chair facing mine. "I want to talk to you."

She sat down, clasping her slender white hands in her lap. In neither face nor pose was there any sign of nervousness, not even of curiosity. And that was overdoing it.

"Where have you cached the plunder?" I asked.

The whiteness of her face was nothing to go by. It had been white as marble since I had first seen her. The darkness of her eyes was as natural. Nothing happened to her other features. Her voice was smoothly cool.

"I am sorry," she said. "The question doesn't convey anything to me."

"Here's the point," I explained. "I'm charging you with complicity in the gutting of Couffignal, and in the murders that went with it. And I'm asking you where the loot has been hidden."

Slowly she stood up, raised her chin, and looked at least a mile down at me.

"How dare you? How dare you speak so to me, a Zhukovski!"

"I don't care if you're one of the Smith Brothers!" Leaning forward, I had pushed my twisted ankle against a leg of the chair, and the resulting agony didn't improve my disposition. "For the purpose of this talk you are a thief and a murderer."

Her strong slender body became the body of a lean crouching animal. Her white face became the face of an enraged animal. One hand—claw now—swept to the heavy pocket of her jacket.

Then, before I could have batted an eye—though my life seemed to depend on my not batting it—the wild animal had vanished. Out of it—and now I know where the writers of the old fairy stories got their ideas—rose the princess again, cool and straight and tall.

She sat down, crossed her ankles, put an elbow on an arm of her chair, propped her chin on the back of that hand, and looked curiously into my face.

"However," she murmured, "did you chance to arrive at so strange and fanciful a theory?"

"It wasn't chance, and it's neither strange nor fanciful," I said. "Maybe it'll save time and trouble if I show you part of the score against you. Then you'll know how you stand and won't waste your brains pleading innocence."

"I shall be grateful," she smiled, "very!"

I tucked my crutch in between one knee and the arm of my chair, so my hands would be free to check off my points on my fingers.

"First—whoever planned the job knew the island—not fairly well, but every inch of it. There's no need to argue about that. Second—the car on which the machine gun was mounted was local property, stolen from the owner here. So was the boat in which the bandits were supposed to have escaped. Bandits from the outside would have needed a car or a boat to bring their machine guns, explosives, and grenades here, and there doesn't seem to be any reason why they shouldn't have used that car or boat instead of stealing a fresh one. Third—there wasn't the least hint of the professional bandit touch on this job. If you ask me, it was a military job from beginning to end. And the worst safe-burglar in the world could have got into both the bank vault and the jeweler's safe without wrecking the buildings. Fourth—bandits from the outside wouldn't have destroyed the bridge. They might have blocked it, but they wouldn't have destroyed it. They'd have saved it in case they had to make their getaway in that direction. Fifth—bandits figuring on a getaway by boat would have cut the job short, wouldn't have spread it over the whole night. Enough racket was made here to wake up California all the way from Sacramento to Los Angeles. What you people did was to send one man out in the boat, shooting, and he didn't go far. As soon as he was at a safe distance, he went overboard, and swam back to the island. Big Ignati could have done it without turning a hair."

That exhausted my right hand. I switched over, counting on my left.

"Sixth—I met one of your party, the lad, down on the beach, and he was coming from the boat. He suggested that we jump it. We were shot at, but the man behind the gun was playing with us. He could have wiped us out in a second if he had been in earnest, but he shot over our heads. Seventh—that same lad is the only man on the island, so far as I know, who saw the departing bandits. Eighth—all of your people that I ran into were especially nice to me, the general even spending an hour talking to me at the reception this afternoon. That's a distinctive amateur crook trait. Ninth—after the machine gun car had been wrecked I chased its occupant. I lost him around this house. The Italian boy I picked up wasn't him. He couldn't have climbed up on the path without my seeing him. But he could have run around to the general's side of the house and vanished indoors there. The general liked him, and would have helped him. I know that, because the general performed a downright miracle by missing him at some six feet with a shotgun. Tenth—you called at Hendrixson's house for no other purpose than to get me away from there."

That finished the left hand. I went back to the right.

"Eleventh—Hendrixson's two servants were killed by someone they knew and trusted. Both were killed at close quarters and without firing a shot. I'd say you got Oliver to let you into the house, and were talking to him when one of your men cut his throat from behind. Then you went upstairs and probably shot the unsuspecting Brophy yourself. He wouldn't have been on his guard against you. Twelfth—but that ought to be enough, and I'm getting a sore throat from listing them."

She took her chin off her hand, took a fat white cigarette out of a think black case, and held it in her mouth while I put a match to the end of it. She took a long pull at it—a draw that accounted for a third of its length—and blew the smoke down at her knees.

"That would be enough," she said when all these things had been done, "if it were not that you yourself know it was impossible for us to have been so engaged. Did you not see us—did not everyone see us—time and time again?"

"That's easy!" I argued. "With a couple of machine guns, a trunkful of grenades, knowing the island from top to bottom, in the darkness and in a storm, against bewildered civilians—it was duck soup. There are nine of you that I know of, including two women. Any five of you could have carried on the work, once it was started, while the others took turns appearing here and there, establishing alibis. And that is what you did. You took turns slipping out to alibi yourselves. Everywhere I went I ran into one of you. And the general! That whiskered old joker running around leading the simple citizens to battle! I'll bet he led 'em plenty! They're lucky there are any of 'em alive this morning!"

She finished her cigarette with another inhalation, dropped the stub on the rug, ground out the light with one foot, sighed wearily, put her hands on her hips, and asked, "And now what?"

"Now I want to know where you have stowed the plunder."

The readiness of her answer surprised me.

"Under the garage, in a cellar we secretly dug there some months ago."

I didn't believe that, of course, but it turned out to be the truth.

I didn't have anything else to say. When I fumbled with my borrowed crutch, preparing to get up, she raised a hand and spoke gently. "Wait a moment, please. I have something to suggest."

Half-standing, I leaned toward her, stretching out one hand until it was close to her side.

"I want the gun," I said.

She nodded, and sat still while I plucked it from her pocket, put it in one of my own, and sat down again.

"You said a little while ago that you didn't care who I was," she began immediately. "But I want you to know. There are so many of us Russians who once were somebodies and who now are nobodies that I won't bore you with the repetition of a tale the world has grown tired of hearing. But you must remember that this weary tale is real to us who are its subjects. However, we fled from Russia with what we could carry of our property, which fortunately was enough to keep us in bearable comfort for a few years.

"In London we opened a Russian restaurant, but London was suddenly full of Russian restaurants, and ours became, instead of a means of livelihood, a source of loss. We tried teaching music and languages, and so on. In short, we hit on all the means of earning our living that other Russian exiles hit upon, and so always found ourselves in overcrowded, and thus unprofitable, fields. But what else did we know—could we do?

"I promised not to bore you. Well, always our capital shrank, and always the day approached on which we should be shabby and hungry, the day when we should become familiar to readers of your Sunday papers—charwomen who had been princesses, dukes who now were butlers. There was no place for us in the world. Outcasts easily become outlaws. Why not? Could it be said that we owed the world any fealty? Had not the world sat idly by and seen us despoiled of place and property and country?

"We planned it before we had heard of Couffignal. We could find a small settlement of the wealthy, sufficiently isolated, and, after establishing ourselves there, we would plunder it. Couffignal, when we found it, seemed to be the ideal place. We leased this house for six months, having just enough capital remaining to do that and to live properly here while our plans matured. Here we spent four months establishing ourselves, collecting our arms and our explosives, mapping our offensive, waiting for a favorable night. Last night seemed to be that night, and we had provided, we thought, against every eventuality. But we had not, of course, provided against your presence and your genius. They were simply others of the unforeseen misfortunes to which we seem eternally condemned."

She stopped, and fell to studying me with mournful large eyes that made me feel like fidgeting.

"It's no good calling me a genius," I objected. "The truth is you people botched your job from beginning to end. Your general would get a big laugh out of a man without military training who tried to lead an army. But here are you people with absolutely no criminal experience trying to swing a trick that needed the highest sort of criminal skill. Look at how you all played around with me! Amateur stuff! A professional crook with any intelligence would have either let me alone or knocked me off. No wonder you flopped! As for the rest of it—your troubles—I can't do anything about them."

"Why?" very softly. "Why can't you?"

"Why should I?" I made it blunt.

"No one else knows what you know." She bent forward to put a white hand on my knee. "There is wealth in that cellar beneath the garage. You may have whatever you ask."

I shook my head.

"You aren't a fool!" she protested. "You know—"

"Let me straighten this out for you," I interrupted. "We'll disregard whatever honesty I happen to have, sense of loyalty to employers, and so on. You might doubt them, so we'll throw them out. Now I'm a detective because I happen to like the work. It pays me a fair salary, but I could find other jobs that would pay more. Even a hundred dollars a month would be twelve hundred a year. Say twenty-five or thirty thousand dollars in the years between now and my sixtieth birthday.

"Now I pass up about twenty-five or thirty thousand of honest gain because I like being a detective, like the work. And liking work makes you want to do it as well as you can. Otherwise there'd be no sense to it. That's the fix I am in. I don't know anything else, don't enjoy anything else, don't want to know or enjoy anything else. You can't weight that against any sum of money. Money is good stuff. I haven't anything against it. But in the past eighteen years I've been getting my fun out of chasing crooks and tackling puzzles, my satisfaction out of catching crooks and solving riddles. It's the only kind of sport I know anything about, and I can't imagine a pleasanter future than twenty-some years more of it. I'm not going to blow that up!"

She shook her head slowly, lowering it, so that now her dark eyes looked up at me under the thin arcs of her brows.

"You speak only of money," she said. "I said you may have whatever you ask."

That was out. I don't know where these women get their ideas.

"You're still all twisted up," I said brusquely, standing now and adjusting my borrowed crutch. "You think I'm a man and you're a woman. That's wrong. I'm a man hunter and you're something that has been running in front of me. There's nothing human about it. You might just as well expect a hound to play tiddledywinks with the fox he's caught. We're wasting time anyway. I've been thinking the police or marines might come up here and save me a walk. You've been waiting for your mob to come back and grab me. I could have told you they were being arrested when I left them."

That shook her. She had stood up. Now she fell back a

step, putting a hand behind her for steadiness, on her chair. An exclamation I didn't understand popped out of her mouth. Russian, I thought, but the next moment I knew it had been Italian.

"Put your hand up." It was Flippo's husky voice. Flippo stood in the doorway, holding an automatic.

I raised my hands as high as I could without dropping my supporting crutch, meanwhile cursing myself for having been too careless, or too vain, to keep a gun in my hand while I talked to the girl.

So this was why she had come back to the house. If she freed the Italian, she had thought, we would have no reason for suspecting that he hadn't been in on the robbery, and so we would look for the bandits among his friends. A prisoner, of course, he might have persuaded us of his innocence. She had given him the gun so he could either shoot his way clear, or, what would help her as much, get himself killed trying.

While I was arranging these thoughts in my head, Flippo had come up behind me. His empty hand passed over my body, taking away my own gun, his, and the one I had taken from the girl.

"A bargain, Flippo," I said when he had moved away from me, a little to one side, where he made one corner of a triangle whose other corners were the girl and I. "You're out on parole, with some years still to be served. I picked you up with a gun on you. That's plenty to send you back to the big house. I know you weren't in on this job. My idea is that you were up here on a smaller one of your own, but I can't prove that and don't want to. Walk out of here, alone and neutral, and I'll forget I saw you."

Little thoughtful lines grooved the boy's round, dark face.

The princess took a step toward him.

"You heard the offer I just now made him?" she asked. "Well, I make that offer to you, if you will kill him."

"There's your choice, Flippo," I summed up for him. "All I can give you is freedom from San Quentin. The princess can give you a fat cut of the profits in a busted caper, with a good chance to get yourself hanged."

The girl, remembering her advantage over me, went at him hot and heavy in Italian, a language in which I know only four words. Two of them are profane and the other two obscene. I said all four.

The boy was weakening. If he had been ten years older, he'd have taken my offer and thanked me for it. But he was young and she—now that I thought of it—was beautiful. The answer wasn't hard to guess.

"But not to bump him off," he said to her in English, for my benefit. "We'll lock him up in there where I was at."

I suspected Flippo hadn't any great prejudice against murder. It was just that he thought this one unnecessary, unless he was kidding me to make the killing easier.

The girl wasn't satisfied with his suggestion. She poured more hot Italian at him. Her game looked surefire, but it had a flaw. She couldn't persuade him that his chances of getting any of the loot away were good. She had to depend on her charms to swing him. And that meant she had to hold his eye.

He wasn't far from me.

She came close to him. She was singing, chanting, crooning Italian syllables into his round face.

She had him.

He shrugged. His whole face said yes. He turned—

I knocked him on the noodle with my borrowed crutch.

The crutch splintered apart. Flippo's knees bent. He stretched up to his full height. He fell on his face on the floor. He lay there, dead-still, except for a thin worm of blood that crawled out of his hair to the rug.

A step, a tumble, a foot or so of hand-and-knee scrambling put me within reach of Flippo's gun.

The girl, jumping out of my path, was halfway to the door when I sat up with the gun in my hand.

"Stop!" I ordered.

"I shan't," she said, but she did, for the time at least. "I am going out."

"You are going out when I take you."

She laughed, a pleasant laugh, low and confident.

"I'm going out before that," she insisted good-naturedly.

I shook my head.

"How do you propose stopping me?" she asked.

"I don't think I'll have to," I told her. "You've got too much sense to try to run while I'm holding a gun on you."

She laughed again, an amused ripple.

"I've got too much sense to stay," she corrected me. "Your crutch is broken, and you're lame. You can't catch me by running after me, then. You pretend you'll shoot me, but I don't believe you. You'd shoot me if I attacked you, of course, but I shan't do that. I shall simply walk out, and you know you won't shoot me for that. You'll wish you could, but you won't. You'll see."

Her face turned over her shoulder, her dark eyes twinkling at me, she took a step toward the door.

"Better not count on that!" I threatened.

For answer to that she gave me a cooing laugh. And took another step.

"Stop, you idiot!" I bawled at her.

Her face laughed over her shoulder at me. She walked without haste to the door, her short skirt of gray flannel shaping itself to the calf of each gray-wool-stockinged leg as its mate stepped forward.

Sweat greased the gun in my hand.

When her right foot was on the doorsill, a little chuckling sound came from her throat.

"Adieu!" she said softly.

And I put a bullet in the calf of her left leg.

She sat down—plump! Utter surprise stretched her white face. It was too soon for pain.

I had never shot a woman before. I felt queer about it.

"You ought to have known I'd do it!" My voice sounded harsh and savage and like a stranger's in my ears. "Didn't I steal a crutch from a cripple?"

ACCIDENT

Agatha Christie

"And I tell you this—it's the same woman—not a doubt of it!" Captain Haydock looked into the eager, vehement face of his friend and sighed. He wished Evans would not be so positive and so jubilant. In the course of a career spent at sea, the old sea captain had learned to leave things that did not concern him well alone. His friend Evans, late CID inspector, had a different philosophy of life. "Acting on information received—" had been his motto in early days, and he had improved upon it to the extent of finding out his own information. Inspector Evans had been a very smart, wide-awake officer, and had justly earned the promotion which had been his. Even now, when he had retired from the force, and had settled down in the country cottage of his dreams, his professional instinct was still active.

"Don't often forget a face," he reiterated complacently.

"Mrs. Anthony—yes, it's Mrs. Anthony right enough. When you said Mrs. Merrowdene—I knew her at once."

Captain Haydock stirred uneasily. The Merrowdenes were his nearest neighbors, barring Evans himself, and this identifying of Mrs. Merrowdene with a former heroine of a *cause célèbre* distressed him.

"It's a long time ago," he said rather weakly.

"Nine years," said Evans, accurate as ever. "Nine years and three months. You remember the case?"

"In a vague sort of way."

"Anthony turned out to be an arsenic eater," said Evans, "so they acquitted her."

"Well, why shouldn't they?"

"No reason in the world. Only verdict they could give on the evidence. Absolutely correct."

"Then, that's all right," said Haydock. "And I don't see what we're bothering about."

"Who's bothering?"

"I thought you were."

"Not at all."

"The thing's over and done with," summed up the captain. "If Mrs. Merrowdene at one time of her life was unfortunate enough to be tried and acquitted of murder—"

"It's not usually considered unfortunate to be acquitted," put in Evans.

"You know what I mean," said Captain Haydock, irritably. "If the poor lady has been through that harrowing experience, it's no business of ours to rake it up, is it?"

Evans did not answer.

"Come now, Evans. The lady was innocent—you've just said so."

"I didn't say she was innocent. I said she was acquitted."

"It's the same thing."

"Not always."

Captain Haydock, who had commenced to tap his pipe out against the side of his chair, stopped, and sat up with a very alert expression.

"Hello-ello-ello," he said. "The wind's in that quarter, is it? You think she wasn't innocent?"

"I wouldn't say that. I just—don't know. Anthony was in the habit of taking arsenic. His wife got it for him. One day, by mistake, he takes far too much. Was the mistake his or his wife's? Nobody could tell, and the jury very properly gave her the benefit of the doubt. That's all quite right and I'm not finding fault with it. All the same—I'd like to know."

Captain Haydock transferred his attention to his pipe once more.

"Well," he said comfortably, "it's none of our business."

"I'm not so sure. . . ."

"But, surely—"

"Listen to me a minute. This man, Merrowdene—in his laboratory this evening, fiddling round with tests—you remember—"

"Yes. He mentioned Marsh's test for arsenic. Said you would know all about it—it was in your line—and chuckled. He wouldn't have said that if he'd thought for one moment—"

Evans interrupted him.

"You mean he wouldn't have said that if he knew. They've been married how long—six years, you told me? I bet you anything he has no idea his wife is the once notorious Mrs. Anthony."

"And he will certainly not know it from me," said Captain Haydock stiffly.

Evans paid no attention, but went on.

"You interrupted me just now. After Marsh's test, Merrowdene heated a substance in a test tube, the metallic residue he dissolved in water and then precipitated it by adding silver nitrate. That was a test for chlorates. A neat, unassuming little test. But I chanced to read these words in a book that stood open on the table. 'H_2SO_4 decomposes chlorates with evolution of Cl_2O_4. If heated, violent explosions occur; the mixture ought therefore to be kept cool and only very small quantities used.'"

Haydock stared at his friend. "Well, what about it?"

"Just this. In my profession we've got tests, too—tests for murder. There's adding up the facts—weighing them, dissecting the residue when you've allowed for prejudice and the general inaccuracy of witnesses. But there's another test for murder—one that is fairly accurate, but rather—dangerous! A murderer is seldom content with one crime. Give him time and a lack of suspicion and he'll commit another. You catch a man—has he murdered his wife or hasn't he?—perhaps the case isn't very black against him. Look into his past—if you find that he's had several wives—and that they've all died, shall we say, rather curiously?—then you know! I'm not speaking legally, you understand. I'm speaking of moral certainty. Once you know, you can go ahead looking for evidence."

"Well?"

"I'm coming to the point. That's all right if there is a past to look into. But suppose you catch your murderer at his or her first crime? Then that test will be one from which you get no reaction. But the prisoner acquitted—starting life under another name. Will or will not the murderer repeat the crime?"

"That's a horrible idea."

"Do you still say it's none of our business?"

"Yes, I do. You've no reason to think that Mrs. Merrowdene is anything but a perfectly innocent woman."

The ex-inspector was silent for a moment. Then he said slowly:

"I told you that we looked into her past and found nothing. That's not quite true. There was a stepfather. As a girl of eighteen she had a fancy for some young man—and her stepfather exerted his authority to keep them apart. She and her stepfather went for a walk along a rather dangerous part of the cliff. There was an accident—the stepfather went too near the edge—it gave way and he went over and was killed."

"You don't think—"

"It was an accident. Accident! Anthony's overdose of arsenic was an accident. She'd never have been tried if it hadn't transpired that there was another man—he sheered off, by the way. Looked as though he weren't satisfied even if the jury were. I tell you, Haydock, where that woman is concerned I'm afraid of another—accident!"

The old captain shrugged his shoulders.

"Well, I don't know how you're going to guard against that."

"Neither do I," said Evans ruefully.

"I should leave well enough alone," said Captain Haydock. "No good ever came of butting into other people's affairs."

But that advice was not palatable to the ex-inspector. He was a man of patience but determination. Taking leave of his friend, he sauntered down to the village, revolving in his mind the possibilities of some kind of successful action.

Turning into the post office to buy some stamps, he ran into the object of his solicitude, George Merrowdene. The ex–chemistry professor was a small, dreamy-looking man, gentle and kindly in manner, and usually completely absent-minded. He recognized the other and greeted him amicably, stooping to recover the letters that the impact had caused him to drop on the ground. Evans stooped also and, more rapid in his movements than the other, secured them first, handing them back to their owner with an apology.

He glanced down at them in doing so, and the address on the topmost suddenly awakened all his suspicions anew. It bore the name of a well-known insurance firm.

Instantly his mind was made up. The guileless George Merrowdene hardly realized how it came about that he and the ex-inspector were strolling down the village together, and still less could he have said how it came about that the conversation should come round to the subject of life insurance.

Evans had no difficulty in attaining his object. Merrowdene of his own accord volunteered the information that he had just insured his life for his wife's benefit and asked Evan's opinion of the company in question.

"I made some rather unwise investments," he explained. "As a result, my income has diminished. If anything were to happen to me, my wife would be left very badly off. This insurance will put things right."

"She didn't object to the idea?" inquired Evans casually. "Some ladies do, you know. Feel it's unlucky—that sort of thing."

"Oh, Margaret is very practical," said Merrowdene, smiling. "Not at all superstitious. In fact, I believe it was her idea originally. She didn't like my being so worried."

Evans had got the information he wanted. He left the other shortly afterwards, and his lips were set in a grim line. The late Mr. Anthony had insured his life in his wife's favor a few weeks before his death.

Accustomed to rely on his instincts, he was perfectly sure in his own mind. But how to act was another matter. He wanted, not to arrest a criminal red-handed, but to prevent a crime being committed and that was a very different and a very much more difficult thing.

All day he was very thoughtful. There was a Primrose League Fete that afternoon held in the grounds of the local squire, and he went to it, indulging in the penny dip, guessing the weight of a pig, and shying at coconuts, all with the same look of abstracted concentration on his face. He even indulged in half a crown's worth of Zara the Crystal Gazer, smiling a little to himself as he did so, remembering his own activities against fortune-tellers in his official days.

He did not pay very much heed to her singsong, droning voice till the end of a sentence held his attention.

"—and you will very shortly—very shortly indeed—be engaged on a matter of life or death—life or death to one person."

"Eh—what's that?" he asked abruptly.

"A decision—you have a decision to make. You must be very careful—very, very careful. . . . If you were to make a mistake—the smallest mistake—"

"Yes?"

The fortune-teller shivered. Inspector Evans knew it was all nonsense, but he was nevertheless impressed.

"I warn you—you must not make a mistake. If you do, I see the result clearly, a death. . . ."

Odd! A death. Fancy her lighting upon that!

"If I make a mistake a death will result? Is that it?"

"Yes."

"In that case," said Evans, rising to his feet and handing over half a crown, "I mustn't make a mistake, eh?"

He spoke lightly enough, but as he went out of the tent, his jaw set determinedly. Easy to say—not so easy to be sure of doing. He mustn't make a slip. A life, a valuable human life depended on it.

And there was no one to help him. He looked across at the figure of his friend Haydock in the distance. No help there. "Leave things alone" was Haydock's motto. And that wouldn't do here.

Haydock was talking to a woman. She moved away from him and came towards Evans, and the inspector recognized her. It was Mrs. Merrowdene. On an impulse he put himself deliberately in her path.

Mrs. Merrowdene was rather a fine-looking woman. She had a broad serene brow, very beautiful brown eyes, and a placid expression. She had the look of an Italian Madonna, which she heightened by parting her hair in the middle and looping it over her ears. She had a deep, rather sleepy voice.

She smiled up at Evans, a contented, welcoming smile.

"I thought it was you, Mrs. Anthony—I mean Mrs. Merrowdene," he said glibly.

He made the slip deliberately, watching her without seeming to do so. He saw her eyes widen, heard the quick intake of her breath. But her eyes did not falter. She gazed at him steadily and proudly.

"I was looking for my husband," she said quietly. "Have you seen him anywhere about?"

"He was over in that direction when I last saw him."

They went side by side in the direction indicated, chatting quietly and pleasantly. The inspector felt his admiration mounting. What a woman! What self-command! What wonderful poise! A remarkable woman—and a very dangerous one. He felt sure—a very dangerous one.

He still felt very uneasy, though he was satisfied with his initial step. He had let her know that he recognized her. That would put her on her guard. She would not dare attempt anything rash. There was the question of Merrowdene. If he could be warned. . . .

They found the little man absently contemplating a china doll which had fallen to his share in the penny dip. His wife suggested home and he agreed eagerly. Mrs. Merrowdene turned to the inspector.

"Won't you come back with us and have a quiet cup of tea, Mr. Evans?"

Was there a faint note of challenge in her voice? He thought there was.

"Thank you, Mrs. Merrowdene. I should like to very much."

They walked there, talking together of pleasant ordinary things. The sun shone, a breeze blew gently, everything around them was pleasant and ordinary.

Their maid was out at the fete, Mrs. Merrowdene explained, when they arrived at the charming Old World cottage. She went into her room to remove her hat, returning to set out tea and boil the kettle on a little silver lamp. From a shelf near the fireplace she took three small bowls and saucers.

"We have some very special Chinese tea," she explained. "And we always drink it in the Chinese manner—out of bowls, not cups."

She broke off, peered into a cup and exchanged it for another, with an exclamation of annoyance.

"George—it's too bad of you. You've been taking these bowls again."

"I'm sorry, dear," said the professor apologetically. "They're such a convenient size. The ones I ordered haven't come."

"One of these days you'll poison us all," said his wife with a half laugh. "Mary finds them in the laboratory and brings them back here and never troubles to wash them out unless they've something very noticeable in them. Why, you were using one of them for potassium cyanide the other day. Really, George, it's frightfully dangerous."

Merrowdene looked a little irritated.

"Mary's no business to remove things from the laboratory. She's not to touch anything there."

"But we often leave our teacups there after tea. How is she to know? Be reasonable, dear."

The professor went into his laboratory murmuring to himself, and with a smile Mrs. Merrowdene poured boiling water on the tea and blew out the flame of the little silver lamp.

Evans was puzzled. Yet a glimmering of light penetrated to him. For some reason or other, Mrs. Merrowdene was showing her hand. Was this to be the "accident"? Was she speaking of all this so as deliberately to prepare her alibi beforehand. So that when, one day, the "accident" happened, he would be forced to give evidence in her favor. Stupid of her, if so, because before that—

Suddenly he drew in his breath. She had poured the tea into the three bowls. One she set before him, one before herself, the other she placed on a little table by the fire near the chair her husband usually sat in, and it was as she placed this last one on the table that a little strange smile curved round her lips. It was the smile that did it.

He knew!

A remarkable woman—a dangerous woman. No waiting—no preparation. This afternoon—this very afternoon—with him here as witness. The boldness of it took his breath away.

It was clever—it was damnably clever. He would be able to prove nothing. She counted on his not suspecting—simply because it was "so soon." A woman of lightning rapidity of thought and action.

He drew a deep breath and leaned forward.

"Mrs. Merrowdene, I'm a man of queer whims. Will you be very kind and indulge me in one of them?"

She looked inquiring but unsuspicious.

He rose, took the bowl from in front of her and crossed to the little table where he substituted it for the other. This other he brought back and placed in front of her.

"I want to see you drink this."

Her eyes met his. They were steady, unfathomable. The color slowly drained from her face.

She stretched out her hand, raised the cup. He held his breath.

Supposing all along he had made a mistake.

She raised it to her lips—at the last moment, with a shudder she leaned forward and quickly poured it into a pot containing a fern. Then she sat back and gazed at him defiantly.

He drew a long sigh of relief, and sat down again.

"Well?" she said.

Her voice had altered. It was slightly mocking—defiant.

He answered her soberly and quietly.

"You are a very clever woman, Mrs. Merrowdene. I think you understand me. There must be no—repetition. You know what I mean?"

"I know what you mean."

Her voice was even, devoid of expression. He nodded his head, satisfied. She was a clever woman, and she didn't want to be hanged.

"To your long life and to that of your husband," he said significantly and raised his tea to his lips.

Then his face changed. It contorted horribly . . . he tried to rise—to cry out. . . . His body stiffened—his face went purple. He fell back sprawling over the chair—his limbs convulsed.

Mrs. Merrowdene leaned forward, watching him. A little smile crossed her lips. She spoke to him—very softly and gently.

"You made a mistake, Mr. Evans. You thought I wanted

to kill George. . . . How stupid of you—how very stupid."

She sat there a minute longer looking at the dead man, the third man who had threatened to cross her path and separate her from the man she loved. . . .

Her smile broadened. She looked more than ever like a Madonna. Unaware of the fate that waited her, she raised her voice and called.

"George—George. . . . Oh! do come here. I'm afraid there's been the most dreadful accident. . . . Poor Mr. Evans. . . "

RED WIND

Raymond Chandler

I

There was a desert wind blowing that night. It was one of
those hot dry Santa Anas that come down through the
mountain passes and curl your hair and make your nerves
jump and your skin itch. On nights like that every booze
party ends in a fight. Meek little wives feel the edge of the
carving knife and study their husbands' necks. Anything can
happen. You can even get a full glass of beer at a cocktail
lounge.

I was getting one in a flossy new place across the street
from the apartment house where I lived. It had been open
about a week and it wasn't doing any business. The kid
behind the bar was in his early twenties and looked as if he
had never had a drink in his life.

There was only one other customer, a souse on a bar-
stool with his back to the door. He had a pile of dimes

stacked neatly in front of him, about two dollars' worth. He was drinking straight rye in small glasses and he was all by himself in a world of his own.

I sat farther along the bar and got my glass of beer and said: "You sure cut the clouds off them, buddy. I will say that for you."

"We just opened up," the kid said. "We got to build up trade. Been in before, haven't you, mister?"

"Uh-huh."

"Live around here?"

"In the Berglund Apartments across the street," I said. "And the name is Philip Marlowe."

"Thanks, mister. Mine's Lew Petrolle." He leaned close to me across the polished dark bar. "Know that guy?"

"No."

"He ought to go home, kind of. I ought to call a taxi and send him home. He's doing his next week's drinking too soon."

"A night like this," I said. "Let him alone."

"It's not good for him," the kid said, scowling at me.

"Rye!" the drunk croaked, without looking up. He snapped his fingers so as not to disturb his piles of dimes by banging on the bar.

The kid looked at me and shrugged. "Should I?"

"Whose stomach is it? Not mine."

The kid poured him another straight rye and I think he doctored it with water down behind the bar because when he came up with it he looked as guilty as if he'd kicked his grandmother. The drunk paid no attention. He lifted coins off his pile with the exact care of a crack surgeon operating on a brain tumor.

The kid came back and put more beer in my glass. Outside the wind howled. Every once in a while it blew the stained-glass door open a few inches. It was a heavy door.

The kid said: "I don't like drunks in the first place and in the second place I don't like them getting drunk in here, and in the third place I don't like them in the first place."

"Warner Brothers could use that," I said.

"They did."

Just then we had another customer. A car squeaked to a stop outside and the swinging door came open. A fellow came in who looked a little in a hurry. He held the door and ranged the place quickly with flat, shiny, dark eyes. He was well set up, dark, good-looking in a narrow-faced, tight-lipped way. His clothes were dark and a white handkerchief peeped coyly from his pocket and he looked cool as well as under a tension of some sort. I guessed it was the hot wind. I felt a bit the same myself only not cool.

He looked at the drunk's back. The drunk was playing checkers with his empty glasses. The new customer looked at me, then he looked along the line of half-booths at the other side of the place. They were all empty. He came on in—down past where the drunk sat swaying and muttering to himself—and spoke to the bar kid.

"Seen a lady in here, buddy? Tall, pretty, brown hair, in a print bolero jacket over a blue crepe silk dress. Wearing a wide-brimmed straw hat with a velvet band." He had a tight voice I didn't like.

"No, sir. Nobody like that's been in," the bar kid said.

"Thanks. Straight Scotch. Make it fast, will you?"

The kid gave it to him and the fellow paid and put the drink down in a gulp and started to go out. He took three or four steps and stopped, facing the drunk. The drunk was grinning. He swept a gun from somewhere so fast that it was just a blur coming out. He held it steady and he didn't look any drunker than I was. The tall dark guy stood quite still and then his head jerked back a little and then he was still again.

A car tore by outside. The drunk's gun was a .22 target automatic, with a large front sight. It made a couple of hard snaps and a little smoke curled—very little.

"So long, Waldo," the drunk said.

Then he put the gun on the barman and me.

The dark guy took a week to fall down. He stumbled,

caught himself, waved one arm, stumbled again. His hat fell off, and then he hit the floor with his face. After he hit it he might have been poured concrete for all the fuss he made.

The drunk slid down off the stool and scooped his dimes into a pocket and slid toward the door. He turned sideways, holding the gun across his body. I didn't have a gun. I hadn't thought I needed one to buy a glass of beer. The kid behind the bar didn't move or make the slightest sound.

The drunk felt the door lightly with his shoulder, keeping his eyes on us, then pushed through it backward. When it was wide a hard gust of air slammed in and lifted the hair of the man on the floor. The drunk said: "Poor Waldo. I bet I made his nose bleed."

The door swung shut. I started to rush it—from long practice in doing the wrong thing. In this case it didn't matter. The car outside let out a roar and when I got onto the sidewalk it was flicking a red smear of taillight around the nearby corner. I got its license number the way I got my first million.

There were people and cars up and down the block as usual. Nobody acted as if a gun had gone off. The wind was making enough noise to make the hard quick rap of .22 ammunition sound like a slammed door, even if anyone heard it. I went back into the cocktail bar.

The kid hadn't moved, even yet. He just stood with his hands flat on the bar, leaning over a little and looking down at the dark guy's back. The dark guy hadn't moved either. I bent down and felt his neck artery. He wouldn't move— ever.

The kid's face had as much expression as a cut of round steak and was about the same color. His eyes were more angry than shocked.

I lit a cigarette and blew smoke at the ceiling and said shortly: "Get on the phone."

"Maybe he's not dead," the kid said.

"When they use a twenty-two that means they don't make mistakes. Where's the phone?"

"I don't have one. I got enough expenses without that. Boy, can I kick eight hundred bucks in the face!"

"You own this place?"

"I did till this happened."

He pulled his white coat off and his apron and came around the inner end of the bar. "I'm locking this door," he said, taking keys out.

He went out, swung the door to and juggled the lock from the outside until the bolt clicked into place. I bent down and rolled Waldo over. At first I couldn't even see where the shots went in. Then I could. A couple of tiny holes in his coat, over his heart. There was a little blood on his shirt.

The drunk was everything you could ask—as a killer.

The prowl-car boys came in about eight minutes. The kid, Lew Petrolle, was back behind the bar by then. He had his white coat on again and he was counting his money in the register and putting it in his pocket and making notes in a little book.

I sat at the edge of one of the half-booths and smoked cigarettes and watched Waldo's face get deader and deader. I wondered who the girl in the print coat was, why Waldo had left the engine of his car running outside, why he was in a hurry, whether the drunk had been waiting for him or just happened to be there.

The prowl-car boys came in perspiring. They were the usual large size and one of them had a flower stuck under his cap and his cap on a bit crooked. When he saw the dead man he got rid of the flower and leaned down to feel Waldo's pulse.

"Seems to be dead," he said, and rolled him around a little more. "Oh, yeah, I see where they went in. Nice clean work. You two see him get it?"

I said yes. The kid behind the bar said nothing. I told them about it, that the killer seemed to have left in Waldo's car.

The cop yanked Waldo's wallet out, went through it

rapidly and whistled. "Plenty of jack and no driver's license." He put the wallet away. "Okay, we didn't touch him, see? Just a chance we could find did he have a car and put it on the air."

"The hell you didn't touch him," Lew Petrolle said.

The cop gave him one of those looks. "Okay, pal," he said softly. "We touched him."

The kid picked up a clean highball glass and began to polish it. He polished it all the rest of the time we were there.

In another minute a homicide fast-wagon sirened up and screeched to a stop outside the door and four men came in, two dicks, a photographer and a laboratory man. I didn't know either of the dicks. You can be in the detecting business a long time and not know all the men on a big-city force.

One of them was a short, smooth, dark, quiet, smiling man, with curly black hair and soft intelligent eyes. The other was big, rawboned, long-jawed, with a veined nose and glassy eyes. He looked like a heavy drinker. He looked tough, but he looked as if he thought he was a little tougher than he was. He shooed me into the last booth against the wall and his partner got the kid up front and the bluecoats went out. The fingerprint man and photographer set about their work.

A medical examiner came, stayed just long enough to get sore because there was no phone for him to call the morgue wagon.

The short dick emptied Waldo's pockets and then emptied his wallet and dumped everything into a large handkerchief on a booth table. I saw a lot of currency, keys, cigarettes, another handkerchief, very little else.

The big dick pushed me back into the end of the half-booth. "Give," he said. "I'm Copernik, Detective Lieutenant."

I put my wallet in front of him. He looked at it, went through it, tossed it back, made a note in a book.

"Philip Marlowe, huh? A shamus. You here on business?"

"Drinking business," I said. "I live just across the street in the Berglund."

"Know this kid up front?"

"I've been in here once since he opened up."

"See anything funny about him now?"

"No."

"Takes it too light for a young fellow, don't he? Never mind answering. Just tell the story."

I told it—three times. Once for him to get the outline, once for him to get the details and once for him to see if I had it too pat. At the end he said: "This dame interests me. And the killer called the guy Waldo, yet didn't seem to be anyways sure he would be in. I mean, if Waldo wasn't sure the dame would be here, nobody could be sure Waldo would be here."

"That's pretty deep," I said.

He studied me. I wasn't smiling. "Sounds like a grudge job, don't it? Don't sound planned. No getaway except by accident. A guy don't leave his car unlocked much in this town. And the killer works in front of two good witnesses. I don't like that."

"I don't like being a witness," I said. "The pay's too low."

He grinned. His teeth had a freckled look. "Was the killer drunk really?"

"With that shooting? No."

"Me too. Well, it's a simple job. The guy will have a record and he's left plenty prints. Even if we don't have his mug here we'll make him in hours. He had something on Waldo, but he wasn't meeting Waldo tonight. Waldo just dropped in to ask about a dame he had a date with and had missed connections on. It's a hot night and this wind would kill a girl's face. She'd be apt to drop in somewhere to wait. So the killer feeds Waldo two in the right place and scrams and don't worry about you boys at all. It's that simple."

"Yeah," I said.

"It's so simple it stinks," Copernik said.

He took his felt hat off and tousled up his ratty blond hair and leaned his head on his hands. He had a long mean horse face. He got a handkerchief out and mopped it, and the back of his neck and the back of his hands. He got a comb out and combed his hair—he looked worse with it combed —and put his hat back on.

"I was just thinking," I said.

"Yeah? What?"

"This Waldo knew just how the girl was dressed. So he must already have been with her tonight."

"So what? Maybe he had to go to the can. And when he came back she's gone. Maybe she changed her mind about him."

"That's right," I said.

But that wasn't what I was thinking at all. I was thinking that Waldo had described the girl's clothes in a way the ordinary man wouldn't know how to describe them. Printed bolero jacket over blue crepe silk dress. I didn't even know what a bolero jacket was. And I might have said blue dress or even blue silk dress, but never blue crepe silk dress.

After a while two men came with a basket. Lew Petrolle was still polishing his glass and talking to the short dark dick.

We all went down to headquarters.

Lew Petrolle was all right when they checked on him. His father had a grape ranch near Antioch in Contra Costa County. He had given Lew a thousand dollars to go into business and Lew had opened the cocktail bar, neon sign and all, on eight hundred flat.

They let him go and told him to keep the bar closed until they were sure they didn't want to do any more printing. He shook hands all around and grinned and said he guessed the killing would be good for business after all, because nobody believed a newspaper account of anything and people would come to him for the story and buy drinks while he was telling it.

"There's a guy won't ever do any worrying," Copernik said, when he was gone. "Over anybody else."

"Poor Waldo," I said. "The prints any good?"

"Kind of smudged," Copernik said sourly. "But we'll get a classification and teletype it to Washington some time tonight. If it don't click, you'll be in for a day on the steel picture racks downstairs."

I shook hands with him and his partner, whose name was Ybarra, and left. They didn't know who Waldo was yet either. Nothing in his pockets told.

II

I got back to my street about 9 P.M. I looked up and down the block before I went into the Berglund. The cocktail bar was farther down on the other side, dark, with a nose or two against the glass, but no real crowd. People had seen the law and the morgue wagon, but they didn't know what had happened. Except the boys playing pinball games in the drugstore on the corner. They know everything, except how to hold a job.

The wind was still blowing, oven-hot, swirling dust and torn paper up against the walls.

I went into the lobby of the apartment house and rode the automatic elevator up to the fourth floor. I unwound the doors and stepped out and there was a tall girl standing there waiting for the car.

She had brown wavey hair under a wide-brimmed straw hat with a velvet band and loose bow. She had wide blue eyes and eyelashes that didn't quite reach her chin. She wore a blue dress that might have been crepe silk, simple in lines but not missing any curves. Over it she wore what might have been a print bolero jacket.

I said: "Is that a bolero jacket?"

She gave me a distant glance and made a motion as if to brush a cobweb out of the way.

"Yes. Would you mind—I'm rather in a hurry. I'd like—"

I didn't move. I blocked her off from the elevator. We stared at each other and she flushed very slowly.

"Better not go out on the street in those clothes," I said.

"Why, how dare you—"

The elevator clanked and started down again. I didn't know what she was going to say. Her voice lacked the edgy twang of a beer parlor frill. It had a soft light sound, like spring rain.

"It's not a make," I said. "You're in trouble. If they come to this floor in the elevator, you have just that much time to get off the hall. First take off the hat and jacket—and snap it up!"

She didn't move. Her face seemed to whiten a little behind the not-too-heavy makeup.

"Cops," I said, "are looking for you. In those clothes. Give me the chance and I'll tell you why."

She turned her head swiftly and looked back along the corridor. With her looks I didn't blame her for trying one more bluff.

"You're impertinent, whoever you are. I'm Mrs. Leroy in Apartment Thirty-one. I can assure—"

"That you're on the wrong floor," I said. "This is the fourth." The elevator had stopped down below. The sound of doors being wrenched open came up the shaft.

"Off!" I rapped. "Now!"

She switched her hat off and slipped out of the bolero jacket, fast. I grabbed them and wadded them into a mess under my arm. I took her elbow and turned her and we were going down the hall.

"I live in Forty-two. The front one across from yours, just a floor up. Take your choice. Once again—I'm not on the make."

She smoothed her hair with that quick gesture, like a bird preening itself. Ten thousand years of practice behind it.

"Mine," she said, and tucked her bag under her arm and strode down the hall fast. The elevator stopped at the floor below. She stopped when it stopped. She turned and faced me.

"The stairs are back by the elevator shaft," I said gently.

"I don't have an apartment," she said.

"I didn't think you had."

"Are they searching for me?"

"Yes, but they won't start gouging the block stone by stone before tomorrow. And then only if they don't make Waldo."

She stared at me. "Waldo?"

"Oh, you don't know Waldo," I said.

She shook her head slowly. The elevator started down in the shaft again. Panic flicked in her blue eyes like a ripple on water.

"No," she said breathlessly, "but take me out of this hall."

We were almost at my door. I jammed the key in and shook the lock around and heaved the door inward. I reached in far enough to switch lights on. She went in past me like a wave. Sandalwood floated on the air, very faint.

I shut the door, threw my hat into a chair and watched her stroll over to a card table on which I had a chess problem set out that I couldn't solve. Once inside, with the door locked, her panic had left her.

"So you're a chess player," she said, in that guarded tone, as if she had come to look at my etchings. I wished she had.

We both stood still then and listened to the distant clang of elevator doors and then steps—going the other way.

I grinned, but with strain, not pleasure, went out into the kitchenette and started to fumble with a couple of glasses and then realized I still had her hat and bolero jacket under my arm. I went into the dressing room behind the wall bed and stuffed them into a drawer, went back out to the kitchenette, dug out some extra-fine Scotch and made a couple of highballs.

When I went in with the drinks she had a gun in her hand. It was a small automatic with a pearl grip. It jumped up at me and her eyes were full of horror.

I stopped, with a glass in each hand, and said: "Maybe

this hot wind has got you crazy too. I'm a private detective.
I'll prove it if you let me."

She nodded slightly and her face was white. I went over
slowly and put a glass down beside her, and went back and
set mine down and got a card out that had no bent corners.
She was sitting down, smoothing one blue knee with her left
hand, and holding the gun on the other. I put the card down
beside her drink and sat with mine.

"Never let a guy get that close to you," I said. "Not if
you mean business. And your safety catch is on."

She flashed her eyes down, shivered, and put the gun
back in her bag. She drank half the drink without stopping,
put the glass down hard and picked the card up.

"I don't give many people that liquor," I said. "I can't
afford to."

Her lips curled. "I supposed you would want money."

"Huh?"

She didn't say anything. Her hand was close to her bag
again.

"Don't forget the safety catch," I said. Her hand
stopped. I went on: "This fellow I called Waldo is quite tall,
say five-eleven, slim, dark, brown eyes with a lot of glitter.
Nose and mouth too thin. Dark suit, white handkerchief
showing and in a hurry to find you. Am I getting anywhere?"

She took her glass again. "So that's Waldo," she said.
"Well, what about him?" Her voice seemed to have a slight
liquor edge now.

"Well, a funny thing. There's a cocktail bar across the
street . . . Say, where have you been all evening?"

"Sitting in my car," she said coldly, "most of the time."

"Didn't you see a fuss across the street up the block?"

Her eyes tried to say no and missed. Her lips said: "I
knew there was some kind of disturbance. I saw policemen
and red searchlights. I supposed someone had been hurt."

"Someone was. And this Waldo was looking for you
before that. In the cocktail bar. He described you and your
clothes."

Her eyes were set like rivets now and had the same amount of expression. Her mouth began to tremble and kept on trembling.

"I was in there," I said, "talking to the kid that runs it. There was nobody in there but a drunk on a stool and the kid and myself. The drunk wasn't paying any attention to anything. Then Waldo came in and asked about you and we said no, we hadn't seen you and he started to leave."

I sipped my drink. I like an effect as well as the next fellow. Her eyes ate me.

"Just started to leave. Then this drunk that wasn't paying any attention to anyone called him Waldo and took a gun out. He shot him twice"—I snapped my fingers twice—"like that. Dead."

She fooled me. She laughed in my face. "So my husband hired you to spy on me," she said. "I might have known the whole thing was an act. You and your Waldo."

I gawked at her.

"I never thought of him as jealous," she snapped. "Not of a man who had been our chauffeur anyhow. A little about Stan, of course—that's natural. But Joseph Coates—"

I made motions in the air. "Lady, one of us has this book open at the wrong page," I grunted. "I don't know anybody named Stan or Joseph Coates. So help me, I didn't even know you had a chauffeur. People around here don't run to them. As for husbands—yeah, we do have a husband once in a while. Not often enough."

She shook her head slowly and her hand stayed near her bag and her blue eyes had glitters in them.

"Not good enough, Mr. Marlowe. No, not nearly good enough. I know you private detectives. You're all rotten. You tricked me into your apartment, if it is your apartment. More likely it's the apartment of some horrible man who will swear anything for a few dollars. Now you're trying to scare me. So you can blackmail me—as well as get money from my husband. All right," she said breathlessly, "how much do I have to pay?"

I put my empty glass aside and leaned back. "Pardon me if I light a cigarette," I said. "My nerves are frayed."

I lit it while she watched me without enough fear for any real guilt to be under it. "So Joseph Coates is his name," I said. "The guy that killed him in the cocktail bar called him Waldo."

She smiled a bit disgustedly, but almost tolerantly. "Don't stall. How much?"

"Why were you trying to meet this Joseph Coates?"

"I was going to buy something he stole from me, of course. Something that's valuable in the ordinary way too. Almost fifteen thousand dollars. The man I loved gave it to me. He's dead. There! He's dead! He died in a burning plane. Now, go back and tell my husband that, you slimy little rat!"

"I'm not little and I'm not a rat," I said.

"You're still slimy. And don't bother about telling my husband. I'll tell him myself. He probably knows anyway."

I grinned. "That's smart. Just what was I supposed to find out?"

She grabbed her glass and finished what was left of her drink. "So he thinks I'm meeting Joseph. Well, perhaps I was. But not to make love. Not with a chauffeur. Not with a bum I picked off the front step and gave a job to. I don't have to dig down that far, if I want to play around."

"Lady," I said, "you don't indeed."

"Now I'm going," she said. "You just try and stop me." She snatched the pearl-handled gun out of her bag. I didn't move.

"Why, you nasty little string of nothing," she stormed. "How do I know you're a private detective at all? You might be a crook. This card you gave me doesn't mean anything. Anybody can have cards printed."

"Sure," I said. "And I suppose I'm smart enough to live here two years because you were going to move in today so I could blackmail you for not meeting a man named Joseph

Coates who was bumped off across the street under the name of Waldo. Have you got the money to buy this something that cost fifteen grand?"

"Oh! You think you'll hold me up, I suppose!"

"Oh!" I mimicked her. "I'm a stickup artist now, am I? Lady, will you please either put that gun away or take the safety catch off? It hurts my professional feelings to see a nice gun made a monkey of that way."

"You're a full portion of what I don't like," she said. "Get out of my way."

I didn't move. She didn't move. We were both sitting down—and not even close to each other.

"Let me in on one secret before you go," I pleaded. "What in hell did you take the apartment down on the floor below for? Just to meet a guy down on the street?"

"Stop being silly," she snapped. "I didn't. I lied. It's his apartment."

"Joseph Coates'?"

She nodded sharply.

"Does my description of Waldo sound like Joseph Coates?"

She nodded sharply again.

"All right. That's one fact learned at last. Don't you realize Waldo described your clothes before he was shot—when he was looking for you—that the description was passed on to the police—that the police don't know who Waldo is—and are looking for somebody in those clothes to help tell them? Don't you get that much?"

The gun suddenly started to shake in her hand. She looked down at it, sort of vacantly, slowly put it back in her bag.

"I'm a fool," she whispered, "to be even talking to you." She stared at me for a long time, then pulled in a deep breath. "He told me where he was staying. He didn't seem afraid. I guess blackmailers are like that. He was to meet me on the street, but I was late. It was full of police when I got here. So I went back and sat in my car for a while. Then I came up to Joseph's apartment and knocked. Then I went back to my car and waited again. I came up here three times in all. The last time I walked up a flight to take the elevator. I had already been seen twice on the third floor. I met you. That's all."

"You said something about a husband," I grunted. "Where is he?"

"He's at a meeting."

"Oh, a meeting," I said nastily.

"My husband's a very important man. He has lots of meetings. He's a hydroelectric engineer. He's been all over the world. I'd have you know—"

"Skip it," I said. "I'll take him to lunch some day and have him tell me himself. Whatever Joseph had on you is dead stock now. Like Joseph."

"He's really dead?" she whispered. "Really?"

"He's dead," I said. "Dead, dead, dead. Lady, he's dead."

She believed it at last. I hadn't thought she ever would somehow. In the silence, the elevator stopped at my floor.

I heard steps coming down the hall. We all have hunches. I put my finger to my lips. She didn't move now. Her face had a frozen look. Her big blue eyes were as black as the shadows below them. The hot wind boomed against the shut windows. Windows have to be shut when a Santa Ana blows, heat or no heat.

The steps that came down the hall were the casual ordinary steps of one man. But they stopped outside my door, and somebody knocked.

I pointed to the dressing room behind the wall bed. She stood up without a sound, her bag clenched against her side. I pointed again, to her glass. She lifted it swiftly, slid across the carpet, through the door, drew the door quietly shut after her.

I didn't know just what I was going to all this trouble for. The knocking sounded again. The backs of my hands were wet. I creaked my chair and stood up and made a loud yawning sound. Then I went over and opened the door— without a gun. That was a mistake.

III

I didn't know him at first. Perhaps for the opposite reason Waldo hadn't seemed to know him. He'd had a hat on all the time over at the cocktail bar and he didn't have one on now. His hair ended completely and exactly where his hat would start. Above that line was hard white sweatless skin almost as glaring as scar tissue. He wasn't just twenty years older. He was a different man.

But I knew the gun he was holding, the .22 target automatic with the big front sight. And I knew his eyes. Bright, brittle, shallow eyes like the eyes of a lizard.

He was alone. He put the gun against my face very lightly and said between his teeth: "Yeah, me. Let's go on in."

I backed in just far enough and stopped. Just the way he would want me to, so he could shut the door without moving much. I knew from his eyes that he would want me to do just that.

I wasn't scared. I was paralyzed.

When he had the door shut he backed me some more, slowly, until there was something against the back of my legs. His eyes looked into mine.

"That's a card table," he said. "Some goon here plays chess. You?"

I swallowed. "I don't exactly play it. I just fool around."

"That means two," he said with a kind of hoarse softness, as if some cop had hit him across the windpipe with a blackjack once, in a third-degree session.

"It's a problem," I said. "Not a game. Look at the pieces."

"I wouldn't know."

"Well, I'm alone," I said, and my voice shook just enough.

"It don't make any difference," he said. "I'm washed up anyway. Some nose puts the bulls on me tomorrow, next week, what the hell? I just didn't like your map, pal. And that smug-faced pansy in the bar coat that played left tackle for Fordham or something. To hell with guys like you guys."

I didn't speak or move. The big front sight raked my cheek lightly, almost caressingly. The man smiled.

"It's kind of good business too," he said. "Just in case. An old con like me don't make good prints—all I got against me is two witnesses. The hell with it."

"What did Waldo do to you?" I tried to make it sound as if I wanted to know, instead of just not wanting to shake too hard.

"Stooled on a bank job in Michigan and got me four years. Got himself a nolle pros. Four years in Michigan ain't no summer cruise. They make you be good in them lifer states."

"How'd you know he'd come in there?" I croaked.

"I didn't. Oh yeah, I was lookin' for him. I was wantin' to see him all right. I got a flash of him on the street night before last but I lost him. Up to then I wasn't lookin' for him. Then I was. A cute guy, Waldo. How is he?"

"Dead," I said.

"I'm still good," he chuckled. "Drunk or sober. Well, that don't make no doughnuts for me now. They make me downtown yet?"

I didn't answer him quick enough. He jabbed the gun into my throat and I choked and almost grabbed for it by instinct.

"Naw," he cautioned me softly. "Naw. You ain't that dumb."

I put my hands back, down at my sides, open, the palms toward him. He would want them that way. He hadn't touched me, except with the gun. He didn't seem to care whether I might have one too. He wouldn't—if he just meant the one thing.

He didn't seem to care very much about anything, coming back on that block. Perhaps the hot wind did something to him. It was booming against my shut windows like the surf under a pier.

"They got prints," I said. "I don't know how good."

"They'll be good enough—but not for teletype work. Take 'em airmail time to Washington and back to check 'em right. Tell me why I came here, pal."

"You heard the kid and me talking in the bar. I told him my name, where I lived."

"That's how, pal. I said why." He smiled at me. It was a lousy smile to be the last one you might see.

"Skip it," I said. "The hangman won't ask you to guess why he's there."

"Say, you're tough at that. After you, I visit that kid. I tailed him home from headquarters, but I figure you're the guy to put the bee on first. I tail him home from the city hall, in the rent car Waldo had. From headquarters, pal. Them funny dicks. You can sit in their laps and they don't know you. Start runnin' for a streetcar and they open up with machine guns and bump two pedestrians, a hacker asleep in his cab, and an old scrubwoman on the second floor workin' a mop. And they miss the guy they're after. Them funny lousy dicks."

He twisted the gun muzzle in my neck. His eyes looked madder than before.

"I got time," he said. "Waldo's rent car don't get a report right away. And they don't make Waldo very soon. I know Waldo. Smart he was. A smooth boy, Waldo."

"I'm going to vomit," I said, "if you don't take that gun out of my throat."

He smiled and moved the gun down to my heart. "This about right? Say when."

I must have spoken louder than I meant to. The door of the dressing room by the wall bed showed a crack of darkness. Then an inch. Then four inches. I saw eyes, but didn't look at them. I stared hard into the bald-headed man's eyes. Very hard. I didn't want him to take his eyes off mine.

"Scared?" he asked softly.

I leaned against his gun and began to shake. I thought he would enjoy seeing me shake. The girl came out through the door. She had her gun in her hand again. I was sorry as hell for her. She'd try to make the door—or scream. Either way it would be curtains—for both of us.

"Well, don't take all night about it," I bleated. My voice sounded far away, like a voice on a radio on the other side of a street.

"I like this, pal," he smiled. "I'm like that."

The girl floated in the air, somewhere behind him. Nothing was ever more soundless than the way she moved. It wouldn't do any good though. He wouldn't fool around with her at all. I had known him all my life but I had been looking into his eyes for only five minutes.

"Suppose I yell," I said.

"Yeah, suppose you yell. Go ahead and yell," he said with his killer's smile.

She didn't go near the door. She was right behind him.

"Well—here's where I yell," I said.

As if that was the cue, she jabbed the little gun hard into his short ribs, without a single sound.

He had to react. It was like a knee reflex. His mouth snapped open and both his arms jumped out from his sides and he arched his back just a little. The gun was pointing at my right eye.

I sank and kneed him with all my strength, in the groin.

His chin came down and I hit it. I hit it as if I was driving the last spike on the first transcontinental railroad. I can still feel it when I flex my knuckles.

His gun raked the side of my face but it didn't go off. He was already limp. He writhed down gasping, his left side against the floor. I kicked his right shoulder—hard. The gun jumped away from him, skidded on the carpet, under a chair. I heard the chessmen tinkling on the floor behind me somewhere.

The girl stood over him, looking down. Then her wide dark horrified eyes came up and fastened on mine.

"That buys me," I said. "Anything I have is yours—now and forever."

She didn't hear me. Her eyes were strained open so hard that the whites showed under the vivid blue iris. She backed quickly to the door with her little gun up, felt behind her for the knob and twisted it. She pulled the door open and slipped out.

The door shut.

She was bareheaded and without her bolero jacket.

She had only the gun, and the safety catch on that was still set so that she couldn't fire it.

It was silent in the room then, in spite of the wind. Then I heard him gasping on the floor. His face had a greenish pallor. I moved behind him and pawed him for more guns, and didn't find any. I got a pair of store cuffs out of my desk and pulled his arms in front of him and snapped them on his wrists. They would hold if he didn't shake them too hard.

His eyes measured me for a coffin, in spite of their suffering. He lay in the middle of the floor, still on his left side, a twisted, wizened, bald-headed little guy with drawn-back lips and teeth spotted with cheap silver fillings. His mouth looked like a black pit and his breath came in little waves, choked, stopped, came on again, limping.

I went into the dressing room and opened the drawer of the chest. Her hat and jacket lay there on my shirts. I put them underneath, at the back, and smoothed the shirts over them. Then I went out to the kitchenette and poured a stiff jolt of whiskey and put it down and stood a moment listening to the hot wind howl against the window glass. A garage door banged, and a power-line wire with too much play between the insulators thumped the side of the building with a sound like somebody beating a carpet.

The drink worked on me. I went back into the living room and opened a window. The guy on the floor hadn't smelled her sandalwood, but somebody else might.

I shut the window again, wiped the palms of my hands and used the phone to dial headquarters.

Copernik was still there. His smart-aleck voice said: "Yeah? Marlowe? Don't tell me. I bet you got an idea."

"Make that killer yet?"

"We're not saying, Marlowe. Sorry as all hell and so on. You know how it is."

"Okay. I don't care who he is. Just come and get him off the floor of my apartment."

"Holy Christ!" Then his voice hushed and went down low. "Wait a minute, now. Wait a minute." A long way off I seemed to hear a door shut. Then his voice again. "Shoot," he said softly.

"Handcuffed," I said. "All yours. I had to knee him, but he'll be all right. He came here to eliminate a witness."

Another pause. The voice was full of honey. "Now listen, boy, who else is in this with you?"

"Who else? Nobody. Just me."

"Keep it that way, boy. All quiet. Okay?"

"Think I want all the bums in the neighborhood in here sight-seeing?"

"Take it easy, boy. Easy. Just sit tight and sit still. I'm practically there. No touch nothing. Get me?"

"Yeah." I gave him the address and apartment number again to save him time.

I could see his big bony face glisten. I got the .22 target gun from under the chair and sat holding it until feet hit the hallway outside my door and knuckles did a quiet tattoo on the door panel.

Copernik was alone. He filled the doorway quickly, pushed me back into the room with a tight grin and shut the door. He stood with his back to it, his hand under the left side of his coat. A big hard bony man with flat cruel eyes.

He lowered them slowly and looked at the man on the floor. The man's neck was twitching a little. His eyes moved in short stabs—sick eyes.

"Sure it's the guy?" Copernik's voice was hoarse.

"Positive. Where's Ybarra?"

"Oh, he was busy." He didn't look at me when he said that. "Those your cuffs?"

"Yeah."

"Key."

I tossed it to him. He went down swiftly on one knee beside the killer and took my cuffs off his wrists, tossed them to one side. He got his own off his hip, twisted the bald man's hands behind him and snapped the cuffs on.

"All right, you bastard," the killer said tonelessly.

Copernik grinned and balled his fist and hit the hand-cuffed man in the mouth a terrific blow. His head snapped back almost enough to break his neck. Blood dribbled from the lower corner of his mouth.

"Get a towel," Copernik ordered.

I got a hand towel and gave it to him. He stuffed it between the handcuffed man's teeth, viciously, stood up and rubbed his bony fingers through his ratty blond hair.

"All right. Tell it."

I told it—leaving the girl out completely. It sounded a little funny. Copernik watched me, said nothing. He rubbed the side of his veined nose. Then he got his comb out and worked on his hair just as he had done earlier in the evening, in the cocktail bar.

I went over and gave him the gun. He looked at it casually, dropped it into his side pocket. His eyes had something in them and his face moved in a hard bright grin.

I bent down and began picking up my chessmen and dropping them into the box. I put the box on the mantel, straightened out a leg of the card table, played around for a while. All the time Copernik watched me. I wanted him to think something out.

At last he came out with it. "This guy uses a twenty-two," he said. "He uses it because he's good enough to get by with that much gun. That means he's good. He knocks at your door, pokes that gat in your belly, walks you back into the room, says he's here to close your mouth for keeps—and yet you take him. You not having any gun. You take him alone. You're kind of good yourself, pal."

"Listen," I said, and looked at the floor. I picked up another chessman and twisted it between my fingers. "I was doing a chess problem," I said. "Trying to forget things."

"You got something on your mind, pal," Copernik said softly. "You wouldn't try to fool an old copper, would you, boy?"

"It's a swell pinch and I'm giving it to you," I said. "What the hell more do you want?"

The man on the floor made a vague sound behind the towel. His bald head glistened with sweat.

"What's the matter, pal? You been up to something?" Copernik almost whispered.

I looked at him quickly, looked away again. "All right," I said. "You know damn well I couldn't take him alone. He had the gun on me and he shoots where he looks."

Copernik closed one eye and squinted at me amiably with the other. "Go on, pal. I kind of thought of that too."

I shuffled around a little more, to make it look good. I said, slowly: "There was a kid here who pulled a job over in Boyle Heights, a heist job. It didn't take. A two-bit service station stickup. I know his family. He's not really bad. He was here trying to beg train money off me. When the knock came he sneaked in—there."

I pointed at the wall bed and the door beside. Copernik's head swiveled slowly, swiveled back. His eyes winked again. "And this kid had a gun," he said.

I nodded. "And he got behind him. That takes guts, Copernik. You've got to give the kid a break. You've got to let him stay out of it."

"Tag out for this kid?" Copernik asked softly.

"Not yet, he says. He's scared there will be."

Copernik smiled. "I'm a homicide man," he said. "I wouldn't know—or care."

I pointed down at the gagged and handcuffed man on the floor. "You took him, didn't you?" I said gently.

Copernik kept on smiling. A big whitish tongue came out and massaged his thick lower lip. "How'd I do it?" he whispered.

"Get the slugs out of Waldo?"

"Sure. Long twenty-twos. One smashed a rib, one good."

"You're a careful guy. You don't miss any angles. You know anything about me? You dropped in on me to see what guns I had."

Copernik got up and went down on one knee again beside the killer. "Can you hear me, guy?" he asked with his face close to the face of the man on the floor.

The man made some vague sound. Copernik stood up and yawned. "Who the hell cares what he says? Go on, pal."

"You wouldn't expect to find I had anything, but you wanted to look around my place. And while you were mousing around in there"—I pointed to the dressing room—"and me not saying anything, being a little sore, maybe, a knock came on the door. So he came in. So after a while you sneaked out and took him."

"Ah." Copernik grinned widely, with as many teeth as a horse. "You're on, pal. I socked him and I kneed him and I took him. You didn't have no gun and the guy swiveled on me pretty sharp and I left-hooked him down the backstairs. Okay?"

"Okay," I said.

"You'll tell it like that downtown?"

"Yeah," I said.

"I'll protect you, pal. Treat me right and I'll always play ball. Forget about that kid. Let me know if he needs a break."

He came over and held out his hand. I shook it. It was as clammy as a dead fish. Clammy hands and the people who own them make me sick.

"There's just one thing," I said. "This partner of yours —Ybarra. Won't he be a bit sore you didn't bring him along on this?"

Copernik tousled his hair and wiped his hatband with a large yellowish silk handkerchief.

"That guinea?" he sneered. "To hell with him!" He came close to me and breathed in my face. "No mistakes, pal —about that story of ours."

His breath was bad. It would be.

IV

There were just five of us in the chief of detectives' office when Copernik laid it before them. A stenographer, the chief, Copernik, myself, Ybarra. Ybarra sat on a chair tilted against the side wall. His hat was down over his eyes but their softness loomed underneath, and the small still smile hung at the corners of the clean-cut Latin lips. He didn't look directly at Copernik. Copernik didn't look at him at all.

Outside in the corridor there had been photos of Copernik shaking hands with me, Copernik with his hat on straight and his gun in his hand and a stern, purposeful look on his face.

They said they knew who Waldo was, but they wouldn't tell me. I didn't believe they knew, because the chief of detectives had a morgue photo of Waldo on his desk. A beautiful job, his hair combed, his tie straight, the light hitting his eyes just right to make them glisten. Nobody would have known it was a photo of a dead man with two bullet holes in his heart. He looked like a dance hall sheik making up his mind whether to take the blonde or the redhead.

It was about midnight when I got home. The apartment door was locked and while I was fumbling for my keys a low voice spoke to me out of the darkness.

All it said was "Please!" but I knew it. I turned and looked at a dark Cadillac coupe parked just off the loading zone. It had no lights. Light from the street touched the brightness of a woman's eyes.

I went over there. "You're a darn fool," I said.

She said: "Get in."

I climbed in and started the car and drove it a block and a half along Franklin and turned down Kingsley Drive. The hot wind still burned and blustered. A radio lilted from an open, sheltered side window of an apartment house. There were a lot of parked cars but she found a vacant space behind a small brand-new Packard cabriolet that had the dealer's sticker on the windshield glass. After she'd jockeyed us up to the curb she leaned back in the corner with her gloved hands on the wheel.

She was all in black now, or dark brown, with a small foolish hat. I smelled the sandalwood in her perfume.

"I wasn't very nice to you, was I?" she said.

"All you did was save my life."

"What happened?"

"I called the law and fed a few lies to a cop I don't like and gave him all the credit for the pinch and that was that. That guy you took away from me was the man who killed Waldo."

"You mean—you didn't tell them about me?"

"Lady," I said again, "all you did was save my life. What else do you want done? I'm ready, willing and I'll try to be able."

She didn't say anything, or move.

"Nobody learned who you are from me," I said. "Incidentally, I don't know myself."

"I'm Mrs. Frank C. Barsaly, Two-twelve Fremont Place, Olympia two-four-five-nine-six. Is that what you wanted?"

"Thanks," I mumbled, and rolled a dry unlit cigarette around in my fingers. "Why did you come back?" Then I snapped the fingers of my left hand. "The hat and jacket," I said. "I'll go up and get them."

"It's more than that," she said. "I want my pearls." I might have jumped a little. It seemed as if there had been enough without pearls.

A car tore by down the street going twice as fast as it should. A thin bitter cloud of dust lifted in the streetlights and whirled and vanished. The girl ran the window up quickly against it.

"All right," I said. "Tell me about the pearls. We have had a murder and a mystery woman and a mad killer and a heroic rescue and a police detective framed into making a false report. Now we will have pearls. All right—feed it to me."

"I was to buy them for five thousand dollars. From the man you call Waldo and I call Joseph Coates. He should have had them."

"No pearls," I said. "I saw what came out of his pockets. A lot of money, but no pearls."

"Could they be hidden in his apartment?"

"Yes," I said. "So far as I know he could have had them hidden anywhere in California except in his pockets. How's Mr. Barsaly this hot night?"

"He's still downtown at his meeting. Otherwise I couldn't have come."

"Well, you could have brought him," I said. "He could have sat in the rumble seat."

"Oh, I don't know," she said. "Frank weighs two hundred pounds and he's pretty solid. I don't think he would like to sit in the rumble seat, Mr. Marlowe."

"What the hell are we talking about anyway?"

She didn't answer. Her gloved hands tapped lightly, provokingly on the rim of the slender wheel. I threw the unlit cigarette out the window, turned a little and took hold of her.

When I let go of her, she pulled as far away from me as she could against the side of the car and rubbed the back of her glove against her mouth. I sat quite still.

We didn't speak for some time. Then she said very slowly: "I meant you to do that. But I wasn't always that way. It's only been since Stan Phillips was killed in his plane. If it hadn't been for that, I'd be Mrs. Phillips now. Stan gave me the pearls. They cost fifteen thousand dollars, he said once. White pearls, forty-one of them, the largest about a third of an inch across. I don't know how many grains. I never had them appraised or showed them to a jeweler, so I don't know those things. But I loved them on Stan's account. I loved Stan. The way you do just the one time. Can you understand?"

"What's your first name?" I asked.

"Lola."

"Go on talking, Lola." I got another dry cigarette out of my pocket and fumbled it between my fingers just to give them something to do.

"They had a simple silver clasp in the shape of a two-bladed propeller. There was one small diamond where the boss would be. I told Frank they were store pearls I had bought myself. He didn't know the difference. It's not so easy to tell, I daresay. You see—Frank is pretty jealous."

In the darkness she came closer to me and her side touched my side. But I didn't move this time. The wind howled and the trees shook. I kept on rolling the cigarette around in my fingers.

"I suppose you've read that story," she said. "About the wife and the real pearls and her telling her husband they were false?"

"I've read it," I said, "Maugham."

"I hired Joseph. My husband was in Argentina at the time. I was pretty lonely."

"*You* should be lonely," I said.

"Joseph and I went driving a good deal. Sometimes we had a drink or two together. But that's all. I don't go around—"

"You told him about the pearls," I said. "And when your two hundred pounds of beef came back from Argentina and kicked him out—he took the pearls, because he knew they were real. And then offered them back to you for five grand."

"Yes," she said simply. "Of course I didn't want to go to the police. And of course in the circumstances Joseph wasn't afraid of my knowing where he lived."

"Poor Waldo," I said. "I feel kind of sorry for him. It was a hell of a time to run into an old friend that had a down on you."

I struck a match on my shoe sole and lit the cigarette. The tobacco was so dry from the hot wind that it burned like grass. The girl sat quietly beside me, her hands on the wheel again.

"Hell with women—these fliers," I said. "And you're still in love with him, or think you are. Where did you keep the pearls?"

"In a Russian malachite jewelry box on my dressing table. With some other costume jewelry. I had to, if I ever wanted to wear them."

"And they were worth fifteen grand. And you think Joseph might have hidden them in his apartment. Thirty-one, wasn't it?"

"Yes," she said. "I guess it's a lot to ask."

I opened the door and got out of the car. "I've been paid," I said. "I'll go look. The doors in my apartment are not very obstinate. The cops will find out where Waldo lived when they publish his photo, but not tonight, I guess."

"It's awfully sweet of you," she said. "Shall I wait here?"

I stood with a foot on the running board, leaning in, looking at her. I didn't answer her question. I just stood there looking in at the shine of her eyes. Then I shut the car door and walked up the street toward Franklin.

Even with the wind shriveling my face I could still smell the sandalwood in her hair. And feel her lips.

I unlocked the Berglund door, walked through the silent lobby to the elevator, and rode up to three. Then I soft-footed along the silent corridor and peered down at the sill of Apartment 31. No light. I rapped—the old light, confidential tattoo of the bootlegger with the big smile and the extra deep hip pockets. No answer. I took the piece of thick hard celluloid that pretended to be a window over the driver's license in my wallet, and eased it between the lock and the jamb, leaning hard on the knob, pushing it toward the hinges. The edge of the celluloid caught the slope of the spring lock and snapped it back with a small brittle sound, like an icicle breaking. The door yielded and I went into near darkness. Street light filtered in and touched a high spot here and there.

I shut the door and snapped the light on and just stood. There was a queer smell in the air. I made it in a moment —the smell of dark-cured tobacco. I prowled over to a smoking stand by the window and looked down at four brown butts—Mexican or South American cigarettes.

Upstairs, on my floor, feet hit the carpet and somebody went into a bathroom. I heard the toilet flush. I went into the bathroom of Apartment 31. A little rubbish, nothing, no place to hide anything. The kitchenette was a longer job, but I only half searched. I knew there were no pearls in that apartment. I knew Waldo had been on his way out and that he was in a hurry and that something was riding him when he turned and took two bullets from an old friend.

I went back to the living room and swung the wall bed and looked past its mirror side into the dressing room for signs of still current occupancy. Swinging the bed farther I was no longer looking for pearls. I was looking at a man.

He was small, middle-aged, iron-gray at the temples, with a very dark skin, dressed in a fawn-colored suit with a wine-colored tie. His neat little brown hands hung limply by his sides. His small feet, in pointed polished shoes, pointed almost at the floor.

He was hanging by a belt around his neck from the metal top of the bed. His tongue stuck out farther than I thought it possible for a tongue to stick out.

He swung a little and I didn't like that, so I pulled the bed shut and he nestled quietly between the two clamped pillows. I didn't touch him yet. I didn't have to touch him to know that he would be cold as ice.

I went around him into the dressing room and used my handkerchief on drawer knobs. The place was stripped clean except for the light litter of a man living alone.

I came out of there and began on the man. No wallet. Waldo would have taken that and ditched it. A flat box of cigarettes, half full, stamped in gold:

LOUIS TAPIA Y CIA
CALLE DE PAYSANDU, 19
MONTEVIDEO

Matches from the Spezzia Club. An underarm holster of dark-grained leather and in it a nine-millimeter Mauser.

The Mauser made him a professional, so I didn't feel so badly. But not a very good professional, or bare hands would not have finished him, with the Mauser—a gun you can blast through a wall with—undrawn in his shoulder holster.

I made a little sense of it, not much. Four of the brown cigarettes had been smoked, so there had been either waiting or discussion. Somewhere along the line Waldo had got the little man by the throat and held him in just the right way to make him pass out in a matter of seconds. The Mauser had been less useful to him than a toothpick. Then Waldo had hung him up by the strap, probably dead already. That would account for haste, cleaning out the apartment, for Waldo's anxiety about the girl. It would account for the car left unlocked outside the cocktail bar.

That is, it would account for these things if Waldo had killed him, if this was really Waldo's apartment—if I wasn't just being kidded.

I examined some more pockets. In the left trouser one I found a gold penknife, some silver. In the left hip pocket a handkerchief, folded, scented. On the right hip another, unfolded but clean. In the right leg pocket four or five tissue handkerchiefs. A clean little guy. He didn't like to blow his nose on his handkerchief. Under these there was a small new keytainer holding four new keys—car keys. Stamped in gold on the keytainer was:

COMPLIMENTS OF R. K. VOGELSANG, INC.
"THE PACKARD HOUSE."

I put everything as I had found it, swung the bed back, used my handkerchief on knobs and other projections, and flat surfaces, killed the light and poked my nose out the door. The hall was empty. I went down to the street and around the corner to Kingsley Drive. The Cadillac hadn't moved. I opened the car door and leaned on it. She didn't seem to have moved, either. It was hard to see any expression on her face. Hard to see anything but her eyes and chin, but not hard to smell the sandalwood.

"That perfume," I said, "would drive a deacon nuts. . . No pearls."

"Well, thanks for trying," she said in a low, soft vibrant voice. "I guess I can stand it. Shall I . . . do we . . . or . . . ?"

"You go on home now," I said. "And whatever happens you never saw me before. Whatever happens. Just as you may never see me again."

"I'd hate that."

"Good luck, Lola." I shut the car door and stepped back.

The lights blazed on, the motor turned over. Against the wind at the corner the big coupe made a slow contemptuous turn and was gone. I stood there by the vacant space at the curb where it had been.

It was quite dark there now. Windows had become blanks in the apartment where the radio sounded. I stood looking at the back of a Packard cabriolet which seemed to be brand-new. I had seen it before—before I went upstairs, in the same place, in front of Lola's car. Parked, dark, silent, with a blue sticker pasted to the right-hand corner of the shiny windshield.

And in my mind I was looking at something else, a set of brand-new car keys in a keytainer stamped "THE PACKARD HOUSE," upstairs, in a dead man's pocket.

I went up to the front of the cabriolet and put a small pocket flash on the blue slip. It was the same dealer all right. Written in ink below his name and slogan was a name and address—Eugénie Kolchenko, 5315 Arvieda Street, West Los Angeles.

It was crazy. I went back up to Apartment 31, jimmied

the door as I had done before, stepped in behind the wall
bed and took the keytainer from the trousers pocket of the
neat brown dangling corpse. I was back down on the street
beside the cabriolet in five minutes. The keys fitted.

V

It was a small house, near a canyon rim out beyond Sawtelle,
with a circle of writhing eucalyptus trees in front of it. Beyond that, on the other side of the street, one of those parties
was going on where they come out and smash bottles on the
sidewalk with a whoop like Yale making a touchdown
against Princeton.

There was a wire fence at my number and some rose
trees, and a flagged walk and a garage that was wide open
and had no car in it. There was no car in front of the house
either. I rang the bell. There was a long wait, then the door
opened rather suddenly.

I wasn't the man she had been expecting. I could see it
in her glittering kohl-rimmed eyes. Then I couldn't see anything in them. She just stood and looked at me, a long, lean,
hungry brunette, with rouged cheekbones, thick black hair
parted in the middle, a mouth made for three-decker sandwiches, coral-and-gold pajamas, sandals—and gilded toenails. Under her earlobes a couple of miniature temple bells
gonged lightly in the breeze. She made a slow disdainful
motion with a cigarette in a holder as long as a baseball bat.

"We-el, what ees it, little man? You want sometheeng?
You are lost from the bee-ootiful party across the street,
hein?"

"Ha-ha," I said. "Quite a party, isn't it? No, I just
brought your car home. Lost it, didn't you?"

Across the street somebody had delirium tremens in the
front yard and a mixed quartet tore what was left of
the night into small strips and did what they could to
make the strips miserable. While this was going on the exotic
brunette didn't move more than one eyelash.

She wasn't beautiful, she wasn't even pretty, but she looked as if things would happen where she was.

"You have said what?" she got out, at last, in a voice as silky as a burned crust of toast.

"Your car." I pointed over my shoulder and kept my eyes on her. She was the type that uses a knife.

The long cigarette holder dropped very slowly to her side and the cigarette fell out of it. I stamped it out, and that put me in the hall. She backed away from me and I shut the door.

The hall was like the long hall of a railroad flat. Lamps glowed pinkly in iron brackets. There was a bead curtain at the end, a tiger skin on the floor. The place went with her.

"You're Miss Kolchenko?" I asked, not getting any more action.

"Ye-es. I am Mees Kolchenko. What the 'ell you want?"

She was looking at me now as if I had come to wash the windows, but at an inconvenient time.

I got a card out with my left hand, held it out to her. She read it in my hand, moving her head just enough. "A detective?" she breathed.

"Yeah."

She said something in a spitting language. Then in English: "Come in! Theese damn wind dry up my skeen like so much teesue paper."

"We're in," I said. "I just shut the door. Snap out of it, Nazi-mova. Who was he? The little guy?"

Beyond the bead curtain a man coughed. She jumped as if she had been stuck with an oyster fork. Then she tried to smile. It wasn't very successful.

"A reward," she said softly. "You weel wait 'ere? Ten dollars it is fair to pay, no?"

"No," I said.

I reached a finger toward her slowly and added: "He's dead."

She jumped about three feet and let out a yell.

A chair creaked harshly. Feet pounded beyond the bead curtain, a large hand plunged into view and snatched it aside, and a big hard-looking blond man was with us. He had a purple robe over his pajamas, his right hand held something in his robe pocket. He stood quite still as soon as he was through the curtain, his feet planted solidly, his jaw out, his colorless eyes like gray ice. He looked like a man who would be hard to take out on an off-tackle play.

"What's the matter, honey?" He had a solid, burring voice, with just the right sappy tone to belong to a guy who would go for a woman with gilded toenails.

"I came about Miss Kolchenko's car," I said.

"Well, you could take your hat off," he said. "Just for a light workout."

I took it off and apologized.

"Okay," he said, and kept his right hand shoved down hard in the purple pocket. "So you came about Miss Kolchenko's car. Take it from there."

I pushed past the woman and went closer to him. She shrank back against the wall and flattened her palms against it. Camille in a high school play. The long holder lay empty at her toes.

When I was six feet from the big man he said easily: "I can hear you from there. Just take it easy. I've got a gun in this pocket and I've had to learn to use one. Now about the car?"

"The man who borrowed it couldn't bring it," I said, and pushed the card I was still holding toward his face. He barely glanced at it. He looked back at me.

"So what?" he said.

"Are you always this tough?" I asked. "Or only when you have your pajamas on?"

"So why couldn't he bring it himself?" he asked. "And skip the mushy talk."

The dark woman made a stuffed sound at my elbow.

"It's all right, honeybunch," the man said. "I'll handle this. Go on."

She slid past both of us and flicked through the bead curtain.

I waited a little while. The big man didn't move a muscle. He didn't look any more bothered than a toad in the sun.

"He couldn't bring it because somebody bumped him off," I said. "Let's see you handle that."

"Yeah?" he said. "Did you bring him with you to prove it?"

"No," I said. "But if you put your tie and crush hat on, I'll take you down and show you."

"Who the hell did you say you were, now?"

"I didn't say. I thought maybe you could read." I held the card at him some more.

"Oh, that's right," he said. "Philip Marlowe, private investigator. Well, well. So I should go with you to look at who, why?"

"Maybe he stole the car," I said.

The big man nodded. "That's a thought. Maybe he did. Who?"

"The little brown guy who had the keys to it in his pocket, and had it parked around the corner from the Berglund Apartments."

He thought that over, without any apparent embarrassment. "You've got something there," he said. "Not much. But a little. I guess this must be the night of the Police Smoker. So you're doing all their work for them."

"Huh?"

"The card says private detective to me," he said. "Have you got some cops outside that were too shy to come in?"

"No, I'm alone."

He grinned. The grin showed white ridges in his tanned skin. "So you find somebody dead and take some keys and find a car and come riding out here—all alone. No cops. Am I right?"

"Correct."

He sighed. "Let's go inside," he said. He yanked the bead curtain aside and made an opening for me to go through. "It might be you have an idea I ought to hear."

I went past him and he turned, keeping his heavy

pocket toward me. I hadn't noticed until I got quite close that there were beads of sweat on his face. It might have been the hot wind but I didn't think so.

We were in the living room of the house.

We sat down and looked at each other across a dark floor, on which a few Navajo rugs and a few dark Turkish rugs made a decorating combination with some well-used overstuffed furniture. There was a fireplace, a small baby grand, a Chinese screen, a tall Chinese lantern on a teakwood pedestal, and gold net curtains against lattice windows. The windows to the south were open. A fruit tree with a whitewashed trunk whipped about outside the screen, adding its bit to the noise from across the street.

The big man eased back into a brocaded chair and put his slippered feet on a footstool. He kept his right hand where it had been since I met him—on his gun.

The brunette hung around in the shadows and a bottle gurgled and her temple bells gonged in her ears.

"It's all right, honeybunch," the man said. "It's all under control. Somebody bumped somebody off and this lad thinks we're interested. Just sit down and relax."

The girl tilted her head and poured half a tumbler of whiskey down her throat. She sighed, said, "Goddam," in a casual voice and curled up on a davenport. It took all of the davenport. She had plenty of legs. Her gilded toenails winked at me from the shadowy corner where she kept herself quiet from then on.

I got a cigarette out without being shot at, lit it and went into my story. It wasn't all true, but some of it was. I told them about the Berglund Apartments and that I had lived there and that Waldo was living there in Apartment 31 on the floor below mine and that I had been keeping an eye on him for business reasons.

"Waldo what?" the blond man put in. "And what business reasons?"

"Mister," I said, "have you no secrets?" He reddened slightly.

I told him about the cocktail lounge across the street from the Berglund and what had happened there. I didn't tell him about the printed bolero jacket or the girl who had worn it. I left her out of the story altogether.

"It was an undercover job—from my angle," I said. "If you know what I mean." He reddened again, bit his teeth. I went on: "I got back from the city hall without telling anybody I knew Waldo. In due time, when I decided they couldn't find out where he lived that night, I took the liberty of examining his apartment."

"Looking for what?" the big man said thickly.

"For some letters. I might mention in passing there was nothing there at all—except a dead man. Strangled and hanging by a belt to the top of the wall bed—well out of sight. A small man, about forty-five, Mexican or South American, well dressed in a fawn-colored—"

"That's enough," the big man said. "I'll bite, Marlowe. Was it a blackmail job you were on?"

"Yeah. The funny part was this little brown man had plenty of gun under his arm."

"He wouldn't have five hundred bucks in twenties in his pocket, of course? Or are you saying?"

"He wouldn't. But Waldo had over seven hundred in currency when he was killed in the cocktail bar."

"Looks like I underrated this Waldo," the big man said calmly. "He took my guy and his payoff money, gun and all. Waldo have a gun?"

"Not on him."

"Get us a drink, honeybunch," the big man said. "Yes, I certainly did sell this Waldo person shorter than a bargain counter shirt."

The brunette unwound her legs and made two drinks with soda and ice. She took herself another gill without trimmings, wound herself back on the davenport. Her big glittering black eyes watched me solemnly.

"Well, here's how," the big man said, lifting his glass in salute. "I haven't murdered anybody, but I've got a divorce suit on my hands from now on. You haven't murdered anybody, the way you tell it, but you laid an egg down at police headquarters. What the hell! Life's a lot of trouble, any way you look at it. I've still got honeybunch here. She's a White Russian I met in Shanghai. She's safe as a vault and she looks as if she could cut your throat for a nickel. That's what I like about her. You get the glamour without the risk."

"You talk damn foolish," the girl spat him.

"You look okay to me." The big man went on ignoring her. "That is, for a keyhole peeper. Is there an out?"

"Yeah. But it will cost a little money."

"I expected that. How much?"

"Say another five hundred."

"Goddam, thees hot wind make me dry like the ashes of love," the Russian girl said bitterly.

"Five hundred might do," the blond man said. "What do I get for it?"

"If I swing it—you get left out of the story. If I don't— you don't pay."

He thought it over. His face looked lined and tired now. The small beads of sweat twinkled in his short blond hair.

"This murder will make you talk," he grumbled. "The second one, I mean. And I don't have what I was going to buy. And if it's a hush, I'd rather buy it direct."

"Who was the little brown man?" I asked.

"Name's Leon Valesanos, a Uruguayan. Another of my importations. I'm in a business that takes me a lot of places. He was working in the Spezzia Club in Chiseltown—you know, the strip of Sunset next to Beverly Hills. Working on roulette, I think. I gave him the five hundred to go down to this—this Waldo—and buy back some bills for stuff Miss Kolchenko had charged to my account and delivered here. That wasn't bright, was it? I had them in my briefcase and this Waldo got a chance to steal them. What's your hunch about what happened?"

I sipped my drink and looked at him down my nose.

"Your Uruguayan pal probably talked cut and Waldo didn't listen good. Then the little guy thought maybe that Mauser might help his argument—and Waldo was too quick for him. I wouldn't say Waldo was a killer—not by intention. A blackmailer seldom is. Maybe he lost his temper and maybe he just held on to the little guy's neck too long. Then he had to take it on the lam. But he had another date, with more money coming up. And he worked the neighborhood looking for the party. And accidentally he ran into a pal who was hostile enough and drunk enough to blow him down."

"There's a hell of a lot of coincidence in all this business," the big man said.

"It's the hot wind." I grinned. "Everybody's screwy tonight."

"For the five hundred you guarantee nothing? If I don't get my cover-up, you don't get your dough. Is that it?"

"That's it," I said, smiling at him.

"Screwy is right," he said, and drained his highball. "I'm taking you up on it."

"There are just two things," I said softly, leaning forward in my chair. "Waldo had a getaway car parked outside the cocktail bar where he was killed, unlocked with the motor running. The killer took it. There's always the chance of a kickback from that direction. You see, all Waldo's stuff must have been in that car."

"Including my bills, and your letters."

"Yeah. But the police are reasonable about things like that—unless you're good for a lot of publicity. If you're not, I think I can eat some stale dog downtown and get by. If you are—that's the second thing. What did you say your name was?"

The answer was a long time coming. When it came I didn't get as much kick out of it as I thought I would. All at once it was too logical.

"Frank C. Barsaly," he said.

After a while the Russian girl called me a taxi. When I

left, the party across the street was doing all that a party could do. I noticed the walls of the house were still standing. That seemed a pity.

VI

When I unlocked the glass entrance door of the Berglund I smelled policeman. I looked at my wristwatch. It was nearly 3 A.M. In the dark corner of the lobby a man dozed in a chair with a newspaper over his face. Large feet stretched out before him. A corner of the paper lifted an inch, dropped again. The man made no other movement.

I went on along the hall to the elevator and rode up to my floor. I soft-footed along the hallway, unlocked my door, pushed it wide and reached in for the light switch.

A chain switch tinkled and light glared from a standing lamp by the easy chair, beyond the card table on which my chessmen were still scattered.

Copernik sat there with a stiff unpleasant grin on his face. The short dark man, Ybarra, sat across the room from him, on my left, silent, half smiling as usual.

Copernik showed more of his big yellow horse teeth and said: "Hi. Long time no see. Been out with the girls?"

I shut the door and took my hat off and wiped the back of my neck slowly, over and over again. Copernik went on grinning. Ybarra looked at nothing with his soft dark eyes.

"Take a seat, pal," Copernik drawled. "Make yourself to home. We got powwow to make. Boy, do I hate this night sleuthing. Did you know you were low on hooch?"

"I could have guessed it," I said. I leaned against the wall.

Copernik kept on grinning. "I always did hate private dicks," he said, "but I never had a chance to twist one like I got tonight."

He reached down lazily beside his chair and picked up

a printed bolero jacket, tossed it on the card table. He reached down again and put a wide-brimmed hat beside it.

"I bet you look cuter than all hell with these on," he said.

I took hold of a straight chair, twisted it around and straddled it, leaned my folded arms on the chair and looked at Copernik.

He got up very slowly—with an elaborate slowness—walked across the room and stood in front of me smoothing his coat down. Then he lifted his open right hand and hit me across the face with it—hard. It stung but I didn't move.

Ybarra looked at the wall, looked at the floor, looked at nothing.

"Shame on you, pal," Copernik said lazily. "The way you was taking care of this nice exclusive merchandise. Wadded down behind your old shirts. You punk peepers always did make me sick."

He stood there over me for a moment. I didn't move or speak. I looked into his glazed drinker's eyes. He doubled a fist at his side, then shrugged and turned and went back to the chair.

"Okay," he said. "The rest will keep. Where did you get these things?"

"They belong to a lady."

"Do tell. They belong to a lady. Ain't you the light-hearted bastard! I'll tell you what lady they belong to. They belong to the lady a guy named Waldo asked about in a bar across the street—about two minutes before he got shot kind of dead. Or would that have slipped your mind?"

I didn't say anything.

"You was curious about her yourself," Copernik sneered on. "But you were smart, pal. You fooled me."

"That wouldn't make me smart," I said.

His face twisted suddenly and he started to get up. Ybarra laughed, suddenly and softly, almost under his breath. Copernik's eyes swung on him, hung there. Then he faced me again, bland-eyed.

"The guinea likes you," he said. "He thinks you're good."

The smile left Ybarra's face, but no expression took its place. No expression at all.

Copernik said: "You knew who the dame was all the time. You knew who Waldo was and where he lived. Right across the hall a floor below you. You knew this Waldo person had bumped a guy off and started to lam, only this broad came into his plans somewhere and he was anxious to meet up with her before he went away. Only he never got the chance. A heist guy from back east named Al Tessilore took care of that by taking care of Waldo. So you met the gal and hid her clothes and sent her on her way and kept your trap glued. That's the way guys like you make your beans. Am I right?"

"Yeah," I said. "Except that I only knew these things very recently. Who was Waldo?"

Copernik bared his teeth at me. Red spots burned high on his sallow cheeks. Ybarra, looking down at the floor, said very softly: "Waldo Ratigan. We got him from Washington by teletype. He was a two-bit porch climber with a few small terms on him. He drove a car in a bank stickup job in Detroit. He turned the gang in later and got a nolle pros. One of the gang was this Al Tessilore. He hasn't talked a word, but we think the meeting across the street was purely accidental."

Ybarra spoke in the soft quiet modulated voice of a man for whom sounds have a meaning. I said: "Thanks, Ybarra. Can I smoke—or would Copernik kick it out of my mouth?"

Ybarra smiled suddenly. "You may smoke, sure," he said.

"The guinea likes you all right," Copernik jeered. "You never know what a guinea will like, do you?"

I lit a cigarette. Ybarra looked at Copernik and said very softly: "The word 'guinea'—you overwork it. I don't like it so well applied to me."

"The hell with what you like, guinea."

Ybarra smiled a little more. "You are making a mistake," he said. He took a pocket nail file out and began to use it, looking down.

Copernik blared: "I smelled something rotten on you from the start, Marlowe. So when we make these two mugs, Ybarra and me think we'll drift over and dabble a few more words with you. I bring one of Waldo's morgue photos—nice work, the light just right in his eyes, his tie all straight and a white handkerchief showing just right in his pocket. Nice work. So on the way up, just as a matter of routine, we rout out the manager here and let him lamp it. And he knows the guy. He's here as A. B. Hummel, Apartment Thirty-one. So we go in there and find a stiff. Then we go round and round with that. Nobody knows him yet, but he's got some swell finger bruises under that strap and I hear they fit Waldo's fingers very nicely."

"That's something," I said. "I thought maybe I murdered him."

Copernik stared at me a long time. His face had stopped grinning and was just a hard brutal face now. "Yeah. We got something else even," he said. "We got Waldo's getaway car —and what Waldo had in it to take with him."

I blew cigarette smoke jerkily. The wind pounded the shut windows. The air in the room was foul.

"Oh, we're bright boys," Copernik sneered. "We never figured you with that much guts. Take a look at this."

He plunged his bony hand into his coat pocket and drew something up slowly over the edge of the card table, drew it along the green top and left it there stretched out, gleaming. A string of white pearls with a clasp like a two-bladed propeller. They shimmered softly in the thick smoky air.

Lola Barsaly's pearls. The pearls the flier had given her. The guy who was dead, the guy she still loved.

I stared at them, but I didn't move. After a long moment Copernik said almost gravely: "Nice, ain't they? Would you feel like telling us a story about now, Mis-ter Marlowe?"

I stood up and pushed the chair from under me, walked slowly across the room and stood looking down at the pearls. The largest was perhaps a third of an inch across. They were pure white, iridescent, with a mellow softness. I lifted them slowly off the card table from beside her clothes. They felt heavy, smooth, fine.

"Nice," I said. "A lot of the trouble was about these. Yeah, I'll talk now. They must be worth a lot of money."

Ybarra laughed behind me. It was a very gentle laugh. "About a hundred dollars," he said. "They're good phonies —but they're phony."

I lifted the pearls again. Copernik's glassy eyes gloated at me. "How do you tell?" I asked.

"I know pearls," Ybarra said. "These are good stuff, the kind women very often have made on purpose, as a kind of insurance. But they are slick like glass. Real pearls are gritty between the edges of the teeth. Try."

I put two or three of them between my teeth and moved my teeth back and forth, then sideways. Not quite biting them. The beads were hard and slick.

"Yes. They are very good," Ybarra said. "Several even have little waves and flat spots, as real pearls might have."

"Would they cost fifteen grand—if they were real?" I asked.

"*Sí.* Probably. That's hard to say. It depends on a lot of things."

"This Waldo wasn't so bad," I said.

Copernik stood up quickly, but I didn't see him swing. I was still looking down at the pearls. His fist caught me on the side of the face, against the molars. I tasted blood at once. I staggered back and made it look like a worse blow than it was.

"Sit down and talk, you bastard!" Copernik almost whispered.

I sat down and used a handkerchief to pat my cheek. I licked at the cut inside my mouth. Then I got up again and went over and picked up the cigarette he had knocked out of my mouth. I crushed it out in a tray and sat down again. Ybarra filed at his nails and held one up against the lamp. There were beads of sweat on Copernik's eyebrows, at the inner ends.

"You found the beads in Waldo's car," I said, looking at Ybarra. "Find any papers?"

He shook his head without looking up.

"I'd believe you," I said. "Here it is. I never saw Waldo until he stepped into the cocktail bar tonight and asked about the girl. I knew nothing I didn't tell. When I got home and stepped out of the elevator this girl, in the printed bolero jacket and the wide hat and the blue silk crepe dress—all as he had described them—was waiting for the elevator, here on my floor. And she looked like a nice girl."

Copernik laughed jeeringly. It didn't make any difference to me. I had him cold. All he had to do was know that. He was going to know it now, very soon.

"I knew what she was up against as a police witness," I said. "And I suspected there was something else to it. But I didn't suspect for a minute that there was anything wrong with her. She was just a nice girl in a jam—and she didn't even know she was in a jam. I got her in here. She pulled a gun on me. But she didn't mean to use it."

Copernik sat up very suddenly and he began to lick his lips. His face had a stony look now. A look like wet gray stone. He didn't make a sound.

"Waldo had been her chauffeur," I went on. "His name was then Joseph Coates. Her name is Mrs. Frank C. Barsaly. Her husband is a big hydroelectric engineer. Some guy gave her the pearls once and she told her husband they were just store pearls. Waldo got wise somehow there was a romance behind them and when Barsaly came home from South America and fired him, because he was too good-looking, he lifted the pearls."

Ybarra lifted his head suddenly and his teeth flashed. "You mean he didn't know they were phony?"

"I thought he fenced the real ones and had imitations fixed up," I said.

Ybarra nodded. "It's possible."

"He lifted something else," I said. "Some stuff from Barsaly's briefcase that showed he was keeping a woman— out in Brentwood. He was blackmailing wife and husband both, without either knowing about the other. Get it so far?"

"I get it," Copernik said harshly, between his tight lips. His face was still wet gray stone. "Get the hell on with it."

"Waldo wasn't afraid of them," I said. "He didn't conceal where he lived. That was foolish, but it saved a lot of finagling, if he was willing to risk it. The girl came down here tonight with five grand to buy back her pearls. She didn't find Waldo. She came here to look for him and walked up a floor before she went back down. A woman's idea of being cagey. So I met her. So I brought her in here. So she was in that dressing room when Al Tessilore visited me to rub out a witness." I pointed to the dressing-room door. "So she came out with her little gun and stuck it in his back and saved my life," I said.

Copernik didn't move. There was something horrible in his face now. Ybarra slipped his nail file into a small leather case and slowly tucked it into his pocket.

"Is that all?" he said gently.

I nodded. "Except that she told me where Waldo's apartment was and I went in there and looked for the pearls. I found the dead man. In his pocket I found new car keys in a case from a Packard agency. And down on the street I found the Packard and took it to where it came from. Barsaly's kept woman. Barsaly had sent a friend from the Spezzia Club down to buy something and he had tried to buy it with his gun instead of the money Barsaly gave him. And Waldo beat him to the punch."

"Is that all?" Ybarra said softly.

"That's all," I said, licking the torn place on the inside of my cheek.

Ybarra said slowly: "What do you want?"

Copernik's face convulsed and he slapped his long hard thigh. "This guy's good," he jeered. "He falls for a stray broad and breaks every law in the book and you ask him what does he want? I'll give him what he wants, guinea!" Ybarra turned his head slowly and looked at him. "I don't think you will," he said. "I think you'll give him a clean bill of health and anything else he wants. He's giving you a lesson in police work."

Copernik didn't move or make a sound for a long minute. None of us moved. Then Copernik leaned forward and his coat fell open. The butt of his service gun looked out of his underarm holster.

"So what do you want?" he asked me.

"What's on the card table there. The jacket and hat and the phony pearls. And some names kept away from the papers. Is that too much?"

"Yeah—it's too much," Copernik said almost gently. He swayed sideways and his gun jumped neatly into his hand. He rested his forearm on his thigh and pointed the gun at my stomach.

"I like better that you get a slug in the guts resisting arrest," he said. "I like that better, because of a report I made out on Al Tessilore's arrest and how I made the pinch. Because of some photos of me that are in the morning sheets going out about now. I like it better that you don't live long enough to laugh about that baby."

My mouth felt suddenly hot and dry. Far off I heard the wind booming. It seemed like the sound of guns.

Ybarra moved his feet on the floor and said coldly: "You've got a couple of cases all solved, policeman. All you do for it is leave some junk here and keep some names from the papers. Which means from the DA. If he gets them anyway, too bad for you."

Copernik said: "I like the other way." The blue gun in his hand was like a rock. "And God help you, if you don't back me up on it."

Ybarra said: "If the woman is brought out into the open,

you'll be a liar on a police report and a chiseler on your own partner. In a week they won't even speak your name at headquarters. The taste of it would make them sick."

The hammer clicked back on Copernik's gun and I watched his big finger slide in farther around the trigger.

Ybarra stood up. The gun jumped at him. He said: "We'll see how yellow a guinea is. I'm telling you to put that gun up, Sam."

He started to move. He moved four even steps. Copernik was a man without a breath of movement, a stone man.

Ybarra took one more step and quite suddenly the gun began to shake.

Ybarra spoke evenly: "Put it up, Sam. If you keep your head everything lies the way it is. If you don't—you're gone."

He took one more step. Copernik's mouth opened wide and made a gasping sound and then he sagged in the chair as if he had been hit on the head. His eyelids dropped.

Ybarra jerked the gun out of his hand with a movement so quick it was no movement at all. He stepped back quickly, held the gun low at his side.

"It's the hot wind, Sam. Let's forget it," he said in the same even, almost dainty voice.

Copernik's shoulders sagged lower and he put his face in his hands. "Okay," he said between his fingers.

Ybarra went softly across the room and opened the door. He looked at me with lazy, half-closed eyes. "I'd do a lot for a woman who saved my life too," he said. "I'm eating this dish, but as a cop you can't expect me to like it."

I said: "The little man in the bed is called Leon Valesanos. He was a croupier at the Spezzia Club."

"Thanks," Ybarra said. "Let's go, Sam."

Copernik got up heavily and walked across the room and out of the open door and out of my sight. Ybarra stepped through the door after him and started to close it.

I said: "Wait a minute."

He turned his head slowly, his left hand on the door, the blue gun hanging down close to his right side.

"I'm not in this for money," I said. "The Barsalys live at Two-twelve Fremont Place. You can take the pearls to her. If Barsaly's name stays out of the paper, I get five Cs. It goes to the Police Fund. I'm not so damn smart as you think. It just happened that way—and you had a heel for a partner."

Ybarra looked across the room at the pearls on the card table. His eyes glistened. "You take them," he said. "The five hundred's okay. I think the fund has it coming."

He shut the door quietly and in a moment I heard the elevator doors clang.

VII

I opened a window and stuck my head out into the wind and watched the squad car tool off down the block. The wind blew in hard and I let it blow. A picture fell off the wall and two chessmen rolled off the card table. The material of Lola Barsaly's bolero jacket lifted and shook.

I went out to the kitchenette and drank some Scotch and went back into the living room and called her—late as it was.

She answered the phone herself, very quickly, with no sleep in her voice.

"Marlowe," I said. "Okay your end?"

"Yes . . . yes," she said. "I'm alone."

"I found something," I said. "Or rather the police did. But your dark boy gypped you. I have a string of pearls. They're not real. He sold the real ones, I guess, and made you up a string of ringers, with your clasp."

She was silent for a long time. Then, a little faintly: "The police found them?"

"In Waldo's car. But they're not telling. We have a deal. Look at the papers in the morning and you'll be able to figure out why."

"There doesn't seem to be anything more to say," she said. "Can I have the clasp?"

"Yes. Can you meet me tomorrow at four in the Club Esquire bar?"

"You're really rather sweet," she said in a dragged-out voice. "I can. Frank is still at his meeting."

"Those meetings—they take it out of a guy," I said. We said good-bye.

I called a West Los Angeles number. He was still there, with the Russian girl.

"You can send me a check for five hundred in the morning," I told him. "Made out to the Police Relief Fund, if you want to. Because that's where it's going."

Copernik made the third page of the morning papers with two photos and a nice half column. The little brown man in Apartment 31 didn't make the paper at all. The Apartment House Association has a good lobby too.

I went out after breakfast and the wind was all gone. It was soft, cool, a little foggy. The sky was close and comfortable and gray. I rode down to the boulevard and picked out the best jewelry store on it and laid a string of pearls on a black velvet mat under a daylight-blue lamp. A man in a wing collar and striped trousers looked down at them languidly.

"How good?" I asked.

"I'm sorry, sir. We don't make appraisals. I can give you the name of an appraiser."

"Don't kid me," I said. "They're Dutch."

He focused the light a little and leaned down and toyed with a few inches of the string.

"I want a string just like them, fitted to that clasp, and in a hurry," I added.

"How, like them?" He didn't look up. "And they're not Dutch. They're Bohemian."

"Okay, can you duplicate them?"

He shook his head and pushed the velvet pad away as if it soiled him. "In three months, perhaps. We don't blow glass like that in this country. If you wanted them matched —three months at least. And this house would not do that sort of thing at all."

"It must be swell to be that snooty," I said. I put a card under his black sleeve. "Give me a name that will—and not in three months—and maybe not exactly like them."

He shrugged, went away with the card, came back in five minutes and handed it back to me. There was something written on the back.

The old Levantine had a shop on Melrose, a junk shop with everything in the window from a folding baby carriage to a French horn, from a mother-of-pearl lorgnette in a faded plush case to one of those .44 Special Single Action six-shooters they still make for Western peace officers whose grandfathers were tough.

The old Levantine wore a skullcap and two pairs of glasses and a full beard. He studied my pearls, shook his head sadly, and said: "For twenty dollars, almost so good. Not so good, you understand. Not so good glass."

"How like will they look?"

He spread his firm strong hands. "I am telling you the truth," he said. "They would not fool a baby."

"Make them up," I said. "With this clasp. And I want the others back, too, of course."

"Yah. Two o'clock," he said.

Leon Valesanos, the little brown man from Uruguay, made the afternoon papers. He had been found hanging in an unnamed apartment. The police were investigating.

At four o'clock I walked into the long cool bar of the Club Esquire and prowled along the row of booths until I found one where a woman sat alone. She wore a hat like a shallow soup plate with a very wide edge, a brown tailor-made suit with a severe mannish shirt and tie.

I sat down beside her and slipped a parcel along the seat. "You don't open that," I said. "In fact you can slip it into the incinerator as is, if you want to."

She looked at me with dark tired eyes. Her fingers twisted a thin glass that smelled of peppermint. "Thanks." Her face was very pale.

I ordered a highball and the waiter went away. "Read the papers?"

"Yes."

"You understand now about this fellow Copernik who stole your act? That's why they won't change the story or bring you into it."

"It doesn't matter now," she said. "Thank you, all the same. Please—please show them to me."

I pulled the string of pearls out of the loosely wrapped tissue paper in my pocket and slid them across to her. The silver propeller clasp winked in the light of the wall bracket. The little diamond winked. The pearls were as dull as white soap. They didn't even match in size.

"You were right," she said tonelessly. "They are not my pearls."

The waiter came with my drink and she put her bag on them deftly. When he was gone she fingered them slowly once more, dropped them into the bag and gave me a dry mirthless smile.

"As you said—I'll keep the clasp."

I said slowly: "You don't know anything about me. You saved my life last night and we had a moment, but it was just a moment. You still don't know anything about me. There's a detective downtown named Ybarra, a Mexican of the nice sort, who was on the job when the pearls were found in Waldo's suitcase. That is in case you would like to make sure—"

She said: "Don't be silly. It's all finished. It was a memory. I'm too young to nurse memories. It may be for the best. I loved Stan Phillips—but he's gone—long gone."

I stared at her, didn't say anything.

She added quietly: "This morning my husband told me something I hadn't known. We are to separate. So I have very little to laugh about today."

"I'm sorry," I said lamely. "There's nothing to say. I may see you sometime. Maybe not. I don't move much in your circle. Good luck."

I stood up. We looked at each other for a moment. "You haven't touched your drink," she said.

"You drink it. That peppermint stuff will just make you sick."

I stood there a moment with a hand hard on the table. "If anybody ever bothers you," I said, "let me know."

I went out of the bar without looking back at her, got into my car and drove west on Sunset and down all the way to the Coast Highway. Everywhere along the way gardens were full of withered and blackened leaves and flowers which the hot wind had burned.

But the ocean looked cool and languid and just the same as ever. I drove on almost to Malibu and then parked and went and sat on a big rock that was inside somebody's wire fence. It was about half tide and coming in. The air smelled of kelp. I watched the water for a while and then I pulled a string of Bohemian glass imitation pearls out of my pocket and cut the knot at one end and slipped the pearls off one by one.

When I had them all loose in my left hand I held them like that for a while and thought. There wasn't really anything to think about. I was sure.

"To the memory of Mr. Stan Phillips," I said aloud. "Just another four-flusher."

I flipped her pearls out into the water one by one at the floating seagulls.

They made little splashes and the seagulls rose off the water and swooped at the splashes.

REAR WINDOW

Cornell Woolrich

I didn't know their names. I'd never heard their voices. I didn't even know them by sight, strictly speaking, for their faces were too small to fill in with identifiable features at that distance. Yet I could have constructed a timetable of their comings and goings, their daily habits and activities. They were the rear-window dwellers around me.

Sure, I suppose it *was* a little bit like prying, could even have been mistaken for the fevered concentration of a Peeping Tom. That wasn't my fault; that wasn't the idea. The idea was, my movements were strictly limited just around this time. I could get from the window to the bed, and from the bed to the window, and that was all. The bay window was about the best feature my rear bedroom had in the warm weather. It was unscreened, so I had to sit with the light out or I would have had every insect in the vicinity in on me.

I couldn't sleep, because I was used to getting plenty of exercise. I'd never acquired the habit of reading books to ward off boredom, so I hadn't that to turn to. Well, what should I do, sit there with my eyes tightly shuttered?

Just to pick a few at random: straight over, and the windows square, there was a young jitter-couple, kids in their teens, only just married. It would have killed them to stay home one night. They were always in such a hurry to go, wherever it was they went, they never remembered to turn out the lights. I don't think it missed once in all the time I was watching. But they never forgot altogether, either. I was to learn to call this delayed action, as you will see. He'd always come skittering madly back in about five minutes, probably from all the way down in the street, and rush around killing the switches. Then fall over something in the dark on his way out. They gave me an inward chuckle, those two.

The next house down, the windows already narrowed a little with perspective. There was a certain light in that one that always went out each night too. Something about it, it used to make me a little sad. There was a woman living there with her child, a young widow I suppose. I'd see her put the child to bed, and then bend over and kiss her in a wistful sort of way. She'd shade the light off her and sit there painting her eyes and mouth. Then she'd go out. She'd never come back till the night was nearly spent. Once I was still up, and I looked and she was sitting there motionless with her head buried in her arms. Something about it, it used to make me a little sad.

The third one down no longer offered any insight, the windows were just slits like in a medieval battlement, due to foreshortening. That brings us around to the one on the end. In that one, frontal vision came back full depth again, since it stood at right angles to the rest, my own included, sealing up the inner hollow all these houses backed on. I could see into it, from the rounded projection of my bay window, as freely as into a dollhouse with its rear wall sliced away. And scaled down to about the same size.

It was a flat building. Unlike all the rest it had been constructed originally as such, not just cut up into furnished rooms. It topped them by two stories and had rear fire escapes to show for this distinction. But it was old, evidently hadn't shown a profit. It was in the process of being modernized. Instead of clearing the entire building while the work was going on, they were doing it a flat at a time, in order to lose as little rental income as possible. Of the six rearward flats it offered to view, the topmost one had already been completed, but not yet rented. They were working on the fifth-floor one now, disturbing the peace of everyone all up and down the "inside" of the block with their hammering and sawing.

I felt sorry for the couple in the flat below. I used to wonder how they stood it with that bedlam going on above their heads. To make it worse the wife was in chronic poor health, too; I could tell that even at a distance by the listless way she moved about over there, and remained in her bathrobe without dressing. Sometimes I'd see her sitting by the window, holding her head. I used to wonder why he didn't have a doctor in to look her over, but maybe they couldn't afford it. He seemed to be out of work. Often their bedroom light was on late at night behind the drawn shade, as though she were unwell and he was sitting up with her. And one night in particular he must have had to sit up with her all night, it remained on until nearly daybreak. Not that I sat watching all that time. But the light was still burning at three in the morning, when I finally transferred from chair to bed to see if I could get a little sleep myself. And when I failed to, and hopscotched back again around dawn, it was still peering wanly out behind the tan shade.

Moments later, with the first brightening of day, it suddenly dimmed around the edges of the shade, and then shortly afterward, not that one, but a shade in one of the other rooms—for all of them alike had been down—went up, and I saw him standing there looking out.

He was holding a cigarette in his hand. I couldn't see it, but I could tell it was that by the quick, nervous little jerks with which he kept putting his hand to his mouth, and the haze I saw rising around his head. Worried about her, I guess. I didn't blame him for that. Any husband would have been. She must have only just dropped off to sleep, after night-long suffering. And then in another hour or so, at the most, that sawing of wood and clattering of buckets was going to start in over them again. Well, it wasn't any of my business, I said to myself, but he really ought to get her out of there. If I had an ill wife on my hands. . . .

He was leaning slightly out, maybe an inch past the window frame, carefully scanning the back faces of all the houses abutting on the hollow square that lay before him. You can tell, even at a distance, when a person is looking fixedly. There's something about the way the head is held. And yet his scrutiny wasn't held fixedly to any one point, it was a slow, sweeping one, moving along the houses on the opposite side from me first. When it got to the end of them, I knew it would cross over to my side and come back along there. Before it did, I withdrew several yards inside my room, to let it go safely by. I didn't want him to think I was sitting there prying into his affairs. There was still enough blue night-shade in my room to keep my slight withdrawal from catching his eye.

When I returned to my original position a moment or two later, he was gone. He had raised two more of the shades. The bedroom one was still down. I wondered vaguely why he had given that peculiar, comprehensive, semicircular stare at all the rear windows around him. There wasn't anyone at any of them, at such an hour. It wasn't important, of course. It was just a little oddity, it failed to blend in with his being worried or disturbed about his wife. When you're worried or disturbed, that's an internal preoccupation, you stare vacantly at nothing at all. When you stare around you in a great sweeping arc at windows, that betrays external preoccupation, outward interest. One doesn't quite jibe with the other. To call such a discrepancy trifling is to add to its importance. Only someone like me, stewing in a vacuum of total idleness, would have noticed it at all.

The flat remained lifeless after that, as far as could be judged by its windows. He must have either gone out or gone to bed himself. Three of the shades remained at normal height, the one masking the bedroom remained down. Sam, my day houseman, came in not long after with my eggs and morning paper, and I had that to kill time with for a while. I stopped thinking about other people's windows and staring at them.

The sun slanted down on one side of the hollow oblong all morning long, then it shifted over to the other side for the afternoon. Then it started to slip off both alike, and it was evening again—another day gone.

The lights started to come on around the quadrangle. Here and there a wall played back, like a sounding board, a snatch of radio program that was coming in too loud. If you listened carefully you could hear an occasional clink of dishes mixed in, faint, far off. The chain of little habits that were their lives unreeled themselves. They were all bound in them tighter than the tightest straitjacket any jailer ever devised, though they all thought themselves free. The jitterbugs made their nightly dash for the great open spaces, forgot their lights, he came careening back, thumbed them out, and their place was dark until the early morning hours. The woman put her child to bed, leaned mournfully over its cot, then sat down with heavy despair to redden her mouth.

In the fourth-floor flat at right angles to the long, interior "street" the three shades had remained up, and the fourth shade had remained at full length, all day long. I hadn't been conscious of that because I hadn't particularly been looking at it, or thinking of it, until now. My eyes may have rested on those windows at times, during the day, but my thoughts had been elsewhere. It was only when a light suddenly went up in the end room behind one of the raised shades, which was their kitchen, that I realized that the shades had been untouched like that all day. That also brought something else to my mind that hadn't been in it until now: I hadn't seen the woman all day. I hadn't seen any sign of life within those windows until now.

He'd come in from outside. The entrance was at the opposite side of their kitchen, away from the window. He'd left his hat on, so I knew he'd just come in from the outside. He didn't remove his hat. As though there was no one there to remove it for anymore. Instead, he pushed it farther to the back of his head by pronging a hand to the roots of his hair. That gesture didn't denote removal of perspiration, I knew. To do that a person makes a sidewise sweep—this was up over his forehead. It indicated some sort of harassment or uncertainty. Besides, if he'd been suffering from excess warmth, the first thing he would have done would be to take off his hat altogether.

She didn't come out to greet him. The first link, of the so-strong chain of habit, of custom, that binds us all, had snapped wide open.

She must be so ill she had remained in bed, in the room behind the lowered shade, all day. I watched. He remained where he was, two rooms away from there. Expectancy became surprise, surprise incomprehension. "Funny," I thought, "that he doesn't go in to her. Or at least go as far as the doorway, look in to see how she is."

Maybe she was asleep, and he didn't want to disturb her. Then immediately: "But how can he know for sure that she's asleep, without at least looking in at her? He just came in himself."

He came forward and stood there by the window, as he had at dawn. Sam had carried out my tray quite some time before, and my lights were out. I held my ground, I knew he couldn't see me within the darkness of the bay window. He stood there motionless for several minutes. And now his attitude was the proper one for inner preoccupation. He stood there looking downward at nothing, lost in thought.

"He's worried about her," I said to myself, "as any man would be. It's the most natural thing in the world. Funny, though, he should leave her in the dark like that, without going near her. If he's worried, then why didn't he at least look in on her on returning?" Here was another of those trivial discrepancies, between inward motivation and outward indication. And just as I was thinking that, the original one, that I had noted at daybreak, repeated itself. His head went up with renewed alertness, and I could see it start to give that slow circular sweep of interrogation around the panorama of rearward windows again. True, the light was behind him this time, but there was enough of it falling on him to show me the microscopic but continuous shift of direction his head made in the process. I remained carefully immobile until the distant glance had passed me safely by. Motion attracts.

"Why is he so interested in other people's windows?" I wondered detachedly. And of course an effective brake to dwelling on that thought too lingeringly clamped down almost at once: "Look who's talking. What about you yourself?"

An important difference escaped me. I wasn't worried about anything. He, presumably, was.

Down came the shades again. The lights stayed on behind their beige opaqueness. But behind the one that had remained down all along, the room remained dark.

Time went by. Hard to say how much—a quarter of an hour, twenty minutes. A cricket chirped in one of the back yards. Sam came in to see if I wanted anything before he went home for the night. I told him no, I didn't—it was all right, run along. He stood there for a minute, head down. Then I saw him shake it slightly, as if at something he didn't like. "What's the matter?" I asked.

"You know what that means? My old mammy told it to me, and she never told me a lie in her life. I never once seen it to miss, either."

"What, the cricket?"

"Any time you hear one of them things, that's a sign of death—someplace close around."

I swept the back of my hand at him. "Well, it isn't in here, so don't let it worry you."

He went out, muttering stubbornly: "It's somewhere close by, though. Somewhere not very far off. Got to be."

The door closed after him, and I stayed there alone in the dark.

It was a stifling night, much closer than the one before. I could hardly get a breath of air even by the open window at which I sat. I wondered how he—that unknown over there—could stand it behind those drawn shades.

Then suddenly, just as idle speculation about this whole matter was about to alight on some fixed point in my mind, crystallize into something like suspicion, up came the shades again, and off it flitted, as formless as ever and without having had a chance to come to rest on anything.

He was in the middle windows, the living room. He'd taken off his coat and shirt, was bare-armed in his undershirt. He hadn't been able to stand it himself, I guess—the sultriness.

I couldn't make out what he was doing at first. He seemed to be busy in a perpendicular, up-and-down way rather than lengthwise. He remained in one place, but he kept dipping down out of sight and then straightening up into view again, at irregular intervals. It was almost like some sort of calisthenic exercise, except that the dips and rises weren't evenly timed enough for that. Sometimes he'd stay down a long time, sometimes he'd bob right up again, sometimes he'd go down two or three times in rapid succession. There was some sort of a widespread black V railing him off from the window. Whatever it was, there was just a sliver of it showing above the upward inclination to which the windowsill deflected my line of vision. All it did was strike off the bottom of his undershirt, to the extent of a sixteenth of an inch maybe. But I hadn't seen it there at other times, and I couldn't tell what it was.

Suddenly he left it for the first time since the shades had gone up, came out around it to the outside, stooped down into another part of the room, and straightened again with an armful of what looked like varicolored pennants at the distance at which I was. He went back behind the V and allowed them to fall across the top of it for a moment, and stay that way. He made one of his dips down out of sight and stayed that way a good while.

The "pennants" slung across the V kept changing color right in front of my eyes. I have very good sight. One moment they were white, the next red, the next blue.

Then I got it. They were a woman's dresses, and he was pulling them down to him one by one, taking the topmost one each time. Suddenly they were all gone, the V was black and bare again, and his torso had reappeared. I knew what it was now, and what he was doing. The dresses had told me. He confirmed it for me. He spread his arms to the ends of the V. I could see him heave and hitch, as if exerting pressure, and suddenly the V had folded up, become a cubed wedge. Then he made rolling motions with his whole upper body, and the wedge disappeared off to one side.

He'd been packing a trunk, packing his wife's things into a large upright trunk.

He reappeared at the kitchen window presently, stood still for a moment. I saw him draw his arm across his forehead, not once but several times, and then whip the end of it off into space. Sure, it was hot work for such a night. Then he reached up along the wall and took something down. Since it was the kitchen he was in, my imagination had to supply a cabinet and a bottle.

I could see the two or three quick passes his hand made to his mouth after that. I said to myself tolerantly: "That's what nine men out of ten would do after packing a trunk—take a good stiff drink. And if the tenth didn't, it would only be because he didn't have any liquor at hand."

Then he came closer to the window again, and standing edgewise to the side of it, so that only a thin paring of his head and shoulder showed, peered watchfully out into the dark quadrilateral, along the line of windows, most of them unlighted by now, once more. He always started on the left-hand side, the side opposite mine, and made his circuit of inspection from there on around.

That was the second time in one evening I'd seen him do that. And once at daybreak made three times altogether. I smiled mentally. You'd almost think he felt guilty about something. It was probably nothing, just an odd little habit, a quirk, that he didn't know he had himself. I had them myself, everyone does.

He withdrew into the room again, and it blacked out. His figure passed into the one that was still lighted next to it, the living room. That blacked next. It didn't surprise me that the third room, the bedroom with the drawn shade, didn't light up on his entering there. He wouldn't want to disturb her, of course—particularly if she was going away tomorrow for her health, as his packing of her trunk showed. She needed all the rest she could get, before making the trip. Simple enough for him to slip into bed in the dark.

It did surprise me, though, when a match-flare winked some time later, to have it still come from the darkened living room. He must be lying down in there, trying to sleep on a sofa or something for the night. He hadn't gone near the bedroom at all, was staying out of it altogether. That puzzled me, frankly. That was carrying solicitude almost too far.

Ten minutes or so later, there was another match-wink, still from that same living room window. He couldn't sleep.

The night brooded down on both of us alike, the curiosity monger in the bay window, the chain smoker in the fourth-floor flat, without giving any answer. The only sound was that interminable cricket.

I was back at the window again with the first sun of morning. Not because of him. My mattress was like a bed of hot coals. Sam found me there when he came in to get things ready for me. "You're going to be a wreck, Mr. Jeff" was all he said.

First, for a while, there was no sign of life over there.

Then suddenly I saw his head bob up from somewhere down out of sight in the living room, so I knew I'd been right; he'd spent the night on a sofa or easy chair in there. Now, of course, he'd look in at her, to see how she was, find out if she felt any better. That was only common ordinary humanity. He hadn't been near her, so far as I could make out, since two nights before.

He didn't. He dressed, and he went in the opposite direction, into the kitchen, and wolfed something in there, standing up and using both hands. Then he suddenly turned and moved off side, in the direction in which I knew the flat entrance to be, as if he had just heard some summons, like the doorbell.

Sure enough, in a moment he came back, and there were two men with him in leather aprons. Expressmen. I saw him standing by while they laboriously maneuvered that cubed black wedge out between them, in the direction they'd just come from. He did more than just stand by. He practically hovered over them, kept shifting from side to side, he was so anxious to see that it was done right.

Then he came back alone, and I saw him swipe his arm across his head, as though it was he, not they, who was all heated up from the effort.

So he was forwarding her trunk, to wherever it was she was going. That was all.

He reached up along the wall again and took something down. He was taking another drink. Two. Three. I said to myself, a little at a loss: "Yes, but he hasn't just packed a trunk this time. That trunk has been standing packed and ready since last night. Where does the hard work come in? The sweat and the need for a bracer?"

Now, at last, after all those hours, he finally did go in to her. I saw his form pass through the living room and go beyond, into the bedroom. Up went the shade that had been down all this time. Then he turned his head and looked around behind him. In a certain way, a way that was unmistakable, even from where I was. Not in one certain direction, as one looks at a person. But from side to side, and up and down, and all around, as one looks at—*an empty room.*

He stepped back, bent a little, gave a fling of his arms, and an unoccupied mattress and bedding upended over the foot of a bed, stayed that way, emptily curved. A second one followed a moment later.

She wasn't in there.

They use the expression "delayed action." I found out then what it meant. For two days a sort of formless uneasiness, a disembodied suspicion, I don't know what to call it, had been flitting and volplaning around in my mind, like an insect looking for a landing place. More than once, just as it had been ready to settle, some slight thing, some slight reassuring thing, such as the raising of the shades after they had been down unnaturally long, had been enough to keep it winging aimlessly, prevent it from staying still long enough for me to recognize it. The point of contact had been there all along, waiting to receive it. Now, for some reason, within a split second after he tossed over the empty mattresses, it landed—*zoom!* And the point of contact expanded—or exploded, whatever you care to call it—into a certainty of murder.

In other words, the rational part of my mind was far behind the instinctive, subconscious part. Delayed action. Now the one had caught up to the other. The thought message that sparked from the synchronization was "He's done something to her!"

I looked down and my hand was bunching the goods over my kneecap, it was knotted so tight. I forced it to open. I said to myself, steadyingly: "Now wait a minute, be careful, go slow. You've seen nothing. You know nothing. You only have the negative proof that you don't see her anymore."

Sam was standing there looking over at me from the pantry way. He said accusingly: "You ain't touched a thing. And your face looks like a sheet."

It felt like one. It had that needling feeling, when the blood has left it involuntarily. It was more to get him out of the way and give myself some elbow room for undisturbed thinking, than anything else, that I said: "Sam, what's the street address of that building down there? Don't stick your head too far out and gape at it."

"Somep'n or other Benedict Avenue." He scratched his neck helpfully.

"I know that. Chase around the corner a minute and get me the exact number on it, will you?"

"Why you want to know that for?" he asked as he turned to go.

"None of your business," I said with the good-natured firmness that was all that was necessary to take care of that once and for all. I called after him just as he was closing the door: "And while you're about it, step into the entrance and see if you can tell from the mailboxes who has the fourth-floor rear. Don't get me the wrong one now. And try not to let anyone catch you at it."

He went out mumbling something that sounded like "When a man ain't got nothing to do but just sit all day, he sure can think up the blamest things—" The door closed and I settled down to some good constructive thinking.

I said to myself: "What are you really building up this monstrous supposition on? Let's see what you've got. Only that there were several little things wrong with the mechanism, the chain-belt, of their recurrent daily habits over there. One, the lights were on all night the first night. Two, he came in later than usual the second night. Three, he left his hat on. Four, she didn't come out to greet him—she hasn't appeared since the evening before the lights were on all night. Five, he took a drink after he finished packing her trunk. But he took three stiff drinks the next morning, immediately after her trunk went out. Six, he was inwardly disturbed and worried, yet superimposed upon this was an unnatural external concern about the surrounding rear windows that was off-key. Seven, he slept in the living room, didn't go near the bedroom, during the night before the departure of the trunk."

Very well. If she had been ill that first night, and he had
sent her away for her health, that automatically canceled
out points 1, 2, 3, 4. It left points 5 and 6 totally unimportant
and unincriminating. But when it came up against 7, it hit
a stumbling block.

If she went away immediately after being ill that first
night, why didn't he want to sleep in their bedroom *last
night*? Sentiment? Hardly. Two perfectly good beds in one
room, only a sofa or uncomfortable easy chair in the other.
Why should he stay out of there if she was already gone? Just
because he missed her, was lonely? A grown man doesn't act
that way. All right, then she was still in there.

Sam came back parenthetically at this point and said:
"That house is Number Five Twenty-five Benedict Avenue.
The fourth-floor rear, it got the name of Mr. and Mrs. Lars
Thorwald up."

"Sh-h," I silenced, and motioned him backhand out of
my ken.

"First he want it, then he don't," he grumbled philo-
sophically, and retired to his duties.

I went ahead digging at it. But if she was still in there,
in that bedroom last night, then she couldn't have gone
away to the country, because I never saw her leave today.
She could have left without my seeing her in the early hours
of yesterday morning. I'd missed a few hours, been asleep.
But this morning I had been up before he was himself, I only
saw his head rear up from that sofa after I'd been at the
window for some time.

To go at all she would have had to go yesterday morning. Then why had he left the bedroom shade down, left the
mattresses undisturbed, until today? Above all, why had he
stayed out of that room last night? That was evidence that
she hadn't gone, was still in there. Then today, immediately
after the trunk had been dispatched, he went in, pulled up
the shade, tossed over the mattresses, and showed that she
hadn't been in there. The thing was like a crazy spiral.

No, it wasn't either. *Immediately after the trunk had
been dispatched—*

The trunk.

That did it.

I looked around to make sure the door was safely closed between Sam and me. My hand hovered uncertainly over the telephone dial a minute. Boyne, he'd be the one to tell about it. He was on Homicide. He had been, anyway, when I'd last seen him. I didn't want to get a flock of strange dicks and cops into my hair. I didn't want to be involved any more than I had to. Or at all, if possible.

They switched my call to the right place after a couple of wrong tries, and I got him finally.

"Look, Boyne? This is Hal Jeffries—"

"Well, where've you been the last sixty-two years?" he started to enthuse.

"We can take that up later. What I want you to do now is take down a name and address. Ready? Lars Thorwald. Five Twenty-five Benedict Avenue. Fourth-floor rear. Got it?"

"Fourth-floor rear. Got it. What's it for?"

"Investigation. I've got a firm belief you'll uncover a murder there if you start digging at it. Don't call on me for anything more than that—just a conviction. There's been a man and wife living there until now. Now there's just the man. Her trunk went out early this morning. If you can find someone who saw *her* leave herself—"

Marshaled aloud like that and conveyed to somebody else, a lieutenant of detectives above all, it did sound flimsy, even to me. He said hesitantly, "Well, but—" Then he accepted it as was. Because I was the source. I even left my window out of it completely. I could do that with him and get away with it because he'd known me years, he didn't question my reliability. I didn't want my room all cluttered up with dicks and cops taking turns nosing out of the window in this hot weather. Let them tackle it from the front.

"Well, we'll see what we see," he said. "I'll keep you posted."

I hung up and sat back to watch and wait events. I had a grandstand seat. Or rather a grandstand seat in reverse. I could only see from behind the scenes, but not from the front. I couldn't watch Boyne go to work. I could only see the results, when and if there were any.

Nothing happened for the next few hours. The police work that I knew must be going on was as invisible as police work should be. The figure in the fourth-floor windows over there remained in sight, alone and undisturbed. He didn't go out. He was restless, roamed from room to room without staying in one place very long, but he stayed in. Once I saw him eating again—sitting down this time—and once he shaved, and once he even tried to read the paper, but he didn't stay with it long.

Little unseen wheels were in motion around him. Small and harmless as yet, preliminaries. If he knew, I wondered to myself, would he remain there quiescent like that, or would he try to bolt out and flee? That mightn't depend so much upon his guilt as upon his sense of immunity, his feeling that he could outwit them. Of his guilt I myself was already convinced, or I wouldn't have taken the step I had.

At three my phone rang. Boyne calling back. "Jeffries? Well, I don't know. Can't you give me a little more than just a bald statement like that?"

"Why?" I fenced. "Why do I have to?"

"I've had a man over there making inquiries. I've just had his report. The building superintendent and several of the neighbors all agree she left for the country, to try and regain her health, early yesterday morning."

"Wait a minute. Did any of them *see* her leave, according to your man?"

"No."

"Then all you've gotten is a secondhand version of an unsupported statement by him. Not an eyewitness account."

"He was met returning from the depot, after he'd bought her ticket and seen her off on the train."

"That's still an unsupported statement, once removed."

"I've sent a man down there to the station to try and check with the ticket agent if possible. After all, he should have been fairly conspicuous at that early hour. And we're keeping him under observation, of course, in the meantime, watching all his movements. The first chance we get we're going to jump in and search the place."

I had a feeling that they wouldn't find anything, even if they did.

"Don't expect anything more from me. I've dropped it in your lap. I've given you all I have to give. A name, an address and an opinion."

"Yes, and I've always valued your opinion highly before now, Jeff—"

"But now you don't, that it?"

"Not at all. The thing is, we haven't turned up anything that seems to bear out your impression so far."

"You haven't gotten very far along, so far."

He went back to his previous cliché. "Well, we'll see what we see. Let you know later."

Another hour or so went by, and sunset came on. I saw him start to get ready to go out, over there. He put on his hat, put his hand in his pocket and stood still looking at it for a minute. Counting change, I guess. It gave me a peculiar sense of suppressed excitement, knowing they were going to come in the minute he left. I thought grimly, as I saw him take a last look around: "If you've got anything to hide, brother, now's the time to hide it."

He left. A breath-holding interval of misleading emptiness descended on the flat. A three-alarm fire couldn't have pulled my eyes off those windows. Suddenly the door by which he had just left parted slightly and two men insinuated themselves, one behind the other. There they were now. They closed it behind them, separated at once, and got busy. One took the bedroom, one the kitchen, and they started to work their way toward one another again from those extremes of the flat. They were thorough. I could see them going over everything from top to bottom. They took the living room together. One cased one side, the other man the other.

They'd already finished before the warning caught

them. I could tell that by the way they straightened up and stood facing one another frustratedly for a minute. Then both their heads turned sharply, as at a tip-off by doorbell that he was coming back. They got out fast.

I wasn't unduly disheartened, I'd expected that. My own feeling all along had been that they wouldn't find anything incriminating around. The trunk had gone.

He came in with a mountainous brown-paper bag sitting in the curve of one arm. I watched him closely to see if he'd discover that someone had been there in his absence. Apparently he didn't. They'd been adroit about it.

He stayed in the rest of the night. Sat tight, safe and sound. He did some desultory drinking, I could see him sitting there by the window and his hand would hoist every once in a while, but not to excess. Apparently everything was under control, the tension had eased, now that—the trunk was out.

Watching him across the night, I speculated: "Why doesn't he get out? If I'm right about him, and I am, why does he stick around—after it?" That brought its own answer: "Because he doesn't know anyone's on to him yet. He doesn't think there's any hurry. To go too soon, right after she has, would be more dangerous than to stay awhile."

The night wore on. I sat there waiting for Boyne's call. It came later than I thought it would. I picked the phone up in the dark. He was getting ready to go to bed, over there, now. He'd risen from where he'd been sitting drinking in the kitchen, and put the light out. He went into the living room, lit that. He started to pull his shirttail up out of his belt. Boyne's voice was in my ear as my eyes were on him, over there. Three-cornered arrangement.

"Hello, Jeff? Listen, absolutely nothing. We searched the place while he was out—"

I nearly said, "I know you did, I saw it," but checked myself in time.

"—and didn't turn up a thing. But—" He stopped as

though this was going to be important. I waited impatiently for him to go ahead.

"Downstairs in his letter box we found a postcard waiting for him. We fished it up out of the slot with bent pins—"

"And?"

"And it was from his wife, written only yesterday from some farm up-country. Here's the message we copied: 'Arrived OK. Already feeling a little better. Love, Anna.'"

I said, faintly but stubbornly: "You say, written only yesterday. Have you proof of that? What was the postmark date on it?"

He made a disgusted sound down in his tonsils. At me, not it. "The postmark was blurred. A corner of it got wet, and the ink smudged."

"All of it blurred?"

"The year date," he admitted. "The hour and the month came out OK. August. And seven-thirty P.M., it was mailed at."

This time I made the disgusted sound, in my larynx. "August, seven-thirty P.M.—1937 or 1939 or 1942. You have no proof how it got into that mailbox, whether it came from a letter carrier's pouch or from the back of some bureau drawer!"

"Give up, Jeff," he said. "There's such a thing as going too far."

I don't know what I would have said. That is, if I hadn't happened to have my eyes on the Thorwald flat living-room windows just then. Probably very little. The postcard *had* shaken me, whether I admitted it or not. But I was looking over there. The light had gone out as soon as he'd taken his shirt off. But the bedroom didn't light up. A match-flare winked from the living room, low down, as from an easy chair or sofa. With two unused beds in the bedroom, he was *still staying out of there.*

"Boyne," I said in a glassy voice, "I don't care what postcards from the other world you've turned up, I say that man has done away with his wife! Trace that trunk he shipped out. Open it up when you've located it—and I think you'll find her!"

And I hung up without waiting to hear what he was going to do about it. He didn't ring back, so I suspected he was going to give my suggestion a spin after all, in spite of his loudly proclaimed skepticism.

I stayed there by the window all night, keeping a sort of deathwatch. There were two more match-flares after the first, at about half-hour intervals. Nothing more after that. So possibly he was asleep over there. Possibly not. I had to sleep some time myself, and I finally succumbed in the flaming light of the early sun. Anything that he was going to do, he would have done under cover of darkness and not waited for broad daylight. There wouldn't be anything much to watch, for a while now. And what was there that he needed to do any more, anyway? Nothing, just sit tight and let a little disarming time slip by.

It seemed like five minutes later that Sam came over and touched me, but it was already high noon. I said irritably: "Didn't you lamp that note I pinned up, for you to let me sleep?"

He said: "Yeah, but it's your old friend Inspector Boyne. I figured you'd sure want to—"

It was a personal visit this time. Boyne came into the room behind him without waiting, and without much cordiality.

I said to get rid of Sam: "Go inside and smack a couple of eggs together."

Boyne began in a galvanized-iron voice: "Jeff, what do you mean by doing anything like this to me? I've made a fool out of myself, thanks to you. Sending my men out right and left on wild-goose chases. Thank God I didn't put my foot in it any worse than I did, and have this guy picked up and brought in for questioning."

"Oh, then you don't think that's necessary?" I suggested, drily.

The look he gave me took care of that. "I'm not alone

in the department, you know. There are men over me I'm accountable to for my actions. That looks great, don't it, sending one of my fellows one-half-a-day's train ride up into the sticks to some godforsaken whistle-stop or other at departmental expense—"

"Then you located the trunk?"

"We traced it through the express agency," he said flintily.

"And you opened it?"

"We did better than that. We got in touch with the various farmhouses in the immediate locality, and Mrs. Thorwald came down to the junction in a produce truck from one of them and opened it for him herself, with her own keys!"

Very few men have ever gotten a look from an old friend such as I got from him. At the door he said, stiff as a rifle barrel: "Just let's forget all about it, shall we? That's about the kindest thing either one of us can do for the other. You're not yourself, and I'm out a little of my own pocket money, time and temper. Let's let it go at that. If you want to telephone me in future I'll be glad to give you my home number."

The door went *whopp!* behind him.

For about ten minutes after he stormed out my numbed mind was in a sort of straitjacket. Then it started to wriggle its way free. "The hell with the police. I can't prove it to them, maybe, but I can prove it to myself, one way or the other, once and for all. Either I'm wrong or I'm right. He's got his armor on against them. But his back is naked and unprotected against me."

I called Sam in. "Whatever became of that spyglass we used to have, when we were bumming around on that cabin cruiser that season?"

He found it some place downstairs and came in with it, blowing on it and rubbing it along his sleeve. I let it lie idle in my lap first. I took a piece of paper and a pencil and wrote six words on it: "What have you done with her?"

I sealed it in an envelope and left the envelope blank. I said to Sam: "Now here's what I want you to do, and I want you to be slick about it. You take this, go in that Building Five Twenty-five, climb the stairs to the fourth-floor rear and ease it under the door. You're fast, at least you used to be. Let's see if you're fast enough to keep from being caught at it. Then when you get safely down again, give the outside doorbell a little poke, to attract attention."

His mouth started to open.

"And don't ask me any questions, you understand? I'm not fooling."

He went, and I got the spyglass ready.

I got him in the right focus after a minute or two. A face leaped up, and I was really seeing him for the first time. Dark-haired, but unmistakable Scandinavian ancestry. Looked like a sinewy customer, although he didn't run to much bulk.

About five minutes went by. His head turned sharply, profileward. That was the bell-poke, right there. The note must be in already.

He gave me the back of his head as he went back toward the flat door. The lens could follow him all the way to the rear, where my unaided eyes hadn't been able to before.

He opened the door first, missed seeing it, looked out on a level. He closed it. Then he dipped, straightened up. He had it. I could see him turning it this way and that.

He shifted in, away from the door, nearer the window. He thought danger lay near the door, safety away from it. He didn't know it was the other way around, the deeper into his own rooms he retreated the greater the danger.

He'd torn it open, he was reading it. God, how I watched his expression. My eyes clung to it like leeches. There was a sudden widening, a pulling—the whole skin of his face seemed to stretch back behind the ears, narrowing his eyes to Mongoloids'. Shock. Panic. His hand pushed out and found the wall, and he braced himself with it. Then he went back toward the door again slowly. I could see him creeping up on it, stalking it as though it were something alive. He opened it so slenderly you couldn't see it at all, peered fearfully through the crack. Then he closed it, and he came back, zigzag, off balance from sheer reflex dismay. He toppled into a chair and snatched up a drink. Out of the bottleneck itself this time. And even while he was holding it to his lips, his head was turned looking over his shoulder at the door that had suddenly thrown his secret in his face.

I put the glass down.

Guilty! Guilty as all hell, and the police be damned!

My hand started toward the phone, came back again. What was the use? They wouldn't listen now any more than they had before. "You should have seen his face," etc. And I could hear Boyne's answer: "Anyone gets a jolt from an anonymous letter, true or false. You would yourself." They had a real live Mrs. Thorwald to show me—or thought they had. I'd have to show them the dead one, to prove that they both weren't one and the same. I, from my window, had to show them a body.

Well, he'd have to show me first.

It took hours before I got it. I kept pegging away at it, pegging away at it, while the afternoon wore away. Meanwhile he was pacing back and forth there like a caged panther. Two minds with but one thought, turned inside-out in my case. How to keep it hidden, how to see that it wasn't kept hidden.

I was afraid he might try to light out, but if he intended doing that he was going to wait until after dark, apparently, so I had a little time yet. Possibly he didn't want to himself, unless he was driven to it—still felt that it was more dangerous than to stay.

The customary sights and sounds around me went on unnoticed, while the main stream of my thoughts pounded like a torrent against that one obstacle stubbornly damming them up: how to get him to give the location away to me, so that I could give it away in turn to the police.

I was dimly conscious, I remember, of the landlord or

somebody bringing in a prospective tenant to look at the sixth-floor apartment, the one that had already been finished. This was two over Thorwald's; they were still at work on the in-between one. At one point an odd little bit of synchronization, completely accidental of course, cropped up. Landlord and tenant both happened to be near the living room windows on the sixth at the same moment that Thorwald was near those on the fourth. Both parties moved onward simultaneously into the kitchen from there, and, passing the blind spot of the wall, appeared next at the kitchen windows. It was uncanny, they were almost like precision strollers or puppets manipulated on one and the same string. It probably wouldn't have happened again just like that in another fifty years. Immediately afterward they digressed, never to repeat themselves like that again.

The thing was, something about it had disturbed me. There had been some slight flaw or hitch to mar its smoothness. I tried for a moment or two to figure out what it had been, and couldn't. The landlord and tenant had gone now, and only Thorwald was in sight. My unaided memory wasn't enough to recapture it for me. My eyesight might have if it had been repeated, but it wasn't.

It sank into my subconscious, to ferment there like yeast, while I went back to the main problem at hand.

I got it finally. It was well after dark, but I finally hit on a way. It mightn't work, it was cumbersome and roundabout, but it was the only way I could think of. An alarmed turn of the head, a quick precautionary step in one certain direction, was all I needed. And to get this brief, flickering, transitory giveaway, I needed two phone calls and an absence of about half an hour on his part between them.

I leafed a directory by matchlight until I'd found what I wanted: "Thorwald, Lars, 525 Bndct . . . SWansea 5–2114."

I blew out the match, picked up the phone in the dark. It was like television. I could see to the other end of my call, only not along the wire but by a direct channel of vision from window to window.

He said "Hullo?" gruffly.

I thought: "How strange this is. I've been accusing him of murder for three days straight, and only now I'm hearing his voice for the first time."

I didn't try to disguise my own voice. After all, he'd never see me and I'd never see him. I said: "You got my note?"

He said guardedly: "Who is this?"

"Just somebody who happens to know."

He said craftily: "Know what?"

"Know what you know. You and I, we're the only ones."

He controlled himself well. I didn't hear a sound. But he didn't know he was open another way too. I had the glass balanced there at proper height on two large books on the sill. Through the window I saw him pull open the collar of his shirt as though its stricture was intolerable. Then he backed his hand over his eyes like you do when there's a light blinding you.

His voice came back firmly. "I don't know what you're talking about."

"Business, that's what I'm talking about. It should be worth something to me, shouldn't it? To keep it from going any further." I wanted to keep him from catching on that it was the windows. I still needed them, I needed them now more than ever. "You weren't very careful about your door the other night. Or maybe the draft swung it open a little."

That hit him where he lived. Even the stomach heave reached me over the wire. "You didn't see anything. There wasn't anything to see."

"That's up to you. Why should I go to the police?" I coughed a little. "If it would pay me not to."

"Oh," he said. And there was relief of a sort in it. "D'you want to—see me? Is that it?"

"That would be the best way, wouldn't it? How much can you bring with you for now?"

"I've only got about seventy dollars around here."

"All right, then we can arrange the rest for later. Do you

know where Lakeside Park is? I'm near there now. Suppose we make it there." That was about thirty minutes away. Fifteen there and fifteen back. "There's a little pavilion as you go in."

"How many of you are there?" he asked cautiously.

"Just me. It pays to keep things to yourself. That way you don't have to divvy up."

He seemed to like that too. "I'll take a run out," he said, "just to see what it's all about."

I watched him more closely than ever, after he'd hung up. He flitted straight through to the end room, the bedroom, that he didn't go near any more. He disappeared into a clothes closet in there, stayed a minute, came out again. He must have taken something out of a hidden cranny or niche in there that even the dicks had missed. I could tell by the pistonlike motion of his hand, just before it disappeared inside his coat, what it was. A gun.

"It's a good thing," I thought, "I'm not out there in Lakeside Park waiting for my seventy dollars."

The place blacked and he was on his way.

I called Sam in. "I want you to do something for me that's a little risky. In fact, damn risky. You might break a leg, or you might get shot, or you might even get pinched. We've been together ten years, and I wouldn't ask you anything like that if I could do it myself. But I can't, and it's got to be done." Then I told him. "Go out the back way, cross the backyard fences, and see if you can get into that fourth-floor flat up the fire escape. He's left one of the windows down a little from the top."

"What do you want me to look for?"

"Nothing." The police had been there already, so what was the good of that? "There are three rooms over there. I want you to disturb everything just a little bit, in all three, to show someone's been in there. Turn up the edge of each rug a little, shift every chair and table around a little, leave the closet doors standing out. Don't pass up a thing. Here, keep your eyes on this." I took off my own wristwatch,

strapped it on him. "You've got twenty-five minutes, starting from now. If you stay within those twenty-five minutes,
nothing will happen to you. When you see they're up, don't
wait any longer, get out and get out fast."

"Climb back down?"

"No." He wouldn't remember, in his excitement, if he'd
left the windows up or not. And I didn't want him to connect
danger with the back of his place, but with the front. I
wanted to keep my own window out of it. "Latch the window down tight, let yourself out the door and beat it out of
the building the front way, for your life!"

"I'm just an easy mark for you," he said ruefully, but he
went.

He came out through our own basement door below
me, and scrambled over the fences. If anyone had chal-
lenged him from one of the surrounding windows, I was
going to backstop for him, explain I'd sent him down to look
for something. But no one did. He made it pretty good for
anyone his age. He isn't so young any more. Even the fire
escape backing the flat, which was drawn up short, he
managed to contact by standing up on something. He got in,
lit the light, looked over at me. I motioned him to go ahead,
not weaken.

I watched him at it. There wasn't any way I could protect him, now that he was in there. Even Thorwald would
be within his rights in shooting him down—this was break
and entry. I had to stay in back behind the scenes, like I
had been all along. I couldn't get out in front of him as a
lookout and shield him. Even the dicks had had a lookout
posted.

He must have been tense, doing it. I was twice as tense,
watching him do it. The twenty-five minutes took fifty to go
by. Finally he came over to the window, latched it fast. The
lights went, and he was out. He'd made it. I blew out a
bellyful of breath that was twenty-five minutes old.

I heard him keying the street door, and when he came
up I said warningly: "Leave the light out in here. Go and

build yourself a great big two-story whiskey punch; you're as close to white as you'll ever be."

Thorwald came back twenty-nine minutes after he'd left for Lakeside Park. A pretty slim margin to hang a man's life on. So now for the finale of the long-winded business, and here was hoping. I got my second phone call in before he had time to notice anything amiss. It was tricky timing but I'd been sitting there with the receiver ready in my hand, dialing the number over and over, then killing it each time. He came in on the 2 of 5–2114, and I saved that much time. The ring started before his hand came away from the light switch.

This was the one that was going to tell the story.

"You were supposed to bring money, not a gun; that's why I didn't show up." I saw the jolt that threw into him. The window still had to stay out of it. "I saw you tap the inside of your coat, where you had it, as you came out on the street." Maybe he hadn't, but he wouldn't remember by now whether he had or not. You usually do when you're packing a gun and aren't an habitual carrier.

"Too bad you had your trip out and back for nothing. I didn't waste my time while you were gone, though. I know more now than I knew before." This was the important part. I had the glass up and I was practically fluoroscoping him. "I've found out where—it is. You know what I mean. I know now where you've got—it. I was there while you were out."

Not a word. Just quick breathing.

"Don't you believe me? Look around. Put the receiver down and take a look for yourself. I found it."

He put it down, moved as far as the living room entrance, and touched off the lights. He just looked around him once, in a sweeping, all-embracing stare, that didn't come to a head on any one fixed point, didn't center at all.

He was smiling grimly when he came back to the phone. All he said, softly and with malignant satisfaction, was "You're a liar."

Then I saw him lay the receiver down and take his hand off it. I hung up at my end.

The test had failed. And yet it hadn't. He hadn't given the location away as I'd hoped he would. And yet that "You're a liar" was a tacit admission that it was there to be found, somewhere around him, somewhere on those premises. In such a good place that he didn't have to worry about it, didn't even have to look to make sure.

So there was a kind of sterile victory in my defeat. But it wasn't worth a damn to me.

He was standing there with his back to me, and I couldn't see what he was doing. I knew the phone was somewhere in front of him, but I thought he was just standing there pensive behind it. His head was slightly lowered, that was all. I'd hung up at my end. I didn't even see his elbow move. And if his index finger did, I couldn't see it.

He stood like that a moment or two, then finally he moved aside. The lights went out over there; I lost him. He was careful not even to strike matches, like he sometimes did in the dark.

My mind no longer distracted by having him to look at, I turned to trying to recapture something else—that troublesome little hitch in synchronization that had occurred this afternoon, when the renting agent and he both moved simultaneously from one window to the next. The closest I could get was this: it was like when you're looking at someone through a pane of imperfect glass, and a flaw in the glass distorts the symmetry of the reflected image for a second, until it has gone on past that point. Yet that wouldn't do, that was not it. The windows had been open and there had been no glass between. And I hadn't been using the lens at the time.

My phone rang. Boyne, I supposed. It wouldn't be anyone else at this hour. Maybe, after reflecting on the way he'd jumped all over me— I said "Hello" unguardedly, in my own normal voice.

There wasn't any answer.

I said: "Hello? Hello? Hello?" I kept giving away samples of my voice.

There wasn't a sound from first to last.

I hung up finally. It was still dark over there, I noticed.

Sam looked in to check out. He was a bit thick-tongued from his restorative drink. He said something about "Awri' if I go now?" I half heard him. I was trying to figure out another way of trapping *him* over there into giving away the right spot. I motioned my consent absently.

He went a little unsteadily down the stairs to the ground floor and after a delaying moment or two I heard the street door close after him. Poor Sam, he wasn't much used to liquor.

I was left alone in the house, one chair the limit of my freedom of movement.

Suddenly a light went on over there again, just momentarily, to go right out again afterward. He must have needed it for something, to locate something that he had already been looking for and found he wasn't able to put his hands on readily without it. He found it, whatever it was, almost immediately, and moved back at once to put the lights out again. As he turned to do so, I saw him give a glance out the window. He didn't come to the window to do it, he just shot it out in passing.

Something about it struck me as different from any of the others I'd seen him give in all the time I'd been watching him. If you can qualify such an elusive thing as a glance, I would have termed it a glance with a purpose. It was certainly anything but vacant or random, it had a bright spark of fixity in it. It wasn't one of those precautionary sweeps I'd seen him give, either. It hadn't started over on the other side and worked its way around to my side, the right. It had hit dead-center at my bay window, for just a split second while it lasted, and then was gone again. And the lights were gone, and he was gone.

Sometimes your senses take things in without your mind translating them into their proper meaning. My eyes saw that look. My mind refused to smelter it properly. "It was meaningless," I thought. "An unintentional bull's-eye that just happened to hit square over here, as he went toward the lights on his way out."

Delayed action. A wordless ring of the phone. To test a voice? A period of bated darkness following that, in which two could have played at the same game—stalking one another's window squares, unseen. A last-moment flicker of the lights, that was bad strategy but unavoidable. A parting glance, radioactive with malignant intention. All these things sank in without fusing. My eyes did their job, it was my mind that didn't—or at least took its time about it.

Seconds went by in packages of sixty. It was very still around the familiar quadrangle formed by the back of the houses. Sort of a breathless stillness. And then a sound came into it, starting up from nowhere, nothing. The unmistakable, spaced clicking a cricket makes in the silence of the night. I thought of Sam's superstition about them that he claimed had never failed to fulfill itself yet. If that was the case, it looked bad for somebody in one of these slumbering houses around here—

Sam had been gone only about ten minutes. And now he was back again, he must have forgotten something. That drink was responsible. Maybe his hat, or maybe even the key to his own quarters uptown. He knew I couldn't come down and let him in, and he was trying to be quiet about it, thinking perhaps I'd dozed off. All I could hear was this faint jiggling down at the lock of the front door. It was one of those old-fashioned stoop houses, with an outer pair of storm doors that were allowed to swing free all night, and then a small vestibule, and then the inner door, worked by a simple iron key. The liquor had made his hand a little unreliable, although he'd had this difficulty once or twice before, even without it. A match would have helped him find the keyhole quicker, but then, Sam doesn't smoke. I knew he wasn't likely to have one on him.

The sound had stopped now. He must have given up,

gone away again, decided to let whatever it was go until
tomorrow. He hadn't gotten in, because I knew his noisy
way of letting doors coast shut by themselves too well, and
there hadn't been any sound of that sort, that loose slap he
always made.

Then suddenly it exploded. Why at this particular moment, I don't know. That was some mystery of the inner
workings of my own mind. It flashed like waiting gunpow-
der which a spark has finally reached along a slow train.
Drove all thoughts of Sam, and the front door, and this and
that completely out of my head. It had been waiting there
since midafternoon today, and only now— More of that
delayed action. Damn that delayed action.

The renting agent and Thorwald had both started even
from the living room window. An intervening gap of blind
wall, and both had reappeared at the kitchen window, still
one above the other. But some sort of a hitch or flaw or jump
had taken place, right there, that bothered me. The eye is
a reliable surveyor. There wasn't anything the matter with
their timing, it was with their parallelness, or whatever the
word is. The hitch had been vertical, not horizontal. There
had been an upward "jump."

Now I had it, now I knew. And it couldn't wait. It was
too good. They wanted a body? Now I had one for them.

Sore or not, Boyne would *have* to listen to me now. I
didn't waste any time, I dialed his precinct house then and
there in the dark, working the slots in my lap by memory
alone. They didn't make much noise going around, just a
light click. Not even as distinct as that cricket out there—

"He went home long ago," the desk sergeant said.

This couldn't wait. "All right, give me his home phone
number."

He took a minute, came back again. "Trafalgar," he
said. Then nothing more.

"Well? Trafalgar what?" Not a sound.

"Hello? Hello?" I tapped it. "Operator, I've been cut off.
Give me that party again." I couldn't get her either.

I hadn't been cut off. My wire had been cut. That had been too sudden, right in the middle of— And to be cut like that it would have to be done somewhere right here inside the house with me. Outside it went underground.

Delayed action. This time final, fatal, altogether too late. A voiceless ring of the phone. A direction finder of a look from over there. "Sam" seemingly trying to get back in a while ago.

Surely, death was somewhere inside the house here with me. And I couldn't move, I couldn't get up out of this chair. Even if I had gotten through to Boyne just now, that would have been too late. There wasn't time enough now for one of those camera finishes in this. I could have shouted out the window to that gallery of sleeping rear-window neighbors around me, I supposed. It would have brought them to the windows. It couldn't have brought them over here in time. By the time they had even figured which particular house it was coming from, it would stop again, be over with. I didn't open my mouth. Not because I was brave, but because it was so obviously useless.

He'd be up in a minute. He must be on the stairs now, although I couldn't hear him. Not even a creak. A creak would have been a relief, would have placed him. This was like being shut up in the dark with the silence of a gliding, coiling cobra somewhere around you.

There wasn't a weapon in the place with me. There were books there on the wall, in the dark, within reach. Me, who never read. The former owner's books. There was a bust of Rousseau or Montesquieu, I'd never been able to decide which, one of those gents with flowing manes, topping them. It was a monstrosity, bisque clay, but it too dated from before my occupancy.

I arched my middle upward from the chair seat and clawed desperately up at it. Twice my fingertips slipped off it, then at the third raking I got it to teeter, and the fourth brought it down into my lap, pushing me down into the chair. There was a steamer rug under me. I didn't need it

around me in this weather, I'd been using it to soften the
seat of the chair. I tugged it out from under and mantled it
around me like an Indian brave's blanket. Then I squirmed
far down in the chair, let my head and one shoulder dangle
out over the arm, on the side next to the wall. I hoisted the
bust to my other, upward shoulder, balanced it there
precariously for a second head, blanket tucked around its
ears. From the back, in the dark, it would look—I hoped—

I proceeded to breathe adenoidally, like someone in
heavy upright sleep. It wasn't hard. My own breath was
coming nearly that labored anyway, from tension.

He was good with knobs and hinges and things. I never
heard the door open, and this one, unlike the one downstairs, was right behind me. A little eddy of air puffed
through the dark at me. I could feel it because my scalp, the
real one, was all wet at the roots of the hair right then.

If it was going to be a knife or head blow, the dodge
might give me a second chance, that was the most I could
hope for, I knew. My arms and shoulders are hefty. I'd bring
him down on me in a bear hug after the first slash or drive,
and break his neck or collarbone against me. If it was going
to be a gun, he'd get me anyway in the end. A difference of
a few seconds. He had a gun, I knew, that he was going to
use on me in the open, over at Lakeside Park. I was hoping
that here, indoors, in order to make his own escape more
practicable—

Time was up.

The flash of the shot lit up the room for a second, it was
so dark. Or at least the corners of it, like flickering, weak
lightning. The bust bounced on my shoulder and disinte-
grated into chunks.

I thought he was jumping up and down on the floor for
a minute with frustrated rage. Then when I saw him dart by
me and lean over the windowsill to look for a way out, the
sound transferred itself rearward and downward, became a
pummeling with hoof and hip at the street door. The camera
finish after all. But he still could have killed me five times.

I flung my body down into the narrow crevice between chair arm and wall, but my legs were still up, and so was my head and that one shoulder.

He whirled, fired at me so close that it was like looking a sunrise in the face. I didn't feel it, so—it hadn't hit.

"You—" I heard him grunt to himself. I think it was the last thing he said The rest of his life was all action, not verbal.

He flung over the sill on one arm and dropped into the yard. Two-story drop. He made it because he missed the cement, landed on the sod strip in the middle. I jacked myself up over the chair arm and flung myself bodily forward at the window, nearly hitting it chin first.

He went all right. When life depends on it, you go. He took the first fence, rolled over that bellyward. He went over the second like a cat, hands and feet pointed together in a spring. Then he was back in the rear yard of his own building. He got up on something, just about like Sam had — The rest was all footwork, with quick little corkscrew twists at each landing stage. Sam had latched his windows down when he was over there, but he'd reopened one of them for ventilation on his return. His whole life depended now on that casual, unthinking little act—

Second, third. He was up to his own windows. He'd made it. Something went wrong. He veered out away from them in another pretzel-twist, flashed up toward the fifth, the one above. Something sparked in the darkness of one of his own windows where he'd been just now, and a shot thudded heavily out around the quadrangle-enclosure like a big bass drum.

He passed the fifth, the sixth, got up to the roof. He'd made it a second time. Gee, he loved life! The guys in his own windows couldn't get him, he was over them in a straight line and there was too much fire escape interlacing in the way.

I was too busy watching him to watch what was going on around me. Suddenly Boyne was next to me, sighting. I heard him mutter: "I almost hate to do this, he's got to fall so far."

He was balanced on the roof parapet up there, with a star right over his head. An unlucky star. He stayed a minute too long, trying to kill before he was killed. Or maybe he was killed, and knew it.

A shot cracked, high up against the sky, the window-pane flew apart all over the two of us and one of the books snapped right behind me.

Boyne didn't say anything more about hating to do it. My face was pressing outward against his arm. The recoil of his elbow jarred my teeth. I blew a clearing through the smoke to watch him go.

It was pretty horrible. He took a minute to show anything, standing up there on the parapet. Then he let his gun go, as if to say: "I won't need this anymore." Then he went after it. He missed the fire escape entirely, came all the way down on the outside. He landed so far out he hit one of the projecting planks, down there out of sight. It bounced his body up, like a springboard. Then it landed again—for good. And that was all.

I said to Boyne: "I got it. I got it finally. The fifth-floor flat, the one over his, that they're still working on. The cement kitchen floor, raised above the level of the other rooms. They wanted to comply with the fire laws and also obtain a dropped living room effect, as cheaply as possible. Dig it up—"

He went right over then and there, down through the basement and over the fences, to save time. The electricity wasn't turned on yet in that one, they had to use their torches. It didn't take them long at that, once they'd got started. In about half an hour he came to the window and wigwagged over for my benefit. It meant yes.

He didn't come over until nearly eight in the morning; after they'd tidied up and taken them away. Both away, the hot dead and the cold dead. He said: "Jeff, I take it all back. That damn fool that I sent up there about the trunk—well, it wasn't his fault, in a way. I'm to blame. He didn't have orders to check on the woman's description, only on the contents of the trunk. He came back and touched on it in a general way. I go home and I'm in bed already, and suddenly pop! into my brain—one of the tenants I questioned two whole days ago had given us a few details and they didn't tally with his on several important points. Talk about being slow to catch on!"

"I've had that all the way through this damn thing," I admitted ruefully. "I call it delayed action. It nearly killed me."

"I'm a police officer and you're not."

"That how you happened to shine at the right time?"

"Sure. We came over to pick him up for questioning. I left them planted there when we saw he wasn't in, and came on over here by myself to square it up with you while we were waiting. How did you happen to hit on that cement floor?"

I told him about the freak synchronization. "The renting agent showed up taller at the kitchen window, in proportion to Thorwald, than he had been a moment before when both were at the living room windows together. It was no secret that they were putting in cement floors, topped by a cork composition, and raising them considerable. But it took on new meaning. Since the top-floor one has been finished for some time, it had to be the fifth. Here's the way I have it lined up, just in theory. She's been in ill health for years, and he's been out of work, and he got sick of that and of her both. Met this other—"

"She'll be here later today, they're bringing her down under arrest."

"He probably insured her for all he could get, and then started to poison her slowly, trying not to leave any trace. I imagine—and remember, this is pure conjecture—she caught him at it that night the light was on all night. Caught on in some way, or caught him in the act. He lost his head, and did the very thing he had wanted all along to avoid

doing. Killed her by violence—strangulation or a blow. The
rest had to be hastily improvised. He got a better break than
he deserved at that. He thought of the apartment upstairs,
went up and looked around. They'd just finished laying the
floor, the cement hadn't hardened yet and the materials
were still around. He gouged a trough out of it just wide
enough to take her body, put her in it, mixed fresh cement
and recemented over her, possibly raising the general level
of the flooring an inch or two so that she'd be safely covered.
A permanent, odorless coffin. Next day the workmen came
back, laid down the cork surfacing on top of it without noticing anything, I suppose he'd used one of their own trowels
to smooth it. Then he sent his accessory upstate fast, near
where his wife had been several summers before, but to a
different farmhouse where she wouldn't be recognized,
along with the trunk keys. Sent the trunk up after her, and
dropped himself an already used postcard into his mailbox,
with the year date blurred. In a week or two she would have
probably committed 'suicide' up there as Mrs. Anna Thorwald. Despondency due to ill health. Written him a farewell
note and left her clothes beside some body of deep water.
It was risky, but they might have succeeded in collecting the
insurance at that."

By nine Boyne and the rest had gone. I was still sitting
there in the chair, too keyed up to sleep. Sam came in and
said: "Here's Doc Preston."

He showed up rubbing his hands, in that way he has.
"Guess we can take that cast off your leg now. You must be
tired of sitting there all day doing nothing."

THE HOUSE IN GOBLIN WOOD

John Dickson Carr

In Pall Mall, that hot July afternoon three years before the war, an open saloon car was drawn up to the curb just opposite the Senior Conservatives' Club.

And in the car sat two conspirators.

It was the drowsy postlunch hour among the clubs, where only the sun remained brilliant. The Rag lay somnolent; the Atheneum slept outright. But these two conspirators, a dark-haired young man in his early thirties and a fair-haired girl perhaps half a dozen years younger, never moved. They stared intently at the Gothic-like front of the Senior Conservatives'.

"Look here, Eve," muttered the young man, and punched at the steering wheel. "Do you think this is going to work?"

"I don't know," the fair-haired girl confessed. "He absolutely *loathes* picnics."

"Anyway, we've probably missed him."

"Why so?"

"He can't have taken as long over lunch as that!" her companion protested, looking at a wristwatch. The young man was rather shocked. "It's a quarter to four! Even if . . ."

"Bill! There! Look there!"

Their patience was rewarded by an inspiring sight.

Out of the portals of the Senior Conservatives' Club, in awful majesty, marched a large, stout, barrel-shaped gentleman in a white linen suit.

His corporation preceded him like the figurehead of a man-of-war. His shell-rimmed spectacles were pulled down on a broad nose, all being shaded by a Panama hat. At the top of the stone steps he surveyed the street with a lordly sneer.

"Sir Henry!" called the girl.

"Hey?" said Sir Henry Merrivale.

"I'm Eve Drayton. Don't you remember me? You knew my father!"

"Oh, ah," said the great man.

"We've been waiting here a terribly long time," Eve pleaded. "Couldn't you see us for just five minutes? . . . The thing to do," she whispered to her companion, "is to keep him in a good humor. Just keep him in a good humor!"

As a matter of fact, H.M. was in a good humor, having just triumphed over the home secretary in an argument. But not even his own mother could have guessed it. Majestically, with the same lordly sneer, he began in grandeur to descend the steps of the Senior Conservatives'. He did this, in fact, until his foot encountered an unnoticed object lying some three feet from the bottom.

It was a banana skin.

"Oh, dear!" said the girl.

Now it must be stated with regret that in the old days certain urchins, of what were then called the "lower orders," had a habit of placing such objects on the steps in the hope that some eminent statesman would take a toss on his way to Whitehall. This was a venial but deplorable practice, probably accounting for what Mr. Gladstone said in 1882.

In any case, it accounted for what Sir Henry Merrivale said now.

From the pavement, where H.M. landed in a seated position, arose in H.M.'s bellowing voice such a torrent of profanity, such a flood of invective and vile obscenities, as has seldom before blasted the holy calm of Pall Mall. It brought the hall porter hurrying down the steps, and Eve Drayton flying out of the car.

Heads were now appearing at the windows of the Atheneum across the street.

"Is it all right?" cried the girl, with concern in her blue eyes. "Are you hurt?"

H.M. merely looked at her. His hat had fallen off, disclosing a large bald head; and he merely sat on the pavement and looked at her.

"Anyway, H.M., get up! Please get up!"

"Yes, sir," begged the hall porter, "for heaven's sake get up!"

"Get up?" bellowed H.M., in a voice audible as far as St. James's Street. "Burn it all, how *can* I get up?"

"But why not?"

"My behind's out of joint," said H.M. simply. "I'm hurt awful bad. I'm probably goin' to have spinal dislocation for the rest of my life."

"But, sir, people are looking!"

H.M. explained what these people could do. He eyed Eve Drayton with a glare of indescribable malignancy over his spectacles.

"I suppose, my wench, *you're* responsible for this?"

Eve regarded him in consternation.

"You don't mean the banana skin?" she cried.

"Oh, yes, I do," said H.M., folding his arms like a prosecuting counsel.

"But we—we only wanted to invite you to a picnic!"

H.M. closed his eyes.

"That's fine," he said in a hollow voice. "All the same, don't you think it'd have been a subtler kind of hint just to pour mayonnaise over my head or shove ants down the back of my neck? Oh, Lord love a duck!"

"I didn't mean that! I meant . . ."

"Let me help you up, sir," interposed the calm, reassuring voice of the dark-haired and blue-chinned young man who had been with Eve in the car.

"So you want to help too, hey? And who are *you*?"

"I'm awfully sorry!" said Eve. "I should have introduced you! This is my fiancé. Dr. William Sage."

H.M.'s face turned purple.

"I'm glad to see," he observed, "you had the uncommon decency to bring along a doctor. I appreciate that, I do. And the car's there, I suppose, to assist with the examination when I take off my pants?"

The hall porter uttered a cry of horror.

Bill Sage, either from jumpiness and nerves or from sheer inability to keep a straight face, laughed loudly.

"I keep telling Eve a dozen times a day," he said, "that I'm not to be called 'Doctor.' I happen to be a surgeon—"

(Here H.M. really did look alarmed.)

"—but I don't think we need operate. Nor, in my opinion," Bill gravely addressed the hall porter, "will it be necessary to remove Sir Henry's trousers in front of the Senior Conservatives' Club."

"Thank you very much, sir."

"We had an infernal nerve to come here," the young man confessed to H.M. "But I honestly think, Sir Henry, you'd be more comfortable in the car. What about it? Let me give you a hand up?"

Yet even ten minutes later, when H.M. sat glowering in the back of the car and two heads were craned round towards him, peace was not restored.

"All right!" said Eve. Her pretty, rather stolid face was flushed; her mouth looked miserable. "If you won't come to the picnic, you won't. But I did believe you might do it to oblige me."

"Well ... now!" muttered the great man uncomfortably.

"And I did think, too, you'd be interested in the other person who was coming with us. But Vicky's—difficult. She won't come either, if you don't."

"Oh? And who's this other guest?"

"Vicky Adams."

H.M.'s hand, which had been lifted for an oratorical gesture, dropped to his side.

"Vicky Adams? That's not the gal who . . . ?"

"Yes!" Eve nodded. "They say it was one of the great mysteries, twenty years ago, that the police failed to solve."

"It was, my wench," H.M. agreed somberly. "It was."

"And now Vicky's grown up. And we thought if you of all people went along, and spoke to her nicely, she'd tell us what really happened on that night."

H.M.'s small, sharp eyes fixed disconcertingly on Eve.

"I say, my wench. What's your interest in all this?"

"Oh, reasons." Eve glanced quickly at Bill Sage, who was again punching moodily at the steering wheel, and checked herself. "Anyway, what difference does it make now? If you won't go with us . . ."

H.M. assumed a martyred air.

"I never said I *wasn't* goin' with you, did I?" he demanded. (This was inaccurate, but no matter.) "Even after you practically made a cripple of me, I never said I *wasn't* goin'." His manner grew flurried and hasty. "But I got to leave now," he added apologetically. "I got to get back to my office."

"We'll drive you there, H.M."

"No, no, no," said the practical cripple, getting out of the car with surprising celerity. "Walkin' is good for my stomach if it's not so good for my behind. I'm a forgivin' man. You pick me up at my house tomorrow morning. G'bye."

And he lumbered off in the direction of the Haymarket.

It needed no close observer to see that H.M. was deeply abstracted. He remained so abstracted, indeed, as to be nearly murdered by a taxi at the Admiralty Arch; and he was halfway down Whitehall before a familiar voice stopped him.

"Afternoon, Sir Henry!"

Burly, urbane, buttoned up in blue serge, with his bowler hat and his boiled blue eye, stood Chief Inspector Masters.

"Bit odd," the chief inspector remarked affably, "to see you taking a constitutional on a day like this. And how are you, sir?"

"Awful," said H.M. instantly. "But that's not the point. Masters, you crawlin' snake! You're the very man I wanted to see."

Few things startled the chief inspector. This one did.

"You," he repeated, "wanted to see *me*?"

"Uh-huh."

"And what about?"

"Masters, do you remember the Victoria Adams case about twenty years ago?"

The chief inspector's manner suddenly changed and grew wary.

"Victoria Adams case?" he ruminated. "No, sir, I can't say I do."

"Son, you're lyin'! You were sergeant to old Chief Inspector Rutherford in those days, and well I remember it!"

Masters stood on his dignity.

"That's as may be, sir. But twenty years ago . . ."

"A little girl of twelve or thirteen, the child of very wealthy parents, disappeared one night out of a country cottage with all the doors and windows locked on the inside. A week later, while everybody was havin' screamin' hysterics, the child reappeared again: through the locks and bolts, tucked up in her bed as usual. And to this day nobody's ever known what really happened."

There was a silence, while Masters shut his jaws hard.

"This family, the Adamses," persisted H.M., "owned the cottage, down Aylesbury way, on the edge of Goblin Wood, opposite the lake. Or was it?"

"Oh, ah," growled Masters. "It was."

H.M. looked at him curiously.

"They used the cottage as a base for bathin' in summer, and ice skatin' in winter. It was black winter when the child vanished, and the place was all locked up inside against drafts. They say her old man nearly went loopy when he found her there a week later, lyin' asleep under the lamp. But all she'd say, when they asked her where she'd been, was *'I don't know.'* "

Again there was a silence, while red buses thundered through the traffic press of Whitehall.

"You've got to admit, Masters, there was a flamin' public rumpus. I say: did you ever read Barrie's *Mary Rose?*"

"No."

"Well, it was a situation straight out of Barrie. Some people, y'see, said that Vicky Adams was a child of faerie who'd been spirited away by the pixies . . ."

Whereupon Masters exploded.

He removed his bowler hat and made remarks about pixies, in detail, which could not have been bettered by H.M. himself.

"I know, son, I know." H.M. was soothing. Then his big voice sharpened. "Now tell me. Was all this talk strictly true?"

"What talk?"

"Locked windows? Bolted doors? No attic trap? No cellar? Solid walls and floor?"

"Yes, sir," answered Masters, regaining his dignity with a powerful effort, "I'm bound to admit it *was* true."

"Then there wasn't any jiggery-pokery about the cottage?"

"In your eye there wasn't," said Masters.

"How d'ye mean?"

"Listen, sir." Masters lowered his voice. "Before the Adamses took over that place, it was a hideout for Chuck Randall. At that time he was the swellest of the swell mob; we lagged him a couple of years later. Do you think Chuck wouldn't have rigged up some gadget for a getaway? Just so! Only . . ."

"Well? Hey?"

"We couldn't find it," grunted Masters.

"And I'll bet that pleased old Chief Inspector Ruther-ford?"

"I tell you straight: he was fair up the pole. Especially as the kid herself was a pretty kid, all big eyes and dark hair. You couldn't help trusting her story."

"Yes," said H.M. "That's what worries me."

"Worries you?"

"Oh, my son!" said H.M. dismally. "Here's Vicky Adams, the spoiled daughter of dotin' parents. She's supposed to be 'odd' and 'fey.' She's even encouraged to be. During her adolescence, the most impressionable time of her life, she gets wrapped round with the gauze of a mystery that people talk about even yet. What's that woman like now, Masters? What's that woman like now?"

"Dear Sir Henry!" murmured Miss Vicky Adams in her softest voice.

She said this just as William Sage's car, with Bill and Eve Drayton in the front seat, and Vicky and H.M. in the back seat, turned off the main road. Behind them lay the smoky-red roofs of Aylesbury, against a brightness of late afternoon. The car turned down a side road, a damp tunnel of greenery, and into another road which was little more than a lane between hedgerows.

H.M.—though cheered by three good-sized picnic hampers from Fortnum & Mason, their wickerwork lids bulging with a feast—did not seem happy. Nobody in that car was happy, with the possible exception of Miss Adams herself.

Vicky, unlike Eve, was small and dark and vivacious. Her large light-brown eyes, with very black lashes, could be arch and coy; or they could be dreamily intense. The late Sir James Barrie might have called her a sprite. Those of more sober views would have recognized a different quality: she had an inordinate sex appeal, which was as palpable as a physical touch to any male within yards. And despite her smallness, Vicky had a full voice like Eve's. All these qualities she used even in so simple a matter as giving traffic directions.

"First right," she would say, leaning forward to put her hands on Bill Sage's shoulders. "Then straight on until the next traffic light. Ah, clever boy!"

"Not at all, not at all!" Bill would disclaim, with red ears and rather an erratic style of driving.

"Oh, yes, you are!" And Vicky would twist the lobe of his ear, playfully, before sitting back again.

(Eve Drayton did not say anything. She did not even turn round. Yet the atmosphere, even of that quiet English picnic party, had already become a trifle hysterical.)

"Dear Sir Henry!" murmured Vicky, as they turned down into the deep lane between the hedgerows. "I do wish you wouldn't be so materialistic! I do, really. Haven't you the tiniest bit of spirituality in your nature?"

"Me?" said H.M. in astonishment. "I got a very lofty spiritual nature. But what I want just now, my wench, is grub. . . . Oi!"

Bill Sage glanced round.

"By that speedometer," H.M. pointed, "we've now come forty-six miles and a bit. We didn't even leave town until people of decency and sanity were having their tea. Where are we *going*?"

"But didn't you know?" asked Vicky, with wide-open eyes. "We're going to the cottage where I had such a dreadful experience when I was a child."

"Was it such a dreadful experience, Vicky dear?" inquired Eve.

Vicky's eyes seemed far away.

"I don't remember, really. I was only a child, you see. I didn't understand. I hadn't developed the power for myself then."

"What power?" H.M. asked sharply.

"To dematerialize," said Vicky. "Of course."

In that warm sun-dusted lane, between the hawthorn hedges, the car jolted over a rut. Crockery rattled.

"Uh-huh. I see," observed H.M. without inflection. "And where do you go, my wench, when you dematerialize?"

"Into a strange country. Through a little door. You wouldn't understand. Oh, you *are* such Philistines!" moaned Vicky. Then, with a sudden change of mood, she leaned forward and her whole physical allurement flowed again towards Bill Sage. "*You* wouldn't like me to disappear, would you, Bill?"

(Easy! Easy!)

"Only," said Bill, with a sort of wild gallantry, "if you promised to reappear again straightaway."

"Oh, I should have to do that." Vicky sat back. She was trembling. "The power wouldn't be strong enough. But even a poor little thing like me might be able to teach you a lesson. Look there!"

And she pointed ahead.

On their left, as the lane widened, stretched the ten-acre gloom of what is fancifully known as Goblin Wood. On their right lay a small lake, on private property and therefore deserted.

The cottage—set well back into a clearing of the wood so as to face the road, screened from it by a line of beeches —was in fact a bungalow of rough-hewn stone, with a slate roof. Across the front of it ran a wooden porch. It had a seedy air, like the long yellow-green grass of its front lawn. Bill parked the car at the side of the road, since there was no driveway.

"It's a bit lonely, ain't it?" demanded H.M. His voice boomed out against that utter stillness, under the hot sun.

"Oh, yes!" breathed Vicky. She jumped out of the car in a whirl of skirts. "That's why *they* were able to come and take me. When I was a child."

"They?"

"Dear Sir Henry! Do I need to explain?"

Then Vicky looked at Bill.

"I must apologize," she said, "for the state the house is in. I haven't been out here for months and months. There's a modern bathroom, I'm glad to say. Only paraffin lamps, of course. But then," a dreamy smile flashed across her face, "you won't need lamps, will you? Unless . . ."

"You mean," said Bill, who was taking a black case out of the car, "unless you disappear again?"

"Yes, Bill. And promise me you won't be frightened when I do."

The young man uttered a ringing oath which was shushed by Sir Henry Merrivale, who austerely said he disapproved of profanity. Eve Drayton was very quiet.

"But in the meantime," Vicky said wistfully, "let's forget it all, shall we? Let's laugh and dance and sing and pretend we're children! And surely our guest must be even more hungry by this time?"

It was in this emotional state that they sat down to their picnic.

H.M., if the truth must be told, did not fare too badly. Instead of sitting on some hummock of ground, they dragged a table and chairs to the shaded porch. All spoke in strained voices. But no word of controversy was said. It was only afterwards, when the cloth was cleared, the furniture and hampers pushed indoors, the empty bottles flung away, that danger tapped a warning.

From under the porch Vicky fished out two half-rotted deck chairs, which she set up in the long grass of the lawn. These were to be occupied by Eve and H.M., while Vicky took Bill Sage to inspect a plum tree of some remarkable quality she did not specify.

Eve sat down without comment. H.M., who was smoking a black cigar opposite her, waited some time before he spoke.

"Y'know," he said, taking the cigar out of his mouth, "you're behavin' remarkably well."

"Yes," Eve laughed. "Aren't I?"

"Are you pretty well acquainted with this Adams gal?"

"I'm her first cousin," Eve answered simply. "Now that her parents are dead, I'm the only relative she's got. I know *all* about her."

From far across the lawn floated two voices saying something about wild strawberries. Eve, her fair hair and fair complexion vivid against the dark line of Goblin Wood, clenched her hands on her knees.

"You see, H.M.," she hesitated, "there was another reason why I invited you here. I—I don't quite know how to approach it."

"I'm the old man," said H.M., tapping himself impressively on the chest. "You tell me."

"Eve, darling!" interposed Vicky's voice, crying across the ragged lawn. "Coo-ee! Eve!"

"Yes, dear?"

"I've just remembered," cried Vicky, "that I haven't shown Bill over the cottage! You don't mind if I steal him away from you for a little while?"

"No, dear! Of course not!"

It was H.M., sitting so as to face the bungalow, who saw Vicky and Bill go in. He saw Vicky's wistful smile as she closed the door after them. Eve did not even look around. The sun was declining, making fiery chinks through the thickness of Goblin Wood behind the cottage.

"I won't let her have him," Eve suddenly cried. "I won't! I won't! I won't!"

"Does she want him, my wench? Or, which is more to the point, does he want her?"

"He never has," Eve said with emphasis. "Not really. And he never will."

H.M., motionless, puffed out cigar smoke.

"Vicky's a faker," said Eve. "Does that sound catty?"

"Not necessarily. I was just thinkin' the same thing myself."

"I'm patient," said Eve. Her blue eyes were fixed. "I'm terribly, terribly patient. I can wait for years for what I want. Bill's not making much money now, and I haven't got a bean. But Bill's got great talent under that easygoing manner of his. He *must* have the right girl to help him. If only . . ."

"If only the elfin sprite would let him alone. Hey?"

"Vicky acts like that," said Eve, "towards practically every man she ever meets. That's why she never married. She says it leaves her soul free to commune with other souls. This occultism—"

Then it all poured out, the family story of the Adamses. This repressed girl spoke at length, spoke as perhaps she had never spoken before. Vicky Adams, the child who wanted to attract attention, her father Uncle Fred and her mother Aunt Margaret seemed to walk in vividness as the shadows gathered.

"I was too young to know her at the time of the 'disappearance,' of course. But, oh, I knew her afterwards! And I thought . . ."

"Well?"

"If I could get *you* here," said Eve, "I thought she'd try to show off with some game. And then you'd expose her. And Bill would see what an awful faker she is. But it's hopeless! It's hopeless!"

"Looky here," observed H.M., who was smoking his third cigar. He sat up. "Doesn't it strike you those two are being a rummy-awful long time just in lookin' through a little bungalow?"

Eve, roused out of a dream, stared back at him. She sprang to her feet. She was not now, you could guess, thinking of any disappearance.

"Excuse me a moment," she said curtly.

Eve hurried across to the cottage, went up on the porch, and opened the front door. H.M. heard her heels rap down the length of the small passage inside. She marched straight back again, closed the front door, and rejoined H.M.

"All the doors of the rooms are shut," she announced in a high voice. "I really don't think I ought to disturb them."

"Easy, my wench!"

"I have absolutely no interest," declared Eve, with the tears coming into her eyes, "in what happens to either of them now. Shall we take the car and go back to town without them?"

H.M. threw away his cigar, got up, and seized her by the shoulders.

"I'm the old man," he said, leering like an ogre. "Will you listen to me?"

"No!"

"If I'm any reader of the human dial," persisted H.M., "that young feller's no more gone on Vicky Adams than I am. He was scared, my wench. Scared." Doubt, indecision crossed H.M.'s face. "I dunno what he's scared of. Burn me, I don't! But . . ."

"Hoy!" called the voice of Bill Sage.

It did not come from the direction of the cottage.

They were surrounded on three sides by Goblin Wood, now blurred with twilight. From the north side the voice bawled at them, followed by crackling in dry undergrowth. Bill, his hair and sports coat and flannels more than a little dirty, regarded them with a face of bitterness.

"Here are her blasted wild strawberries," he announced, extending his hand. "Three of 'em. The fruitful (excuse me) result of three quarters of an hour's hard labor. I absolutely refuse to chase 'em in the dark."

For a moment Eve Drayton's mouth moved without speech.

"Then you weren't . . . in the cottage all this time?"

"In the cottage?" Bill glanced at it. "I was in that cottage," he said, "about five minutes. Vicky had a woman's whim. She wanted some wild strawberries out of what she called the 'forest.' "

"Wait a minute, son!" said H.M. very sharply. "You didn't come out that front door. Nobody did."

"No! I went out the back door! It opens straight on the wood."

"Yes. And what happened then?"

THE HOUSE IN GOBLIN WOOD

"Well, I went to look for these damned . . ."

"No, no! What did *she* do?"

"Vicky? She locked and bolted the back door on the inside. I remember her grinning at me through the glass panel. She—"

Bill stopped short. His eyes widened, and then narrowed, as though at the impact of an idea. All three of them turned to look at the rough-stone cottage.

"By the way," said Bill. He cleared his throat vigorously. "By the way, have you seen Vicky since then?"

"No."

"This couldn't be . . . ?"

"It could be, son," said H.M. "We'd all better go in there and have a look."

They hesitated for a moment on the porch. A warm, moist fragrance breathed up from the ground after sunset. In half an hour it would be completely dark.

Bill Sage threw open the front door and shouted Vicky's name. That sound seemed to penetrate, reverberating, through every room. The intense heat and stuffiness of the cottage, where no window had been raised in months, blew out at them. But nobody answered.

"Get inside," snapped H.M. "And stop yowlin'." The Old Maestro was nervous. "I'm dead sure she didn't get out by the front door; but we'll just make certain there's no slippin' out now."

Stumbling over the table and chairs they had used on the porch, he fastened the front door. They were in a narrow passage, once handsome with parquet floor and pine-paneled walls, leading to a door with a glass panel at the rear. H.M. lumbered forward to inspect this door and found it locked and bolted, as Bill had said.

Goblin Wood grew darker.

Keeping well together, they searched the cottage. It was not large, having two good-sized rooms on one side of the passage, and two small rooms on the other side, so as to make space for bathroom and kitchenette. H.M., raising fogs of dust, ransacked every inch where a person could possibly hide.

And all the windows were locked on the inside. And the chimney flues were too narrow to admit anybody.

And Vicky Adams wasn't there.

"Oh, my eye!" breathed Sir Henry Merrivale.

They had gathered, by what idiotic impulse not even H.M. could have said, just outside the open door of the bathroom. A bath tap dripped monotonously. The last light through a frosted-glass window showed three faces hung there as though disembodied.

"Bill," said Eve in an unsteady voice, "this is a trick. Oh, I've longed for her to be exposed! This is a trick!"

"Then where is she?"

"H.M. can tell us! Can't you, H.M.?"

"Well . . . now," muttered the great man.

Across H.M.'s Panama hat was a large black handprint, made there when he had pressed down the hat after investigating a chimney. He glowered under it.

"Son," he said to Bill, "there's just one question I want you to answer in all this hokey-pokey. When you went out pickin' wild strawberries, will you swear Vicky Adams didn't go with you?"

"As God is my judge, she didn't," returned Bill, with fervency and obvious truth. "Besides, how the devil could she? Look at the lock and bolt on the back door!"

H.M. made two more violent black handprints on his hat.

He lumbered forward, his head down, two or three paces in the narrow passage. His foot half skidded on something that had been lying there unnoticed, and he picked it up. It was a large, square section of thin, waterproof oilskin, jagged at one corner.

"Have you found anything?" demanded Bill in a strained voice.

"No. Not to make any sense, that is. But just a minute!"

At the rear of the passage, on the left-hand side, was the

bedroom from which Vicky Adams had vanished as a child. Though H.M. had searched this room once before, he opened the door again.

It was almost dark in Goblin Wood.

He saw dimly a room of twenty years before: a room of flounces, of lace curtains, of once-polished mahogany, its mirrors glimmering against white-papered walls. H.M. seemed especially interested in the windows.

He ran his hands carefully round the frame of each, even climbing laboriously up on a chair to examine the tops. He borrowed a box of matches from Bill; and the little spurts of light, following the rasp of the match, rasped against nerves as well. The hope died out of his face, and his companions saw it.

"H.M.," Bill said for the dozenth time, "where is she?"

"Son," replied H.M. despondently, "I don't know."

"Let's get out of here," Eve said abruptly. Her voice was a small scream. "I kn-know it's all a trick! I know Vicky's a faker! But let's get out of here. For God's sake let's get out of here!"

"As a matter of fact," Bill cleared his throat, "I agree. Anyway, we won't hear from Vicky until tomorrow morning."

"Oh, yes, you will," whispered Vicky's voice out of the darkness.

Eve screamed.

They lighted a lamp.

But there was nobody there.

Their retreat from the cottage, it must be admitted, was not very dignified.

How they stumbled down that ragged lawn in the dark, how they piled rugs and picnic hampers into the car, how they eventually found the main road again, is best left undescribed.

Sir Henry Merrivale has since sneered at this—"a bit of a goosey feeling; nothin' much"—and it is true that he has no nerves to speak of. But he can be worried, badly worried; and that he was worried on this occasion may be deduced from what happened later.

H.M., after dropping in at Claridge's for a modest late supper of lobster and *pêche Melba*, returned to his house in Brook Street and slept a hideous sleep. It was three o'clock in the morning, even before the summer dawn, when the ringing of the bedside telephone roused him.

What he heard sent his blood pressure soaring.

"Dear Sir Henry!" crooned a familiar and spritelike voice.

H.M. was himself again, full of gall and bile. He switched on the bedside lamp and put on his spectacles with care, so as adequately to address the phone.

"Have I got the honor," he said with dangerous politeness, "of addressin' Miss Vicky Adams?"

"Oh, yes!"

"I sincerely trust," said H.M., "you've been havin' a good time? Are you materialized yet?"

"Oh, yes!"

"Where are you now?"

"I'm afraid," there was coy laughter in the voice, "that must be a little secret for a day or two. I want to teach you a really *good* lesson. Blessings, dear."

And she hung up the receiver.

H.M. did not say anything. He climbed out of bed. He stalked up and down the room, his corporation majestic under an old-fashioned nightshirt stretching to his heels. Then, since he himself had been waked up at three o'clock in the morning, the obvious course was to wake up somebody else; so he dialed the home number of Chief Inspector Masters.

"No, sir," retorted Masters grimly, after coughing the frog out of his throat, "I do *not* mind you ringing up. Not a bit of it!" He spoke with a certain pleasure. "Because I've got a bit of news for you."

H.M. eyed the phone suspiciously.

"Masters, are you tryin' to do me in the eye again?"

"It's what you always try to do to me, isn't it?"

"All right, all right!" growled H.M. "What's the news?"

"Do you remember mentioning the Vicky Adams case yesterday?"

"Sort of. Yes."

"Oh, ah! Well, I had a word or two round among our people. I was tipped the wink to go and see a certain solicitor. He was old Mr. Fred Adams's solicitor before Mr. Adams died about six or seven years ago."

Here Masters's voice grew triumphant.

"I always said, Sir Henry, that Chuck Randall had planted some gadget in that cottage for a quick getaway. And I was right. The gadget was . . ."

"You were quite right, Masters. The gadget was a trick window."

The telephone, so to speak, gave a start.

"What's that?"

"A trick window." H.M. spoke patiently. "You press a spring. And the whole frame of the window, two leaves locked together, slides down between the walls far enough so you can climb over. Then you push it back up again."

"How in lum's name do you know that?"

"Oh, my, son! They used to build windows like it in country houses during the persecution of Catholic priests. It was a good enough *second* guess. Only . . . it won't work."

Masters seemed annoyed. "It won't work now," Masters agreed. "And do you know why?"

"I can guess. Tell me."

"Because, just before Mr. Adams died, he discovered how his darling daughter had flummoxed him. He never told anybody except his lawyer. He took a handful of four-inch nails, and sealed up the top of that frame so tight an orangutan couldn't move it, and painted 'em over so they wouldn't be noticed."

"Uh-huh. You can notice 'em now."

"I doubt if the young lady herself ever knew. But, by

George!" Masters said savagely. "I'd like to see anybody try the same game now!"

"You would, hey? Then will it interest you to know that the same gal has just disappeared out of the same house *again*?"

H.M. began a long narrative of the facts, but he had to break off because the telephone was raving.

"Honest, Masters," H.M. said seriously, "I'm not jokin'. She didn't get out through that window. But she did get out. You'd better meet me," he gave directions, "tomorrow morning. In the meantime, son, sleep well."

It was, therefore, a worn-faced Masters who went into the Visitors' Room at the Senior Conservatives' Club just before lunch on the following day.

The Visitors' Room is a dark sepulchral place, opening on an air well, where the visitor is surrounded by pictures of dyspeptic-looking gentlemen with beards. It has a pervading mustiness of wood and leather. Though whiskey and soda stood on the table, H.M. sat in a leather chair far away from it, ruffling his hands across his bald head.

"Now, Masters, keep your shirt on!" he warned. "This business may be rummy. But it's not a police matter—yet."

"I know it's not a police matter," Masters said grimly. "All the same, I've had a word with the superintendent at Aylesbury."

"Fowler?"

"You know him?"

"Sure. I know everybody. Is he going to keep an eye out?"

"He's going to have a look at that ruddy cottage. I've asked for any telephone calls to be put through here. In the meantime, sir—"

It was at this point, as though diabolically inspired, that the telephone rang. H.M. reached it before Masters.

"It's the old man," he said, unconsciously assuming a stance of grandeur. "Yes, yes! Masters is here, but he's drunk. You tell me first. What's that?"

The telephone talked thinly.

"Sure I looked in the kitchen cupboard," bellowed H.M. "Though I didn't honestly expect to find Vicky Adams hidin' there. What's that? Say it again! Plates? Cups that had been . . ."

An almost frightening change had come over H.M.'s expression. He stood motionless. All the posturing went out of him. He was not even listening to the voice that still talked thinly, while his eyes and his brain moved to put together facts. At length (though the voice still talked) he hung up the receiver.

H.M. blundered back to the center table, where he drew out a chair and sat down.

"Masters," he said very quietly, "I've come close to makin' the silliest mistake of my life."

He cleared his throat.

"I shouldn't have made it, son. I really shouldn't. But don't yell at me for cuttin' off Fowler. I can tell you now how Vicky Adams disappeared. And she said one true thing when she said she was goin' into a strange country."

"How do you mean?"

"She's dead," answered H.M.

The word fell with heavy weight into that dingy room, where the bearded faces looked down.

"Y'see," H.M. went on blankly, "a lot of us were right when we thought Vicky Adams was a faker. She was. To attract attention to herself, she played that trick on her family with the hocused window. She's lived and traded on it ever since. That's what sent me straight in the wrong direction. I was on the alert for some *trick* Vicky Adams might play. So it never occurred to me that this elegant pair of beauties, Miss Eve Drayton and Mr. William Sage, were deliberately conspirin' to murder *her.*"

Masters got slowly to his feet.

"Did you say . . . murder?"

"Oh, yes."

Again H.M. cleared his throat.

"It was all arranged beforehand for me to be a witness. They knew Vicky Adams couldn't resist a challenge to disappear, especially as Vicky always believed she could get out by the trick window. They wanted Vicky to *say* she was goin' to disappear. They never knew anythin' about the trick window, Masters. But they knew their own plan very well.

"Eve Drayton even told me the motive. She hated Vicky, of course. But that wasn't the main point. She was Vicky Adams's only relative; she'd inherit an awful big scoopful of money. Eve said she could be patient. (And, burn me, how her eyes meant it when she said that!) Rather than risk any slightest suspicion of murder, she was willin' to wait seven years until a disappeared person can be presumed dead.

"Our Eve, I think, was the fiery drivin' force of that conspiracy. She was only scared part of the time. Sage was scared all of the time. But it was Sage who did the real dirty work. He lured Vicky Adams into that cottage, while Eve kept me in close conversation on the lawn. . . ."

H.M. paused.

Intolerably vivid in the mind of Chief Inspector Masters, who had seen it years before, rose the picture of the rough-stone bungalow against the darkling wood.

"Masters," said H.M., "why should a bath tap be drippin' in a house that hadn't been occupied for months?"

"Well?"

"Sage, y'see, is a surgeon. I saw him take his black case of instruments out of the car. He took Vicky Adams into that house. In the bathroom he stabbed her, he stripped her, and *he dismembered her body in the bathtub*—easy, son!"

"Go, on," said Masters without moving.

"The head, the torso, the folded arms and legs, were wrapped up in three large, square pieces of thin transparent oilskin. Each was sewed up with coarse thread so the blood wouldn't drip. Last night I found one of the oilskin pieces he'd ruined when his needle slipped at the corner. Then he

walked out of the house, with the back door still standin'
unlocked, to get his wild-strawberry alibi."

"Sage went out of there," shouted Masters, "leaving the
body in the house?"

"Oh, yes," agreed H.M.

"But where did he leave it?"

H.M. ignored this.

"In the meantime, son, what about Eve Drayton? At
the end of the arranged three quarters of an hour, she indicated there was hanky-panky between her fiancé and
Vicky Adams. She flew into the house. But what did
she do?

"She walked to the back of the passage. I heard her.
There she simply locked and bolted the back door. And then
she marched out to join me with tears in her eyes. And these
two beauties were ready for investigation."

"Investigation?" said Masters. *"With that body still in
the house?"*

"Oh, yes."

Masters lifted both fists.

"It must have given young Sage a shock," said H.M.,
"when I found that piece of waterproof oilskin he'd washed
but dropped. Anyway, these two had only two more bits of
hokey-pokey. The 'vanished' gal had to speak—to show she
was still alive. If you'd been there, son, you'd have noticed
that Eve Drayton's got a voice just like Vicky Adams's. If
somebody speaks in a dark room, carefully imitatin' a coy
tone she never uses herself, the illusion's goin' to be pretty
good. The same goes for a telephone.

"It was finished, Masters. All that had to be done was
remove the body from the house, and get it far away from
there. . . ."

"But that's just what I'm asking you, sir! Where was the
body all this time? And who in blazes *did* remove the body
from the house?"

"All of us did," answered H.M.

"What's that?"

"Masters," said H.M., "aren't you forgettin' the picnic hampers?"

And now, the chief inspector saw, H.M. was as white as a ghost. His next words took Masters like a blow between the eyes.

"Three good-sized wickerwork hampers, with lids. After our big meal on the porch, those hampers were shoved inside the house where Sage could get at 'em. He had to leave most of the used crockery behind, in a kitchen cupboard. But three wickerwork hampers from a picnic, and three butchers' parcels to go inside 'em. I carried one down to the car myself. It felt a bit funny. . . ."

H.M. stretched out his hand, not steadily, towards the whiskey.

"Y'know," he said, "I'll always wonder if I was carryin' the—head."

DON'T LOOK BEHIND YOU

Fredric Brown

Just sit back and relax, now. Try to enjoy this; it's going to be the last story you ever read, or nearly the last. After you finish it you can sit there and stall awhile, you can find excuses to hang around your house, or your room, or your office, wherever you're reading this; but sooner or later you're going to have to get up and go out. That's where I'm waiting for you: outside. Or maybe closer than that. Maybe in this room.

You think that's a joke of course. You think this is just a story in a book, and that I don't really mean you. Keep right on thinking so. But be fair; admit that I'm giving you fair warning.

Harley bet me I couldn't do it. He bet me a diamond he's told me about, a diamond as big as his head. So you see why I've got to kill you. And why I've got to tell you how and why and all about it first. That's part of the bet. It's just the kind of idea Harley would have.

I'll tell you about Harley first. He's tall and handsome, and suave and cosmopolitan. He looks something like Ronald Colman, only he's taller. He dresses like a million dollars, but it wouldn't matter if he didn't; I mean that he'd look distinguished in overalls. There's a sort of magic about Harley, a mocking magic in the way he looks at you; it makes you think of palaces and far-off countries and bright music.

It was in Springfield, Ohio, that he met Justin Dean. Justin was a funny-looking little runt who was just a printer. He worked for the Atlas Printing & Engraving Company. He was a very ordinary little guy, just about as different as possible from Harley; you couldn't pick two men more different. He was only thirty-five, but he was mostly bald already, and he had to wear thick glasses because he'd worn out his eyes doing fine printing and engraving. He was a good printer and engraver; I'll say that for him.

I never asked Harley how he happened to come to Springfield, but the day he got there, after he'd checked in at the Castle Hotel, he stopped in at Atlas to have some calling cards made. It happened that Justin Dean was alone in the shop at the time, and he took Harley's order for the cards; Harley wanted engraved ones, the best. Harley always wants the best of everything.

Harley probably didn't even notice Justin; there was no reason why he should have. But Justin noticed Harley all right, and in him he saw everything that he himself would like to be, and never would be, because most of the things Harley has, you have to be born with.

And Justin made the plates for the cards himself and printed them himself, and he did a wonderful job—something he thought would be worthy of a man like Harley Prentice. That was the name engraved on the card, just that and nothing else, as all really important people have their cards engraved.

He did fine-line work on it, freehand cursive style, and

used all the skill he had. It wasn't wasted, because the next day when Harley called to get the cards he held one and stared at it for a while, and then he looked at Justin, seeing him for the first time. He asked, "Who did this?"

And little Justin told him proudly who had done it, and Harley smiled at him and told him it was the work of an artist, and he asked Justin to have dinner with him that evening after work, in the Blue Room of the Castle Hotel.

That's how Harley and Justin got together, but Harley was careful. He waited until he'd known Justin awhile before he asked him whether or not he could make plates for five- and ten-dollar bills. Harley had the contacts; he could market the bills in quantity with men who specialized in passing them, and—most important—he knew where he could get paper with the silk threads in it, paper that wasn't quite the genuine thing, but was close enough to pass inspection by anyone but an expert.

So Justin quit his job at Atlas and he and Harley went to New York, and they set up a little printing shop as a blind, on Amsterdam Avenue south of Sherman Square, and they worked at the bills. Justin worked hard, harder than he had ever worked in his life, because besides working on the plates for the bills, he helped meet expenses by handling what legitimate printing work came into the shop.

He worked day and night for almost a year, making plate after plate, and each one was a little better than the last, and finally he had plates that Harley said were good enough. That night they had dinner at the Waldorf-Astoria to celebrate and after dinner they went the rounds of the best nightclubs, and it cost Harley a small fortune, but that didn't matter because they were going to get rich.

They drank champagne, and it was the first time Justin ever drank champagne and he got disgustingly drunk and must have made quite a fool of himself. Harley told him about it afterward, but Harley wasn't mad at him. He took him back to his room at the hotel and put him to bed, and Justin was pretty sick for a couple of days. But that didn't matter, either, because they were going to get rich.

Then Justin started printing bills from the plates, and they got rich. After that, Justin didn't have to work so hard, either, because he turned down most jobs that came into the print shop, told them he was behind schedule and couldn't handle any more. He took just a little work, to keep up a front. And behind the front, he made five- and ten-dollar bills, and he and Harley got rich.

He got to know other people whom Harley knew. He . met Bull Mallon, who handled the distribution end. Bull Mallon was built like a bull, that was why they called him that. He had a face that never smiled or changed expression at all except when he was holding burning matches to the soles of Justin's bare feet. But that wasn't then; that was later, when he wanted Justin to tell him where the plates were.

And he got to know Captain John Willys of the police department, who was a friend of Harley's, to whom Harley gave quite a bit of the money they made, but that didn't matter either, because there was plenty left and they all got rich. He met a friend of Harley's who was a big star of the stage, and one who owned a big New York newspaper. He got to know other people equally important, but in less respectable ways.

Harley, Justin knew, had a hand in lots of other enterprises besides the little mint on Amsterdam Avenue. Some of these ventures took him out of town, usually over weekends. And the weekend that Harley was murdered Justin never found out what really happened, except that Harley went away and didn't come back. Oh, he knew that he was murdered, all right, because the police found his body— with three bullet holes in his chest—in the most expensive suite of the best hotel in Albany. Even for a place to be found dead in Harley Prentice had chosen the best.

All Justin ever knew about it was that a long-distance call came to him at the hotel where he was staying, the night that Harley was murdered—it must have been a matter of minutes, in fact, before the time the newspapers said Harley was killed.

It was Harley's voice on the phone, and his voice was debonair and unexcited as ever. But he said, "Justin? Get to the shop and get rid of the plates, the paper, everything. Right away. I'll explain when I see you." He waited only until Justin said, "Sure, Harley," and then he said, "Attaboy" and hung up.

Justin hurried around to the printing shop and got the plates and the paper and a few thousand dollars' worth of counterfeit bills that were on hand. He made the paper and bills into one bundle and the copper plates into another, smaller one, and he left the shop with no evidence that it had ever been a mint in miniature.

He was very careful and very clever in disposing of both bundles. He got rid of the big one first by checking in at a big hotel, not one he or Harley ever stayed at, under a false name, just to have a chance to put the big bundle in the incinerator there. It was paper and it would burn. And he made sure there was a fire in the incinerator before he dropped it down the chute.

The plates were different. They wouldn't burn, he knew, so he took a trip to Staten Island and back on the ferry and, somewhere out in the middle of the bay, he dropped the bundle over the side into the water.

Then, having done what Harley had told him to do, and having done it well and thoroughly, he went back to the hotel—his own hotel, not the one where he had dumped the paper and the bills—and went to sleep.

In the morning he read in the newspapers that Harley had been killed, and he was stunned. It didn't seem possible. He couldn't believe it; it was a joke someone was playing on him. Harley would come back to him, he knew. And he was right; Harley did, but that was later, in the swamp.

But anyway, Justin had to know, so he took the very next train for Albany. He must have been on the train when the police went to his hotel, and at the hotel they must have learned he'd asked at the desk about trains for Albany, because they were waiting for him when he got off the train there.

They took him to a station and they kept him there a long, long time, days and days, asking him questions. They found out, after a while, that he couldn't have killed Harley because he'd been in New York City at the time Harley was killed in Albany but they knew, also, that he and Harley had been operating the little mint, and they thought that might be a lead to who killed Harley, and they were interested in ⁻ the counterfeiting, too, maybe even more than in the murder. They asked Justin Dean questions, over and over and over, and he couldn't answer them, so he didn't. They kept him awake for days at a time, asking him questions over and over. Most of all they wanted to know where the plates were. He wished he could tell them that the plates were safe where nobody could ever get them again, but he couldn't tell them that without admitting that he and Harley had been counterfeiting, so he couldn't tell them.

They located the Amsterdam shop, but they didn't find any evidence there, and they really had no evidence to hold Justin on at all, but he didn't know that, and it never occurred to him to get a lawyer.

He kept wanting to see Harley, and they wouldn't let him; then, when they learned he really didn't believe Harley could be dead, they made him look at a dead man they said was Harley, and he guessed it was, although Harley looked different dead. He didn't look magnificent, dead. And Justin believed, then, but still didn't believe. And after that he just went silent and wouldn't say a word, even when they kept him awake for days and days with a bright light in his eyes, and kept slapping him to keep him awake. They didn't use clubs or rubber hoses, but they slapped him a million times and wouldn't let him sleep. And after a while he lost track of things and couldn't have answered their questions even if he'd wanted to.

For a while after that, he was in a bed in a white room,

and all he remembers about that are nightmares he had, and calling for Harley and an awful confusion as to whether Harley was dead or not, and then things came back to him gradually and he knew he didn't want to stay in the white room; he wanted to get out so he could hunt for Harley. And if Harley was dead, he wanted to kill whoever had killed Harley, because Harley would have done the same for him.

So he began pretending, and acting, very cleverly, the way the doctors and nurses seemed to want him to act, and after a while they gave him his clothes and let him go.

He was becoming cleverer now. He thought, "What would Harley tell me to do?" And he knew they'd try to follow him because they'd think he might lead them to the plates, which they didn't know were at the bottom of the bay, and he gave them the slip before he left Albany, and he went first to Boston, and from there by boat to New York, instead of going direct.

He went first to the print shop, and went in the back way after watching the alley for a long time to be sure the place wasn't guarded. It was a mess; they must have searched it very thoroughly for the plates.

Harley wasn't there, of course. Justin left and from a phone booth in a drugstore, he telephoned their hotel and asked for Harley and was told Harley no longer lived there; and to be clever and not let them guess who he was, he asked for Justin Dean, and they said Justin Dean didn't live there anymore either.

Then he moved to a different drugstore and from there he decided to call up some friends of Harley's, and he phoned Bull Mallon first and because Bull was a friend, he told him who he was and asked if he knew where Harley was.

Bull Mallon didn't pay any attention to that; he sounded excited, a little, and he asked, "Did the cops get the plates, Dean?" and Justin said they didn't, that he wouldn't tell them, and he asked again about Harley.

Bull asked, "Are you nuts, or kidding?" And Justin just

asked him again, and Bull's voice changed and he said, "Where are you?" and Justin told him. Bull said, "Harley's here. He's staying under cover, but it's all right if you know, Dean. You wait right there at the drugstore, and we'll come and get you."

They came and got Justin, Bull Mallon and two other men in a car, and they told him Harley was hiding out way deep in New Jersey and that they were going to drive there now. So he went along and sat in the back seat between two men he didn't know, while Bull Mallon drove.

It was late afternoon then, when they picked him up, and Bull drove all evening and most of the night and he drove fast, so he must have gone farther than New Jersey, at least into Virginia or maybe farther, into the Carolinas.

The sky was getting faintly gray with first dawn when they stopped at a rustic cabin that looked like it had been used as a hunting lodge. It was miles from anywhere, there wasn't even a road leading to it, just a trail that was level enough for the car to be able to make it.

They took Justin into the cabin and tied him to a chair, and they told him Harley wasn't there, but Harley had told them that Justin would tell them where the plates were, and he couldn't leave until he did tell.

Justin didn't believe them; he knew then that they'd tricked him about Harley, but it didn't matter, as far as the plates were concerned. It didn't matter if he told them what he'd done with the plates, because they couldn't get them again, and they wouldn't tell the police. So he told them, quite willingly.

But they didn't believe him. They said he'd hidden the plates and was lying. They tortured him to make him tell. They beat him, and they cut him with knives, and they held burning matches and lighted cigars to the soles of his feet, and they pushed needles under his fingernails. Then they'd rest and ask him questions and if he could talk, he'd tell them the truth, and after a while they'd start to torture him again.

It went on for days and weeks—Justin doesn't know how long, but it was a long time. Once they went away for several days and left him tied up with nothing to eat or drink. They came back and started in all over again. And all the time he hoped Harley would come to help him, but Harley didn't come, not then.

After a while what was happening in the cabin ended, or anyway he didn't know any more about it. They must have thought he was dead; maybe they were right, or anyway not far from wrong.

The next thing he knows was the swamp. He was lying in shallow water at the edge of deeper water. His face was out of the water; it woke him when he turned a little and his face went under. They must have thought him dead and thrown him into the water, but he had floated into the shallow part before he had drowned, and a last flicker of consciousness had turned him over on his back with his face out.

I don't remember much about Justin in the swamp; it was a long time, but I just remember flashes of it. I couldn't move at first; I just lay there in the shallow water with my face out. It got dark and it got cold, I remember, and finally my arms would move a little and I got farther out of the water, lying in the mud with only my feet in the water. I slept or was unconscious again and when I woke up it was getting gray dawn, and that was when Harley came. I think I'd been calling him, and he must have heard.

He stood there, dressed as immaculately and perfectly as ever, right in the swamp, and he was laughing at me for being so weak and lying there like a log, half in the dirty water and half in the mud, and I got up and nothing hurt anymore.

We shook hands and he said, "Come on, Justin, let's get you out of here," and I was so glad he'd come that I cried a little. He laughed at me for that and said I should lean on him and he'd help me walk, but I wouldn't do that, because I was coated with mud and filth of the swamp and he was so clean and perfect in a white linen suit, like an ad in a magazine. And all the way out of that swamp, all the days and nights we spent there, he never even got mud on his trouser cuffs, nor his hair mussed.

I told him just to lead the way, and he did, walking just ahead of me, sometimes turning around, laughing and talking to me and cheering me up. Sometimes I'd fall but I wouldn't let him come back and help me. But he'd wait patiently until I could get up. Sometimes I'd crawl instead when I couldn't stand up anymore. Sometimes I'd have to swim streams that he'd leap lightly across.

And it was day and night and day and night, and sometimes I'd sleep, and things would crawl across me. And some of them I caught and ate, or maybe I dreamed that. I remember other things, in that swamp, like an organ that played a lot of the time, and sometimes angels in the air and devils in the water, but those were delirium, I guess.

Harley would say, "A little farther, Justin; we'll make it. And we'll get back at them, at all of them."

And we made it. We came to dry fields, cultivated fields with waist-high corn, but there weren't ears on the corn for me to eat. And then there was a stream, a clear stream that wasn't stinking water like the swamp, and Harley told me to wash myself and my clothes and I did, although I wanted to hurry on to where I could get food.

I still looked pretty bad; my clothes were clean of mud and filth but they were mere rags and wet, because I couldn't wait for them to dry, and I had a ragged beard and I was barefoot.

But we went on and came to a little farm building, just a two-room shack, and there was a smell of fresh bread just out of an oven, and I ran the last few yards to knock on the door. A woman, an ugly woman, opened the door and when she saw me she slammed it again before I could say a word.

Strength came to me from somewhere, maybe from Harley, although I can't remember him being there just then. There was a pile of kindling logs beside the door. I picked one of them up as though it were no heavier than a broomstick, and I broke down the door and killed the woman. She screamed a lot, but I killed her. Then I ate the hot fresh bread.

I watched from the window as I ate, and saw a man running across the field toward the house. I found a knife, and I killed him as he came in at the door. It was much better, killing with the knife; I liked it that way.

I ate more bread, and kept watching from all the windows, but no one else came. Then my stomach hurt from the hot bread I'd eaten and I had to lie down, doubled up, and when the hurting quit, I slept.

Harley woke me up, and it was dark. He said, "Let's get going; you should be far away from here before it's daylight."

I knew he was right, but I didn't hurry away. I was becoming, as you see, very clever now. I knew there were things to do first. I found matches and a lamp, and lighted the lamp. Then I hunted through the shack for everything I could use. I found clothes of the man, and they fitted me not too badly except that I had to turn up the cuffs of the trousers and the shirt. His shoes were big, but that was good because my feet were so swollen.

I found a razor and shaved; it took a long time because my hand wasn't steady, but I was very careful and didn't cut myself much.

I had to hunt hardest for their money, but I found it finally. It was sixty dollars.

And I took the knife, after I had sharpened it. It isn't fancy; just a bone-handled carving knife, but it's good steel. I'll show it to you, pretty soon now. It's had a lot of use.

Then we left and it was Harley who told me to stay away from the roads, and find railroad tracks. That was easy because we heard a train whistle far off in the night and knew which direction the tracks lay. From then on, with Harley helping, it's been easy.

You won't need the details from here. I mean, about the brakeman, and about the tramp we found asleep in the empty reefer, and about the near thing I had with the police in Richmond. I learned from that; I learned I mustn't talk to Harley when anybody else was around to hear. He hides himself from them; he's got a trick and they don't know he's there, and they think I'm funny in the head if I talk to him. But in Richmond I bought better clothes and got a haircut and a man I killed in an alley had forty dollars on him, so I had money again. I've done a lot of traveling since then. If you stop to think you'll know where I am right now.

I'm looking for Bull Mallon and the two men who helped him. Their names are Harry and Carl. I'm going to kill them when I find them. Harley keeps telling me that those fellows are big time and that I'm not ready for them yet. But I can be looking while I'm getting ready so I keep moving around. Sometimes I stay in one place long enough to hold a job as a printer for a while. I've learned a lot of things. I can hold a job and people don't think I'm too strange; they don't get scared when I look at them like they sometimes did a few months ago. And I've learned not to talk to Harley except in our own room and then only very quietly so people in the next room won't think I'm talking to myself.

And I've kept in practice with the knife. I've killed lots of people with it, mostly on the streets at night. Sometimes because they look like they might have money on them, but mostly just for practice and because I've come to like doing it. I'm really good with the knife by now. You'll hardly feel it.

But Harley tells me that kind of killing is easy and that it's something else to kill a person who's on guard, as Bull and Harry and Carl will be.

And that's the conversation that led to the bet I mentioned. I told Harley that I'd bet him that, right now, I could warn a man I was going to use the knife on him and even tell him why and approximately when, and that I could still kill him. And he bet me that I couldn't and he's going to lose that bet.

He's going to lose it because I'm warning you right now and you're not going to believe me. I'm betting that you're going to believe that this is just another story in a book. That you won't believe that this is the *only* copy of this book that contains this story and that this story is true. Even when I tell you how it was done, I don't think you'll really believe me.

You see I'm putting it over on Harley, winning the bet, by putting it over on you. He never thought, and you won't realize, how easy it is for a good printer, who's been a counterfeiter too, to counterfeit one story in a book. Nothing like as hard as counterfeiting a five-dollar bill.

I had to pick a book of short stories and I picked this one because I happened to notice that the last story in the book was titled "Don't Look Behind You" and that was going to be a good title for this. You'll see what I mean in a few minutes.

I'm lucky that the printing shop I'm working for now does book work and had a typeface that matches the rest of this book. I had a little trouble matching the paper exactly, but I finally did and I've got it ready while I'm writing this. I'm writing this directly on a Linotype, late at night in the shop where I'm working days. I even have the boss's permission, told him I was going to set up and print a story that a friend of mine had written, as a surprise for him, and that I'd melt the type metal back as soon as I'd printed one good copy.

When I finish writing this I'll make up the type in pages to match the rest of the book and I'll print it on the matching paper I have ready. I'll cut the new pages to fit and bind them in; you won't be able to tell the difference, even if a faint suspicion may cause you to look at it. Don't forget I made five- and ten-dollar bills you couldn't have told from the original, and this is kindergarten stuff compared to that job. And I've done enough bookbinding that I'll be able to take the last story out of the book and bind this one in instead of it and you won't be able to tell the difference no matter how closely you look. I'm going to do a perfect job of it if it takes me all night.

And tomorrow I'll go to some bookstore, or maybe a newsstand or even a drugstore that sells books and has other copies of this book, ordinary copies, and I'll plant this one there. I'll find myself a good place to watch from, and I'll be watching when you buy it.

The rest I can't tell you yet because it depends a lot on circumstances, whether you went right home with the book or what you did. I won't know till I follow you and keep watch till you read it—and I see that you're reading the last story in the book.

If you're home while you're reading this, maybe I'm in the house with you right now. Maybe I'm in this very room, hidden, waiting for you to finish the story. Maybe I'm watching through a window. Or maybe I'm sitting near you on the streetcar or train, if you're reading it there. Maybe I'm on the fire escape outside your hotel room. But wherever you're reading it, I'm near you, watching and waiting for you to finish. You can count on that.

You're pretty near the end now. You'll be finished in seconds and you'll close the book, still not believing. Or, if you haven't read the stories in order, maybe you'll turn back to start another story. If you do, you'll never finish it.

But don't look around; you'll be happier if you don't know, if you don't see the knife coming. When I kill people from behind they don't seem to mind so much.

Go on, just a few seconds or minutes, thinking this is just another story. Don't look behind you. Don't believe this—*until you feel the knife.*

THE NINE MILE WALK

Harry Kemelman

I had made an ass of myself in a speech I had given at the Good Government Association dinner, and Nicky Welt had cornered me at breakfast at the Blue Moon, where we both ate occasionally, for the pleasure of rubbing it in. I had made the mistake of departing from my prepared speech to criticize a statement my predecessor in the office of county attorney had made to the press. I had drawn a number of inferences from his statement and had thus left myself open to a rebuttal, which he had promptly made and which had the effect of making me appear intellectually dishonest. I was new to this political game, having but a few months before left the law school faculty to become the Reform party candidate for county attorney. I said as much in extenuation, but Nicholas Welt, who could never drop his pedagogical manner (he was Snowdon Professor of English

363

Language and Literature), replied in much the same tone that he would dismiss a request from a sophomore for an extension on a term paper, "That's no excuse."

Although he is only two or three years older than I, in his late forties, he always treats me like a schoolmaster hectoring a stupid pupil. And I, perhaps because he looks so much older with his white hair and lined, gnomelike face, suffer it.

"They were perfectly logical inferences," I pleaded.

"My dear boy," he purred, "although human intercourse is well-nigh impossible without inference, most inferences are usually wrong. The percentage of error is particularly high in the legal profession, where the intention is not to discover what the speaker wishes to convey, but rather what he wishes to conceal."

I picked up my check and eased out from behind the table.

"I suppose you are referring to cross-examination of witnesses in court. Well, there's always an opposing counsel who will object if the inference is illogical."

"Who said anything about logic?" he retorted. "An inference can be logical and still not be true."

He followed me down the aisle to the cashier's booth. I paid my check and waited impatiently while he searched in an old-fashioned change purse, fishing out coins one by one and placing them on the counter beside his check, only to discover that the total was insufficient. He slid them back into his purse and with a tiny sigh extracted a bill from another compartment of the purse and handed it to the cashier.

"Give me any sentence of ten or twelve words," he said, "and I'll build you a logical chain of inferences that you never dreamed of when you framed the sentence."

Other customers were coming in, and since the space in front of the cashier's booth was small, I decided to wait outside until Nicky completed his transaction with the cashier. I remember being mildly amused at the idea that he probably thought I was still at his elbow and was going right ahead with his discourse.

When he joined me on the sidewalk I said, "A nine mile walk is no joke, especially in the rain."

"No, I shouldn't think it would be," he agreed absently. Then he stopped in his stride and looked at me sharply. "What the devil are you talking about?"

"It's a sentence and it has eleven words," I insisted. And I repeated the sentence, ticking off the words on my fingers. "What about it?"

"You said that given a sentence of ten or twelve words—"

"Oh, yes." He looked at me suspiciously. "Where did you get it?"

"It just popped into my head. Come on now, build your inferences."

"You're serious about this?" he asked, his little blue eyes glittering with amusement. "You really want me to?"

It was just like him to issue a challenge and then to appear amused when I accepted it. And it made me angry.

"Put up or shut up," I said.

"All right," he said mildly. "No need to be huffy. I'll play. Hm-m, let me see, how did the sentence go? 'A nine mile walk is no joke, especially in the rain.' Not much to go on there."

"It's more than ten words," I rejoined.

"Very well." His voice became crisp as he mentally squared off to the problem. "First inference: the speaker is aggrieved."

"I'll grant that," I said, "although it hardly seems to be an inference. It's really implicit in the statement."

He nodded impatiently. "Next inference: the rain was unforeseen, otherwise he would have said, 'A nine mile walk in the rain is no joke,' instead of using the 'especially' phrase as an afterthought."

"I'll allow that," I said, "although it's pretty obvious."

"First inferences should be obvious," said Nicky tartly.

I let it go at that. He seemed to be floundering and I didn't want to rub it in.

"Next inference: the speaker is not an athlete or an outdoorsman."

"You'll have to explain that one," I said.

"It's the 'especially' phrase again," he said. "The speaker does not say that a nine mile walk in the rain is no joke, but merely the walk—just the distance, mind you—is no joke. Now, nine miles is not such a terribly long distance. You walk more than half that in eighteen holes of golf—and golf is an old man's game," he added slyly. *I* play golf.

"Well, that would be all right under ordinary circumstances," I said, "but there are other possibilities. The speaker might be a soldier in the jungle, in which case nine miles would be a pretty good hike, rain or no rain."

"Yes," and Nicky was sarcastic, "and the speaker might be one-legged. For that matter, the speaker might be a graduate student writing a Ph.D. thesis on humor and starting by listing all the things that are not funny. See here, I'll have to make a couple of assumptions before I continue."

"How do you mean?" I asked, suspiciously.

"Remember, I'm taking this sentence *in vacuo*, as it were. I don't know who said it or what the occasion was. Normally a sentence belongs in the framework of a situation."

"I see. What assumptions do you want to make?"

"For one thing, I want to assume that the intention was not frivolous, that the speaker is referring to a walk that was actually taken, and that the purpose of the walk was not to win a bet or something of that sort."

"That seems reasonable enough," I said.

"And I also want to assume that the locale of the walk is here."

"You mean here in Fairfield?"

"Not necessarily. I mean in this general section of the country."

"Fair enough."

"Then, if you grant those assumptions, you'll have to accept my last inference that the speaker is no athlete or outdoorsman."

"Well, all right, go on."

"Then my next inference is that the walk was taken very late at night or very early in the morning—say, between midnight and five or six in the morning."

"How do you figure that one?" I asked.

"Consider the distance, nine miles. We're in a fairly well-populated section. Take any road and you'll find a community of some sort in less than nine miles. Hadley is five miles away, Hadley Falls is seven and a half, Goreton is eleven, but East Goreton is only eight and you strike East Goreton before you come to Goreton. There is local train service along the Goreton road and bus service along the others. All the highways are pretty well traveled. Would anyone have to walk nine miles in a rain unless it were late at night when no buses or trains were running and when the few automobiles that were out would hesitate to pick up a stranger on the highway?"

"He might not have wanted to be seen," I suggested.

Nicky smiled pityingly. "You think he would be less noticeable trudging along the highway than he would be riding in a public conveyance where everyone is usually absorbed in his newspaper?"

"Well, I won't press the point," I said brusquely.

"Then try this one: he was walking toward a town rather than away from one."

I nodded. "It is more likely, I suppose. If he were in a town, he could probably arrange for some sort of transportation. Is that the basis for your inference?"

"Partly that," said Nicky, "but there is also an inference to be drawn from the distance. Remember, it's a *nine* mile walk and nine is one of the exact numbers."

"I'm afraid I don't understand."

That exasperated schoolteacher-look appeared on Nicky's face again. "Suppose you say, 'I took a ten mile walk' or 'a hundred mile drive'; I would assume that you actually walked anywhere from eight to a dozen miles, or that you rode between ninety and a hundred and ten miles. In other words, *ten* and *hundred* are round numbers. You might have walked *exactly* ten miles or just as likely you might have walked *approximately* ten miles. But when you speak of walking *nine* miles, I have a right to assume that you have named an exact figure. Now, we are far more likely to know the distance of the city from a given point than we are to know the distance of a given point from the city. That is, ask anyone in the city how far out Farmer Brown lives, and if he knows him, he will say, 'Three or four miles.' But ask Farmer Brown how far he lives from the city and he will tell you, 'Three and six-tenths miles—measured it on my speedometer many a time.' "

"It's weak, Nicky," I said.

"But in conjunction with your own suggestion that he could have arranged transportation if he had been in a city—"

"Yes, that would do it," I said. "I'll pass it. Any more?"

"I've just begun to hit my stride," he boasted. "My next inference is that he was going to a definite destination and that he had to be there at a particular time. It was not a case of going off to get help because his car broke down or his wife was going to have a baby or somebody was trying to break into his house."

"Oh, come now," I said, "the car breaking down is really the most likely situation. He could have known the exact distance from having checked the mileage just as he was leaving the town."

Nicky shook his head. "Rather than walk nine miles in the rain, he would have curled up on the backseat and gone to sleep, or at least stayed by his car and tried to flag another motorist. Remember, it's nine miles. What would be the least it would take him to hike it?"

"Four hours," I offered.

He nodded. "Certainly no less, considering the rain.

We've agreed that it happened very late at night or very early in the morning. Suppose he had his breakdown at one o'clock in the morning. It would be five o'clock before he would arrive. That's daybreak. You begin to see a lot of cars on the road. The buses start just a little later. In fact, the first buses hit Fairfield around five-thirty. Besides, if he were going for help, he would not have to go all the way to town —only as far as the nearest telephone. No, he had a definite appointment, and it was in a town, and it was for some time before five-thirty."

"Then why couldn't he have got there earlier and waited?" I asked. "He could have taken the last bus, arrived around one o'clock, and waited until his appointment. He walks nine miles in the rain instead, and you said he was no athlete."

We had arrived at the Municipal Building, where my office is. Normally, any arguments begun at the Blue Moon ended at the entrance to the Municipal Building. But I was interested in Nicky's demonstration and I suggested that he come up for a few minutes.

When we were seated I said, "How about it, Nicky, why couldn't he have arrived early and waited?"

"He could have," Nicky retorted. "But since he did not, we must assume that he was either detained until after the last bus left, or that he had to wait where he was for a signal of some sort, perhaps a telephone call."

"Then according to you, he had an appointment some time between midnight and five-thirty—"

"We can draw it much finer than that. Remember, it takes him four hours to walk the distance. The last bus stops at twelve-thirty A.M. If he doesn't take that, but starts at the same time, he won't arrive at his destination until four-thirty. On the other hand, if he takes the first bus in the morning, he will arrive around five-thirty. That would mean that his appointment was for some time between four-thirty and five-thirty."

"You mean that if his appointment was earlier than

four-thirty, he would have taken the last night bus, and if it was later than five-thirty, he would have taken the first morning bus?"

"Precisely. And another thing: if he was waiting for a signal or a phone call, it must have come not much later than one o'clock."

"Yes, I see that," I said. "If his appointment is around five o'clock and it takes him four hours to walk the distance, he'd have to start around one."

He nodded, silent and thoughtful. For some queer reason I could not explain, I did not feel like interrupting his thoughts. On the wall was a large map of the county and I walked over to it and began to study it.

"You're right, Nicky," I remarked over my shoulder, "there's no place as far as nine miles away from Fairfield that doesn't hit another town first. Fairfield is right in the middle of a bunch of smaller towns."

He joined me at the map. "It doesn't have to be Fairfield, you know," he said quietly. "It was probably one of the outlying towns he had to reach. Try Hadley."

"Why Hadley? What would anyone want in Hadley at five o'clock in the morning?"

"The *Washington Flyer* stops there to take on water about that time," he said quietly.

"That's right, too," I said. "I've heard that train many a night when I couldn't sleep. I'd hear it pulling in and then a minute or two later I'd hear the clock on the Methodist church banging out five." I went back to my desk for a timetable. "The *Flyer* leaves Washington at twelve forty-seven A.M. and gets into Boston at eight A.M."

Nicky was still at the map measuring distances with a pencil.

"Exactly nine miles from Hadley is the Old Sumter Inn," he announced.

"Old Sumter Inn," I echoed. "But that upsets the whole theory. You can arrange for transportation there as easily as you can in a town."

He shook his head. "The cars are kept in an enclosure and you have to get an attendant to check you through the gate. The attendant would remember anyone taking out his car at a strange hour. It's a pretty conservative place. He could have waited in his room until he got a call from Washington about someone on the *Flyer*—maybe the number of the car and the berth. Then he could just slip out of the hotel and walk to Hadley."

I stared at him, hypnotized.

"It wouldn't be difficult to slip aboard while the train was taking on water, and then if he knew the car number and the berth—"

"Nicky," I said portentously, "as the Reform district attorney who campaigned on an economy program, I am going to waste the taxpayers' money and call Boston long distance. It's ridiculous, it's insane—but I'm going to do it!"

His little blue eyes glittered and he moistened his lips with the tip of his tongue.

"Go ahead," he said hoarsely.

I replaced the telephone in its cradle.

"Nicky," I said, "this is probably the most remarkable coincidence in the history of criminal investigation: *a man was found murdered in his berth on last night's twelve forty-seven from Washington!* He'd been dead about three hours, which would make it exactly right for Hadley."

"I thought it was something like that," said Nicky. "But you're wrong about its being a coincidence. It can't be. Where did you get that sentence?"

"It was just a sentence. It simply popped into my head."

"It couldn't have! It's not the sort of sentence that pops into one's head. If you had taught composition as long as I have, you'd know that when you ask someone for a sentence of ten words or so, you get an ordinary statement such as 'I like milk'—with the other words made up by a modifying clause like 'because it is good for my health.' The sentence you offered related to a *particular situation*."

"But I tell you I talked to no one this morning. And I was alone with you at the Blue Moon."

"You weren't with me all the time I paid my check," he said sharply. "Did you meet anyone while you were waiting on the sidewalk for me to come out of the Blue Moon?"

I shook my head. "I was outside for less than a minute before you joined me. You see, a couple of men came in while you were digging out your change and one of them bumped me, so I thought I'd wait—"

"Did you ever see them before?"

"Who?"

"The two men who came in," he said, the note of exasperation creeping into his voice again.

"Why, no—they weren't anyone I knew."

"Were they talking?"

"I guess so. Yes, they were. Quite absorbed in their conversation, as a matter of fact—otherwise, they would have noticed me and I would not have been bumped."

"Not many strangers come into the Blue Moon," he remarked.

"Do you think it was they?" I asked eagerly. "I think I'd know them again if I saw them."

Nicky's eyes narrowed. "It's possible. There had to be two—one to trail the victim in Washington and ascertain his berth number, the other to wait here and do the job. The Washington man would be likely to come down here afterward. If there was theft as well as murder, it would be to divide the spoils. If it was just murder, he would probably have to come down to pay off his confederate."

I reached for the telephone.

"We've been gone less than half an hour," Nicky went on. "They were just coming in and service is slow at the Blue Moon. The one who walked all the way to Hadley must certainly be hungry and the other probably drove all night from Washington."

"Call me immediately if you make an arrest," I said into the phone and hung up.

Neither of us spoke a word while we waited. We paced the floor, avoiding each other almost as though we had done something we were ashamed of.

The telephone rang at last. I picked it up and listened. Then I said, "Okay," and turned to Nicky.

"One of them tried to escape through the kitchen but Winn had someone stationed at the back and they got him."

"That would seem to prove it," said Nicky with a frosty little smile.

I nodded agreement.

He glanced at his watch. "Gracious," he exclaimed, "I wanted to make an early start on my work this morning, and here I've already wasted all this time talking with you."

I let him get to the door. "Oh, Nicky," I called, "what was it you set out to prove?"

"That a chain of inferences could be logical and still not be true," he said.

"Oh."

"What are you laughing at?" he asked snappishly. And then he laughed too.

THE SPECIALTY OF THE HOUSE

Stanley Ellin

"And this," said Laffler, "is Sbirro's." Costain saw a square brownstone facade identical with the others that extended from either side into the clammy darkness of the deserted street. From the barred windows of the basement at his feet, a glimmer of light showed behind heavy curtains.

"Lord," he observed, "it's a dismal hole, isn't it?"

"I beg you to understand," said Laffler stiffly, "that Sbirro's is the restaurant without pretensions. Besieged by these ghastly, neurotic times, it has refused to compromise. It is perhaps the last important establishment in this city lit by gas jets. Here you will find the same honest furnishings, the same magnificent Sheffield service, and possibly, in a far corner, the very same spider webs that were remarked by the patrons of a half century ago!"

"A doubtful recommendation," said Costain, "and hardly sanitary."

"When you enter," Laffler continued, "you leave the insanity of this year, this day, and this hour, and you find yourself for a brief span restored in spirit, not by opulence, but by dignity, which is the lost quality of our time."

Costain laughed uncomfortably. "You make it sound more like a cathedral than a restaurant," he said.

In the pale reflection of the street lamp overhead, Laffler peered at his companion's face. "I wonder," he said abruptly, "whether I have not made a mistake in extending this invitation to you."

Costain was hurt. Despite an impressive title and large salary, he was no more than clerk to this pompous little man, but he was impelled to make some display of his feelings. "If you wish," he said coldly, "I can make other plans for my evening with no trouble."

With his large, cowlike eyes turned up to Costain, the mist drifting into the ruddy, full moon of his face, Laffler seemed strangely ill at ease. Then "No, no," he said at last, "absolutely not. It's important that you dine at Sbirro's with me." He grasped Costain's arm firmly and led the way to the wrought-iron gate of the basement. "You see, you're the sole person in my office who seems to know anything at all about good food. And on my part, knowing about Sbirro's, but not having some appreciative friend to share it, is like having a unique piece of art locked in a room where no one else can enjoy it."

Costain was considerably mollified by this. "I understand there are a great many people who relish that situation."

"I'm not one of that kind!" Laffler said sharply. "And having the secret of Sbirro's locked in myself for years has finally become unendurable." He fumbled at the side of the gate and from within could be heard the small, discordant jangle of an ancient pull bell. An interior door opened with a groan, and Costain found himself peering into a dark face whose only discernible feature was a row of gleaming teeth.

"Sair?" said the face.

"Mr. Laffler and a guest."

"Sair," the face said again, this time in what was clearly an invitation. It moved aside and Costain stumbled down a single step behind his host. The door and gate creaked behind him, and he stood blinking in a small foyer. It took him a moment to realize that the figure he now stared at was his own reflection in a gigantic pier glass that extended from floor to ceiling. "Atmosphere," he said under his breath and chuckled as he followed his guide to a seat.

He faced Laffler across a small table for two and peered curiously around the dining room. It was no size at all, but the half-dozen guttering gas jets which provided the only illumination threw such a deceptive light that the walls flickered and faded into uncertain distance.

There were no more than eight or ten tables about, arranged to insure the maximum privacy. All were occupied, and the few waiters serving them moved with quiet efficiency. In the air was a soft clash and scrape of cutlery and a soothing murmur of talk. Costain nodded appreciatively.

Laffler breathed an audible sigh of gratification. "I knew you would share my enthusiasm," he said. "Have you noticed, by the way, that there are no women present?"

Costain raised inquiring eyebrows.

"Sbirro," said Laffler, "does not encourage members of the fair sex to enter the premises. And, I can tell you, his method is decidedly effective. I had the experience of seeing a woman get a taste of it not long ago. She sat at a table for not less than an hour waiting for service which was never forthcoming."

"Didn't she make a scene?"

"She did." Laffler smiled at the recollection. "She succeeded in annoying the customers, embarrassing her partner, and nothing more."

"And what about Mr. Sbirro?"

"He did not make an appearance. Whether he directed affairs from behind the scenes, or was not even present during the episode, I don't know. Whichever it was, he won a complete victory. The woman never reappeared nor, for that matter, did the witless gentleman who by bringing her was really the cause of the entire contretemps."

"A fair warning to all present," laughed Costain.

A waiter now appeared at the table. The chocolate-dark skin, the thin, beautifully molded nose and lips, the large liquid eyes, heavily lashed, and the silver-white hair so heavy and silken that it lay on the skull like a cap all marked him definitely as an East Indian. The man arranged the stiff table linen, filled two tumblers from a huge, cut-glass pitcher, and set them in their proper places.

"Tell me," Laffler said eagerly, "is the special being served this evening?"

The waiter smiled regretfully and showed teeth as spectacular as those of the majordomo. "I am sorry, sair. There is no special this evening."

Laffler's face fell into lines of heavy disappointment. "After waiting so long. It's been a month already, and I hoped to show my friend here . . ."

"You understand the difficulties, sair."

"Of course, of course," Laffler looked at Costain sadly and shrugged. "You see, I had in mind to introduce you to the greatest treat that Sbirro's offers, but unfortunately it isn't on the menu this evening."

The waiter said: "Do you wish to be served now, sair?" and Laffler nodded. To Costain's surprise the waiter made his way off without waiting for any instructions.

"Have you ordered in advance?" he asked.

"Ah," said Laffler, "I really should have explained. Sbirro's offers no choice whatsoever. You will eat the same meal as everyone else in this room. Tomorrow evening you would eat an entirely different meal, but again without designating a single preference."

"Very unusual," said Costain, "and certainly unsatisfactory at times. What if one doesn't have a taste for the particular dish set before him?"

"On that score," said Laffler solemnly, "you need have no fears. I give you my word that no matter how exacting your tastes, you will relish every mouthful you eat in Sbirro's."

Costain looked doubtful, and Laffler smiled. "And consider the subtle advantages of the system," he said. "When you pick up the menu of a popular restaurant, you find yourself confronted with innumerable choices. You are forced to weigh, to evaluate, to make uneasy decisions which you may instantly regret. The effect of all this is a tension which, however slight, must make for discomfort.

"And consider the mechanics of the process. Instead of a hurly-burly of sweating cooks rushing about a kitchen in a frenzy to prepare a hundred varying items, we have a chef who stands serenely alone, bringing all his talents to bear on one task, with all assurance of a complete triumph!"

"Then you have seen the kitchen?"

"Unfortunately, no," said Laffler sadly. "The picture I offer is hypothetical, made of conversational fragments I have pieced together over the years. I must admit, though, that my desire to see the functioning of the kitchen here comes very close to being my sole obsession nowadays."

"But have you mentioned this to Sbirro?"

"A dozen times. He shrugs the suggestion away."

"Isn't that a rather curious foible on his part?"

"No, no," Laffler said hastily, "a master artist is never under the compulsion of petty courtesies. Still," he sighed, "I have never given up hope."

The waiter now reappeared bearing two soup bowls, which he set in place with mathematical exactitude, and a small tureen, from which he slowly ladled a measure of clear, thin broth. Costain dipped his spoon into the broth and tasted it with some curiosity. It was delicately flavored, bland to the verge of tastelessness. Costain frowned, tentatively reached for the salt and pepper cellars, and discovered there were none on the table. He looked up, saw Laffler's eyes on him, and although unwilling to compromise with his own tastes, he hesitated to act as a damper on Laffler's enthusiasm. Therefore he smiled and indicated the broth.

"Excellent," he said.

Laffler returned his smile. "You do not find it excellent at all," he said coolly. "You find it flat and badly in need of condiments. I know this," he continued as Costain's eyebrows shot upward, "because it was my own reaction many years ago, and because like yourself I found myself reaching for salt and pepper after the first mouthful. I also learned with surprise that condiments are not available in Sbirro's."

Costain was shocked. "Not even salt!" he exclaimed.

"Not even salt. The very fact that you require it for your soup stands as evidence that your taste is unduly jaded. I am confident that you will now make the same discovery that I did: by the time you have nearly finished your soup, your desire for salt will be nonexistent."

Laffler was right; before Costain had reached the bottom of his plate, he was relishing the nuances of the broth with steadily increasing delight. Laffler thrust aside his own empty bowl and rested his elbows on the table. "Do you agree with me now?"

"To my surprise," said Costain, "I do."

As the waiter busied himself clearing the table, Laffler lowered his voice significantly. "You will find," he said, "that the absence of condiments is but one of several noteworthy characteristics which mark Sbirro's. I may as well prepare you for these. For example, no alcoholic beverages of any sort are served here, nor for that matter any beverage except clear, cold water, the first and only drink necessary for a human being."

"Outside of mother's milk," suggested Costain dryly.

"I can answer that in like vein by pointing out that the average patron of Sbirro's has passed that primal stage of his development."

Costain laughed. "Granted," he said.

"Very well. There is also a ban on the use of tobacco in any form."

"But good heavens," said Costain, "doesn't that make Sbirro's more a teetotaler's retreat than a gourmet's sanctuary?"

"I fear," said Laffler solemnly, "that you confuse the words 'gourmet' and 'gourmand.' The gourmand, through glutting himself, requires a wider and wider latitude of experience to stir his surfeited senses, but the very nature of the gourmet is simplicity. The ancient Greek in his coarse chiton savoring the ripe olive; the Japanese in his bare room contemplating the curve of a single flower stem—these are the true gourmets."

"But an occasional drop of brandy, or pipeful of tobacco," said Costain dubiously, "are hardly overindulgences."

"By alternating stimulant and narcotic," said Laffler, "you seesaw the delicate balance of your taste so violently that it loses its most precious quality: the appreciation of fine food. During my years as a patron of Sbirro's, I have proved this to my satisfaction."

"May I ask," said Costain, "why you regard the ban on these things as having such deep esthetic motives? What about such mundane reasons as the high cost of a liquor license, or the possibility that patrons would object to the smell of tobacco in such confined quarters?"

Laffler shook his head violently. "If and when you meet Sbirro," he said, "you will understand at once that he is not the man to make decisions on a mundane basis. As a matter of fact, it was Sbirro himself who first made me cognizant of what you call 'aesthetic' motives."

"An amazing man," said Costain as the waiter prepared to serve the entrée.

Laffler's next words were not spoken until he had savored and swallowed a large portion of meat. "I hesitate to use superlatives," he said, "but to my way of thinking, Sbirro represents man at the apex of his civilization!"

Costain cocked an eyebrow and applied himself to his roast, which rested in a pool of stiff gravy ungarnished by green or vegetable. The thin steam rising from it carried to his nostrils a subtle, tantalizing odor which made his mouth water. He chewed a piece as slowly and thoroughly as if he were analyzing the intricacies of a Mozart symphony. The range of taste he discovered was really extraordinary, from the pungent nip of the crisp outer edge to the peculiarly flat yet soul-satisfying ooze of blood which the pressure of his jaws forced from the half-raw interior.

Upon swallowing he found himself ferociously hungry for another piece, and then another, and it was only with an effort that he prevented himself from wolfing down all his share of the meat and gravy without waiting to get the full voluptuous satisfaction from each mouthful. When he had scraped his platter clean, he realized that both he and Laffler had completed the entire course without exchanging a single word. He commented on this, and Laffler said: "Can you see any need for words in the presence of such food?"

Costain looked around at the shabby, dimly lit room, the quiet diners, with a new perception. "No," he said humbly, "I cannot. For any doubts I had I apologize unreservedly. In all your praise of Sbirro's there was not a single word of exaggeration."

"Ah," said Laffler delightedly. "And that is only part of the story. You heard me mention the special which unfortunately was not on the menu tonight. What you have just eaten is nothing when compared to the absolute delights of that special!"

"Good Lord!" cried Costain; "What is it? Nightingales' tongues? Filet of unicorn?"

"Neither," said Laffler. "It is lamb."

"Lamb?"

Laffler remained lost in thought for a minute. "If," he said at last, "I were to give you in my own unstinted words my opinion of this dish, you would judge me completely insane. That is how deeply the mere thought of it affects me. It is neither the fatty chop, nor the too solid leg; it is, instead, a select portion of the rarest sheep in existence and is named after the species—lamb Amirstan."

Costain knit his brows. "Amirstan?"

"A fragment of desolation almost lost on the border which separates Afghanistan and Russia. From chance remarks dropped by Sbirro, I gather it is no more than a plateau which grazes the pitiful remnants of a flock of superb sheep. Sbirro, through some means or other, obtained rights to the traffic in this flock and is, therefore, the sole restauranteur ever to have lamb Amirstan on his bill of fare. I can tell you that the appearance of this dish is a rare occurrence indeed, and luck is the only guide in determining for the clientele the exact date when it will be served."

"But surely," said Costain, "Sbirro could provide some advance knowledge of this event."

"The objection to that is simply stated," said Laffler. "There exists in this city a huge number of professional gluttons. Should advance information slip out, it is quite likely that they will, out of curiosity, become familiar with the dish and thenceforth supplant the regular patrons at these tables."

"But you don't mean to say," objected Costain, "that these few people present are the only ones in the entire city, or for that matter, in the whole wide world, who know of the existence of Sbirro's!"

"Very nearly. There may be one or two regular patrons who, for some reason, are not present at the moment."

"That's incredible."

"It is done," said Laffler, the slightest shade of menace in his voice, "by every patron making it his solemn obligation to keep the secret. By accepting my invitation this evening, you automatically assume that obligation. I hope you can be trusted with it."

Costain flushed. "My position in your employ should vouch for me. I only question the wisdom of a policy which keeps such magnificent food away from so many who would enjoy it."

"Do you know the inevitable result of the policy *you* favor?" asked Laffler bitterly. "An influx of idiots who would nightly complain that they are never served roast duck with chocolate sauce. Is that picture tolerable to you?"

"No," admitted Costain, "I am forced to agree with you."

Laffler leaned back in his chair wearily and passed his hand over his eyes in an uncertain gesture. "I am a solitary man," he said quietly, "and not by choice alone. It may sound strange to you, it may border on eccentricity, but I feel to my depths that this restaurant, this warm heaven in a coldly insane world, is both family and friend to me."

And Costain, who to this moment had never viewed his companion as other than tyrannical employer or officious host, now felt an overwhelming pity twist inside his comfortably expanded stomach.

By the end of two weeks the invitations to join Laffler at Sbirro's had become something of a ritual. Every day, at a few minutes after five, Costain would step out into the office corridor and lock his cubicle behind him; he would drape his overcoat neatly over his left arm, and peer into the glass of the door to make sure his Homburg was set at the proper angle. At one time he would have followed this by lighting a cigarette, but under Laffler's prodding he had decided to give abstinence a fair trial. Then he would start down the corridor, and Laffler would fall in step at his elbow, clearing his throat. "Ah, Costain. No plans for this evening, I hope."

"No," Costain would say, "I'm footloose and fancy-free," or "At your service," or something equally inane. He wondered at times whether it would not be more tactful to vary the ritual with an occasional refusal, but the glow with which Laffler received his answer, and the rough friendliness of Laffler's grip on his arm, forestalled him.

Among the treacherous crags of the business world, reflected Costain, what better way to secure your footing than friendship with one's employer. Already, a secretary close to the workings of the inner office had commented publicly on

Laffler's highly favorable opinion of Costain. That was all to the good.

And the food! The incomparable food at Sbirro's! For the first time in his life, Costain, ordinarily a lean and bony man, noted with gratification that he was certainly gaining weight; within two weeks his bones had disappeared under a layer of sleek, firm flesh, and here and there were even signs of incipient plumpness. It struck Costain one night, while surveying himself in his bath, that the rotund Laffler, himself, might have been a spare and bony man before discovering Sbirro's.

So there was obviously everything to be gained and nothing to be lost by accepting Laffler's invitations. Perhaps after testing the heralded wonders of lamb Amirstan and meeting Sbirro, who thus far had not made an appearance, a refusal or two might be in order. But certainly not until then.

That evening, two weeks to a day after his first visit to Sbirro's, Costain had both desires fulfilled: he dined on lamb Amirstan, and he met Sbirro. Both exceeded all his expectations.

When the waiter leaned over their table immediately after seating them and gravely announced: "Tonight is special, sair," Costain was shocked to find his heart pounding with expectation. On the table before him he saw Laffler's hands trembling violently. "But it isn't natural," he thought suddenly: "two full-grown men, presumably intelligent and in the full possession of their senses, as jumpy as a pair of cats waiting to have their meat flung to them!"

"This is it!" Laffler's voice startled him so that he almost leaped from his seat. "The culinary triumph of all times! And faced by it you are embarrassed by the very emotions it distills."

"How did you know that?" Costain asked faintly.

"How? Because a decade ago I underwent your embarrassment. Add to that your air of revulsion and it's easy to see how affronted you are by the knowledge that man has not yet forgotten how to slaver over his meat."

"And these others," whispered Costain, "do they all feel the same thing?"

"Judge for yourself."

Costain looked furtively around at the nearby tables. "You are right," he finally said. "At any rate, there's comfort in numbers."

Laffler inclined his head slightly to the side. "One of the numbers," he remarked, "appears to be in for a disappointment."

Costain followed the gesture. At the table indicated a gray-haired man sat conspicuously alone, and Costain frowned at the empty chair opposite him.

"Why, yes," he recalled, "that very stout, bald man, isn't it? I believe it's the first dinner he's missed here in two weeks."

"The entire decade more likely," said Laffler sympathetically. "Rain or shine, crisis or calamity, I don't think he's missed an evening at Sbirro's since the first time I dined here. Imagine his expression when he's told that on his very first defection, lamb Amirstan was the *plat du jour.*"

Costain looked at the empty chair again with a dim discomfort. "His very first?" he murmured.

"Mr. Laffler! And friend! I am so pleased. So very, very pleased. No, do not stand; I will have a place made." Miraculously a seat appeared under the figure standing there at the table. "The lamb Amirstan will be an unqualified success, hurr? I myself have been stewing in the miserable kitchen all the day, prodding the foolish chef to do everything just so. The just so is the important part, hurr? But I see your friend does not know me. An introduction, perhaps?"

The words ran in a smooth, fluid eddy. They rippled, they purred, they hypnotized Costain so that he could do no more than stare. The mouth that uncoiled this sinuous monologue was alarmingly wide, with thin mobile lips that curled and twisted with every syllable. There was a flat nose with a straggling line of hair under it; wide-set eyes, almost Oriental in appearance, that glittered in the unsteady flare of gaslight; and long, sleek hair that swept back from high on the unwrinkled forehead—hair so pale that it might have been bleached of all color. An amazing face surely, and the sight of it tortured Costain with the conviction that it was somehow familiar. His brain twitched and prodded but could not stir up any solid recollection.

Laffler's voice jerked Costain out of his study. "Mr. Sbirro. Mr. Costain, a good friend and associate." Costain rose and shook the proffered hand. It was warm and dry, flint-hard against his palm.

"I am so very pleased, Mr. Costain. So very, very pleased," purred the voice. "You like my little establishment, hurr? You have a great treat in store, I assure you."

Laffler chuckled. "Oh, Costain's been dining here regularly for two weeks," he said. "He's by way of becoming a great admirer of yours, Sbirro."

The eyes were turned on Costain. "A very great compliment. You compliment me with your presence and I return same with my food, hurr? But the lamb Amirstan is far superior to anything of your past experience, I assure you. All the trouble of obtaining it, all the difficulty of preparation, is truly merited."

Costain strove to put aside the exasperating problem of that face. "I have wondered," he said, "why with all these difficulties you mention, you even bother to present lamb Amirstan to the public. Surely your other dishes are excellent enough to uphold your reputation."

Sbirro smiled so broadly that his face became perfectly round. "Perhaps it is a matter of the psychology, hurr? Someone discovers a wonder and must share it with others. He must fill his cup to the brim, perhaps, by observing the so evident pleasure of those who explore it with him. Or," he shrugged, "perhaps it is just a matter of good business."

"Then in the light of all this," Costain persisted, "and considering all the conventions you have imposed on your customers, why do you open the restaurant to the public instead of operating it as a private club?"

The eyes abruptly glinted into Costain's, then turned away. "So perspicacious, hurr? Then I will tell you. Because there is more privacy in a public eating place than in the most exclusive club in existence! Here no one inquires of your affairs; no one desires to know the intimacies of your life. Here the business is eating. We are not curious about names and addresses or the reasons for the coming and going of our guests. We welcome you when you are here; we have no regrets when you are here no longer. That is the answer, hurr?"

Costain was startled by this vehemence. "I had no intention of prying," he stammered.

Sbirro ran the tip of his tongue over his thin lips. "No, no," he reassured, "you are not prying. Do not let me give you that impression. On the contrary, I invite your questions."

"Oh, come, Costain," said Laffler. "Don't let Sbirro intimidate you. I've known him for years and I guarantee that his bark is worse than his bite. Before you know it, he'll be showing you all the privileges of the house—outside of inviting you to visit his precious kitchen, of course."

"Ah," smiled Sbirro, "for that, Mr. Costain may have to wait a little while. For everything else I am at his beck and call."

Laffler slapped his hand jovially on the table. "What did I tell you!" he said. "Now let's have the truth, Sbirro. Has anyone, outside of your staff, ever stepped into the sanctum sanctorum?"

Sbirro looked up. "You see on the wall above you," he said earnestly, "the portrait of one to whom I did the honor. A very dear friend and a patron of most long standing, he is evidence that my kitchen is not inviolate."

Costain studied the picture and started with recognition. "Why," he said excitedly, "that's the famous writer—you know the one, Laffler—he used to do such wonderful short stories and cynical bits and then suddenly took himself off and disappeared in Mexico!"

"Of course!" cried Laffler, "and to think I've been sitting under his portrait for years without even realizing it!" He turned to Sbirro. "A dear friend, you say? His disappearance must have been a blow to you."

Sbirro's face lengthened. "It was, it was, I assure you. But think of it this way, gentlemen: he was probably greater in his death than in his life, hurr? A most tragic man, he often told me that his only happy hours were spent here at this very table. Pathetic, is it not? And to think the only favor I could ever show him was to let him witness the mysteries of my kitchen, which is, when all is said and one, no more than a plain, ordinary kitchen."

"You seem very certain of his death," commented Costain. "After all, no evidence has ever turned up to substantiate it."

Sbirro contemplated the picture. "None at all," he said softly. "Remarkable, hurr?"

With the arrival of the entrée Sbirro leaped to his feet and set about serving them himself. With his eyes alight he lifted the casserole from the tray and sniffed at the fragrance from within with sensual relish. Then, taking great care not to lose a single drop of gravy, he filled two platters with chunks of dripping meat. As if exhausted by this task, he sat back in his chair, breathing heavily. "Gentlemen," he said, "to your good appetite."

Costain chewed his first mouthful with great deliberation and swallowed it. Then he looked at the empty tines of his fork with glazed eyes.

"Good God!" he breathed.

"It is good, hurr? Better than you imagined?"

Costain shook his head dazedly. "It is as impossible," he said slowly, "for the uninitiated to conceive the delights of lamb Amirstan as for mortal man to look into his own soul."

"Perhaps," Sbirro thrust his head so close that Costain

could feel the warm, fetid breath tickle his nostrils, "perhaps you have just had a glimpse into your soul, hurr?"

Costain tried to draw back slightly without giving offense. "Perhaps," he laughed, "and a gratifying picture it made: all fang and claw. But without intending any disrespect, I should hardly like to build my church on lamb *en casserole.*"

Sbirro rose and laid a hand gently on his shoulder. "So perspicacious," he said. "Sometimes when you have nothing to do, nothing, perhaps, but sit for a very little while in a dark room and think of this world—what it is and what it is going to be—then you must turn your thoughts a little to the significance of the Lamb in religion. It will be so interesting. And now," he bowed deeply to both men, "I have held you long enough from your dinner. I was most happy"—he nodded to Costain—"and I am sure we will meet again." The teeth gleamed, the eyes glittered, and Sbirro was gone down the aisle of tables.

Costain twisted around to stare after the retreating figure. "Have I offended him in some way?" he asked.

Laffler looked up from his plate. "Offended him? He loves that kind of talk. Lamb Amirstan is a ritual with him; get him started and he'll be back at you a dozen times worse than a priest making a conversion."

Costain turned to his meal with the face still hovering before him. "Interesting man," he reflected. "Very."

It took him a month to discover the tantalizing familiarity of that face, and when he did, he laughed aloud in his bed. Why, of course! Sbirro might have sat as the model for the Cheshire cat in *Alice!*

He passed this thought on to Laffler the very next evening as they pushed their way down the street to the restaurant against a chill, blustering wind. Laffler only looked blank.

"You may be right," he said, "but I'm not a fit judge. It's a far cry back to the days when I read the book. A far cry, indeed."

As if taking up his words, a piercing howl came ringing down the street and stopped both men short in their tracks. "Someone's in trouble there," said Laffler. "Look!"

Not far from the entrance to Sbirro's two figures could be seen struggling in the near darkness. They swayed back and forth and suddenly tumbled into a writhing heap on the sidewalk. The piteous howl went up again, and Laffler, despite his girth, ran toward it at a fair speed with Costain tagging cautiously behind.

Stretched out full length on the pavement was a slender figure with the dusky complexion and white hair of one of Sbirro's servitors. His fingers were futilely plucking at the huge hands which encircled his throat, and his knees pushed weakly up at the gigantic bulk of a man who brutally bore down with his full weight.

Laffler came up panting. "Stop this!" he shouted. "What's going on here?"

The pleading eyes almost bulging from their sockets turned toward Laffler. "Help, sair. This man—drunk—"

"Drunk am I, ya dirty—" Costain saw now that the man was a sailor in a badly soiled uniform. The air around him reeked with the stench of liquor. "Pick me pocket and then call me drunk, will ya!" He dug his fingers in harder, and his victim groaned.

Laffler seized the sailor's shoulder. "Let go of him, do you hear! Let go of him at once!" he cried, and the next instant was sent careening into Costain, who staggered back under the force of the blow.

The attack on his own person sent Laffler into immediate and berserk action. Without a sound he leaped at the sailor, striking and kicking furiously at the unprotected face and flanks. Stunned at first, the man came to his feet with a rush and turned on Laffler. For a moment they stood locked together, and then as Costain joined the attack, all three went sprawling to the ground. Slowly Laffler and Costain got to their feet and looked down at the body before them.

"He's either out cold from liquor," said Costain, "or he

struck his head going down. In any case, it's a job for the police."

"No, no, sair!" The waiter crawled weakly to his feet, and stood swaying. "No police, sair. Mr. Sbirro do not want such. You understand, sair." He caught hold of Costain with a pleading hand, and Costain looked at Laffler.

"Of course not," said Laffler. "We won't have to bother with the police. They'll pick him up soon enough, the murderous sot. But what in the world started all this?"

"That man, sair. He make most erratic way while walking, and with no meaning I push against him. Then he attack me, accusing me to rob him."

"As I thought." Laffler pushed the waiter gently along. "Now go on in and get yourself attended to."

The man seemed ready to burst into tears. "To you, sair, I owe my life. If there is anything I can do—"

Laffler turned into the areaway that led to Sbirro's door. "No, no, it was nothing. You go along, and if Sbirro has any questions send him to me. I'll straighten it out."

"My life, sair," were the last words they heard as the inner door closed behind them.

"There you are, Costain," said Laffler, as a few minutes later he drew his chair under the table: "civilized man in all his glory. Reeking with alcohol, strangling to death some miserable innocent who came too close."

Costain made an effort to gloss over the nerve-shattering memory of the episode. "It's the neurotic cat that takes to alcohol," he said. "Surely there's a reason for that sailor's condition."

"Reason? Of course there is. Plain atavistic savagery!" Laffler swept his arm in an all-embracing gesture. "Why do we all sit here at our meat? Not only to appease physical demands, but because our atavistic selves cry for release. Think back, Costain. Do you remember that I once described Sbirro as the epitome of civilization? Can you now see why? A brilliant man, he fully understands the nature of human beings. But unlike lesser men he bends all his efforts to the satisfaction of our innate natures without resultant harm to some innocent bystander."

"When I think back on the wonders of lamb Amirstan," said Costain, "I quite understand what you're driving at. And, by the way, isn't it nearly due to appear on the bill of fare? It must have been over a month ago that it was last served."

The waiter, filling the tumblers, hesitated. "I am so sorry, sair. No special this evening."

"There's your answer," Laffler grunted, "and probably just my luck to miss out on it altogether the next time."

Costain stared at him. "Oh, come, that's impossible."

"No, blast it." Laffler drank off half his water at a gulp and the waiter immediately refilled the glass. "I'm off to South America for a surprise tour of inspection. One month, two months, Lord knows how long."

"Are things that bad down there?"

"They could be better." Laffler suddenly grinned. "Mustn't forget it takes very mundane dollars and cents to pay the tariff at Sbirro's."

"I haven't heard a word of this around the office."

"Wouldn't be a surprise tour if you had. Nobody knows about this except myself—and now you. I want to walk in on them completely unsuspected. Find out what flimflammery they're up to down there. As far as the office is concerned, I'm off on a jaunt somewhere. Maybe recuperating in some sanatorium from my hard work. Anyhow, the business will be in good hands. Yours, among them."

"Mine?" said Costain, surprised.

"When you go in tomorrow you'll find yourself in receipt of a promotion, even if I'm not there to hand it to you personally. Mind you, it has nothing to do with our friendship either; you've done fine work, and I'm immensely grateful for it."

Costain reddened under the praise. "You don't expect to be in tomorrow. Then you're leaving tonight?"

Laffler nodded. "I've been trying to wangle some reservations. If they come through, well, this will be in the nature of a farewell celebration."

"You know," said Costain slowly, "I devoutly hope that your reservations don't come through. I believe our dinners here have come to mean more to me than I ever dared imagine."

The waiter's voice broke in. "Do you wish to be served now, sair?" and they both started.

"Of course, of course," said Laffler sharply, "I didn't realize you were waiting."

"What bothers me," he told Costain as the waiter turned away, "is the thought of the lamb Amirstan I'm bound to miss. To tell you the truth, I've already put off my departure a week, hoping to hit a lucky night, and now I simply can't delay any more. I do hope that when you're sitting over your share of lamb Amirstan, you'll think of me with suitable regrets."

Costain laughed. "I will indeed," he said as he turned to his dinner.

Hardly had he cleared the plate when a waiter silently reached for it. It was not their usual waiter, he observed; it was none other than the victim of the assault.

"Well," Costain said, "how do you feel now? Still under the weather?"

The waiter paid no attention to him. Instead, with the air of a man under great strain, he turned to Laffler. "Sair," he whispered. "My life. I owe it to you. I can repay you!"

Laffler looked up in amazement, then shook his head firmly. "No," he said; "I want nothing from you, understand? You have repaid me sufficiently with your thanks. Now get on with your work and let's hear no more about it."

The waiter did not stir an inch, but his voice rose slightly. "By the body and blood of your God, sair, I will help you even if you do not want! *Do not go into the kitchen, sair.* I trade you my life for yours, sair, when I speak this. Tonight or any night of your life, do not go into the kitchen at Sbirro's!"

Laffler sat back, completely dumbfounded. "Not go into the kitchen? Why shouldn't I go into the kitchen if Mr. Sbirro ever took it into his head to invite me there? What's all this about?"

A hard hand was laid on Costain's back, and another gripped the waiter's arm. The waiter remained frozen to the spot, his lips compressed, his eyes downcast.

"What is all *what* about, gentlemen?" purred the voice. "So opportune an arrival. In time as ever, I see, to answer all the questions, hurr?"

Laffler breathed a sigh of relief. "Ah, Sbirro, thank heaven you're here. This man is saying something about my not going into your kitchen. Do you know what he means?"

The teeth showed in a broad grin. "But of course. This good man was giving you advice in all amiability. It so happens that my too emotional chef heard some rumor that I might have a guest into his precious kitchen, and he flew into a fearful rage. Such a rage, gentlemen! He even threatened to give notice on the spot, and you can understand what that should mean to Sbirro's, hurr? Fortunately, I succeeded in showing him what a signal honor it is to have an esteemed patron and true connoisseur observe him at his work firsthand, and now he is quite amenable. Quite, hurr?"

He released the waiter's arm. "You are at the wrong table," he said softly. "See that it does not happen again."

The waiter slipped off without daring to raise his eyes and Sbirro drew a chair to the table. He seated himself and brushed his hand lightly over his hair. "Now I am afraid that the cat is out of the bag, hurr? This invitation to you, Mr. Laffler, was to be a surprise; but the surprise is gone, and all that is left is the invitation."

Laffler mopped beads of perspiration from his forehead. "Are you serious?" he said huskily. "Do you mean that we are really to witness the preparation of your food tonight?"

Sbirro drew a sharp fingernail along the tablecloth, leaving a thin, straight line printed in the linen. "Ah," he said, "I am faced with a dilemma of great proportions." He studied the line soberly. "You Mr. Laffler, have been my guest for ten long years. But our friend here—"

Costain raised his hand in protest. "I understand perfectly. This invitation is solely to Mr. Laffler, and naturally my presence is embarrassing. As it happens, I have an early engagement for this evening and must be on my way anyhow. So you see there's no dilemma at all, really."

"No," said Laffler, "absolutely not. That wouldn't be fair at all. We've been sharing this until now, Costain, and I won't enjoy this experience half as much if you're not along. Surely Sbirro can make his conditions flexible, this one occasion."

They both looked at Sbirro who shrugged his shoulders regretfully.

Costain rose abruptly. "I'm not going to sit here, Laffler, and spoil your great adventure. And then too," he bantered, "think of that ferocious chef waiting to get his cleaver on you. I prefer not to be at the scene. I'll just say good-bye," he went on, to cover Laffler's guilty silence, "and leave you to Sbirro. I'm sure he'll take pains to give you a good show." He held out his hand and Laffler squeezed it painfully hard.

"You're being very decent, Costain," he said. "I hope you'll continue to dine here until we meet again. It shouldn't be too long."

Sbirro made way for Costain to pass. "I will expect you," he said. *"Au 'voir."*

Costain stopped briefly in the dim foyer to adjust his scarf and fix his Homburg at the proper angle. When he turned away from the mirror, satisfied at last, he saw with a final glance that Laffler and Sbirro were already at the kitchen door; Sbirro holding the door invitingly wide with one hand, while the other rested, almost tenderly, on Laffler's meaty shoulders.

LOVE LIES BLEEDING

Philip MacDonald

Cyprian didn't like rushing over dinner, so they had eaten early. And now, at eight o'clock, he was alone with coffee in Astrid's living room while Astrid herself was in the bedroom out of sight and sound, changing into some frock suitable for the rather tedious party they were going to together.

It was very quiet in Astrid's apartment, very comfortable. The maid had gone as soon as they had finished eating, so there weren't even sounds of movement from dining room and kitchen to disturb the peace. And there was plenty of time. Plenty. Because they needn't arrive at the Ballards' before nine-thirty at the earliest.

Cyprian stretched luxuriously. He picked his coffee cup from the mantel and drained it and set it down again, his fingers momentarily caressing the delicate texture of the thin china.

He strolled about the room, thinking how well Astrid had done with it, taking pleasure in the blendings and contrasts of color under the soft lights, the balance and position of furniture, the choice and subject of the few paintings.

He went back to the mantel, and took the fragile, thistle-shaped liqueur glass from beside his empty coffee cup. He couldn't remember what was in it, and sniffed at it, his thin sensitive nostrils quivering a little as the sharp, bitter-orange aroma stung them pleasantly. He smiled; he should have known that Astrid wouldn't make mistakes.

He sipped slowly, letting the hot stringency slide over his tongue. He turned his back to the room and faced himself in the big mirror over the mantel and was pleased by what he saw. He could find this evening nothing at variance with the appearance of Cyprian Morse as he wished it to be. With absorbed interest he studied Cyprian—the graceful, high-shouldered slenderness so well set off by the dinner jacket of midnight blue; the fine-textured pallor of the odd, high-cheekboned face with its heavy-lidded eyes and chiseled mouth which seemed to lift at one corner in satire perpetual but never overstressed; the long slim fingers of the hand which twitched with languid dexterity at the tie which so properly enhanced the silken snowy richness of the shirt and its collar.

The blue gleam of the carved lapis lazuli in his signet ring made him think of Charles, and the time when Charles had given it to him. He turned away from the mirror and sipped at the liqueur again and wished Charles were here and wondered how long it would be before Charles returned from Venezuela. He was looking forward to Charles and Astrid meeting, though he wasn't too sure what Charles's initial reaction would be. Astrid would be all right, of course—and, after all, Charles would very soon find out what she was like, just an awfully nice girl, and a great, an inspired designer. He toyed with visions of making Charles work too. With Astrid doing the sets, and Charles letting himself go on weird, macabre décor, Cyprian Morse's

Abanazar could well be the most sensational production ever seen in the theater.

Cyprian finished the liqueur, and set down the glass. Still musing on the possibilities of *Abanazar*, he dropped into a big low chair, and found himself—his eyes almost level with a coffee table—looking straight at a photograph of Astrid he hadn't seen before. It was an excellent portrait, oddly and interestingly lighted, and the camera had caught and registered that somehow astringent little smile which some people said spoiled her looks, but which had always been for Cyprian a sort of epitome of why he liked her. He went on looking at it now, and thought, as he had thought many times looking at her in life, how necessary a smile it was. Without it there would be no way of knowing that the full-blown and almost aggressive femininity of Astrid's structure was merely an accident in design; no way of telling that in fact she had no nonsense about her but was simply the best of designers and—he was beginning to believe more and more as their association developed—the best of friends.

He stretched again and relaxed in the chair. He was in the after-dinner mood which he liked best, and which only seemed to come when he had had exactly the right amount of a-little-too-much-to-drink. All his senses, all his perceptions, were sharpened to a fine edge beneath a placid sheath of contentment. There was a magazine lying on the table near the photograph, and he reached out a lazy arm and picked it up. It was last month's *Manhattan,* and it fell open in his hands to the theatrical page and the beginning of Burn Heyward's long glowing review of *The Square Triangle.* He knew it nearly by heart, but nevertheless began to read and savor it afresh, starting with the headline, CYPRIAN MORSE DOES IT AGAIN, and going through its delicious paeans to the shiny super-plum of the very last paragraph, ". . . There is no doubt left that, despite his youth and (in this instance at least) his dubious choice of subject, Morse is one of the really important playwrights of the day, certainly the most significant in America. . . ."

He heard the door open behind him, and let the magazine fall shut on his knee and said, "Ready?" without turning around.

"*Cyprian!*" said Astrid's voice.

There was something strange about the sound, a quality which inexplicably, as if it had been some dreadful psychic emanation, seemed to change the shape of his every thought and sensation, so that where he had been relaxed and warmly content, he was now tense and chill with formless apprehension.

"*Cyprian!*" said the voice again, and he came to his feet in a single spasmodic movement, turning to face Astrid as he rose.

He stared at her in stunned amazement and a useless hope of disbelief. His flesh crept, and he seemed to feel the hairs on his neck rising like the hackles on a dog.

She came toward him, slowly—and he backed away. She mustn't touch him; she mustn't touch him.

She drew inexorably closer. She held out her arms to him. He didn't know he was still moving away until the edge of the mantelshelf came hard against his shoulders. He could feel sweat clammy-cold on his forehead, his upper lip, his neck. Desperately, his mind struggled for mastery over his body. His mind knew that, in reality, this was merely a distressing incident hardly removed from the commonplace. His mind knew that a few simple words, a curl of the lip, a lift of the shoulders—any or all of these would free him not only now but forever. But the words had to be uttered, the gestures made—and his body refused the tasks.

She was close now. Very close. She was going to touch him.

She said, in the same thick voice, "Cyprian! Don't look at me like that." And she said, "I love you, Cyprian, you must know that. . . ."

There was a ringing in his ears, and the tight grip of nausea in his stomach. His throat worked as he tried to speak, but no words came from his mouth.

She touched him. She was close against him. His body could feel the dreadful soft warmness of her. There was a mist over his eyes and he could hardly see her through it. And then her arms were around his neck, soft but implacably strong. His mind screamed something, but the arms tightened their hold. She was speaking, but he couldn't hear through the roaring in his head. Somehow, he tore himself free. Forgetting, he tried to retreat, and thudded against the brick of the mantel. With a scrabbling lunge, he went sideways—and almost fell.

He clutched wildly. His left hand caught the edge of the mantelshelf and checked his fall. His right hand, swinging, struck against something metallic and closed around it.

"Cyprian—" said the voice. *"Cyprian!"*

She was going to touch him again. Through the haze he could see her, the arms reaching.

There was a clatter of metal as the rest of the fire irons fell, and his right hand, still grasping the log pick it had closed around, raised itself above his head and swung downward, with more than all his force.

Through the rushing in his ears, through the red-flecked haze over his eyes, he heard the sick dull crushing of the first blow, saw the slender shape crumple and collapse . . .

The haze and the roaring faded, and he found himself standing half-crouched over the thing on the floor—striking down at it again and again. It was as if some outside power had taken charge of him, so that the blows came without his conscious volition—thudding with the broadside of the heavy bar, then thrusting, slashing, tearing with the sharp point of the spike . . .

Then, piercing the haze and thrusting him back into knowledge of himself, there was a sharp pain in his shoulder as a muscle twisted and cramped.

The log pick fell from his hands, thudding onto the thick carpet. He looked down at what he had done—and then, an arm flung across his eyes, he turned and ran, stumbling and wavering, for the outer door of the apartment.

He smashed into it—scrabbled with shaking hands for the latch—tore it open—plunged out into the corridor—and, sightless, witless, came into heavy collision with a man and a woman just passing the door.

The woman lurched against the opposite wall. Cursing, the man snarled at Cyprian and caught him by the shoulder and straightened his slim bent body and thrust him back against the doorjamb. The woman took one horrified look at Cyprian and screamed. The man stared and said, "What in the name of—"

Cyprian swayed. Everything—the figures facing him, the walls and doors, the lights overhead, the pattern of the corridor carpet—all swung crazily together before his eyes; swung and tilted so that he reeled, and clutched vainly for support—and slid down against the jamb to sit sprawled and ungainly on the floor, clutching at his whirling head.

The woman said, "Look at him. *Look* at him!" in a shaking voice. "That's *blood!*"—and the man said heavily, "What goes on around here?"

Cyprian moaned—and began to vomit. Above him the man said, "I'm going to take a look in there," and moved through the open doorway.

The woman went after him, and there glowed in Cyprian's mind the first sudden and frightful awareness of his danger. Even as another spasm shook him, a tiny self-preservatory spark was born, and when the woman began to scream just inside the door, he was already mumbling to himself, "*. . . There was a man . . . he went through the window . . .*"

And then the beginning of the long nightmare.

The man and woman rushing out of the apartment. Shouting. Doors opening. People. More screaming. Trying to get to his feet and failing. More men, one in shirt sleeves, another in a robe, standing over him like guards. Sirens wailing outside. Whistles. Noise. Voices. Elevator doors clanging and heavy feet tramping down the corridor. New voices, harsh and different. Men in uniform. The other faces going, the new faces staring down at him, looming behind the harsh voices. A hand as ruthless as God's pulling him to his feet . . .

He wanted help. He craved succor. *". . . There was a man . . . he went through the window . . ."*

He wanted a friend. He wanted Charles. Charles would know what to do. Charles would deal with these bullying louts.

". . . There was a man . . . he went through the window . . ."

And Charles was thousands of miles away.

The nightmare went on. The questions. First in the room where men—not in uniform now—worked over the horror on the floor, muttering to each other, measuring, flashing lights, pointing cameras, scribbling in notebooks.

Then in another room, after a hellish, siren-screaming journey in a crowded car. Questions, questions. All framed with the certainty, the *knowledge,* that he had done what he must not admit having done.

Questions. And the white light aching in his eyes. His throat stiff and his lips unmanageable. His whole body shaking, shaking. The inside of his head shaking too.

—Why did you kill her?

—What time did you kill her?

—What did you kill her for? What had she done?

—How long after ya killed her before you run out?

—*I didn't. I didn't. . . . There was a man . . . he went through the window . . .*

—All right—so there was a man. An' he went outa the window. Whaddud he do? Jump? Fly?

—You don't expect us to swallow that, do you?

—Yeah. How d'ya figure this sorta hooey's goin' to help?

—*I tell you there was a man . . . he went through the window . . . down the fire escape . . .*

—He did? Leavin' your prints all over the poker?

—Yeah. An' splashin' her blood all over ya?

—Now, listen, Mr. Morse: it's completely certain that you killed this woman. The evidence is overwhelming. Can't you realize that you're doing yourself no good by your attitude?

—*I'm telling the truth. There was a man. I—I was in the bathroom. I heard a noise. I ran in. I saw Astrid. There was a man. He climbed out of the window. I'm telling the truth.*

—Very well. So you're telling the truth. Which window did this man go out?

—Yeah? And how come he locked it behind him?

—Never mind that, Mr. Morse. Answer the other question. Which window?

—*I—I don't know.... The window in the—the end wall . . . next to the fire escape . . .*

—Which window? The right as you face? Or the left?

—Yeah. Which? One of 'em was locked, bud. Which?

Questions. And the light. Questions all around him. Questions from faces. Coarse, brutal faces. Sharp fox faces. They began to associate themselves with the voices.

And another face with wise gray eyes that watched him always. A face with no voice. A face in the corner. A face more to be feared than all the faces with voices.

Questions. And the light. Time standing still, immobilized. He had always been here. He would always be here. "*. . . There was a man . . . he went through the window . . .*"

It was a pattern, diabolic and infinite: Fear—questions —fear fear—light—fear fear fear—fatigue.

Fatigue. First a dull dead core of exhaustion, but now beginning to reach out all around itself, encroaching more and more on all other feeling.

Until even fear was going . . . going . . . almost gone—

—Why don't we wind this up, Morse?

—Yes. We know you killed her, and you know we know. Why not get it over with?

—Yeah. How's about it, fella? Why doncha come clean, so's we can let up on ya?

Fear flickering again, momentarily reborn.

—*I didn't I didn't I didn't . . . There was a man. When I ran in, he was climbing out of the window . . .*

For an instant a picture forming behind his eyes. An

image of Charles—tall, tough, elegant, dangerous, one shoulder lifting higher than the other, a cigarette jutting from the corner of his long mouth, his creased face creasing more in a mastering smile. Charles coming through the door, being suddenly framed in the doorway, standing and looking down at the faces, the stupid crafty animal faces—

Then his eyes closing. His head falling forward. Then nothing. Except the hard scratched feeling of the tabletop against his cheek. And a ghost smell of soap and pencils and agony.

A rough hand biting into his shoulder. Shaking. His head lolling, jerking back and forward like a marionette's—

Then a new voice, quiet, sharp, charged with authority.

—That's enough. Let him alone. Schraff, you go find Dr. Innes. This isn't any Bowery bum you're handling.

His head resting on the table again. The voices muttering all around him, not thrusting at him now.

Conscious of someone standing over him. Not touching him. Just standing.

Opening his eyes. Forcing muscles to roll up the ton-weight lids. Seeing the wise gray eyes looking down at him, contemplating him, understanding everything.

Staring dully up into the gray eyes for a moment, dully wondering. Then letting the heavy lids fold down over his own eyes again.

The door opening, and brisk footsteps. And quick impersonal hands upon him. Doctor's hands. Feeling at his temples, his wrist. Tilting back his unbearably heavy head, with a deft thumb rolling back those eyelids.

Then muttering above his head. His coat being eased off, shirt sleeve rolled up.

Indefinite pause—and then the fingers on his arm, and the sting of the needle . . .

When he waked it was to grayness. A gray blanket over him; gray walls; a door of gray bars; gray light filtering through a small grilled window.

For some timeless interval the drug held memory in

check. But at last, with a sick gray emptiness in his stomach, recollection came. And fear again, all the worse because its edges were dulled now and instead of it being so intense that there was no room in him for other emotions, it was now entangled and heightened by remorse and shame and horror.

He threw off the blanket and swung his feet to the floor and propped his elbows on his knees and dropped his face into his hands.

There was a clanging sound, and he started convulsively and raised his head and saw a uniformed guard coming into the cell. The man was carrying a big suitcase which he put down as he closed the barred door. On the side of the case were the initials C.M., and Cyprian saw with dull surprise that it was his own, the one Charles had given him in London. He heard himself saying, "Where did you get that?" and the fellow looked at him and said, "Came from y'r apartment. There's clothes an' shaving tack an' setra." He had a strange manner, at once meaning and noncommittal, official and yet faintly sycophantic.

He came closer to Cyprian and looked down at him. He said, "Mr. Friar fixed it. An' about sendin' out for what you want."

A little faint glow of warmth came to life somewhere in Cyprian's coldness. "Trust John Friar," he thought.

The guard said, "You like anything now? Breakfast? Or just coffee?"

Cyprian went on staring at him: it was as if his mind was so full that he didn't hear words until long after they had been spoken.

"Coffee," he said at last. "Just coffee."

The man nodded, and went to the door and opened it again, and paused. "Like to see the papers?" he said over his shoulder.

This time the words penetrated fast. Cyprian recoiled from them as if they were blows. "No!" he said. "No—*no!*"

He closed his eyes and held them screwed shut until he

had heard the door open and clang shut, and then receding footsteps echoing. A shudder shook him at the thought of newspapers, and once more he covered his face with his hands. Headlines—as if on an endless ticker tape—began to unroll behind his eyes, running the gamut from the sober through the sensational to the nadir of the tabloid—

—FAMOUS PLAYWRIGHT HELD ON MURDER CHARGE. DESIGNER SLAIN. . . .

—CYPRIAN MORSE ARRAIGNED FOR MURDER. GIRL ASSOCIATE BRUTALLY BATTERED TO DEATH. . . .

—PARK AVENUE LOVE-FIEND MURDER. NUDE THEATER BEAUTY SLASHED. MORSE, BROADWAY FIGURE, JAILED. . . .

He groaned and twisted his body this way and that and desperately pressed the heels of his palms against his eyes until a spark-shot red mist seemed to swim under the lids. But the tape went on unrolling—a ceaseless stream of words.

He jumped up and began to pad about the cell—and then mercifully heard footsteps in the corridor again and mastered himself and was sitting on the edge of the gray cot when the guard reappeared with a tray.

He mumbled thanks and reached for the coffeepot. But his hand trembled so badly that, without speaking, the man filled a cup for him.

He drank greedily, and felt strength coming back to him. He looked up and said, "Can I—would—is it allowed to send a cablegram?"

"Could be. With an okay from the warden's office." The fellow reached into a pocket, produced a little memo pad and a stump of pencil. "Want to write it down?"

Cyprian took the things. Once more he mumbled thanks. He didn't look at the man; he didn't like his eyes. He began to write, not having to think, letting the pencil print the words—

CHARLES DE LASTRO HOTEL CASTILIA VENEZUELA IN TERRIBLE TROUBLE NEED YOU DESPERATELY PLEASE COME REPLY CARE JOHN FRIAR CYPRIAN.

He handed the pad and pencil back, and watched while

what he had written was read. He said, "Well—?" and met the eyes again as they flickered over him.

"Seems like this'll be okay." The guard turned a blue-clad back and went to the door. "I'll look after it."

Once more the clanging, the footsteps dying away—and Cyprian was alone again. His hand steadier now, he poured himself more coffee. Anything, any action, to keep him from thought.

He drained the cup. He picked up the suitcase and set it on the cot and opened it. Forcing himself to activity, he washed and shaved and put on the clothes he found packed. A suit of dark blue flannel—a white silk shirt—a plain maroon tie.

He felt a little better. It was easier to believe that this was Cyprian Morse—and he gave silent thanks to John Friar.

But there was nothing to do now—and if he weren't careful he might have to start thinking. He lit a cigarette from the box in the suitcase and began to pace the cell. There were five steps one way and six the other. . . .

So this was Cyprian Morse. Perhaps he did feel better after all. Perhaps—

Footsteps in the corridor again. One, two, three sets.

John Friar himself, with another man and the guard. Who opened the door, and stood aside to let the visitors in, and clanged the door shut again and stood outside, his back to it.

John Friar took Cyprian's hand in both of his and gripped hard. He was white-faced, strained. He looked less like a successful producer than ever, and more like a truncated and careworn Abe Lincoln. The man with him towered over him, a lank, loose-limbed, stooping giant with a thatch of white hair and a seamed, unlikely face which was neither saint's nor gargoyle's but something of both.

John Friar said, "Cyprian!" in a voice which wasn't quite steady. He made a gesture including the third man. He said, "Julius, meet Cyprian Morse. . . . Cyprian, this is Julius Magnussen."

Again Cyprian's hand was taken, and enveloped in a vast paw which gripped firmly but with surprising gentleness. And Cyprian found himself looking up, tall though he was, into dark unreadable eyes which seemed jet-black under the shaggy white brows.

John Friar said, "Julius is taking on your def—your case, Cyprian. And you know what that means!"

"I most definitely do!" Cyprian hoped they wouldn't hear the trembling in his throat. "Is there anyone in America who doesn't?"

Magnussen grunted. He turned away and folded his length in the middle and sat on the edge of the gray bed. He looked at Cyprian and said, "Better tell me about it," then moved a little and added, "Sit down here."

Cyprian found himself obeying. But he couldn't keep on meeting the dark eyes, and gave up trying to. He looked up at John Friar and essayed a smile. He said, "Of course," in Magnussen's direction—and then, faintly, all the fear and horror of memory breaking loose in his head again, "Where —where—d'you want me to start?"

"At the beginning, Mr. Morse," Magnussen said, and Cyprian drew a deep breath to still the quaking inside him.

But it wouldn't be stilled. It spread from his body to his mind. He was being thrust into nightmare again—

—I can't. . . . I can't. . . .

—Would it be easier if I asked you questions?

Questions. The pattern returning. Fear—questions— fear fear—fatigue. But worse now. Hiding from friends, not enemies.

—I have to ask you this: did you kill this woman Astrid Halmar?

—No—no—no! . . . *There was a man . . . he went through the window . . .*

—You know of no enemies Miss Halmar might have had?

—No. How should I? I—

—So you think the murderer was a stranger, a prowler?

—How—how do I know what he was! Or who! I don't know anything. . . .

Questions. Questions. Fear. Thinking furiously before each answer without letting the pause be evident. Trying to screen the vortex of his mind with caution. Time standing still again. He had always been here. He would always be here.

—So you were in the bathroom for more than an hour?

—Yes—yes. I went there just after dinner. Just as—just after the maid left the apartment.

—Were you feeling unwell? Is that why you stayed so long? Had something you ate upset your stomach?

A straw. A solid straw. Snatch it!

—Yes. That's right. I was sick. . . . It was the oysters. . . .

More questions. More fear. Feeling the dark eyes always on his face. Not meeting them.

—And you were just about to come out of the bathroom when you heard a cry. Am I right?

Another straw. Snatch it!

—Yes. Yes. Astrid screamed . . .

—And you ran out, and along the passage to the living room?

—Yes.

—While you were running along the passage, did you happen to notice Miss Halmar's robe, lying on the floor?

—Robe? What—no, I don't think—

—Her robe was found by the door to the living room. The killer—however he gained entry to the apartment—must have struggled with her, snatched at her, in the passageway there, pulling off the robe as she fled into the living room. I am wondering—did you notice it?

A straw?

—I think I did. There was something—soft on the floor. It caught my shoe. . . .

—Now, Mr. Morse, as you entered the living room, you saw the figure of a man just disappearing out of the window?

—Yes. Yes.

—And you saw Miss Halmar's body on the floor and ran to it?

—Yes. Of course I did. I—I had to try and help her . . .

—Naturally. Now, as your fingerprints are on the log pick, Mr. Morse, you must have handled it? Maybe you touched it—picked it up—when you went to her? It was in your way, was it?

A sudden lightening. As if some frightful pressure were easing. Fear actually receding. Knowing now that these were no accidental straws, but material for a raft. A life raft.

—Yes. That was it. I remember now. It—it was lying across her body. I—I picked it up and—threw it down, away from her.

—And in your shock and horror, when you found she was dead, you forgot the telephone and ran blindly out to seek help, and then collapsed?

—Yes. Yes. That's it—exactly.

Questions. Questions. But not minding them now. Being eager for them. And being able to meet the dark eyes, keeping his own eyes on them.

The pattern had changed. Fear was there, as a permanent lowering background, but in front of it was hope. . . .

The hope persisted, even when he was alone once more. It seemed to widen the cell, and raise its roof. It set the blood flowing through his head again, so that his brain worked fast and clear and he started to elaborate on the structure Julius Magnussen had begun to build for him.

This work—and work it was—carried him through the dragging days and weeks with a surprising minimum of anguish. It even fortified him to some extent against the shock of the answering cablegram from Charles, which didn't arrive until several days after he had expected it.

The cable ran: HOSPITALIZED BAD KICKUP MALARIA FLYING BACK IMMEDIATELY RELEASED MAYBE TWO WEEKS HANG ON CHARLES.

And that, of course, was bad news. Bad from two angles

—that he would have to wait before Charles could get to him, that poor Charles was sick.

But whereas before the first meeting with Julius Magnussen, Cyprian would have been crushed almost to extinction by these twin misfortunes, now they seemed merely to serve as a spur to his fortitude and his hope and his labor. So that he clenched his teeth and redoubled his efforts to produce appropriate "memories"—until he reached the point of being sure that at least Friar and Magnussen believed him, that he almost believed himself.

But it was as well for him that he wasn't present at any of the several meetings between Julius Magnussen and John Friar alone, or he would have heard talk which would have turned his hope-lightened purgatory into hopeless hell.

—A bad case, John. Don't hide it from yourself. We'll need a miracle.

—Good God, Julius, d'you mean you yourself don't believe—

—Stop. That's not a question I want to be asked. Or answer. Leave it at what I said. A bad case. No case at all.

—But the evidence against him's all circumstantial!

—And therefore the best, in spite of what they say in novels.

—But surely it's all open to two interpretations! Like—like his fingerprints on that poker.

—*And* the splashes of blood on him and his clothing? Have you thought of that, John? *Splashes.* Not smears, which are what should be there from raising her, examining her, trying to help her . . .

—But the boy's *gentle,* Julius! There's no violence in him. He couldn't even kill a fly that was pestering him.

—Maybe not. And don't think that's not going to be used. For more than all it's worth. For God's sake, it's practically all we have! You know the young man, John: tell me, how would he react to the suggestion of an alternative plea?

—You mean "not guilty, or guilty by reason of insanity"!

—that gag! Good God, Julius—he wouldn't go for that if you tortured him.

—Hmm. I was afraid that would be the answer.

—Look now, what is all this? What are you trying to do —tell me you won't take the case after all? Is that it?

—Cool off, John. I'm trying to save your prodigy's life, that's all.

—I don't get this! Julius Magnussen, of all people, scared of a setup like this! . . . Remember that police photograph you showed me? Well, think of it. Not the head wounds, the others. Think of 'em! Cyprian could not have been responsible for that frightful *sort* of brutality. Think of what was done to that girl, man! . . . Can't you see—can't you?

—Oh, yes, John, I can see. A great many things . . .

But Cyprian knew nothing of such conversations, and it seemed to him, every time he saw his counsel, that more and more confidence radiated from that towering, loose-limbed figure; that the penetrating dark eyes looked always more cheerful.

So he rode out the rest of the dragging days and nights and came in good enough order to the morning when the trial was to open. It was a Thursday, and he liked that because he had had a fancy, since an episode in his boyhood, that Thor's was his lucky day. Further, a bright autumnal sun was glittering over New York and even—a rare occurrence in the weeks he had been there—pushing rays through the bars of the small window high up in the wall of the cell.

He dressed with great, almost finicking care. He drank a whole pot of coffee and then sent for more. He even ate a little of his breakfast.

He was ready and waiting a full half hour before they came for him. He spent it pacing the cell, smoking too much and too fast, glancing occasionally toward the pile of letters which he hadn't read and had no more intention of ever reading than he had of looking in court at any of the reporters' faces. He didn't think of what was before him today. He daren't think of that, in the same way—only infinitely multiplied—that he never thought about what was coming on a first night.

So he considered, with furious intensity, anything and everything except what was coming. The sure hope at the back of his mind must be kept inviolate.

He came naturally to thoughts of Charles. Every day he had been sure this must be the day when he would hear again—and every day he had been disappointed. He had wired again, and he had written—just a note which John Friar had airmailed for him. But still no answer. Charles must be very ill indeed. Or—a wonderful idea which he dare not dwell upon for more than one delicious instant—Charles was well again and had arrived in New York, and was on his way here.

The third alternative he shuddered away from. The thought of Charles dead was so black, so bleak, so dreadful that it would have driven him back in escape to thoughts of the immediate future if he hadn't been saved by the arrival of his guard.

For once he was glad to see the fellow. He said, "Do we start now?" and moved toward the door.

But the man shook his head. "They ain't here yet," he said. "Take it easy." He drew a folded yellow envelope from a pocket and held it out to Cyprian. "Sent over from Friar's," he said. "He reckoned you might like to have it right away."

Cyprian almost snatched it from the outstretched hand. His heart was pounding, and sudden color had tinged his pallid face. With fingers which he didn't know were shaking, he fumbled at the flimsy envelope, ripped it open at last, and unfolded the sheet it contained.

And read: BETTER OUT NEXT WEDNESDAY WILL FLY ARRIVING THURSDAY CHARLES.

The new color deepened in Cyprian's face. He read the cable again—and again. Here was the best of all possible omens. Almost as good as his wild daydream of a few moments before—that perhaps Charles would arrive in person. On second thought, perhaps better. Because now he was supremely confident, and he would so far prefer to have all this ugliness behind him when Charles returned; out of sight and wrapped up and put away, to be disinterred and examined, if ever, at a safe distance in time and then only for personal historic interest.

He moved his shoulders unconsciously, as if in reflex to the removal of a heavy weight. He folded the strip of paper carefully, and stowed it away in his breast pocket. And then looked at the guard and smiled, and said softly, "Thank you. Thank you very much. . . ."

There was a tramping of feet in the corridor—and two uniformed men he had never seen before. One of them pushed the cell door wide and looked at him with no expression and said, "All set?"

Cyprian smiled at this man too, and walked out into the corridor quickly, lightly, almost jauntily. . . .

But there was no lightness in him when he came back eight hours later, and no square of sunshine from the barred window. There was only night outside and here the hard cold light of the single bulb overhead.

His face was lined and wax-white. His shoulders sagged and his body seemed not to fill his clothes. He lurched on his feet while they opened the door of the cell, and one of the men gripped his arm and said, "Take it easy."

They put him inside and he dropped on the edge of his cot and sat there limp and head hanging, his eyes wide and staring at the floor and not seeing it.

The escort went away and his own guard came, and sometime later the doctor. He couldn't get food down, and they put him to bed and gave him a sedative. He slept almost at once, and they left him.

He lay like a log for three hours, until the deadly numbness of fatigue had gone and the drug had eased its grip. And then he began to murmur and thrash around on the cot— and in a moment gave a harsh choked cry and sat upright, awake.

He remembered. He tried not to, he fought, but he couldn't stop memory from working. He remembered everything—at first in jumbled pictures, then in echoing phrases; at last, concentrated upon the gray-haired, gray-eyed figure of the district attorney, he recalled the whole of the clear and ruthlessly dispassionate opening for the prosecution. The speech which, period by period, point by careful point, had not only stripped Cyprian Morse of all cover but had shattered all remnant of hope in him.

What had happened after the speech didn't matter. The irreparable damage to Cyprian Morse, the conviction of Cyprian Morse, had been brought about; those witnesses, the silly endless procession of them who answered silly endless questions, they were just so many more nails in his coffin. After the speech, which showed such complete, such eerie knowledge and understanding, as if the speaker had not only seen everything that had happened but had seen it with Cyprian's mind and Cyprian's eyes—after that, all else seemed time-prolonging and sadistic anticlimax. . . .

He didn't move. He sat as he was, and stared into the abyss. . . .

Morning came, and daylight, and people he heard and saw as if from a long distance. He moved then but was almost unconscious of moving. It was as if his body were an automaton and his mind a separate entity outside it, which had no concern with the robot movements.

The automaton clothed itself, and ate and drank, and went with his mind and the uniformed men and sat in the crowded courtroom in the same place as his undivided self had sat the day before.

The automaton sat still and went through motions—of listening to friends and counsel, of answering them when necessary, of looking attentive to the gabber-jab of the unending witnesses, of considering thoughtfully the closing speech for the prosecution, of hearing the crabbed judge rule that the court, this being Friday, should recess until the morning of Monday . . .

But his mind, his actual self, was in hell without a permit. For sixty-two hours the automaton made all the foolish gestures of living; for uncountable stages of distorted time his mind gazed into the pit.

The Monday came, and the automaton moved accordingly. But the clean-cut edges of the schism between body and mind began to waver before the two parts of him left the cell, as if something had happened which demanded they should be joined again. Resisting the pull, his mind began to wonder what had caused it. His refusal to see John Friar or Magnussen during the recess? The odd, almost excited manner of his guard on bringing a newspaper to the cell and trying to insist on the automaton reading it? The looks which both his escorts cast at the automaton in the car on the way to court?

He didn't want the union. He would break, he felt, if he couldn't keep up the separation. But the pull grew stronger with every foot of the way, and almost irresistible as he entered the courtroom itself, and his mind felt a difference —a strange, disturbing, agitated alteration—in the other minds behind the faces staring at him.

And then, with a shivering, nauseating shock, his resistance went and he was swept back into his body once more, so that he was stripped and next to the world again with no transparent armor between.

It was the face of Magnussen's wizened clerk which brought it about, a face which always before had been harassed and grave and filled with foreboding, but which now was gay and eager and irradiated by a tremendous gnomelike smile. As Cyprian was about to take his seat, this smile was turned full on him, and his hand was surreptitiously taken and earnestly squeezed, and through the smile a voice came whispering something which couldn't be distinguished but all the same was pregnant with the most extreme importance.

Cyprian sat down, weakly. Once again, he had no strength. He looked up into the little clerk's face and muttered something—he wasn't sure of the words himself.

An astonished change came over the puckered visage. "Mr. Morse!" The voice cracked in amazement. "Do you mean to say you haven't *heard!*"

Dumbly Cyprian shook his head, the small movement leaving him exhausted.

"Not about the—the other killings!... Mr. Morse! There have been two more murders of unfortunate girls! In every respect the same as Miss Halmar's—even the—the mutilations identical. . . . On Saturday night the first victim was found; and another discovered in the early hours of this morning!"

Cyprian went on staring up into the excited, agitated face.

"D-don't you realize what this m-means!" The voice was stammering now. "All three deaths must be linked. *You* couldn't have caused the others! They're the work of a maniac—a Jack the Ripper!" Fluttering hands produced a newspaper, unfolded it, waved it. "Look here, Mr. Morse!"

There were black heavy headlines. They wavered in front of Cyprian's eyes, then focused sharply and made him catch at his breath.

POLICE CLUELESS IN NEW FIEND SLAYINGS! MORSE RELEASE DEMANDED BY PUBLIC!

"Oh," said Cyprian, his lips barely moving. "Oh, I see. . . ." His whole body began to tingle, as if circulation had been withheld from it until now. He said, a little louder, "What—what will happen?"

The clerk sat down beside him. His hoarse whispering was as clear now as a shout in Cyprian's ears. "What will happen? I'll tell you, Mr. Morse. I'll tell you exactly. The DA will withdraw—and not long after Mr. Magnussen's opened. He'll withdraw, Mr. Morse, you mark my words!"

The words coincided with a stentorian bellow from the back of the courtroom, followed by a stamping rustle as everyone stood up—and Justice swept to its throne in a dusty black robe. . . .

And Cyprian, life welling up in him, found himself

caught in a whirling timeless jumble of fact and feeling and emotion, a maelstrom which was in effect the precise opposite of the long nightmare succeeding his arrest—

Julius Magnussen towering on his feet, speaking of Cyprian Morse's innocence with an almost contemptuous certainty. Julius Magnussen examining detectives on the witness stand, forcing them to prove all three killings had been identical. Julius Magnussen calling more witnesses, then looking around haughtily at the prosecution when the court was asked to hear a statement. The district attorney himself, gray eyes not understanding now but puzzled and confused, muttering that the state withdrew its case against Cyprian Morse. The judge speaking, bestowing commiseration on Cyprian Morse, laudation on Julius Magnussen, censure upon their opponents—

Then bedlam breaking loose, himself the center. Friends. Strangers. Acquaintances. Reporters. All crowding, jabbering, laughing. Women weeping. Flashbulbs exploding. John Friar pumping both his hands. Magnussen clapping him on the shoulder. Himself the center of a wedge of policemen, struggling for the exit. An odd little instant of comparative quiet in the hallway, and hearing Magnussen say to John Friar behind him, "An apology, John, you were right."

Then John's big car, and the soft-cushioned seat supporting him. And quietness, with the tires singing on the road and time to draw breath—and taste freedom. . . .

All horror was behind him and it was Wednesday evening and Charles was coming home. From John Friar's house in Westchester, in John Friar's car, driven by John Friar's chauffeur.

It was deepening dusk when they pulled into the parking lot behind the apartment house. Cyprian peered, and saw no sign of any human being and was pleased. He got out and smiled at the chauffeur and said warmly, "Thank you, Maurice. Thank you very much. . . ." and thrust a lavish tip into the man's gloved hand and waved a cheerful salute and walked off toward the rear entrance of the building. His footsteps rang crisply on the concrete, and a faint, wreath-like mist from his breathing hung on the autumn air. He suppressed an impulse to stop and crane his neck to look up to the penthouse and see the warm lights glowing out from it. He knew they were there, because he had heard John Friar telephoning to his servant, telling him when Mr. Morse was to be expected.

"Good old John," he thought. "Thoughtful John!" And then forgot John completely as he entered the service door, and still met no one and found one of the service elevators empty and waiting.

He forgot John. He forgot everyone and everything— except Charles.

And Charles would be here tomorrow. That was why Cyprian had insisted upon coming home tonight—so that he could supervise preparation.

He hurried the elevator with his mind, and when it reached the rear hallway of his penthouse, threw open the gate—and was faced, not by light and an open door and Walter's white-smiling black face, but by cold unwelcoming darkness.

He stepped out of the elevator and groped for the light switch and pressed it and blinked at the sudden glare. Frowning, he tried the door to the kitchen. It wasn't locked, but when he opened it there was more darkness. And no sound. No sound at all.

A chill settled on his mind. The warm excited glow which had been growing inside him evaporated with un-nerving suddenness. He switched on more lights and went quickly through the bright-tiled neatness and threw open an inner door and called, "Walter! Walter, where are you?" into more darkness still.

Not such absolute darkness this time, but the more disturbing for that. The curtains across the big windows at the west side of the living room had not been drawn and there was still a sort of gray luminosity in the air.

Cyprian took two or three paces into the room. He called, "Walter!" again, and heard his own voice go up too high at the end of the word.

And another voice spoke from behind him—a cracked and casual voice.

"I sent him out for an hour or two," it said. "Hope you don't mind."

Cyprian started violently. He gasped, *"Charles!"* And wheeled around and saw a tall figure looming in the grayness. His heart pounded in his ears and he felt a swaying in his head.

There was no answering sound—and he said, "Charles!" again and moved toward a table near the figure and reached out for the lamp he knew was on it.

But his shoulder was caught in a grip which checked him completely. Long fingers strong as steel bit into his flesh, and Charles's voice said, "Take it easy. We don't need light just yet."

Cyprian felt cold. His head still whirled. He couldn't understand, and the grip on his shoulder seemed to be paralyzing him and he was afraid with that worst of all fears which hasn't any shape.

He said wildly, "Charles, I don't understand—I—" and couldn't get out any more words. He contorted all the muscles in his face in a useless attempt to see Charles's face.

"You will," said Charles's voice. "Do you remember once telling me you'd never lie to me again?"

"Yes," Cyprian whispered—and then, his mouth drying with fear, "Let me go. You're hurting me. . . ."

"Did you mean it?" The hand didn't relax its grip.

"Of course. . . . And I never have lied to you since! I don't understand—"

"You will." The grip tightened and Cyprian caught his breath. "I want a truthful answer to one question. Will you give it?"

"Yes. Yes. Of course I will. . . ."

"Did you kill that Halmar woman?"

"No—no—*there was a man . . . he went through the window . . .*"

"I thought you weren't going to lie to me. Did you kill her?"

"*No!* I—" The steel fingers bit deeper and Cyprian sobbed.

"Did you kill her? Don't lie to me."

"Yes! *Yes!*" Cyprian's face was writhing. His eyes stung with tears and his lips were trembling. "Yes, I killed her! I killed her—*I killed her! . . .*"

The grip eased. The hand lifted from his shoulder. He tottered on uncertain feet, and the lamp on the table jumped suddenly into life and through the mist over his eyes he saw Charles for the first time—and then heard Charles's voice say, easily and softly and with the old-time chuckle hidden somewhere in it:

"Well, that's that. Just so long as we know. . . . I'd like a drink."

He turned away from Cyprian and crossed with his lounging walk to the bar—the lounging walk which always reminded Cyprian of the stalking of a cat—

And suddenly Cyprian knew.

He knew, and in the same moment that understanding flooded his mind, he thought—for the first time actively thought—of those other two deaths which had saved him from death.

A scream came to his throat and froze there. He shrank into himself as he stood there—and Charles turned, glass in hand, and looked at him.

His eyes burned in his head. He couldn't move their gaze from Charles's face. He said:

"You did it. You killed those two women. You weren't ill. You got someone else to send those cables. You heard about Astrid and you flew back without anyone knowing. And you plotted and planned and stalked—and did that. As if they were animals. You did that!"

His voice died in his throat. All strength went out of him

and he tottered to a chair and doubled up in it and sat crumpled.

"Don't fret, my dear Cyprian." Charles drank, looking at him over the rim of the glass. "We sit tight—and live happily ever after. . . ."

Cyprian dropped his head into his hands.

"Oh, my God!" he said. "Oh, my God!"

LAMB TO THE SLAUGHTER

Roald Dahl

The room was warm and clean, the curtains drawn, the two table lamps alight—hers and the one by the empty chair opposite. On the sideboard behind her, two tall glasses, soda water, whiskey. Fresh ice cubes in the Thermos bucket.

Mary Maloney was waiting for her husband to come home from work.

Now and again she would glance up at the clock, but without anxiety, merely to please herself with the thought that each minute gone by made it nearer the time when he would come. There was a slow smiling air about her, and about everything she did. The drop of the head as she bent over her sewing was curiously tranquil. Her skin—for this was her sixth month with child—had acquired a wonderful translucent quality, the mouth was soft, and the eyes, with their new placid look, seemed larger, darker than before.

When the clock said ten minutes to five, she began to listen, and a few moments later, punctually as always, she heard the tires on the gravel outside, and the car door slamming, the footsteps passing the window, the key turning in the lock. She laid aside her sewing, stood up, and went forward to kiss him as he came in.

"Hello darling," she said.

"Hello," he answered.

She took his coat and hung it in the closet. Then she walked over and made the drinks, a strongish one for him, a weak one for herself; and soon she was back again in her chair with the sewing, and he in the other, opposite, holding the tall glass with both his hands, rocking it so the ice cubes tinkled against the side.

For her, this was always a blissful time of day. She knew he didn't want to speak much until the first drink was finished, and she, on her side, was content to sit quietly, enjoying his company after the long hours alone in the house. She loved to luxuriate in the presence of this man, and to feel—almost as a sunbather feels the sun—that warm male glow that came out of him to her when they were alone together. She loved him for the way he sat loosely in a chair, for the way he came in a door, or moved slowly across the room with long strides. She loved the intent, far look in his eyes when they rested on her, the funny shape of the mouth, and especially the way he remained silent about his tiredness, sitting still with himself until the whiskey had taken some of it away.

"Tired, darling?"

"Yes," he said. "I'm tired." And as he spoke, he did an unusual thing. He lifted his glass and drained it in one swallow although there was still half of it, at least half of it left. She wasn't really watching him, but she knew what he had done because she heard the ice cubes falling back against the bottom of the empty glass when he lowered his arm. He paused a moment, leaning forward in the chair, then he got up and went slowly over to fetch himself another.

"I'll get it!" she cried, jumping up.

"Sit down," he said.

When he came back, she noticed that the new drink was dark amber with the quantity of whiskey in it.

"Darling, shall I get your slippers?"

"No."

She watched him as he began to sip the dark yellow drink, and she could see little oily swirls in the liquid because it was so strong.

"I think it's a shame," she said, "that when a policeman gets to be as senior as you, they keep him walking about on his feet all day long."

He didn't answer, so she bent her head again and went on with her sewing; but each time he lifted the drink to his lips, she heard the ice cubes clinking against the side of the glass.

"Darling," she said. "Would you like me to get you some cheese? I haven't made any supper because it's Thursday."

"No," he said.

"If you're too tired to eat out," she went on, "it's still not too late. There's plenty of meat and stuff in the freezer, and you can have it right here and not even move out of the chair."

Her eyes waited on him for an answer, a smile, a little nod, but he made no sign.

"Anyway," she went on, "I'll get you some cheese and crackers first."

"I don't want it," he said.

She moved uneasily in her chair, the large eyes still watching his face. "But you *must* have supper. I can easily do it here. I'd like to do it. We can have lamb chops. Or pork. Anything you want. Everything's in the freezer."

"Forget it," he said.

"But darling, you *must* eat! I'll fix it anyway, and then you can have it or not, as you like."

She stood up and placed her sewing on the table by the lamp.

"Sit down," he said. "Just for a minute, sit down."

It wasn't till then that she began to get frightened.

"Go on," he said. "Sit down."

She lowered herself back slowly into the chair, watching him all the time with those large, bewildered eyes. He had finished the second drink and was staring down into the glass, frowning.

"Listen," he said. "I've got something to tell you."

"What is it, darling? What's the matter?"

He had now become absolutely motionless, and he kept his head down so that the light from the lamp beside him fell across the upper part of his face, leaving the chin and mouth in shadow. She noticed there was a little muscle moving near the corner of his left eye.

"This is going to be a bit of a shock to you, I'm afraid," he said. "But I've thought about it a good deal and I've decided the only thing to do is tell you right away. I hope you won't blame me too much."

And he told her. It didn't take long, four or five minutes at most, and she sat very still through it all, watching him with a kind of dazed horror as he went further and further away from her with each word.

"So there it is," he added. "And I know it's kind of a bad time to be telling you, but there simply wasn't any other way. Of course I'll give you money and see you're looked after. But there needn't really be any fuss. I hope not anyway. It wouldn't be very good for my job."

Her first instinct was not to believe any of it, to reject it all. It occurred to her that perhaps he hadn't even spoken, that she herself had imagined the whole thing. Maybe, if she went about her business and acted as though she hadn't been listening, then later, when she sort of woke up again, she might find none of it had ever happened.

"I'll get the supper," she managed to whisper, and this time he didn't stop her.

When she walked across the room she couldn't feel her feet touching the floor. She couldn't feel anything at all—

except a slight nausea and a desire to vomit. Everything was automatic now—down the steps to the cellar, the light switch, the deep freeze, the hand inside the cabinet taking hold of the first object it met. She lifted it out, and looked at it. It was wrapped in paper, so she took off the paper and looked at it again.

A leg of lamb.

All right then, they would have lamb for supper. She carried it upstairs, holding the thin bone-end of it with both her hands, and as she went through the living-room, she saw him standing over by the window with his back to her, and she stopped.

"For God's sake," he said, hearing her, but not turning round. "Don't make supper for me. I'm going out."

At that point, Mary Maloney simply walked up behind him and without any pause she swung the big frozen leg of lamb high in the air and brought it down as hard as she could on the back of his head.

She might just as well have hit him with a steel club.

She stepped back a pace, waiting, and the funny thing was that he remained standing there for at least four or five seconds, gently swaying. Then he crashed to the carpet.

The violence of the crash, the noise, the small table overturning helped bring her out of the shock. She came out slowly, feeling cold and surprised, and she stood for a while blinking at the body, still holding the ridiculous piece of meat tight with both hands.

"All right," she told herself. "So I've killed him."

It was extraordinary, now, how clear her mind became all of a sudden. She began thinking very fast. As the wife of a detective, she knew quite well what the penalty would be. That was fine. It made no difference to her. In fact, it would be a relief. On the other hand, what about the child? What were the laws about murderers with unborn children? Did they kill them both—mother and child? Or did they wait until the tenth month? What did they do?

Mary Maloney didn't know. And she certainly wasn't prepared to take a chance.

She carried the meat into the kitchen, placed it in a pan, turned the oven on high, and shoved it inside. Then she washed her hands and ran upstairs to the bedroom. She sat down before the mirror, tidied her hair, touched up her lips and face. She tried a smile. It came out rather peculiar. She tried again.

"Hello, Sam," she said brightly, aloud.

The voice sounded peculiar too.

"I want some potatoes please, Sam. Yes, and I think a can of peas."

That was better. Both the smile and the voice were coming out better now. She rehearsed it several times more. Then she ran downstairs, took her coat, went out the back door, down the garden, into the street.

It wasn't six o'clock yet and the lights were still on in the grocery shop.

"Hello, Sam," she said brightly, smiling at the man behind the counter.

"Why, good evening, Mrs. Maloney. How're *you*?"

"I want some potatoes please, Sam. Yes, and I think a can of peas."

The man turned and reached up behind him on the shelf for the peas.

"Patrick's decided he's tired and doesn't want to eat out tonight," she told him. "We usually go out Thursdays, you know, and now he's caught me without any vegetables in the house."

"Then how about meat, Mrs. Maloney?"

"No, I've got meat, thanks. I got a nice leg of lamb from the freezer."

"Oh."

"I don't much like cooking it frozen, Sam, but I'm taking a chance on it this time. You think it'll be all right?"

"Personally," the grocer said, "I don't believe it makes any difference. You want these Idaho potatoes?"

"Oh yes, that'll be fine. Two of those."

"Anything else?" The grocer cocked his head on one side, looking at her pleasantly. "How about afterwards? What you going to give him for afterwards?"

"Well—what would you suggest, Sam?"

The man glanced around his shop. "How about a nice big slice of cheesecake? I know he likes that."

"Perfect," she said. "He loves it."

And when it was all wrapped and she had paid, she put on her brightest smile and said, "Thank you, Sam. Good night."

"Good night, Mrs. Maloney. And thank *you.*"

And now, she told herself as she hurried back, all she was doing now, she was returning home to her husband and he was waiting for his supper; and she must cook it good, and make it as tasty as possible because the poor man was tired; and if, when she entered the house, she happened to find anything unusual, or tragic, or terrible, then naturally it would be a shock and she'd become frantic with grief and horror. Mind you, she wasn't *expecting* to find anything. She was just going home with the vegetables. Mrs. Patrick Maloney going home with the vegetables on Thursday evening to cook supper for her husband.

"That's the way," she told herself. "Do everything right and natural. Keep things absolutely natural and there'll be no need for any acting at all."

Therefore, when she entered the kitchen by the back door, she was humming a little tune to herself and smiling.

"Patrick!" she called. "How are you, darling?"

She put the parcel down on the table and went through into the living room; and when she saw him lying there on the floor with his legs doubled up and one arm twisted back underneath his body, it really was rather a shock. All the old love and longing for him welled up inside her, and she ran over to him, knelt down beside him, and began to cry her heart out. It was easy. No acting was necessary.

A few minutes later she got up and went to the phone.

She knew the number of the police station, and when the man at the other end answered, she cried to him, "Quick! Come quick! Patrick's dead!"

"Who's speaking?"

"Mrs. Maloney. Mrs. Patrick Maloney."

"You mean Patrick Maloney's dead?"

"I think so," she sobbed. "He's lying on the floor and I think he's dead."

"Be right over," the man said.

The car came very quickly, and when she opened the front door, two policemen walked in. She knew them both —she knew nearly all the men at that precinct—and she fell right into Jack Noonan's arms, weeping hysterically. He put her gently into a chair, then went over to join the other one, who was called O'Malley, kneeling by the body.

"Is he dead?" she cried.

"I'm afraid he is. What happened?"

Briefly, she told her story about going out to the grocer and coming back to find him on the floor. While she was talking, crying and talking, Noonan discovered a small patch of congealed blood on the dead man's head. He showed it to O'Malley, who got up at once and hurried to the phone.

Soon, other men began to come into the house. First a doctor, then two detectives, one of whom she knew by name. Later, a police photographer arrived and took pictures, and a man who knew about fingerprints. There was a great deal of whispering and muttering beside the corpse, and the detectives kept asking her a lot of questions. But they always treated her kindly. She told her story again, this time right from the beginning, when Patrick had come in, and she was sewing, and he was tired, so tired he hadn't wanted to go out for supper. She told how she'd put the meat in the oven—"It's there now, cooking"—and how she'd slipped out to the grocer for vegetables, and come back to find him lying on the floor.

"Which grocer?" one of the detectives asked.

She told him, and he turned and whispered something

to the other detective, who immediately went outside into the street.

In fifteen minutes he was back with a page of notes, and there was more whispering, and through her sobbing she heard a few of the whispered phrases—". . . acted quite normal . . . very cheerful . . . wanted to give him a good supper . . . peas . . . cheesecake . . . impossible that she . . ."

After a while, the photographer and the doctor departed and two other men came in and took the corpse away on a stretcher. Then the fingerprint man went away. The two detectives remained, and so did the two policemen. They were exceptionally nice to her, and Jack Noonan asked if she wouldn't rather go somewhere else, to her sister's house perhaps, or to his own wife, who would take care of her and put her up for the night.

No, she said. She didn't feel she could move even a yard at the moment. Would they mind awfully if she stayed just where she was until she felt better? She didn't feel too good at the moment, she really didn't.

Then hadn't she better lie down on the bed? Jack Noonan asked.

No, she said. She'd like to stay right where she was, in this chair. A little later perhaps, when she felt better, she would move.

So they left her there while they went about their business, searching the house. Occasionally one of the detectives asked her another question. Sometimes Jack Noonan spoke at her gently as he passed by. Her husband, he told her, had been killed by a blow on the back of the head administered with a heavy blunt instrument, almost certainly a large piece of metal. They were looking for the weapon. The murderer may have taken it with him, but on the other hand he may've thrown it away or hidden it somewhere on the premises.

"It's the old story," he said. "Get the weapon, and you've got the man."

Later, one of the detectives came up and sat beside her.

Did she know, he asked, of anything in the house that could've been used as the weapon? Would she mind having a look around to see if anything was missing—a very big spanner, for example, or a heavy metal vase.

They didn't have any heavy metal vases, she said.

"Or a big spanner?"

She didn't think they had a big spanner. But there might be some things like that in the garage.

The search went on. She knew that there were other policemen in the garden all around the house. She could hear their footsteps on the gravel outside, and sometimes she saw the flash of a torch through a chink in the curtains. It began to get late, nearly nine she noticed by the clock on the mantle. The four men searching the rooms seemed to be growing weary, a trifle exasperated.

"Jack," she said, the next time Sergeant Noonan went by. "Would you mind giving me a drink?"

"Sure I'll give you a drink. You mean this whiskey?"

"Yes, please. But just a small one. It might make me feel better."

He handed her the glass.

"Why don't you have one yourself," she said. "You must be awfully tired. Please do. You've been very good to me."

"Well," he answered. "It's not strictly allowed, but I might take just a drop to keep me going."

One by one the others came in and were persuaded to take a little nip of whiskey. They stood around rather awkwardly with the drinks in their hands, uncomfortable in her presence, trying to say consoling things to her. Sergeant Noonan wandered into the kitchen, came out quickly and said, "Look, Mrs. Maloney. You know that oven of yours is still on, and the meat still inside."

"Oh, *dear* me!" she cried. "So it is!"

"I better turn it off for you, hadn't I?"

"Will you do that, Jack? Thank you so much."

When the sergeant returned the second time, she looked at him with her large, dark, tearful eyes. "Jack Noonan," she said.

"Yes?"

"Would you do me a small favor—you and these others?"

"We can try, Mrs. Maloney."

"Well," she said. "Here you all are, and good friends of dear Patrick's too, and helping to catch the man who killed him. You must be terribly hungry by now because it's long past your suppertime, and I know Patrick would never forgive me, God bless his soul, if I allowed you to remain in his house without offering you decent hospitality. Why don't you eat up that lamb that's in the oven? It'll be cooked just right by now."

"Wouldn't dream of it," Sergeant Noonan said.

"Please," she begged. "Please eat it. Personally I couldn't touch a thing, certainly not what's been in the house when he was here. But it's all right for you. It'd be a favor to me if you'd eat it up. Then you can go on with your work again afterwards."

There was a good deal of hesitating among the four policemen, but they were clearly hungry, and in the end they were persuaded to go into the kitchen and help themselves. The woman stayed where she was, listening to them through the open door, and she could hear them speaking among themselves, their voices thick and sloppy because their mouths were full of meat.

"Have some more, Charlie?"

"No. Better not finish it."

"She *wants* us to finish it. She said so. Be doing her a favor."

"Okay then. Give me some more."

"That's a hell of a big club the guy must've used to hit poor Patrick," one of them was saying. "The doc says his skull was smashed all to pieces just like from a sledgehammer."

"That's why it ought to be easy to find."

"Exactly what I say."

"Whoever done it, they're not going to be carrying a thing like that around with them longer than they need."

One of them belched.

"Personally, I think it's right here on the premises."

"Probably right under our very noses. What you think, Jack?"

And in the other room, Mary Maloney began to giggle.

NO PARKING

Ellery Queen

Modesta Ryan played her greatest role not on a Broadway stage but in her penthouse on Madison Avenue. The performance took place one midsummer night against a backdrop of flooding rain, thunder, and lightning; power failures darkened some buildings in the Central Park area; and, of course, the Athenia Apartments was one of them. So Modesta even got to play her big scene by the light of candles, a surefire touch.

Ellery was not surprised. Modesta Ryan specialized in melodrama. Everything she touched went off like a rocket. She could not walk her dog without landing on the front page. Her last pet had broken his leash on Fifth Avenue and been run over by a car carrying the ambassador of an Iron Curtain country.

Modesta was spectacularly unlucky in love. She had

never married. The men she wanted always seemed to prefer lisping ingenues or hatcheck girls, and those who wanted her she could not stand. Her suitors ran to handkissers, cigarette holder smokers, jodhpur wearers, and gloomy college boys with mother fixations.

But suddenly, there he was. It was too impossibly wonderful. There he was—all three of him.

For naturally, when the right man did come along, two others equally right showed up, too.

It was a typical Modesta Ryan sensation, and for some months Broadway speculated on little else. Which of the three would she marry?

Jock Shanville was male lead in the new play Modesta was rehearsing, a costume piece set in medieval Venice. It was type casting, for besides flaunting a doge's profile, a wicked eye, and a fine leg in tights, Shanville excelled in scene stealing, reputation poisoning, character assassination, and other closet arts of the theater. Jock had a wife, an ex–show girl named Pearline, but she was no problem; his rapier tongue had been backing her toward the nearest divorce court long before he decided on Modesta Ryan as her successor.

Then there was Kid Catt, a black-browed fighting machine who dealt bloody unconsciousness from both fists with a cold smile that had become his TV trademark. The Kid's body was his god, self-denial his creed; and women sat high on his proscribed list. So when he fell in love with Modesta it was with the violent passion of a fallen monk. Modesta found holding the beautiful young brute at bay an enchanting experience.

Richard Van Olde II, however, was a quite different temptation. Van Olde was a soft-spoken tyrant of position and wealth. Modesta Ryan was the first woman he had wanted since the death of his wife a dozen years before, and he meant to have her. He was a man of instant, irrevocable decisions, and he offered Modesta marriage from the first, courting her tirelessly. There was something about his lashless eyes and noiseless personality that made her shiver like an inexperienced girl.

Jock Shanville fitted her like a glove; young Catt excited her; Van Olde fascinated her.

Which should she accept?

The phone rang just as Ellery was stooping to unlace his shoes.

"It's for you," Inspector Queen called from the other bedroom.

"At a quarter to twelve?" Ellery used the extension. "Yes?"

"Ellery? Modesta Ryan . . ."

"Modesta." Ellery fingered his tie automatically. He had known her for years, and each time he heard her voice was like the first time. Tonight the throaty tones had a throb in them, subdued and offbeat. "What's wrong?"

"Ellery, I'm in trouble," she whispered. "Can you come right over to my apartment? Please."

"Of course. But what kind of trouble?"

"I can't talk. I'm not alone—"

"This marriage business?"

"Yes, I decided today. Gave the other two their walking papers. But hurry!"

"Modesta, wait. Just tell me who's with you—"

But the phone went dead. Ellery grabbed his raincoat and ran.

The streets were empty rivers, and he roared east toward Central Park leaving a wake like a power launch. He was through the park transverse and across Fifth and Madison Avenues in a matter of minutes. Sixty seconds later he was sloshing around the corner of Park Avenue into a one-way westbound street in the East Eighties, peering through his streaming windshield for a parking space.

As far down the street as he could see, the curbs were jammed with cars bumper to bumper.

Ellery cruised, trying to control his temper. You could

never find a parking space in New York, least of all when you were in a hurry. And when it rained—

The Athenia Apartments was on the northeast corner, just off Madison Avenue. Between the corner and the Athenia's canopy he sighted empty curb and he stepped on the gas. But when he got there he saw a No Parking sign; it was a crosstown bus stop. Wouldn't you know! Back into Madison Avenue he drove, and he circumnavigated the block, ready to settle for a dozen feet of curb anywhere. But the curbs were all occupied. He turned into Modesta's street again, worried and furious.

"God knows what's happening up there," he thought angrily. He was tempted to park at the bus stop; but a family respect for the law, and the prospect of squatting half a day in traffic court, dissuaded him.

No miracle had happened. There was still no place to park on Modesta's street. Groaning, Ellery turned up Madison Avenue again.

"This is my last time on this merry-go-round," he promised himself grittily. "Modesta must think I'm coming by pack mule. I'll double-park."

The last time around he had noticed one car illegally parked. At the curb between the Athenia's canopy and the entrance of the next building stood three cars in a row, and a fourth was double-parked by the side of the middle one. The double-parked car bore an M.D. license plate.

Again Ellery drove up the block from Park Avenue toward Madison. He was about to pull in behind the doctor's car when two young couples dashed out of the apartment house on the southeast corner, splashed toward the Athenia's canopy, and jumped into the first of the three parked cars.

"Hurray," Ellery said sourly; and when his rescuers pulled away he shot around the double-parked car and backed like a fireman into the vacated space nearest the canopy.

Five minutes past midnight! He had lost ten minutes finding a space. And he'd been lucky at that.

Ellery was under the Athenia's canopy in two jumps. He ran into the lobby, swishing the water off his hat. The lobby was dark. Basement flooded, probably, shorting the power mains.

"Doorman?" he shouted into the darkness.

"Comin'." A flashlight snapped on and bobbed quickly toward him. "Who'd you want to see, sir?"

"Miss Ryan, penthouse. Elevator out?"

"Uh-huh." The doorman seemed dubious. "It's pretty late. The house phone's not workin', either."

"I'm expected," said Ellery. "Where's the stairway? Speak up!"

The doorman stared, then mumbled, "This way."

The man shuffled toward the rear of the lobby past the dead switchboard, flashing his light behind him for Ellery. As they reached the emergency door it opened and a male figure hurried past them and vanished in the darkness. Ellery caught one glimpse of the figure as it scuttled by— stooped over, so that his height and age were impossible to guess, wearing a double-breasted tan trench coat buttoned up the left side to the chin, and a tan stetson pulled well down over his face.

Something about the man bothered Ellery, but he had no time to analyze.

He ran up marble stairs endlessly, praying that the battery of his pencil-flashlight would hold out. When he reached the penthouse landing eleven flights up he was seeing phosphorescent confetti in the darkness. Breathing hard, he swept his light about, located the push button near the service door, and leaned on it. He heard a buzz inside the apartment, but nothing else.

He tried the door. It was unlocked.

Ellery stepped into Modesta Ryan's country-style kitchen. A candle glass was wavering eerily on the fireplace mantel; a bed of briquettes had burned to embers.

"Modesta?"

He stepped through the swinging door into her dining room, feeling his scalp tickle. A candlestick on the sideboard illuminated the room fitfully. The hall beyond was dark.

"*Modesta?*"

He groped along the passage, playing his flash, no longer calling. He kept telling himself as the shadows parted in his path that Modesta was quite capable of an elaborate joke, picking a night like this for atmosphere.

For a moment, as he stepped into her living room, he was sure of it. Two seven-branched candelabra blazed, and in the focus of their flames, in an exquisite negligee, lay Modesta's lovely body. She was crumpled on the Italian tile floor beside her mother-of-pearl grand piano. On the breast of her negligee there was an illusion of a bullet wound and blood. . . . Ellery knelt. The stuff staining her breast looked exactly like ketchup.

But it was not. And the silk was scorched around a very real hole.

He hunted for her pulse. There it was!—but it was flickering like the candles. She was barely alive.

Ellery ran to the phone more out of habit than conviction. To his surprise it was working. He made two calls—one for an emergency ambulance, the other to his father; and then he tore through the apartment to the service door and began leaping down the eleven flights like a mountain goat.

"If she dies," he was thinking, "those parked cars around here ought to be tagged as accessories." The ten minutes he had lost looking for a parking space might have saved what was left of Modesta Ryan's life.

He plunged out under the canopy, followed by the astonished doorman. Nothing had changed. The cloudburst continued to swab down the streets. The same three cars were lined up between the Athenia's entrance and the adjoining building, his own foremost; the same doctor's car was still double-parked beside the middle car of the three, boxing it in.

Of course the man in the trench coat was gone.

"Then this is the way it went, Wladeczki?" Inspector Queen said to the doorman in the light of the police torches.

"You were on duty since four P.M., due to go off at midnight, but you stayed on because the storm held up your relief man. You didn't leave this lobby at any time. Nobody could have sneaked past you, you say. All right.

"Miss Ryan come home from rehearsal in a taxi about seven P.M. She was alone. About eight her maid left for the night. Between eight and a few minutes past eleven only five people entered or left the building. They are all long time tenants. At eleven-thirty Mr. Trench Coat walks into the lobby. Five minutes later an M.D. on emergency call to an old lady tenant—who's very sick in 4–G—drives up and complains to you he can't find space for his car. You let the doctor double-park—"

"And he's still up in 4–G," said Sergeant Velie. "The other five, the tenants, alibi okay, too."

"Now about Mr. Trench Coat. He didn't come by cab, you say. You don't get a real good look at him by your flash, the way he has his hat pulled down and his collar turned up. He talks in a croaky whisper, as if he has a bad cold. He says he has an appointment with Miss Modesta Ryan, you tell him he'll have to walk up to the penthouse, he goes up the stairway, and that's the last you see of him till a few minutes past midnight when he ducks out the stairway door under your nose—and the nose," added the inspector gently, "of the eminent Mr. Queen here."

Ellery gave his father a wan look. "Did you notice," he asked the doorman, "how wet his trench coat and hat were when he first came into the lobby?"

"No wetter than yours was, Mr. Queen," said the doorman. "Got my name spelled right, Sergeant?"

"Time will tell," said the sergeant. "Hey, Goldie. Well?"

Detective Goldberg came in, shaking himself like a dog. He had found Modesta Ryan's maid asleep in her Harlem flat, he reported; the maid knew nothing except that on Miss Ryan's arrival home she had made three phone calls—one to Kid Catt, one to Mr. Shanville, and the last to Mr. Van Olde. But the maid hadn't listened to the con-

versations, so she couldn't say which ones Miss Ryan had
given the heave and which one she'd made the happy
man.

"Any report from the hospital yet?" muttered the inspector.

"She's this way that way," said Sergeant Velie.

"But did she talk?"

"She's got all she can do to keep on breathing, Inspector. She's still unconscious."

"Then we do it the hard way," said the old man gloomily. "It's a cinch Trench Coat was one of Modesta's two
rejects. He didn't waste any time, did he? As soon as those
three are brought in, have 'em taken up to the penthouse.
Coming, Ellery?"

His son sighed. "If I could have found a place to park as
soon as I got here . . ."

Hollow laughter followed him to the stairway door.

At twenty minutes after two the inspector finished with
the last of the three interrogations. He found Ellery in
Modesta Ryan's living room staring reproachfully at her
phone.

"Any luck?"

"I've called every columnist in town, all her close
friends. She just didn't tell anybody."

The old man grunted. He stuck his head into the hall.
"Get those cuties in here."

Shanville made his entrance with a rather set smile. The
disheveled blond hair was all dagger points, and with the
slight upcurve of his lips he looked satanic.

"What now?" he asked. "The rack?"

About Kid Catt there was a look of astounded suffering,
as if he had just been knocked down. His powerful frame
sagged into a chair and his black eyes stared dully at the
chalk marks on the tiles near the piano.

"Who did it?" the fighter mumbled. "Just tell me which
one of these two—did it."

"Underplay, Kid," said the actor pleasantly. "This is a professional audience."

The black eyes looked at him. "Lay off, actor," the Kid said.

"Or else?" smiled Shanville.

"I'm leaving," said Richard Van Olde II abruptly.

The tycoon was very angry. His naturally pale skin was almost green, the lashless eyes murderous.

"Just another few minutes, Mr. Van Olde," said Inspector Queen.

"A very few, please. Then I either walk out of here unmolested or I telephone my attorneys and the commissioner."

"Yes, *sir*. Now, gentlemen, each of you wanted to marry Miss Ryan—bad. And each of you got a phone call from her tonight. One she told she'd finally decided to marry. Two— the other two—she brushed. One of those two promptly came here tonight and shot her.

"You think you've got us stymied," the inspector went on, showing his dentures. "Each man was found home in bed. And while we have the bullet—probably from a 38—search of your respective premises has failed to turn up the gun. Or the trench coat or stetson. On top of that, each claims *he* was the man Modesta told over the phone she was accepting! Two of those claims are lies, of course, to take the heat off. But right now we can't tell which two.

"Gentlemen, I have news for you," said Inspector Queen softly. "Thrown-away guns, coats, and hats have a way of turning up. And you've got no alibis for the time of the shooting. You were home in bed, say all of you, but none of you can prove it, not even you, Shanville, because you occupy a separate bedroom and weren't even heard coming home—"

"Are you quite finished?" asked Richard Van Olde.

"Not yet, sir!"

"Dad."

The inspector looked around, surprised. Ellery was on his feet, the picture of wry hopelessness.

"I don't see any point to going any further with this now, do you? Let's call it a night. These gentlemen won't run away, and we can all use some sleep."

The old man blinked.

"All right," he said.

But when the three had gone, he growled to his son, "And what's the big plot, Mastermind?"

"It's simple enough," Ellery said as they crouched near the glass outer doors of the lobby. It was after three, the rain had stopped, and the chrome on the dark cars outside winked damply in the street lights. "We're waiting for our friend to come back."

"Come *back?*" said Sergeant Velie. "What is he, goofed?"

"Case of necessity, Velie," murmured Ellery. "Consider. How did Trench Coat get to the Athenia last night?"

"*Get* here?"

"Yes. By cab? No, says the doorman. On foot? No, because if he'd walked or even run from as close by as the corner of Madison he'd have been soaked in that downpour, whereas the doorman said his trench coat and hat were no wetter than mine when I got here—and I had to make only two jumps from my car to get under the canopy. Conclusion? *Trench Coat came in a car, and he parked almost as close to the canopy as I did.*"

His father made a strangled sort of sound.

"Now, the nearest parked cars are those four between the Athenia's canopy and the next building—my car, the two behind mine, and the M.D.'s, double-parked beside the one behind mine. Well, which of the four was Trench Coat's? Not mine, of course, or the car mine replaced—the people who drove off in that one came from the building across the street; what's more, they drove away before Trench Coat left the Athenia.

"So Trench Coat's car must be one of the other three. Which one?

"Let's see. Trench Coat made his escape just as I was going up to Modesta's apartment. You'd expect him to jump into his car—one of those three—and drive off. Did he? No —when I rushed downstairs after finding Modesta shot, all three cars were still parked. Why didn't he take his car for his getaway? *Obviously, because he couldn't.* His car must be the one behind mine, the middle one of the three at the curb—the one that's boxed in by the doctor's car!"

The inspector sounded punchy. "So that's why you moved your jalopy away . . . to give him room to get his car out when he thinks the coast is clear."

"That's the idea," said Ellery.

"Now all you have to do," said the sergeant, not without bitterness, "is tell us who you see in your crystal ball."

"Why, So-and-so," replied Ellery, naming a name; and at their exclamations he grinned. "At least, I'm ninety-nine percent sure."

At 4:15 A.M. a furtive figure skulked suddenly past the Athenia, darted into the designated car, and fought cattishly but in vain to shake off Sergeant Velie's paralyzing clutch.

It was, as Ellery had predicted, So-and-so.

By the time they booked their catch downtown and sat in on the confession, the city was driving to work. They crawled uptown in Ellery's car to the hospital.

It was while Inspector Queen went off to inquire about Modesta that Sergeant Velie seemed to come out of a fog. "Can I be *that* stupid, Ellery? I still don't see how you could—"

"Console yourself," soothed Ellery. "The doorman and I saw Trench Coat; you didn't. When he hurried past us at the stairway door, I was bothered by something in his appearance. Later I realized what it had been: he'd had his double-breasted coat buttoned down the *left* side. It's women who are left-side buttoners; men are the reverse. So

I knew Trench Coat was a woman dressed as a man. Which woman? Van Olde's a widower, Kid Catt's a bachelor, and neither has any entangling alliances. But Jock Shanville's married, so his wife was an odds-on bet. As she told us, she eavesdropped on Modesta's call, heard that she was through as Mrs. Shanville, and proceeded—with the help of her theatrical training—to do something about it."

The sergeant was still shaking his head when the inspector came back, all smiles. Modesta would live—although she'd have to have new evening gowns designed—and she had satisfactorily fingered Pearline Shanville as the jealous witch who had ruined her décolletage.

Then they shuffled blearily out to Ellery's car and he found a ticket on it for parking in a restricted hospital zone.

THE OBLONG ROOM

Edward D. Hoch

It was Fletcher's case from the beginning, but Captain Leopold rode along with him when the original call came in. The thing seemed open and shut, with the only suspect found literally standing over his victim, and on a dull day Leopold thought that a ride out to the university might be pleasant.

Here, along the river, the October color was already in the trees, and through the park a slight haze of burning leaves clouded the road in spots. It was a warm day for autumn, a sunny day. Not really a day for murder.

"The university hasn't changed much," Leopold commented, as they turned into the narrow street that led past the fraternity houses to the library tower. "A few new dorms, and a new stadium. That's about all."

"We haven't had a case here since that bombing four or

five years back," Fletcher said. "This one looks to be a lot easier, though. They've got the guy already. Stabbed his roommate and then stayed right there with the body."

Leopold was silent. They'd pulled up before one of the big new dormitories that towered toward the sky like some middle-income housing project, all brick and concrete and right now surrounded by milling students. Leopold pinned on his badge and led the way.

The room was on the fourth floor, facing the river. It seemed to be identical to all the others—a depressing oblong with bunk beds, twin study desks, wardrobes, and a large picture window opposite the door. The medical examiner was already there, and he looked up as Leopold and Fletcher entered. "We're ready to move him. All right with you, Captain?"

"The boys get their pictures? Then it's fine with me. Fletcher, find out what you can." Then, to the medical examiner, "What killed him?"

"A couple of stab wounds. I'll do an autopsy, but there's not much doubt."

"How long dead?"

"A day or so."

"A day!"

Fletcher had been making notes as he questioned the others. "The precinct men have it pretty well wrapped up for us, Captain. The dead boy is Ralph Rollings, a sophomore. His roommate admits to being here with the body for maybe twenty hours before they were discovered. Roommate's name is Tom McBern. They've got him in the next room."

Leopold nodded and went through the connecting door. Tom McBern was tall and slender, and handsome in a dark, collegiate sort of way. "Have you warned him of his rights?" Leopold asked a patrolman.

"Yes, sir."

"All right." Leopold sat down on the bed opposite McBern. "What have you got to say, son?"

The deep brown eyes came up to meet Leopold's. "Nothing, sir. I think I want a lawyer."

"That's your privilege, of course. You don't wish to make any statement about how your roommate met his death, or why you remained in the room with him for several hours without reporting it?"

"No, sir." He turned away and stared out the window.

"You understand we'll have to book you on suspicion of homicide."

The boy said nothing more, and after a few moments Leopold left him alone with the officer. He went back to Fletcher and watched while the body was covered and carried away. "He's not talking. Wants a lawyer. Where are we?"

Sergeant Fletcher shrugged. "All we need is motive. They probably had the same girl or something."

"Find out."

They went to talk with the boy who occupied the adjoining room, the one who'd found the body. He was sandy-haired and handsome, with the look of an athlete, and his name was Bill Smith.

"Tell us how it was, Bill," Leopold said.

"There's not much to tell. I knew Ralph and Tom slightly during my freshman year, but never really well. They stuck pretty much together. This year I got the room next to them, but the connecting door was always locked. Anyway, yesterday neither one of them showed up at class. When I came back yesterday afternoon I knocked at the door and asked if anything was wrong. Tom called out that they were sick. He wouldn't open the door. I went into my own room and didn't think much about it. Then, this morning, I knocked to see how they were. Tom's voice sounded so . . . strange."

"Where was your own roommate all this time?"

"He's away. His father died and he went home for the funeral." Smith's hands were nervous, busy with a shredded piece of paper. Leopold offered him a cigarette and he took it. "Anyway, when he wouldn't open the door I became quite concerned and told him I was going for help. He opened it then—and I saw Ralph stretched out on the bed, all bloody and . . . dead."

Leopold nodded and went to stand by the window. From here he could see the trees down along the river, blazing gold and amber and scarlet as the October sun passed across them. "Had you heard any sounds the previous day? Any argument?"

"No. Nothing. Nothing at all."

"Had they disagreed in the past about anything?"

"Not that I knew of. If they didn't get along, they hardly would have asked to room together again this year."

"How about girls?" Leopold asked.

"They both dated occasionally, I think."

"No special one? One they both liked?"

Bill Smith was silent for a fraction too long. "No."

"You're sure?"

"I told you I didn't know them very well."

"This is murder, Bill. It's not a sophomore dance or Class Day games."

"Tom killed him. What more do you need?"

"What's her name, Bill?"

He stubbed out the cigarette and looked away. Then finally he answered. "Stella Banting. She's a junior."

"Which one did she go with?"

"I don't know. She was friendly with both of them. I think she went out with Ralph a few times around last Christmas, but I've seen her with Tom lately."

"She's older than them?"

"No. They're all twenty. She's just a year ahead."

"All right," Leopold said. "Sergeant Fletcher will want to question you further."

He left Smith's room and went out in the hall with Fletcher. "It's your case, Sergeant. About time I gave it to you."

"Thanks for the help, Captain."

"Let him talk to a lawyer and then see if he has a story. If he still won't make a statement, book him on suspicion. I don't think there's any doubt we can get an indictment."

"You going to talk to that girl?"

Leopold smiled. "I just might. Smith seemed a bit shy about her. Might be a motive there. Let me know as soon as the medical examiner has something more definite about the time of death."

"Right, Captain."

Leopold went downstairs, pushing his way through the students and faculty members still crowding the halls and stairways. Outside he unpinned the badge and put it away. The air was fresh and crisp as he strolled across the campus to the administration building.

Stella Banting lived in the largest sorority house on campus, a great columned building of ivy and red brick. But when Captain Leopold found her she was on her way back from the drugstore, carrying a carton of cigarettes and a bottle of shampoo. Stella was a tall girl with firm, angular lines and a face that might have been beautiful if she ever smiled.

"Stella Banting?"

"Yes?"

"I'm Captain Leopold. I wanted to talk to you about the tragedy over at the men's dorm. I trust you've heard about it?"

She blinked her eyes and said, "Yes. I've heard."

"Could we go somewhere and talk?"

"I'll drop these at the house and we can walk if you'd like. I don't want to talk there."

She was wearing faded Bermuda shorts and a bulky sweatshirt, and walking with her made Leopold feel young again. If only she smiled occasionally—but perhaps this was not a day for smiling. They headed away from the main campus, out toward the silent oval of the athletic field and sports stadium. "You didn't come over to the dorm," he said to her finally, breaking the silence of their walk.

"Should I have?"

"I understood you were friendly with them—that you dated the dead boy last Christmas and Tom McBern more recently."

"A few times. Ralph wasn't the sort anyone ever got to know very well."

"And what about Tom?"

"He was a nice fellow."

"*Was?*"

"It's hard to explain. Ralph did things to people, to everyone around him. When I felt it happening to me, I broke away."

"What sort of things?"

"He had a power—a power you wouldn't believe any twenty-year-old capable of."

"You sound as if you've known a lot of them."

"I have. This is my third year at the university. I've grown up a lot in that time. I think I have anyway."

"And what about Tom McBern?"

"I dated him a few times recently just to confirm for myself how bad things were. He was completely under Ralph's thumb. He lived for no one but Ralph."

"Homosexual?" Leopold asked.

"No, I don't think it was anything as blatant as that. It was more the relationship of teacher and pupil, leader and follower."

"Master and slave?"

She turned to smile at him. "You do seem intent on midnight orgies, don't you?"

"The boy is dead, after all."

"Yes. Yes, he is." She stared down at the ground, kicking randomly at the little clusters of fallen leaves. "But you see what I mean? Ralph was always the leader, the teacher—for Tom, almost the messiah."

"Then why would he have killed him?" Leopold asked.

"That's just it—he wouldn't! Whatever happened in

that room, I can't imagine Tom McBern ever bringing himself to kill Ralph."

"There is one possibility, Miss Banting. Could Ralph Rollings have made a disparaging remark about you? Something about when he was dating you?"

"I never slept with Ralph, if that's what you're trying to ask me. With either of them, for that matter."

"I didn't mean it that way."

"It happened just the way I've told you. If anything, I was afraid of Ralph. I didn't want him getting that sort of hold over me."

Somehow he knew they'd reached the end of their stroll, even though they were still in the middle of the campus quadrangle, some distance from the sports arena. "Thank you for your help, Miss Banting. I may want to call on you again."

He left her there and headed back toward the men's dorm, knowing that she would watch him until he was out of sight.

Sergeant Fletcher found Leopold in his office early the following morning, reading the daily reports of the night's activities. "Don't you ever sleep, Captain?" he asked, pulling up the faded leather chair that served for infrequent visitors.

"I'll have enough time for sleeping when I'm dead. What have you got on McBern?"

"His lawyer says he refuses to make a statement, but I gather they'd like to plead him not guilty by reason of insanity."

"What's the medical examiner say?"

Fletcher read from a typed sheet. "Two stab wounds, both in the area of the heart. He apparently was stretched out on the bed when he got it."

"How long before they found him?"

"He'd eaten breakfast maybe an hour or so before he died, and from our questioning that places the time of death at about ten o'clock. Bill Smith went to the door and got McBern to open it at about eight the following morning. Since we know McBern was in the room the previous evening when Smith spoke to him through the door, we can assume he was alone with the body for approximately twenty-two hours."

Leopold was staring out the window, mentally comparing the city's autumn gloom with the colors of the countryside that he'd witnessed the previous day. Everything dies, only it dies a little sooner, a bit more drably, in the city. "What else?" he asked Fletcher, because there obviously was something else.

"In one of the desk drawers," Fletcher said, producing a little evidence envelope. "Six sugar cubes, saturated with LSD."

"All right." Leopold stared down at them. "I guess that's not too unusual on campuses these days. Has there ever been a murder committed by anyone under the influence of LSD?"

"A case out west somewhere. And I think another one over in England."

"Can we get a conviction, or is this the basis of the insanity plea?"

"I'll check on it, Captain."

"And one more thing—get that fellow Smith in here. I want to talk with him again."

Later, alone, Leopold felt profoundly depressed. The case bothered him. McBern had stayed with Rollings's body for twenty-two hours. Anybody that could last that long would have to be crazy. He was crazy and he was a killer and that was all there was to it.

When Fletcher ushered Bill Smith into the office an hour later, Leopold was staring out the window. He turned and motioned the young man to a chair. "I have some further questions, Bill."

"Yes?"

"Tell me about the LSD."

"What?"

Leopold walked over and sat on the edge of the desk. "Don't pretend you never heard of it. Rollings and McBern had some in their room."

Bill Smith looked away. "I didn't know. There were rumors."

"Nothing else? No noise through that connecting door?"

"Noise, yes. Sometimes it was . . ."

Leopold waited for him to continue, and when he did not, said, "This is a murder investigation, Bill."

"Rollings . . . he deserved to die, that's all. He was the most completely evil person I ever knew. The things he did to poor Tom . . ."

"Stella Banting says Tom almost worshiped him."

"He did, and that's what made it all the more terrible."

Leopold leaned back and lit a cigarette. "If they were both high on LSD, almost anyone could have entered that room and stabbed Ralph."

But Bill Smith shook his head. "I doubt it. They wouldn't have dared unlock the door while they were turned on. Besides, Tom would have protected him with his own life."

"And yet we're to believe that Tom killed him? That he stabbed him to death and then spent a day and a night alone with the body? Doing what, Bill? Doing what?"

"I don't know."

"Do you think Tom McBern is insane?"

"No, not really. Not legally." He glanced away. "But on the subject of Rollings, he was pretty far gone. Once, when we were still friendly, he told me he'd do anything for Rollings—even trust him with his life. And he did, one time. It was during the spring weekend and everybody had been drinking a lot. Tom hung upside down out of the dorm window with Rollings holding his ankles. That's how much he trusted him."

"I think I'll have to talk with Tom McBern again," Leopold said. "At the scene of the crime."

Fletcher brought Tom McBern out to the campus in handcuffs, and Captain Leopold was waiting for them in the oblong room on the fourth floor. "All right, Fletcher," Leopold said. "You can leave us alone. Wait outside."

McBern had lost a good deal of his previous composure, and now he faced Leopold with red-ringed eyes and a lip that trembled when he spoke. "What . . . what did you want to ask me?"

"A great many things, son. All the questions in the world."

Leopold sighed and offered the boy a cigarette. "You and Rollings were taking LSD, weren't you?"

"We took it, yes."

"Why? For kicks?"

"Not for kicks. You don't understand about Ralph."

"I understand that you killed him. What more is there to understand? You stabbed him to death right over there on that bed."

Tom McBern took a deep breath. "We didn't take LSD for kicks," he repeated. "It was more to heighten the sense of religious experience—a sort of mystical involvement that is the whole meaning of life."

Leopold frowned down at the boy. "I'm only a detective, son. You and Rollings were strangers to me until yesterday, and I guess now he'll always be a stranger to me. That's one of the troubles with my job. I don't get to meet people until it's too late, until the damage"—he gestured toward the empty bed—"is already done. But I want to know what happened in this room, between you two. I don't want to hear about mysticism or religious experience. I want to hear what happened—why you killed him and why you sat here with the body for twenty-two hours."

Tom McBern looked up at the walls, seeing them perhaps for the first and thousandth time. "Did you ever think about this room? About the shape of it? Ralph used to say it reminded him of a story by Poe, 'The Oblong Box.' Remember that story? The box was on board a ship, and of course it contained a body. Like Queequeg's coffin which rose from the sea to rescue Ishmael."

"And this room was Ralph's coffin?" Leopold asked quietly.

"Yes." McBern stared down at his handcuffed wrists. "His tomb."

"You killed him, didn't you?"

"Yes."

Leopold looked away. "Do you want your lawyer?"

"No. Nothing."

"My God! Twenty-two hours!"

"I was—"

"I know what you were doing. But I don't think you'll ever tell it to a judge and jury."

"I'll tell you, because maybe you can understand." And he began to talk in a slow, quiet voice, and Leopold listened because that was his job. Toward evening, when Tom McBern had been returned to his cell and Fletcher sat alone with Leopold, he said, "I've called the district attorney, Captain. What are you going to tell him?"

"The facts, I suppose. McBern will sign a confession of just how it happened. The rest is out of our hands."

"Do you want to tell me about it, Captain?"

"I don't think I want to tell anyone about it. But I suppose I have to. I guess it was all that talk of religious experience and coffins rising from the ocean that tipped me off. You know that Rollings pictured their room as a sort of tomb."

"For him it was."

"I wish I'd known him, Fletcher. I only wish I'd known him in time."

"What would you have done?"

"Perhaps only listened and tried to understand him."

"McBern admitted killing him?"

Leopold nodded. "It seems that Rollings asked him to, and Tom McBern trusted him more than life itself."

"Rollings asked to be stabbed through the heart?"

"Yes."

"Then why did McBern stay with the body so long? For a whole day and night?"

"He was waiting," Leopold said quietly, looking at nothing at all. "He was waiting for Rollings to rise from the dead."

SWEET FEVER

Bill Pronzini

Quarter before midnight, like on every evening except the Sabbath or when it's storming or when my rheumatism gets to paining too bad, me and Billy Bob went down to the Chigger Mountain railroad tunnel to wait for the night freight from St. Louis. This here was a fine summer evening, with a big old fat yellow moon hung above the pines on Hankers Ridge and mockingbirds and cicadas and toads making a soft ruckus. Nights like this, I have me a good feeling, hopeful, and I know Billy Bob does too.

They's a bog hollow on the near side of the tunnel opening, and beside it a woody slope, not too steep. Halfway down the slope is a big catalpa tree, and that was where we always set, side by side with our backs up against the trunk.

So we come on down to there, me hobbling some with my cane and Billy Bob holding onto my arm. That moon was so bright you could see the melons lying in Ferdie Johnson's patch over on the left, and the rail tracks had a sleek oiled look coming out of the tunnel mouth and leading off toward the Sabreville yards a mile up the line. On the far side of the tracks, the woods and the rundown shacks that used to be a hobo jungle before the county sheriff closed it off thirty years back had them a silvery cast, like they was all coated in winter frost.

We set down under the catalpa tree and I leaned my head back to catch my wind. Billy Bob said, "Granpa, you feeling right?"

"Fine, boy."

"Rheumatism ain't started paining you?"

"Not a bit."

He give me a grin. "Got a little surprise for you."

"The hell you do."

"Fresh plug of blackstrap," he said. He come out of his pocket with it. "Mr. Cotter got him in a shipment just today down at his store."

I was some pleased. But I said, "Now you hadn't ought to go spending your money on me, Billy Bob."

"Got nobody else I'd rather spend it on."

I took the plug and unwrapped it and had me a chew. Old man like me ain't got many pleasures left, but fresh blackstrap's one; good corn's another. Billy Bob gets us all the corn we need from Ben Logan's boys. They got a pretty good sized still up on Hankers Ridge, and their corn is the best in this part of the hills. Not that either of us is a drinking man, now. A little touch after supper and on special days is all. I never did hold with drinking too much, or doing anything too much, and I taught Billy Bob the same.

He's a good boy. Man couldn't ask for a better grandson. But I raised him that way—in my own image, you might say —after both my own son Rufus and Billy Bob's ma got taken from us in 1947. I reckon I done a right job of it, and I couldn't be less proud of him than I was of his pa, or love him no less, either.

Well, we set there and I worked on the chew of black-strap and had a spit every now and then, and neither of us said much. Pretty soon the first whistle come, way off on the other side of Chigger Mountain. Billy Bob cocked his head and said, "She's right on schedule."

"Mostly is," I said, "this time of year."

That sad lonesome hungry ache started up in me again —what my daddy used to call the "sweet fever." He was a railroad man, and I grew up around trains and spent a goodly part of my early years at the roundhouse in the Sabreville yards. Once, when I was ten, he let me take the throttle of the big 2-8-0 Mogul steam locomotive on his highballing run to Eulalia, and I can't recollect no more finer experience in my whole life. Later on I worked as a callboy, and then as a fireman on a 2-10-4, and put in some time as a yard tender engineer, and I expect I'd have gone on in railroading if it hadn't been for the Depression and getting myself married and having Rufus. My daddy's short-line company folded up in 1931, and half a dozen others too, and wasn't no work for either of us in Sabreville or Eulalia or anywheres else on the iron. That squeezed the will right out of him, and he took to ailing, and I had to accept a job on Mr. John Barnett's truck farm to support him and the rest of my family. Was my intention to go back into railroading, but the Depression dragged on, and my daddy died, and a year later my wife Amanda took sick and passed on, and by the time the war come it was just too late.

But Rufus got him the sweet fever too, and took a switchman's job in the Sabreville yards, and worked there right up until the night he died. Billy Bob was only three then; his own sweet fever comes most purely from me and what I taught him. Ain't no doubt trains been a major part of all our lives, good and bad, and ain't no doubt neither they get into a man's blood and maybe change him, too, in one way and another. I reckon they do.

The whistle come again, closer now, and I judged the St. Louis freight was just about to enter the tunnel on the other side of the mountain. You could hear the big wheels singing on the track, and if you listened close you could just about hear the banging of couplings and the hiss of air brakes as the engineer throttled down for the curve. The tunnel don't run straight through Chigger Mountain; she comes in from the north and angles to the east, so that a big freight like the St. Louis got to cut back to quarter speed coming through.

When she entered the tunnel, the tracks down below seemed to shimmy, and you could feel the vibration clear up where we was sitting under the catalpa tree. Billy Bob stood himself up and peered down toward the black tunnel mouth like a bird dog on a point. The whistle come again, and once more, from inside the tunnel, sounding hollow and miseried now. Every time I heard it like that, I thought of a body trapped and hurting and crying out for help that wouldn't come in the empty hours of the night. I swallowed and shifted the cud of blackstrap and worked up a spit to keep my mouth from drying. The sweet fever feeling was strong in my stomach.

The blackness around the tunnel opening commenced to lighten, and got brighter and brighter until the long white glow from the locomotive's headlamp spilled out onto the tracks beyond. Then she come through into my sight, her light shining like a giant's eye, and the engineer give another tug on the whistle, and the sound of her was a clattering rumble as loud to my ears as a mountain rockslide. But she wasn't moving fast, just kind of easing along, pulling herself out of that tunnel like a night crawler out of a mound of earth.

The locomotive clacked on past, and me and Billy Bob watched her string slide along in front of us. Flats, boxcars, three tankers in a row, more flats loaded down with pine logs big around as a privy, a refrigerator car, five coal gondolas, another link of boxcars. Fifty in the string already, I thought. She won't be dragging more than sixty, sixty-five. . . .

Billy Bob said suddenly, "Granpa, look yonder!"

He had his arm up, pointing. My eyes ain't so good no

more, and it took me a couple of seconds to follow his point,
over on our left and down at the door of the third boxcar in
the last link. It was sliding open, and clear in the moonlight
I saw a man's head come out, then his shoulders.

"It's a floater, Granpa," Billy Bob said, excited. "He's
gonna jump. Look at him holding there—he's gonna jump."

I spit into the grass. "Help me up, boy."

He got a hand under my arm and lifted me up and held
me until I was steady on my cane. Down there at the door
of the boxcar, the floater was looking both ways along the
string of cars and down at the ground beside the tracks. That
ground was soft loam, and the train was going slow enough
that there wasn't much chance he would hurt himself jumping off. He come to that same idea, and as soon as he did he
flung himself off the car with his arms spread out and his hair
and coattails flying in the slipstream. I saw him land solid
and go down and roll over once. Then he knelt there, shaking his head a little, looking around.

Well, he was the first floater we'd seen in seven months.
The yard crews seal up the cars nowadays, and they ain't
many ride the rails anyhow, even down in our part of the
country. But every now and then a floater wants to ride bad
enough to break a seal, or hides himself in a gondola or on
a loaded flat. Kids, old-time hoboes, wanted men. They's still
a few.

And some of 'em get off right down where this one had,
because they know the St. Louis freight stops in Sabreville
and they's yardmen there that check the string, or because
they see the rundown shacks of the old hobo jungle or
Ferdie Johnson's melon patch. Man rides a freight long
enough, no provisions, he gets mighty hungry; the sight of
a melon patch like Ferdie's is plenty enough to make him
jump off.

"Billy Bob," I said.

"Yes, Granpa. You wait easy now."

He went off along the slope, running. I watched the
floater, and he come up on his feet and got himself into a

clump of bushes alongside the tracks to wait for the caboose to pass so's he wouldn't be seen. Pretty soon the last of the cars left the tunnel, and then the caboose with a signalman holding a red-eye lantern out on the platform. When she was down the tracks and just about beyond my sight, the floater showed himself again and had him another look around. Then, sure enough, he made straight for the melon patch.

Once he got into it I couldn't see him, because he was in close to the woods at the edge of the slope. I couldn't see Billy Bob neither. The whistle sounded one final time, mournful, as the lights of the caboose disappeared, and a chill come to my neck and set there like a cold dead hand. I closed my eyes and listened to the last singing of the wheels fade away.

It weren't long before I heard footfalls on the slope coming near, then the angry sound of a stranger's voice, but I kept my eyes shut until they walked up close and Billy Bob said, "Granpa." When I opened 'em the floater was standing three feet in front of me, white face shining in the moonlight —scared face, angry face, evil face.

"What the hell is this?" he said. "What you want with me?"

"Give me your gun, Billy Bob," I said.

He did it, and I held her tight and lifted the barrel. The ache in my stomach was so strong my knees felt weak and I could scarcely breathe. But my hand was steady.

The floater's eyes come wide open and he backed off a step. "Hey," he said, "hey, you can't—"

I shot him twice.

He fell over and rolled some and come up on his back. They wasn't no doubt he was dead, so I give the gun back to Billy Bob and he put it away in his belt. "All right, boy," I said.

Billy Bob nodded and went over and hoisted the dead floater onto his shoulder. I watched him trudge off toward the bog hollow, and in my mind I could hear the train whistle as she'd sounded from inside the tunnel. I thought again, as I had so many times, that it was the way my boy Rufus and Billy Bob's ma must have sounded that night in 1947, when the two floaters from the hobo jungle broke into their home and raped her and shot Rufus to death. She lived just long enough to tell us about the floaters, but they was never caught. So it was up to me, and then up to me and Billy Bob when he come of age.

Well, it ain't like it once was, and that saddens me. But they's still a few that ride the rails, still a few take it into their heads to jump off down there when the St. Louis freight slows coming through the Chigger Mountain tunnel.

Oh my yes, they'll *always* be a few for me and Billy Bob and the sweet fever inside us both.